Praise for the Johanne

"Fans of Howard's witty prose and m... appointed; his characteristic blend of horror, comedy, fantasy, and drama is particularly effective in this installment. Cabal remains an entertaining antihero whose complexities have deepened over time, and the conclusion of the narrative threads that have spanned the previous four Cabal books is both satisfying and touching."

—*Publishers Weekly*

"Howard makes it look easy to paint a soul-stealing, murdering necromancer as a sympathetic character; that, folks, is worth the price of admission." —*The San Diego Union-Tribune*

"Howard is a supremely talented writer and the Johannes Cabal series makes for superb reading. It would be easy at this point to say if you like Rankin or Fforde or Pratchett or Holt, then you will love these books, but while it may well be true, it would be doing Howard a disservice." —*Sci-Fi-London*

"Howard's Dreamlands will thrill fans of H. P. Lovecraft, but Cabal leaves a permanent mark on even the most fluid of landscapes, and Howard's writing shines, sketching out a personality both fascinating and heartbreaking." —*BookGeeks*

"Cabal, the detective and necromancer, is full of charismatic amorality, making him both a classical and refreshing antihero."

—*Time Out Chicago*

"Jonathan L. Howard has such an effortless way with monsters and the undead that you might suspect him of being, like his creation, Johannes Cabal, a necromancer. The series is addictive."

—Richard Kadrey, author of the Sandman Slim series

"In the vein of the comic horror-fantasies of Tom Holt and Christopher Moore but substantially weirder." —*Booklist*

"Johannes Cabal would kill me for saying this, but he's my favorite zeppelin-hopping detective. The fellow has got all the charm of Bond and the smarts of Holmes—without the pesky morality."

—Daniel H. Wilson, author of *Robopocalypse*

Also by Jonathan L. Howard

THE JOHANNES CABAL SERIES

Johannes Cabal the Necromancer

Johannes Cabal the Detective

Johannes Cabal: The Fear Institute

The Brothers Cabal

STAND-ALONE NOVEL

Carter & Lovecraft

YOUNG ADULT NOVELS

Katya's World

Katya's War

THE FALL OF THE HOUSE OF

Cabal

JONATHAN L. HOWARD

Thomas Dunne Books
St. Martin's Griffin
New York

This is a work of fiction. All of the characters, organizations, and events portrayed in this novel are either products of the author's imagination or are used fictitiously.

THOMAS DUNNE BOOKS.
An imprint of St. Martin's Press.

 For information, address St. Martin's Press, 175 Fifth Avenue, New York, N.Y. 10010.

www.thomasdunnebooks.com
www.stmartins.com

Illustrations by Linda "Snugbat" Smith

The Library of Congress has cataloged the hardcover edition as follows:

Names: Howard, Jonathan L., author.
Title: The fall of the House of Cabal / Jonathan L. Howard.
Description: First edition. | New York : Thomas Dunne Books/St. Martin's Press, 2016. | Series: Johannes Cabal novels ; 5
Identifiers: LCCN 2016013061 | ISBN 9781250069979 (hardcover) | ISBN 9781466879850 (ebook)
Subjects: LCSH: Cabal, Johannes (Fictitious character)—Fiction. | Quests (Expeditions)—Fiction. | Voyages and travels—Fiction. | Vampires—Fiction. | Devil—Fiction. | BISAC: FICTION / Horror. | FICTION / Ghost. | GSAFD: Fantasy fiction. | Occult fiction.
Classification: LCC PR6108.O928 F35 2016 | DDC 823/.92—dc23
LC record available at https://lccn.loc.gov/2016013061

ISBN 978-1-250-14499-7 (trade paperback)

Our books may be purchased in bulk for promotional, educational, or business use. Please contact your local bookseller or the Macmillan Corporate and Premium Sales Department at 1-800-221-7945, extension 5442, or by email at MacmillanSpecialMarkets@macmillan.com.

First St. Martin's Griffin Edition: November 2017

P1

For my sister, Paula

CONTENTS

Preface xi

THE GRAND PLAN 1
THE FIRST WAY: JOHANNES CABAL, THE NECROPOLITAN 59
THE SECOND WAY: LEONIE BARROW, GREAT DETECTIVE 99
THE THIRD WAY: ZARENYIA, PRINCESS OF HELL 139
THE FOURTH WAY: HORST CABAL, LORD OF THE DEAD 211
THE FIFTH WAY: *RUBRUM IMPERATRIX* 265
THE FALL OF THE HOUSE OF CABAL 343

Afterword 369

Acknowledgements 371

At the foot of Mount Olympus bubbles up a spring that changes
its flavour hour by hour, night and day, and the spring is scarcely
three days' journey from Paradise, out of which Adam
was driven. If anyone has tasted thrice of the fountain,
from that day he will feel no fatigue, but will, as long
as he lives, be as a man of thirty years.
—From the wonderful letter of Presbyter Johannes sent
to various Christian princes in 1165

PREFACE

My Lords, Ladies, and Gentlemen, Boys and Girls, and Folk of All Other Persuasions.

You are about to embark on an adventure wherein risks are taken, and do not always succeed. Where danger haunts every decision, where the stakes are high and the odds are long. You, at least, are in the happy position of not being in any personal peril during this tale, despite my suggestion to the publisher that one in a thousand copies should be impregnated with dimethylmercury just to give a *frisson* to book purchasing. 'You can't just go around killing readers,' they said.

'Not until you're selling more units, anyway,' they added.

Every Cabal novel that I have written has been very different from the one before it. This is partially out of deference to you, the reader—Why would you want to read the same novel (but for cosmetic differences) time and time again?—and partially for me—Why would I wish to write the same novel (but for cosmetic differences) time and time again? Thus, you will be delighted or appalled to discover that the novel you currently hold—with surgical gloves if you have any sense—is not just the same as the one that precedes it, or the one before that, or the one before that, or—I feel compelled to say, although I'm as bored with this sentence as you—the one before that. This novel is its own creature.

It is also, however, a tying up of threads as a tapestry reaches its conclusion. It is not necessarily the last Johannes Cabal novel, although it might be. It is certainly, however, the end of a phase. In the following story, the reader who has read the previous novels (and, ideally, the short stories, although that isn't a requisite) will see many things that are familiar: some ideas are revisited and maliciously subverted; some old characters will re-emerge. Pieces slot into place, the clockwork grates, the chimes play. The penny tableau that began with *Johannes Cabal the Necromancer* comes to an end of sorts, the curtain rattles down, and you may all sprint for the exit before the national anthem plays.

Zoltán Kodály started his opera *Háry János* with a sneeze, a nod to an old Hungarian superstition that a statement preceded or followed by a sneeze is the truth. He had an orchestra to perform an instrumental sneeze; I have a computer and an overabundance of fancy. Thus, I sneeze a cloud of electrons upon the backlit LCD screen, and the following tale's truth is assured, just as much as the historical truth that Napoleon was captured by a lone Hungarian. We all knew that, didn't we? Of course.

Here, then, is the fifth major undertaking of the necromancer Johannes Cabal. May you enjoy it in the knowledge that it is the absolute, unvarnished truth in every respect.

THE GRAND PLAN

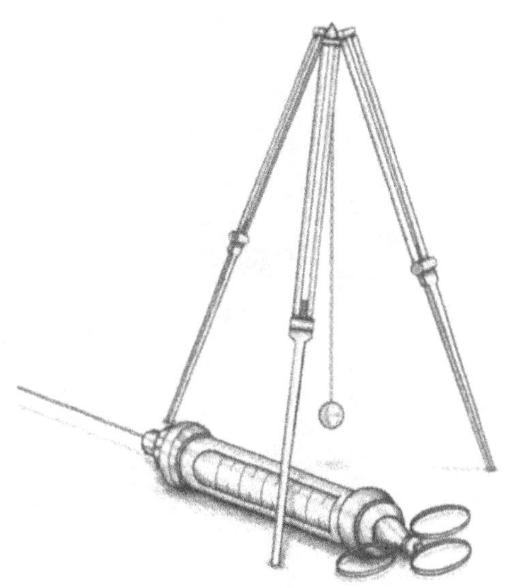

It is a damned place, is Perkis Moor. Perched high on the spine of the country, there is little up there but sheep and the crows that feed upon the corpses of sheep fallen in gorges, trapped in gullies, tumbled down scree. The shepherds do a good enough job, but they do not enjoy their work and are happy to retire of a night to their huts of millstone grit and turfed rooves, brutal little boxes with small windows in hulking walls that seem as much defensive as simply shelters.

The wind blows across Perkis Moor; it is the only thing that wanders freely, for it is a damned place, and even ramblers show little inclination to labour across the broken, unhappy earth. Ask a local—which is to say, ask anyone who lives by the moor, for no one would claim to live upon it, only to sojourn briefly until they can return to a proper place, fit for decent souls—ask a local why the place feels so baleful, so full of mindless, lolling hatefulness, and they will tell you it is haunted. The spirits of five thousand pagan dead are trapped there, so they say, from a time before Constantine, from before Christ. A great battle, fought with weapons of wood and rough iron, took place there. The culmination of a war between nameless tribes, for unknown reasons, they met there and offered no quarter. Five thousand dead and the grass fed by gallons of their gore. A terrible thing that scarred the land itself, a festering wound that seeps spectral blood into the here and now still, after all these years.

The shepherds say sometimes at night they hear the cries in strange languages long lost from the throats of living men, the screams, the clash of weapons. The shepherds know better than to look out of the small windows in the hulking walls of their millstone grit huts on such cursed nights or storm-threatened days. What they may see can do them no good, and an immortal soul is worth far more than assuaging a moment's curiosity.

The locals say no merchant travelling with his wares will cross the moor, not even in daytime, for fear of making poor progress and still being upon it when the sun dips below the distant horizon. Once, an itinerant tinker did, they say. He scoffed at the legend and set out upon the dreary sheep path with liquor in him when he really needed wit. The shepherds found him the next day, cold and dead by the path, staring up at the grey clouds, eyes and mouth open to gather the drizzle. All the rain in the world could not wash away that expression of terror, though, the outward signifier of an experience that froze his blood and stopped his heart.

The archaeologists say 'Bollocks' to all that. There isn't a shred of empirical evidence that such a battle ever took place. They say that it's a myth and the old tales of a great spectral battle fought periodically upon Perkis Moor are simply the product of bored people in a boring place making things up to entertain themselves. In this, they are largely correct.

But not entirely.

The tall, pale man in the black suit and walking boots caused a huge sensation amongst the locals of the Perkis Path Inn, which is to say they went a little quieter when he entered, nodded covertly at him to their drinking partners when his back was turned, and marvelled at his accent, which was as alien to them as Ancient Assyrian. That the accent was German says little for the cosmopolitan nature of the locals.

'You'll be wanting a room, then?' The landlord leaned heavily upon the counter and glowered at the strange stranger, with his fancy spectacles and gloves. The locals didn't hold with such fripperies; if the Good Lord intended one to be terribly myopic, then it was not given to man to correct this defect. Much better that man wander around tripping over things. He might fall down the stairs or use bleach for flour, but at least he wouldn't die horribly in a graceless state.

The man removed the blue-tinted spectacles, and it became apparent to the landlord that they were intended to protect the man's eyes from the glare of daylight. He himself had never seen the glare of daylight, but his grandfather had once told him that the sun was actually a fiercely radiant object in the sky and not merely one area of the permanent overcast that glowed slightly more strongly than the rest. In some distant, foreign places like Egypt or China or Barnoldswick, it was said that sometimes the cloud cleared away and you could see the sky above, and the sun, and—at night—bright objects that defied rational explanation. The landlord had always been of the opinion that his grandfather had been making a joke. As if such things might be in a godly world.

Looking at the stranger's strikingly blue eyes, eyes that hinted at an incisive mind and a calloused soul, it occurred to the landlord that there might be many ungodly things in a godly world, after all.

'I shall,' said the man in his ungodly accent, removing his ungodly gloves, and casting an ungodly eye upon the regulars, who returned their attention to their dominoes rather than suffer it for longer than necessary. He turned and looked through the mullion window, the road beyond distorted by the bullseye panes and thereby rendered far more interesting than the reality. 'The moor is in that direction, isn't it?'

'It is. Thinking of going for a walk there later?'

'I was considering it.'

'Don't,' said the landlord, with a great satisfaction that echoed around every local's heart in the public bar.

'You don't want to go up there,' said a drinker. 'Not good to go on the moor if you don't need to.'

'Perhaps,' said the stranger, 'I need to.'

'Don't look much like a shepherd t'me,' said a dominoes player, and there was much amusement at this *bon mot*, the merriest thing ever said within those walls since they were raised 234 years earlier.

'Why?' The stranger's tone was neutral. 'Is it haunted?'

The landlord leaned yet more heavily upon the counter. It would have groaned under the stress if it had been some profane, foreign wood, like Norwegian pine from a profane fittings showroom. But it was good English oak, and it was used to the meaty forearms of stout English yeomanry leaning heavily upon it.

'What if it is?'

The cold blue eyes turned to regard him. 'Tell me all about it.' And he produced a good stout English ten-bob note, and all animosities were shortly forgotten.

The stranger left the tavern some hours later, a room for the night secured and the locals rendered glazed and garrulous by the application of a multitude of ten-bob notes and the ale thus purchased.

In truth, they had told him little he did not already know, but the investigation was not purely based upon what they said, but upon how they said it. They believed every word of it, that much was plain. Every word was, of course, nonsense, but they held those words with a fervent regard. Even the most aggressively masculine of them would not venture upon the moor at night without an excellent reason, and that intrigued and satisfied the stranger, who was Johannes Cabal,* a

* It is to be hoped that, by this juncture, the revelation of the stranger's identity causes the reader little or no surprise. This is, after all, the fifth novel in the series. If this is the first Cabal novel the reader has read, the author strongly advises that you go off and read the others first. Also any other novels the author has written. This latter point is unnecessary to the reader's

necromancer of some little infamy. This job description he left off the battered ledger the inn used as a guest book, instead entering 'Gentleman scientist'. In a rational and well-ordered world, he would have been perfectly happy to write 'Necromancer', but the world was not rational, and little enough of it was in any sort of order of which he could approve. Had he used that word, he would likely have received sour looks, poor service, and a lynch party, and so he did not.

The landlord looked at the not entirely inaccurate substitute term and wrinkled his brow. 'So what are you doing here?' Clearly the locals didn't hold with any of that newfangled science stuff like evolution or gravity.

'My current interest is folklore and legends,' replied Cabal. 'The tales of the moor drew my attention. I am considering a monograph upon the subject.'

'A monograph?'

'A monograph, yes.'

They looked at one another, both men with secrets. Cabal's was that he had no intention of writing a monograph. The landlord's, that he had no idea what a monograph was.

Presently, Cabal left the inn to 'go for a walk' and 'get a breath of fresh air'. These claims were true, as both were unavoidable. His main aim was to carry out an experiment that was esoteric in both field and morality, true, but he would have to walk to get to the location he had chosen for the experiment and would doubtless have to breathe one or more times *en route*.

Cabal wore a soft Homburg in a dark grey bearing a sedate curve, an unimposing pinch, and a small black feather in the band, the loss of which had surely not inconvenienced the bird from which it came in the slightest. His suit was dour, but hard-wearing, and his boots—as

---

understanding of the plot in progress, but it would make me happy, and what soulless creature would miss an opportunity to make me happy? Certainly not the reader, I'm sure, who is wise, just, intelligent, and of above-average appearance.

mentioned previously—eminently suitable for tramping around on rough terrains. He carried a Gladstone bag and a cane topped with a tarnished silver skull. If one maintained a mental image of how a gentleman scientist might conceivably appear, it would certainly have been along the lines of Cabal's wardrobe.

He walked in a brisk line along the road that bordered Perkis Moor until he was safely out of sight of the pub, and then performed a sharp left-hand turn that took him directly onto it. There was not a great deal of daylight left, but that was all to plan.

He did not need to go far onto the moor itself, just up onto a ridge at its edge that he had noted on the Ordnance Survey map of the area. The area it overlooked was a natural arena, a wide, flat depression rising into the flat of the main part of the moor. A natural arena, or perhaps 'theatre' was a better term. The vast majority of sightings of the unusual happened in or near this area. The closeness of the road was perhaps the primary explanation for the place having the most witnesses. The closeness of the pub was often mooted as the primary explanation for the sightings themselves, perhaps unkindly.

Perhaps not. Having found himself a dry spot at the ridge's edge to sit upon, Cabal wasted no time tying a length of rubber tubing around his bicep, flicked the skin of the inside of the elbow to bring up a vein, and injected himself there with a syringe he drew from a sterile metal cylinder he took from his bag. The syringe contained a rare and potent narcotic that might threaten addiction if overindulged. This was not a concern; Cabal did little enough for recreational purposes as it was, and even amongst these rare hobbies and pastimes, becoming a junkie came very low upon his list of life goals.

The act done, he loosened the tubing and placed it, the syringe, and its container back within the Gladstone bag. In their stead he removed a small tripod with telescoping legs and set it up by him. From its apex dangled a length of fine silver chain and upon its end a small silver sphere, its surface regularly pitted and a seam around its equator, where it might be unscrewed. Thus prepared, he relaxed and allowed himself to take in his surroundings, looking without seeing, hearing without listening.

The day died around him, and the night grew in its stead, unhurried and unheralded. Somewhere a lonely meadow pipit called. The sound was allowed into his ears and to merge with his awareness without him troubling to identify the bird, even down to naming it (*Anthus pratensis*) as was his usual wont. In the common run of things, this degree of mental slackness would have been impossible to him. It was the duty of the drug he had taken intravenously to render his mind less focussed, less capable, less analytical, or—to put it differently—more like those of normal people.

He relaxed as deeply as he was capable, a great deal more deeply than he might have managed without narcotic aid, and measured his breaths, focusing entirely on the steady metre of inhalation, exhalation. He allowed the outside world to become nothing, the interior not much more than that. He sought a state of semi-consciousness, in which his awareness of the mundane was blunted, and his perception of those things less mundane equivalently sharpened.

Beside him, the silver plumb upon its silver chain swung gently in the light evening breeze that blew up across from the moor before him. Presently it stopped moving with a sudden shudder and hung canted at an angle of some twenty or so degrees from the vertical. Slowly, quivering as if base iron in a strong magnetic field, it swung degree by degree upwards further still, up until it was pointing directly into the centre of the large, low basin before him.

Cabal was unaware of it, but that didn't matter. The tripod was not some manner of indicator, although it could fulfil that role, too. It was more in the nature of bait.

Somewhere far, far away and yet so very close at hand, the note of a sword striking a sword sounded. Cabal heard it, but his eyes had sunk shut and he did not trouble to open them. Not yet. The time was not yet.

A scream now. A single solitary scream of mortal agony and the fear of death brought close and immediate. It died away, as the man who had once screamed it must also have died away. The whinnying of terrified horses rose in a faint chorus, borne to him on the breeze. The clang of swords, both great and broad, echoed above it, the dull battering of a struck shield, the rattling of the horses' tack and barding. Cabal's face showed some small phantom of emotion. Specifically, disgust.

There was a sound like thunder, but it was the roar of cannon. Ancient artillery firing in an ancient battle. Cabal's pupils could be discerned through his eyelids as small bumps in the skin, and these bumps swung high and around. Cabal was rolling his eyes.

The individual sounds grew together, forming a soundscape, an auditory painting in action. Men grunted, horses snickered, blows were given and taken, warriors killed and died. The timbre grew, the sounds became more distinct, the silver pendulum pulled so hard towards the sounds, so filled with unnatural vivacity, that only the fact that the tripod's legs ended in spikes driven into the sod kept it upright at all.

When the phantom battle was all but bellowing in Cabal's face, he deigned to open his eyes.

And there it was in all its spectral glory, the great battle of Perkis Moor more sharply defined than any man or woman had ever seen, this thanks to the precision of Cabal's preparations. Men-at-arms clashed with knights, musketeers of the English Civil War engaged Roman legionaries, naked men painted in blue woad charged Napoleonic artillery pieces and were duly cut down by grapeshot. It was, in purely historical terms at any rate, bollocks, just as the archaeologists had always said. It was also, just as they had said, very exciting indeed if one's job consisted of watching sheep for lengthy periods.

Perhaps once, a very long time ago, there had been some small fight here. Not even necessarily a fatal one. Perhaps Og of the stone tribe had grunted something needlessly deprecatory about Ug of the fur tribe's mother, and Ug—who loved his mother dearly although not in the manner alluded to by Og—had struck him smartly in the face, putting him on his arse with a split lip.

In the retelling, the blow had become a fight, the fight a skirmish, the skirmish a battle, a pebble of truth gathering the moss of invention as it rolled down the years. And people were *so* stupid, they couldn't tell one period from another. Cabal had once seen an early medieval Bible lovingly illustrated with men and women dressed in clothes contemporaneous with the age in which it was created. Jericho was shown being besieged with siege engines a thousand years out of their time. In uncountable minds' eyes down the centuries, the Battle of Perkis Moor was fought in whatever best pleased the daydreamer. Knights in gleaming armour to please the heart of Malory, soldiers of the War of the Roses, swords and spears, crossbows and muskets, rocks and rockets.

It hardly mattered; all that was important was that the device worked. He wasn't even convinced that the drug had been necessary and would try the operation again the following evening, this time without. In the meantime, the drug hadn't so purged him of reason that he couldn't be judgemental of the sideshow for fools playing out before him. This was the least of examples, he was sure. One clumsily glued together by generations of unimpressive intellects. He was after greater fare. Out there were five particular sites, and his suspicion was that they had been created deliberately by methods that escaped him. Not that he needed to know, of course. He had no great interest in replicating such things, only in exploiting them. Exploiting five. It was no small undertaking. They would be cathedrals of the intellect as compared to Perkis Moor's small mud hut.

In a single movement Cabal took up the tripod and slid home its legs against a stone, closed it, flicked some small fragments of soil adhering to the spikes clear with a gloved finger, and put the device back into his bag. As he did so, the battle suddenly attenuated, its combatants thinning out like magic lantern projections when the curtain is drawn back and the daylight re-enters the room. Now they looked like ghosts, and now they looked like suggestive shapes in the evening mist rising from the damp land, and now they were gone altogether.

Cabal cared not a jot. His main concern was how on earth he was supposed to entertain himself for a full day in a place as devoid of interest as Perkis Moor. After all, it was only haunted, and the ghosts were boring.

* * *

A week later, two mourners stood by an open grave in a concrete field, and looked down upon a glass coffin that held a beautiful corpse.

'My God,' said one, dead himself. 'She's perfect. Just as she was.'

'I made no mistake,' said the other, dead himself once, half-dead on enough occasions to be worth several more extinctions. Yet now he was living and vital, because some people are just jammy like that. 'I have never made a mistake where she was concerned. At least,' and here he paused and frowned at painful memory, 'no mistake in method or theory. There are other mistakes possible, however. The metaphysics of my endeavours are far from clear or simple.'

The first man, a monster by some authorities, a good chap by all the rest, smiled a sympathetic smile. 'You speak of the morality of it?'

'I do.' The second man was only considered a monster by the law and most churches, and who were they to judge him, anyway? 'It used to be simple. She is dead, therefore I move heaven and earth to save her.'

'Simple . . .' echoed the other.

'And yet, despite the clear practical problems involved in my practises, it transpires there are philosophical matters to consider, too. Once I discounted philosophy as a pastime for earnest young men with unconvincing beards and the be-sweatered young women who hang upon their every word, for old men in barrels or on top of pillars. I have made war upon angels and demons and, worst of them all, humans to arrive at this juncture, and yet it was only recently that I realised there is a pressing question that I had never once addressed nor even considered.

'Would she actually wish to be brought back to the land of the living?'

'Those are heavy matters indeed,' said the first, who was a vampire. A nice one.

'Indeed,' said the second, who was a necromancer.

They pondered in silence.

Finally, the vampire said to the necromancer, his brother, 'Is "be-sweatered" actually a word?'

They replaced the great stone cover upon the concrete grave—and went to leave the hidden laboratory adjoining the cellar of the house of Johannes Cabal, the necromancer. As they left the laboratory and made their way through the cellar, the vampire, Horst, paused by a large barrel, a butt of the type popular for the drowning of dukes. This example, however, did not contain an awkward rival for the throne of Richard III pickled in Malmsey wine.

Horst laid his hand on the wood of the barrel's head a little guiltily. 'This seems very undignified in comparison.'

Cabal knew his brother well enough to detect the forced lightness in his tone; he did not comment on it. Instead he said, 'Practicality was the concern. The barrel was handy, and undoubtedly made its . . . *her* transport across the Continent a great deal easier. It's just as good a container as a glass coffin. Better, perhaps. It's certainly a great deal less fragile.'

'You're not going to—' Horst made vague gestures with his hands, as if pouring out a bucket—'decant her, then?'

'I am not,' said Cabal. 'Doing so would be a risky operation and for little gain beyond, I admit, the aesthetic. In any case, from what I know of Fräulein Bartos's personality, I think she would prefer the barrel. Glass coffins are for fairy-tale princesses. Not someone as pragmatic as she.'

Horst nodded, reassured. It wasn't necessary for his brother to explicitly state that Alisha Bartos had been a trained killer, practised agent, and decent conversationalist. Had been, and would be again if Johannes Cabal could keep his promise.

In an ideal world, the reader would have the common courtesy to have read all the previous novels in this series and retained sufficient of the plot that a pithy summation would be unnecessary.

As has been noted by observers more perspicacious than the

author, however, it is far from an ideal world, and a distinct proportion of those reading these words will have had more pressing matters than to avail themselves of the four novels preceding this one. To these people, the author says, 'Yes, *four.* You jumped in at Book Five. What are you like?'

Thus, it falls upon the author (as diligent and kind as he is handsome and effortlessly virile) to offer a brief summation of previous events to aid these readers—Who starts reading at Book Five, I ask you?—as well as those who have read the preceding novels and would simply like their memories refreshed.

Johannes Cabal was once very nearly a solicitor, but a kindly fate saved him from this terrible future by killing his best beloved. She drowned, should you be curious, or just morbid.

Grief stricken, Cabal refused to accept the generally accepted absoluteness of death, and instead turned to certain esoteric, occult, and highly illegal paths of possibility. One such path took him to a remote, shunned graveyard where he was forced to abandon his brother, Horst, in a crypt wherein dwelt a vampire. Horst destroyed the monster, but not before he was contaminated.

Thus, Horst vanished from the purview of man. Missing, believed dead (which was both true and not true), his loss splintered *die Familie Cabal:* his father sank into a dreadful melancholy that ended with his premature death; his mother denounced the younger and less favoured son, Johannes, before leaving England and returning to her birthplace in Hesse, Germany.

All of this troubled Johannes Cabal less than perhaps it ought. Rather than doing anything to rectify matters, he instead relocated the family house by curious means from the middle of a terrace in a provincial English town to a lonely hillside in open country, by which he gained the solitude necessary to continue his studies.

He gained the knowledge to perform such research and, indeed, commit wanton acts of urban redevelopment by the simple expedient of selling his soul. Presently it transpired that this was a mistake, and that his soul was actually of use to him. Using a potent mix of ruthlessness, immorality, deception, diablerie, and candyfloss, he was able to reclaim his soul. In so doing, he upset Satan. If only that were the only time he had upset a major otherworldly entity.

At least Cabal had recovered his brother, Horst, from the ancient crypt in which he had been abandoned, albeit for selfish ends. Unhappily, there were words and hurt feelings, and Horst died, utterly and finally.

Until he got better. This was as great a surprise to him as to anyone else. Resurrected by a shadowy conspiracy (as distinct, presumably, from one of those highly publicised conspiracies), Horst was put in the difficult position of asking his brother to help save the world from the machinations of the conspiracy in general and of its prime mover in particular, a woman of means, intellect, and profound wickedness known as the 'Red Queen'.

To his surprise, Johannes seemed older (this was because he was older), wiser, and altogether more human than Horst remembered, his experiences having mellowed him at least a little. He readily agreed to help Horst and his allies, and the world was saved. Saved again, strictly speaking, as it turned out Johannes Cabal had done it a couple of times before, usually by accident.

The victory was not without sacrifices, however. One such was Alisha Bartos, currently perfectly preserved by a strange chemical in a large barrel. Horst had developed a fondness for her—she had once shot him, then apologised nicely—but more pressingly felt responsible for her death.

Nor, however, was the victory without spoils. Johannes Cabal had recovered a book so rare that he had believed every copy had long since been lost or destroyed: *The One True Account of Presbyter Johannes by His Own Hand*.

This, you may rest assured, is a very important book. Why that should be has not been revealed to date, but probably shall be sooner rather than later. After all, Johannes Cabal, a necromancer of some little infamy, has rested much stock upon it and enthused in uncharacteristically vigorous terms how it changes everything without actually being overly specific about why that should be.

And so, we are up to date. If you have read the previous novels,

I hope that has successfully refreshed your memory. If you have not, and have just lurched in here like a drunk into a cinema half an hour after the programme began, sit down and shut up. You are disturbing the patrons.

We may now continue.

The grandfather clock chimed midnight as they emerged from the cellar door and made their way to the front parlour. Cabal was nocturnal by habit (it was when the cemeteries and graveyards were most fruitful for his visits) and Horst by nature (sunlight caused him to burn rather than tan; burn in a brief moment of incandescence leaving naught but dust and regrets).

Horst was taking things as restfully as possible, delaying the inevitable moment when needs be he would seek blood. Even when that happened, he would take it carefully, a jigger here, a mouthful there, so as not to inconvenience anyone. His brother's material needs were less troublesome, and he went to the kitchen to assuage them with a pot of Assam tea and a plate of cold meat and pickles.

Horst sank into his favourite armchair and awaited Cabal's return. While he waited, he regarded the deep alcove by the fireplace and the high shelf there. Upon it was a row of three wooden boxes, each large enough to contain a human head. This is not a fanciful metric; two did contain human heads and the third something head-like that may well have been a head. Johannes Cabal was cagey on the subject of its contents. Whatever it was, it had a good singing voice. To the right of it was the living skull of the hermit and sage Ercusides, whose voice was a little reedy, but he tried all the same, bless him. The third box contained the living head of Rufus Maleficarus, although his was not the spirit that animated it. That was an entity of awful malevolence that had sought on several previous occasions to bring the apocalypse to earth, that loathed Johannes Cabal with a savage intensity, and that couldn't carry a tune in a bucket. Now it was forced to occupy the head of a former rival of Cabal's, and spent its days sulking, voicing threats and imprecations, and utterly failing to hit even middle C with any reliability.

The thing in the first box's hopes for, with the addition of a hypothetical future fourth box, a barbershop quartet had foundered on the head of Rufus Maleficarus massacring 'Carolina Moon'.

For the moment, however, the boxes were quiet but for a quiet burring snore from the second and subdued spasmodic expletives from the third.

Cabal returned with his supper. As he arranged his plate and saucer to his satisfaction upon the table, he noted Horst's languid gaze up at the shelf. 'The erstwhile Herr Maleficarus turns out to be as poor a loser in the afterlife as he ever was when he had a body beneath his neck,' Cabal commented. 'His father was no better.'

'You decapitated him, too?' Horst's tone was no more astonished than if his brother had suggested he had taken up golf. Far less so, in fact.

'I did not. I don't make a habit of that, you know.'

Horst regarded the row of boxes. 'Of course you don't.'

'There is a certain degree of coincidence with regard to living heads in my line of work, I'll grant you. Still, they are hardly unknown in occult circles. Bacon's head of brass leaps to mind, for example.'

'Hmmmm.' Horst was not agreeing, as he had no idea as to whom Cabal referred. He was, however, remembering that he had once liked bacon and grieved privately that it could no longer be part of his diet.

'So,' he said, stirring himself from memories of bacon sandwiches past, 'has that book turned out to be as useful as you thought it would be? Are the secrets of the universe there unveiled?'

'No,' said Johannes Cabal.

'Too easy, eh?'

'Too easy. I'm sure I have impressed upon you in the past what the word "occult" actually means?'

'You have. It means "hidden".' He saw Cabal's raised eyebrow. 'You see? I do listen. Now and then.'

'Much of that "hidden" quality is not on the part of nature, or the supernatural. Wizards, sorcerers, witches, and oracles have seen things for which the common herd are neither prepared nor tolerant.

For their own safety, such people are inclined towards secrecy. I can only sympathise; many of my more potentially . . . contentious—'

'Incriminating . . .'

'—notes are enciphered for exactly those reasons.'

'So Presbyterian Jack's big book of magic is in code, is that what you are saying?'

'Presbyter Johannes, often called Prester John.'

'Let's call him Prester John to avoid confusion.'

'Quite, yes. That would be sensible.' Cabal stirred his tea and took a sip. 'It isn't exactly enciphered, but it is in code. It uses allegory and allusion to hide its truths, mostly very esoteric imagery. Highly arcane. I have been working to squeeze sense from it.'

Horst could see this was no more than the truth. Cabal's sunken face and darkly rimmed eyes betokened near exhaustion. Horst was dead to the world during the hours of light and could not know what his brother did in that time, but it seemed to contain little enough sleep.

'You should rest, Johannes.' He said it gently. 'You are no use to anyone if you burn the candle at both ends.'

'I have no time for rest.'

'Make some.' The gentle tone slipped a little, leaving something steelier in its place. 'Don't make me compel you.'

Cabal looked up sharply at him. 'You wouldn't dare.'

'I'm still the elder of us, even if you're the one who looks older now. I won't watch you work yourself to death, especially having brought you back from the brink once recently already. I have better things to do than nurse you through another convalescence.'

'Don't even joke about exerting any of your . . . talents upon me, brother. I do not take well to coercion.'

There was an awkward silence. In truth, Horst had indeed used his vampiric powers to force his brother into deep recuperative sleep when he had been seriously ill some weeks before. This, he would never tell Johannes. For his part, Johannes had strong suspicions that Horst had done exactly that. This, he would never tell Horst. He was damned sure he would never permit it while in good or, at least, moderate health, however.

Cabal coughed. 'In any case, it would be an unnecessary measure. I have wrung what truth I can from the book. I am reasonably confident that I have all of it. I shall attend to my health and well-being at this point. You are, quite accidentally, right for once. The trials I foresee shall require my constitution to be at a peak.'

Horst, who had been slouching back with his hands behind his head, sat up. 'Trials? What do you mean? I thought that book was meant to be the be-all and end-all. The Philosopher's Stone, you called it. The Fountain of Youth.'

'So I believed. I was wrong, but in some ways right. I have told you of my time in the Dreamlands?'

Horst nodded. 'Zebras.'

'Of all the aspects of that long and perilous journey, your first thought is of the zebras. Yes, then. The place with the zebras. The nature of the Dreamlands is that they are formed from the will of sleepers, not all benevolent, not all human. It is concrete enough, but mutable, and that mutability is a function of belief. The Dreamlands gain much of their permanence from being what they are anticipated to be.'

'Yes,' said Horst slowly, uncertain as to the relevance.

'The waking world impinges upon the Dreamlands. Indeed, many physical entities may gain entrance directly to them. Ghouls, for example.' Here a glimmer of fond remembrance passed across his face. 'And gods.' The glimmer vanished. Cabal stared at a cold cut of beef and its pickled red cabbage accompaniment as if he held it personally responsible for some tragedy in his life. He sighed. 'The point is that what is not, may be, and that which is, may not.'

'Oh,' said Horst.

They sat in silence for a minute.

'You have no idea what I'm talking about, do you?' said Cabal.

'Not a sausage.'

'I am trying to say, in words of as few syllables as possible, that the principles of the Dreamlands hold some sway in the waking world. They may even be extrusions. This latter point I do not know, and nor do I care to find out. That they exist is all that matters.'

Now Horst started to get an inkling of what his brother was proposing, and his expression was suitably startled at the revelation.

'Hold on. Are you suggesting that there are places in the world that don't actually exist?'

Cabal looked at him coldly. 'If you say, "Like Norwich," or similar, I shall not be responsible for my actions.'

Horst seemed insulted. 'The very thought.'

He had been about to moot Swindon.

'As I say, I do not know whether these locations are outposts of the Dreamlands or simply called into being by a similar process. It hardly matters. They will not be found on any map, that much I know. They exist in between the here and the now, edge on like the blade of a knife. If you don't know where to find them, you never shall.'

'How did this Prester John fellow find all these places?'

'He didn't.'

'He wrote a book about it.'

'He didn't exist. He never existed.'

Horst took in this intelligence with difficulty. 'How did he manage to write a book, then?'

'You're forgetting that of which I spoke earlier. Allegory and allusion. Have you ever heard of Prester John before?'

Horst shrugged. 'I don't know. I *think* I have, probably. Sounds familiar. Something to do with the Crusades, wasn't he?'

'Yes. Gold star.'

'I would ask you not to patronise me,' said Horst, 'but that would be like asking you not to breathe. Carry on.'

'Simply put—'

'Thanks *ever* so . . .'

'Simply put, he was the great hope of Christian Europe when the Moslems were being such a threat to them in the thirteenth century. They had the Holy Lands, they had spread along North Africa and into Spain, and there was the real possibility that they would spread further still. The Crusades were partially about reclaiming the Holy Lands in general and Jerusalem in particular, but the core of their purpose was to halt the threat. It was a real threat, too. The forces arrayed under the crescent were far more coherent than those under the cross. The royal houses of Europe had spent so long bickering and warring amongst themselves, they were taken by surprise by an external threat. They were desperate.

'So, when a rumour of a previously unknown Christian empire in the East started to circulate, people were desperate enough to believe in it. An empire under a Christian ruler popularly known as Prester John, who had successfully defeated the Moslem in the East, and now wished to ally himself with Europe to fight the Moslem in the West.' Cabal drank some tea. 'A shame, then, that he didn't exist, and neither did his empire.'

'That must have been a bit of a blow.'

'You know how the Crusades turned out. Yes, I think we can safely say it was a bit of a blow. That didn't stop people believing in Prester John, however. It didn't stop them from *wanting* to believe. A letter was delivered decades later, claiming to be from the same Prester John. You see how wishful thinking starts to develop supernatural overtones? In this letter, the author describes "his" empire. It is full of the most remarkable wonders, including'—and here Cabal paused dramatically—'the Fountain of Youth.'

'So the Fountain of Youth *doesn't* exist?'

'Did I say that?'

'You said Prester John's empire didn't exist.'

'I said Prester John didn't exist. Attend more closely, Horst.'

Horst huffed with exasperation. 'May I just say that I am very confused at this juncture?'

'That is why I am a scientist and you are a fop. Now, the Orient was becoming less of a mystery to Europeans by this time, and its lands were being mapped. Cartographers looked around and saw there was no possible place that this marvellous empire could possibly exist, and reported as such. This, again, constituted "a bit of a blow".'

'So, that was it for the legend of Prester John . . .'

'No.'

'No?' Horst's expression was of somebody trying to play a game wherein the other player keeps 'remembering' rules that tip things in his favour.

'No. They just looked for another bit of *terra incognita* and stuck it in there instead. The mysterious empire of Prester John and all its marvels did a moonlight flit. Popular delusion lifted it bodily from the Orient and placed it in Africa instead. So, you see the significance of the book's title now?'

Horst looked like he'd been slapped with a halibut. Cabal pressed on regardless.

'*The One True Account of Presbyter Johannes by His Own Hand* is not about Presbyter Johannes at all. His legend is used as an extended allegory to hide from the ignorant and illuminate to the wise that such places of such potentiality actually exist. The wonders listed in the letter purporting to be from Prester John are not parts of a single empire; they are all pockets of ontological happenstance. Including . . .'

He looked keenly at Horst. For once, his brother did not disappoint him.

'The Fountain of Youth?'

Cabal smiled a smile of harsh satisfaction. 'And what is youth if not vitality? What is it if not life?' The smile faltered. 'My tea's gone cold.'

This was not the most glamorous job they had ever been engaged upon, but for the two men lurking in shrubbery just below the crest of the hill, nor was it the worst. They were encamped on the other side of the hill, and only lit a fire during the hours of darkness, its light baffled by an impromptu wall of stones, its smoke hidden by the night. They had food for a few days, and supplemented it with locally caught rabbits, roots, and berries. They were used to living rough, and the English countryside was a great deal less rugged than the Katamenian forests to which they were accustomed. It was, therefore, something of a busman's holiday to them, used as they were to living hand to mouth, waylaying strangers, and avoiding the law. All they had to do was keep an eye on the house across the valley from their encampment and, should the owner leave, go to the nearby village and report the fact by telegram. Leave, that is, with luggage. Their leader, their employer, their *owner* was not interested in trips to buy a bottle of milk and a loaf. These were logged in haltingly formed letters scrawled into a notebook, but were of insufficient import for concern. If, however, he left with luggage including—probably—something coffin-sized and likely at night, they were to report this with alacrity. It did not do to fail in orders, not even in the slightest detail. Their employment was profitable, it was true, far more than they would have believed possible even a year before. But the other side of the coin was a level of discipline to which the wise had adjusted quickly.

It was after all a dangerous, even fatal, mistake to disappoint the Red Queen.

'The book details . . .' Cabal paused to reconsider his words. 'The book *implies* methods by which these splinters may be located.'

'Are these like pocket universes, Johannes?' Horst had his best serious face on, and it was a reasonable question. 'Like that one with the drizzle and the croquet?'

'You remembered that? No. Not really. The Eternal Garden and its cousins—'

'That place has a name?'

'It does. I just coined it. The Eternal Garden and its cousins are constructs, very deliberately created by wit, wile, and a lot of mathematics. The splinters of reality to which the book refers are more natural in their creation. They are literally the stuff of legend. The creations of a mass *gestalt*, not necessarily—as I hinted earlier—of human intellect. They are of a feather to the hidden places of the fey, and share many of the same dangers.'

'Oh, goody,' said Horst. 'I was wondering when we'd get onto the dangers. Come on, then. What are we likely to encounter?'

Cabal was pleased that his brother was so engaged upon the project at hand that he easily used 'we' when describing the approaching travails. He gave no indication of that pleasure, however. It would never do to give Horst the impression, truthful though it might have been, that he both required and wished his brother's involvement.

'The usual. Monsters, deathtraps, riddles, plentiful opportunities for derring-do.'

'What an interesting definition of "usual" you have . . .'

'It isn't by choice, brother. These are places created, as much as anything, by an unconscious yearning for the impossible, and the certainty that any fruit worth the taking will not be easily plucked. We shall be confronting the results of millennia of human ingenuity, wilfulness, and malice. Nor just that of humans. We shall tread in the shadows cast by campfires and their stories, of the tales of minstrels, of every idiotic blood-soaked fable told by an elder sibling to terrify the younger.'

Here Horst scratched his jaw, and regarded Cabal from under a censorious brow. 'You're not still looking under the bed before retiring, are you? Anyway, given your line of work, I'd have thought that was a good habit to get into. Lord only knows what ghosties and ghoulies and long-legged beasties *you've* stirred up in your time.'

'I tend to shoot them at the time of stirring. It saves later unpleasantness.'

'Never put off an unpleasantness until tomorrow when you can be unpleasant today?'

Cabal shrugged. 'In principle, yes. There is another consideration.'

'Thank heavens. It was all beginning to sound so easy.'

'The Lady Ninuka.'

Horst sat up suddenly. 'The Red Queen?'

'I suppose she's a *de facto* queen, now. Queen Ninuka of Mirkarvia. That country seems to have no luck at all. If only you had slain her while you had the chance.'

It was an unwise thing to say. 'I *didn't* have a chance. You weren't there. Don't be so bloody ignorant.' Horst sank back into a louring attitude, unusual for him.

Cabal belatedly remembered something he'd come across once.

It was called 'diplomacy' and it was, in principle, lying as an instrument for making people feel not quite so ill done to. This would seem to be an ideal situation on which to ply such a discipline, as it occurred to Cabal that not only had Horst failed to kill Ninuka, which was embarrassing enough, but that the woman Alisha Bartos, currently to be found occupying a barrel in the cellar, had died in that encounter, and that Horst may have harboured some sort of emotional attachment to her. Perhaps diplomacy was the correct tactic to employ at that moment, Cabal concluded. Thus steeled in his intent, he hazarded an attempt at this exciting new conversational form.

'It wasn't your fault,' he said, and rested from his labours.

It didn't seem to have entirely worked. 'I didn't want to kill Ninuka, anyway. That's not the sort of person I am, Johannes. I'd, y'know, sort of had vague ideas of arresting her. Capturing her. The Mirkarvians have been hurt by her far more than anyone else; they deserved to put her up on trial. If they want to string her up at the end of it, that's their concern. I'm not some sort of executioner.'

Cabal was hardly listening. Horst had entirely failed to appreciate the delicacy and elegance of his utterance and was instead blathering about failing to kill Ninuka. Holding down his exasperation at his brother's arrant twittery, he said, 'No, no. I wasn't talking about Ninuka. I was talking about you getting the Bartos woman killed.'

The short pause that ensued was more than sufficient to assure Cabal that there was far more to this 'diplomacy' malarkey than he had perhaps given credence.

'Not that you did,' he added.

Horst's anger flared across his face and passed in a flicker to be replaced by a dour acceptance that this was his brother he was talking to, and the lifetime of making allowances that this betokened.

'That's your idea of diplomacy, is it?' he asked. Cabal shrugged; *perhaps*. 'Let's just skip that whole unhappy episode and get back to what you were saying, shall we?' Cabal shrugged; *yes, let us do that*.

'Notes. There were none. Ninuka's scientific library was . . . idiosyncratic, to say the least. About a third of the books made no sense in context. Popular histories, dreadful calumnies, much the same where necromancy is concerned. They had no place there. The rest, however, were sensible choices, including a couple of rarities.'

'Like the Prester John book?'

Here Cabal paused and seemed troubled. 'No. It is a great rarity to be sure. Indeed, the only extant copy as far as I know. But, it is not a book of necromancy. I only recognised its great utility to my researches due to a great deal of reading and peripheral references.' He looked deeply perplexed. 'It has taken me years to reach that point, Horst. Is she really such an extraordinary prodigy as a necromantrix that she arrived at the same conclusion so much more quickly and then was able to actually procure this rarest of texts?'

'It's . . . possible?' said Horst, deploying the meanest slivers of tact under the circumstances. If he meant to sting his brother by the unavoidable implication, he was disappointed. Cabal was too wrapped up in conjecture to notice.

'Possible, of course. Probable . . . its probability concerns me. What I understand of Ninuka's intelligence is that, while she is by no means stupid, her nous is not of the academic variety. Indeed, before she was—'

'Provoked?' offered Horst.

'—*inspired* to take up necromancy by—'

'You murdering her father?'

'—*circumstances*, she seemed to have no scientific interests at all. Apart from a very specific branch of biology, at any rate.' He glanced at Horst, whose left eyebrow had risen on a tide of curiosity. 'You would have liked her then.'

'Ah,' said Horst, to whom all had become clear.

'From Lady Bountiful to an evil fairy-tale queen in a single bound seems prodigious.' He nodded, conceding the point. 'But not impossible.'

'You should be proud, Johannes.' Horst's tone was hardly conciliatory. 'She is your creation, after all.'

At this, Cabal coloured slightly, but then subsided quickly. 'Unkind, but true, I regret to say. Most of my more malignant creations are more easily dealt with, too.'

'I doubt she's going to succumb to a few sharp blows with a retort stand, no.'

'Oh, she probably would. Getting within a country mile of her with a retort stand is the issue. I digress. The point I was making is that her notes were nowhere to be found in her laboratory. Whatever she had culled from her books and her researches is contained within them, and those notes represent the nucleus of the threat she represents.'

'Threat? What threat? She's in Mirkarvia, we're in England's green and pleasant land. She's a long way away.'

Here Johannes Cabal furnished his brother with a look that spoke of disappointment largely with himself at trying to talk to Horst when he could be talking to some lichen, which would probably understand the situation better.

'She's very rich, ruthless, and motivated. Mirkarvia really isn't that far away when one has access to at least one fast air vehicle. I doubt the *Catullus* is the only thing she appropriated from the Mirkarvian aeronavy, either. If she but knew of this house, a stick of bombs descending upon it from a cloudless sky would be a likely outcome. And don't tell me that she wouldn't risk the ire of the Royal Aeroforce by doing so; losing a ship would be a small price for her as long as she was not aboard.

'I don't believe revenge is her main concern at present, however. She must know I have *Presbyter Johannes*, and that will inform her actions. She knows I shall attempt to seek out the Fountain of Youth, be it actual or figurative. She will attempt to beat me to it. I am sure of it.'

'But you don't know where it is.'

'I know several places where it *might* be. They will have to be investigated until the correct one is found.'

'How many is "several"?'

'Five, scattered across Europe, Asia, and Africa.'

Horst blanched. 'That will take years!'

'Months, but too many months. Given her resources, Ninuka will almost certainly find the majority before us.'

Horst rose and paced up and down. 'Well, here's a pretty problem.'

'Not at all. If the sites are explored sequentially, yes. If, however, two expeditions go forth, then I think that tips matters back in our favour.'

Horst stopped in his pacing. 'We split up? I'm not sure that is a very good idea, Johannes. For one thing, there's the way I tend to burst into flames in daylight. That's limiting. And, to be honest, I'm not sure I'd recognise a knife-thin sliver of a conjectural reality if it bit me.'

Cabal smiled at him or, at least, the furthermost point of his mouth rose. 'Trust you to do this by yourself? Ever the joker, Horst.'

'Thanks.' Horst said it without a reciprocating smile.

'No, there will be physical danger, and there will be challenges of an intellectual nature. You can surely handle the former, but with all due respect . . .'

He did not finish the sentence, nor did he need to.

Horst sat down heavily and crossed his arms.

'In truth, I have the opposite problem. There are things in this and others worlds that are unimpressed by even a Webley .577. What I propose, therefore, are two teams of two. We shall procure the services of somebody able to look after themselves and me into the bargain for one duo, and somebody with perspicacity, wit, and intelligence to make up for your shortcomings in those attributes to join you in the other.'

Horst shrugged off the slurs upon his intellect with brotherly ease. 'That's another quest in itself, surely? By the time you've found these paragons, we might as well have tried to do it all ourselves in any case.'

'I know where to find them already,' said Cabal. 'That is not the hurdle. Persuading them is the rub. Well, for one, at least. The other will certainly prove more enthusiastic.'

At this point, Cabal's face did a strange thing, a sudden flexion and tautening that was brief, but that filled his brother with wonder.

'Did you just *smile?* I mean, really smile? Not one of those things you call a smile that frightens donkeys, but a real, actual smile?'

To which Johannes Cabal said nothing, but the ghost of that fleeting expression glowed upon his countenance for some time after.

It was an unassuming cottage overlooking an unassuming little market town, but it was homely and comfortable and a pleasant enough place in which to spend one's retirement. It had once been visited by a small bit of elemental evil that had disported itself around the fireplace and almost resulted in a death and a damnation, but that was years ago, and one has to let these things go ultimately, doesn't one? The reminders crop up now and then, and dreams sometimes colour into nightmares at what almost was and what awful thing might have been. The day comes, and the half-remembered blows away, dust on the breeze. The calamity did not come to pass. The agent of evil turned out to be wrought with internal conflict. The last hope was fruitful.

Still, for all this, Frank Barrow was only momentarily surprised when that agent reappeared on his doorstep, bearing flowers, a bottle of decent wine, and asking curtly if politely if his daughter, Leonie, happened to be in residence. This moment of surprise passed easily from Barrow to Cabal, as he punched the necromancer a beautiful right straight to the jaw that felled him like an ox introduced to a poleaxe.

Barrow stood over Cabal, fists up and furious. 'Get up, you bastard! Get up so I can knock you down again!'

Cabal blinked to dispel stars, but was only partially successful. He tried his jaw with his hand to make sure it was still there. Remarkably, it was; retired he might be, but ex–detective inspector Francis Barrow was still not a man to invite into a physical contretemps lightly.

'I shall stay down here in that case,' said Cabal. 'I have no desire to be knocked down again.'

Here, Barrow made the shade of the Marquess of Queensberry

very sad by kicking his opponent in the ribs. Cabal, however, had not lived as long as he had without allowing for contingencies. Mr Barrow being rather put out to see him had not even been a very unlikely one. Cabal reached inside his jacket and, when his hand reappeared, it bore a businesslike semi-automatic pistol of Italian pedigree. This he aimed at Barrow's head in a manner that implied a second kick would be unwise.

Barrow backed away a step. 'Why have you come back, Cabal? You're not bloody welcome here.'

'So I gather.' He took up the bottle—unbroken due to a fall into a rose bed—and the bouquet—dishevelled, but still presentable—in his off hand and showed them to Barrow. 'I brought peace offerings. I understood that was the done thing.'

'Cabal?'

Frank Barrow looked back. In the corridor behind him stood his daughter, Leonie, her unruly blond hair temporarily corralled in a ponytail. 'I'll deal with this, love,' he said. He might have been talking about a dog's leaving upon the garden path.

'Fräulein Barrow,' said Cabal, 'always a pleasure. I would rise, but your father has promised to knock me down again.'

'You're pointing a gun at him, Cabal.'

'I am, yes.'

'Last time I saw you, you were pointing a gun at me then, too, you pallid bastard,' said Barrow.

'So I was. You're right; it's unfriendly. I shall suggest a compromise. I shall put the gun away, and you do not kick or punch me or otherwise do me harm. Is that acceptable?'

It was barely that. Barrow stood pale and almost quivering with rage over Cabal's prone form. It was left to Leonie to say, 'Yes, it is. Dad, step away from him, for heaven's sake.'

'What?' Barrow swung his head to face her, disbelief in his eyes. 'You can't want to take this evil bugger's side?'

'I'm not taking anyone's side,' she said. 'But look at the pair of you. I don't want to have to clear up any blood. You're all set to beat him into a pulp, and believe you me, I know Cabal would shoot you without hesitation. I don't want to have to deal with any corpses today, thank you. We have enough trouble getting the dustbin men to take away extra rubbish at the best of times.'

Barrow knew his daughter of old, and so backed down first. He made a show of unclenching his fists and nodded at Cabal. 'Put yon gun away. I'll not hit you. Though God knows you deserve it.'

More quickly than he might once have done, Cabal accepted Barrow's acquiescence. He smartly aimed the gun away, lowered its hammer, re-engaged the safety catch, and returned it to its holster. 'May I get up now?'

Barrow snorted, which was the closest to an affirmative he felt like giving at that moment. Cabal carefully and without sudden moves climbed to his feet. He addressed Leonie. 'I brought wine. And flowers. You may wish to place them in a vase. With water. They are already dead in any real sense, but the water will preserve the appearance of life for a little longer.'

Leonie accepted them despite a warning glance from her father. 'Why, Mr Cabal. How romantic. Please, come in.'

'Leonie!' Barrow stepped into Cabal's path as he tried to follow her into the house. 'This is my house and that . . . man is not coming in. Have you forgotten what he did? What he *is*?'

Cabal's eyes narrowed suspiciously. 'You speak of the carnival?'

'Of course! What else?'

Cabal leaned slightly to look at Leonie past Barrow. 'You haven't told him?'

Barrow's brow fogged with confusion. 'Haven't told me what?' he demanded of his daughter.

She smiled at him, a little weakly.

It took longer than it needed to, to tell Frank Barrow of the fact that Leonie, his daughter and only child, had actually met Cabal twice in the intervening years, and had kept it from him because, 'I thought it would upset you.' In this, she was absolutely correct.

'Twice?' Barrow was not sure what he ought to be most horrified by; that she had met Cabal again on two occasions that might reasonably be described as fraught, that she had kept this intelligence from him, her own father, or that she had come away from these encounters with a growingly positive view of a man whose business included body snatching and consorting with supernatural minions of diabolical evil. He inwardly decided it was all pretty ghastly and said as much at regular intervals, hence the reason the history of the aeroship the *Princess Hortense* and the curious business of the Christmas at Maple Durham took so long to recount.

Throughout these recollections, Cabal remained quiet, less due to consideration of Barrow's pained feelings as a desire not to get punched again. A painful jaw and some bruised ribs spoke volubly that Barrow's feeling towards him were not the finest. Even where his recollection of events differed from Leonie Barrow's or where he disagreed with her interpretation (the latter was the more common), he maintained a silence birthed of self-preservation.

When she had at last finished, there was a heavy silence that Cabal punctured by saying, 'Would anyone like a glass of wine?'

'The kitchen's through there,' said Leonie with a nod. 'Corkscrew's in the cutlery drawer by the cooker. Wine glasses are in the cabinet over the worktop.' Cabal rose uncertainly and went to fetch them. As he reached the door, she added, 'Take your time.'

Barely was the door shut behind him when he heard Barrow's voice lift. 'How could you? He's a bloody monster!'

'He *was* a monster,' he heard her reply, and he was inexplicably heartened by this. He set off to find the corkscrew and glasses, and he took his time doing so.

He found them immediately, and dawdled for a few minutes, watching the day dim though the kitchen window as the sun touched the horizon. When the voices from the parlour had diminished from full rancour to an aggrieved resentment communicated in mutters and sharp rejoinders, he judged the time right to return.

'I'll be mother,' said Leonie, taking the corkscrew from Cabal and using its blade to break the wax around the bottle's cork. Barrow occupied the time by glaring at Cabal, Cabal by finding almost everything in the room of interest with the exception of Barrow's face if the line of his wandering gaze was to be believed.

Leonie passed a filled glass to Cabal and slid one to her father across the tabletop when he seemed not to notice it proffered to him.

'My daughter,' said Barrow in clear syllables that brooked no interruption, 'tells me that you're not such a bastard any more.'

Cabal shrugged modestly. 'Well, I—'

'My daughter,' said Barrow, 'tells me you don't work for . . . a certain entity any more.'

'That was more of a temporary arrange—'

'My daughter,' said Barrow, 'tells me that you have done *good.*'

Here, Cabal paused. Yes, he had done good. By accident, as a by-product, by serendipity. But yes, he had done good. He just didn't see why people kept wanting to rub his nose in it.

Unsure how to answer, he said nothing, and inadvertently seemed modest by it. All unaware, he sat cloaked in unwitting humility.

Barrow took up his glass. 'All right, then. Let's hear it.' Cabal looked inquisitively at him. 'What are you doing here, man?'

Explaining the concept to Horst had taken long enough. Horst, for his part, was a moderately intelligent man who was also a vampire; a man who had encountered werewolves, *döppelgangers,* creatures from beyond the veil of our reality and a fell beast that was half-man, half-badger. He was alive, or at least undead to the possibilities of the eldritch. Frank Barrow was a former police officer who lived in a cottage, and to whom the only thing he might consider truly unusual in his life had consisted largely of Johannes Cabal and the travelling entourage he nominally managed at the time.

He still cottoned on to what Cabal was asking faster than Horst had, and Leonie was a few seconds ahead of him.

'The secret of life itself?' said Barrow. 'That's what you're after?'

Cabal raised his hands modestly. It was a modest enough goal, after all.

'But you have no idea what form this secret might take?' added Leonie.

'None. The text from which I am working is long on symbolism, short on detail. It may be a principle. It may be a literal fountain. I tend towards the former view.'

'And what will you do with this secret, assuming there even is a secret, and assuming you get your grubby little paws on it?' Frank Barrow was still not convinced that Cabal was anything other than the soul-stealing huckster he had once been and made few pains to hide it. 'Sell it? Use it for nefarious ends?' Barrow had once heard a chief constable speak of nefarious ends and been impressed by the phrase. Whatever these ends were, they sounded like they were an end unto themselves, self-contained little parcels of villainy that malefactors collected as a scout collects badges.

Cabal started to reply, but was overcome by nonplussedness for a moment. When he recovered his wherewithal, he asked, 'What sort of "nefarious ends", exactly?'

Barrow grimaced at such sophistry. Inwardly, he imagined one nefarious end being *The Commission of Arson Using Only Two Matches.* 'You know full well what I'm talking about.'

'In the first instance, Herr Barrow, you may have been led astray by my activities when first we met. I am not usually engaged in business, not even the running of a carnival. Money matters little to me. I only seek to save someone.'

'Who?'

'That,' said Cabal, a little steel showing in his voice, 'is my concern. You need not worry that I intend to raise some dreadful dictator or similar from the grave. Politics concerns me fractionally less than business, and business concerns me not at all.'

'Not good enough. You can't expect my daughter to go along with your schemes without so much as a hint as to the reason for it all.'

'I don't need to know,' said Leonie. 'You're a man of honour, Dad. I've always respected that. Well, this is my honour, and Cabal . . . Mr Cabal saved my life. I owe him a debt.'

Cabal shook his head. 'No. I make no claim upon any such debt, not least because you saved my life, too.'

'I did?' Leonie looked astonished.

'You could have reported me to the authorities at any point. I doubt my life would have seen out an hour subsequent such a denunciation. That is by the bye. Even if a debt did stand, I cannot impose upon you to help me in this undertaking from any sense of obligation. There will undoubtedly be danger. I hope and trust the goal will be more than worth any such peril, but the peril will be real, nonetheless. You must make your decision based upon whatever merits you see in this enterprise.'

'And if I think it's a fool's errand?'

'Then you would be a fool to agree.'

'Very well.' Leonie sat back, cosseting her wine glass. 'Convince me. Why should I help?'

'Simply put, because lives depend upon it. Two lives.'

Leonie glanced at her father and back at Cabal. 'That's not some sort of ham-fisted threat, is it?'

Cabal was silent for a moment while he digested the implication. 'No, no. As I think I said to your father once, I really do not care for threats very much. Warnings, perhaps, but threats, no. The lives to which I allude are already extinguished. Unfairly, and before their time.'

'Life's unfair,' said Barrow. He regarded his hands clasped together on his lap, anything to avoid looking at the picture of his wife on the mantel. 'Death twice as much. You can't go gallivanting around undermining eternal verities just because they happen to nark you off a bit.'

'Two questions, Mr Barrow. Firstly, why ever not? All science is based on the precept that we know too little. Ignorance is not bliss. It is only ignorance. Its bed partner may be the inertia of the conservative. Often it is only fear. If death may be cured, why should we regard it as anything different from curing the common cold, or cancer? Secondly, if an eternal verity turns out to be neither eternal nor true, why defend it? It is said that death and taxes are the only inevitabilities in life. It is, I understand, meant in a jocular manner, but nevertheless, if there was some miraculous economic formula that meant you never had to pay a penny in taxes ever again, yet there were no dreadful repercussions, no collapse in public services, would you not rush to embrace it?'

'That's chalk and cheese—'

'Is it? What, then, is your objection?'

'This thing you're looking for, it's against nature.'

'If the mechanism exists, it is part of nature. By definition, it cannot be anything but natural.'

Barrow's face flushed. 'It's against God's law.'

It was possibly not the best argument to employ against a necromancer. Still, by a remarkable feat of self-control and a mental image of Horst slowly mouthing the word *Diplomacy*, Cabal managed not to burst out in peals of bitter laughter.

'Mr Barrow, I appreciate that God's opinion probably matters a great deal to you, but—truly—He doesn't care. If the object of this quest is against God's notoriously morphic and ill-defined law, it wouldn't exist. The only promise we have from the mouth of that deity worth spit is that of free will and self-determination. Everything else is open to negotiation.'

'You're a blasphemous bugger, Cabal.'

'I'm rational, unlike your God. Really, when has He ever stuck to His word?'

Barrow smiled grimly. Finally, Sunday school was going to prove its worth. 'The Flood. God promised never to do it again.' He crossed his arms. 'And He never has.'

Cabal was underwhelmed by this argument. 'Really. And when somebody drowns in a natural flash flood, say, what's that? A white lie? No, Mr Barrow, the only time your God takes a blind bit of notice of you is when you die. Either you go off to the petty sadist in the other place—'

'You mean the devil? Satan?'

'The devil, yes. Satan, I'm no longer so sure. I'm beginning to think it's a job description rather than a personality.' He waved an impatient hand, as if wafting away a cloud of dumbstruck theologians. 'But that is neither here nor there. Or, as I was saying, you end up in the personal collection of the entity you call "God". He . . . it chamfers off any awkward corners that might indicate bothersome traces of individuality, and stacks the homogenised souls into the eternal equivalent of pigeonholes.'

Barrow flinched at Cabal's description of Heaven. 'You can't know that.'

'I know enough to know God does us no favours. The heavenly afterlife is very much what atheists have long suspected: nothingness. Where they are wrong is that it isn't the simple cessation of all sensation and awareness, but the engineered nothingness of an entity who hates mess and fuss. Consciousness . . . poo. Will . . . won't need that. Memories of life and love and everything . . . tiresome. God is not your friend. God has *never* been your friend.'

The room grew quiet.

'Perhaps,' said Leonie, 'perhaps working to undermine my father's faith wasn't the best way to talk me into coming along.'

'Wasn't it?' Cabal thought about it, and salted that information away for some future date when it might come in useful. 'Oh.' He nodded at Frank Barrow. 'Well, he started it, believing in nonsense.'

'Not an improvement. Look, Cabal, you're setting about this all wrong. I'm not very interested in having you gain the secrets of life, whether it be bringing back the dead in a way that doesn't involve brain-eating, or potentially immortality. For one thing, just think what it'll do to the population figures.'

'I wasn't planning on marketing it . . .'

'I appreciate that. No matter what, it's not my concern. It has never been my concern.'

'Ah.' Cabal picked up his glass as if considering finishing the drop of wine at the bottom, but put it down again undrained. 'I'm sorry to hear it, Fräulein Barrow. I am sorry I've wasted your time. Mine, too, but I regarded it as necessary.' He rose awkwardly. 'I shall see myself out.'

Leonie watched him complacently. 'You're adorable when you do that, you know? Your injured-pride face would melt a puppy.'

Cabal's expression was uncertain; he had seen a molten puppy once, and it hadn't been *that* adorable.

'Sit down,' she said. 'We're not done yet.'

'With respect, Fräulein Barrow, I understood that we were. You do not wish to help me. I shall have to look for aid elsewhere.'

'I said nothing of the sort. You forget, Cabal, I'm a scientist myself.'

'Criminology, I believe?'

'You remembered.' She smiled a sweet smile like icing on a razor. 'I have my own interests. For one thing, bringing back the dead would make my job a lot easier. Or, I admit, obsolete.' She adopted a poor workable Cockney accent. "Orright, Bert, 'oo did you in?" "It were 'im, guv'nor! Stabbed me to death good and proper an' dropped me in the river. I'll swear to it in court." '

She observed conflicting expressions on the faces of Cabal and her father, the former somewhat taken aback by the amateur dramatics, the latter suddenly remembering a few old cold cases from his career that might finally be brought to book by this development.

'But that's not what I'm talking about in this case. These fragments of myth of yours, Cabal. They exist?'

'I believe so, yes. I believe so very strongly. I have seen variants of the same mechanism; these "fragments" are hybrids of the two. The only reason that they are not generally known is because they are not easily discovered or entered.'

'Now *they* fascinate me.' She shrugged. 'Who wouldn't be by the thought that our world contains such things, like reading a novel and finding pages of another book mixed in?'

'It's dangerous,' both men chorused and looked at one another.

'Life is brief, opportunities to see the extraordinary are rare. It's not as if I'll be by myself, Dad. Cabal here is a rare survivor. If I have his word that he will not abandon me, that's good enough for me.'

'Ah,' said Cabal slowly. 'That's not *quite* the plan.' He looked out of the window. Beyond the net curtains, dusk deepened.

'It isn't?' said Leonie.

'Not quite. Pardon me a moment.'

Cabal rose and left the room. They heard him go to the door and open it. Frank and Leonie Barrow heard Cabal speak in lowered tones. A voice, male, answered him. The Barrows looked at one another with cautious surprise. A moment later Cabal re-entered the room.

'I should like to introduce you to my brother, Horst,' he said.

A tall man in his early twenties, handsome, pale, and with curls of light brown hair curling out from beneath his hat stepped into the room. He was dressed well in a suit of black with flashes of imperial purple at the breast pocket and lapels, the left of which bore a clove-red carnation as a *boutonnière*. He doffed his hat, and bowed to the Barrows.

'Hullo,' said Horst. 'More of a reintroduction, I think? We've met before.' He smiled, and his eye teeth seemed somewhat pronounced, yet it was no less charming a smile for all that. 'Hullo.'

It took a week to settle matters. Frank Barrow spent two full days of this trying to talk Leonie out of what he sincerely believed to be a disastrous decision. To his every argument, she would smile consolingly and answer with a counterargument that always, reduced to its most fundamental terms, ran thus: 'Science.'

To this, he had no response.

When it became apparent that no appeal to intellect, sympathy, or sentiment (he was too good a man to resort to emotional blackmail, no matter how profoundly he feared her loss) would dissuade her, he instead turned his attention to improving the odds of her safe return. The first step of this was when, on the morning of the third day, he came to her bearing, not argumentation, but a well-crafted but undecorated box of pale, varnished wood.

They sat together at the breakfast table, and he opened it. Inside lay a .38 revolver in a shaped covert lined with green felt. Around it, also snuggled into slots and alcoves, were the accoutrements of maintenance, and six live rounds.

Leonie looked at it for a long moment, expressionless. Then she took it up to examine it. 'Webley Mk.1,' she said. 'Cabal would approve. He usually carries a Webley .577.'

'I'm not giving it to you for his bloody approval.' It disconcerted him to see a firearm in his daughter's hands, frightened him, and he sat down to forestall the desire to take it from her. She was a grown woman, after all. She had an M.Phil and was working on a Ph.D. She wasn't his baby any more. Would never be his baby again.

'I thought you didn't like guns, Dad.'

'I don't. Bought that after . . . after the last time.'

He didn't clarify this, but he didn't need to. *The last time Cabal came into our lives.*

She weighed the weapon in her hand a moment longer, and returned it to its case. 'It's a kind thought, Dad, but I'm not taking this.'

'You need to be able to protect yourself. God only knows what sort of mess that maniac wants to drag you into. A vampire!' He looked around helplessly, as if something in the kitchen would appreciate his discontent. 'A bloody vampire he's got you running off with!'

'Horst seems nice enough,' said Leonie carelessly. 'He never wanted to become one.'

'Oh? So how did *that* happen? Caught vampirism off a toilet seat or something?'

'No. I *think* it was his brother's fault. Some experiment or something that went wrong.'

'Cabal made his own brother into a blood-sucking monster? Well, that makes me so much more confident about the whole thing now. If only he'd said, I'd have offered to go along myself.' He paused. 'I should go with you.'

'Dad, we've been through this. You're in your sixties, now, and—be honest—you've not kept yourself in the best condition.' Barrow looked down at his gut glumly; even his own adipose was betraying him. 'Cabal's a planner. He doesn't take risks he doesn't have to. And, when all's said and done, Horst is a blood-sucking monster, yes, but he's *our* blood-sucking monster. I'll be safe.'

'I'd be happier if you had a gun.'

'Dad.' She sat opposite him and took his hands in hers. 'I've *got* a gun.'

Barrow's mouth dropped open. 'You've what?'

'Senzan 8mm automatic. The man sold me a box of dumdums under the counter.'

'Dumdums? Bloody hell! How long have you had that?'

Leonie shrugged. 'Bought it after . . . after the last time.'

She didn't clarify this, but she didn't need to. *The last time Cabal came into my life.*

The brothers Cabal were staying in the next town, as they were not remembered entirely fondly in Penlow on Thurse where the Barrows lived. There had been the business with the exploding carnival, the giant ape, the demons, and so forth. It had even made the front page of the *Penlow Reporter*; FUSS CAUSED, screamed the headline on the story. THREE NOISE COMPLAINTS RECEIVED. Admittedly it had been a sidebar to a more pressing story about a small fire in a hayrick that had been put out quite quickly. They took their hayricks seriously in Penlow on Thurse.

So, Johannes Cabal had taken a room in a bed-and-breakfast establishment while Horst found a fairly comfortable and long disused tomb in the local cemetery, and the two brothers waited, one more patiently than the other. Finally, a telegram of acquiescence arrived, and Cabal met Leonie at the Penlow railway station, a station the railway company had been astonished to discover was not as decommissioned and demolished as their records showed and so quietly returned it to the schedules. Somebody had clearly blundered and, on the off chance it was somebody important, it was better to just let things be.

Cabal was pleased—perhaps even *very* pleased—to see Leonie, less so to see her father.

'Mr Barrow,' he said. He didn't trouble himself to fabricate even one of his least convincing smiles for the greeting. The two men understood one another completely.

Frank Barrow placed the end of one fingertip a quivering sixteenth of an inch from the tip of Cabal's nose.

'One hair. So much as one bloody hair on my daughter's head is harmed, and I will hunt you down to world's end. Do you understand me?'

'Of course.' Cabal took a half step back to remove his nose from the finger's proximity. 'And you should understand that no part of my plans involve anyone getting hurt.'

'You just look after her.'

'I shall not. My brother shall. He is to be her bodyguard and to sport his not inconsiderable abilities as and when they are required.'

Barrow's eyes narrowed. Horst struck him as possibly a bit of a lady's man, vampire or not. 'What sort of abilities?'

'Strength, alacrity, mesmerism, acute senses. He's rather impressive; I don't say that lightly.'

'I'll be okay, Dad,' said Leonie, returning from the kiosk with a magazine to read. 'Where is Horst, anyway?'

Cabal nodded towards the rear of the train. 'In the baggage car. The sun is up, and it and he are not especially compatible.' He picked up Leonie's valises and frowned. 'I suggested that you pack lightly, Miss Barrow. Money is not a concern, and the intention is that we buy supplies as and when they are required. What do you have in these bags, anyway?'

'Well,' she said brightly, placing a fingertip to her chin, 'the *brown* one has all my dresses and frillies and girly things in it. And the *cream* one, why, that holds my ammunition.' She smiled sweetly. 'All aboard!' She climbed up into the carriage, leaving an astonished Cabal in her wake.

Barrow smiled at him, not kindly. 'She's not even joking, Mr Cabal. Do not upset my little girl.'

Cabal hefted the bags onto the carriage and turned on the step to address Barrow. 'You will not believe it, I am sure, sir, but I hold your daughter in the highest regard. If any harm befalls her and it was in my power to protect her, you need not hunt me at all, for I shall already have died in her unsuccessful defence.'

As the train pulled away, Leonie waved at her father, and he waved back, albeit with a somewhat dumbfounded expression. She watched him vanish from view as the train left Penlow on Thurse Station and then Penlow on Thurse proper before turning to Cabal and regarding him with suspicion.

'Just *what* did you say to my father?'

'Oh, merely a bitter exchange of insults. The usual.' Cabal shrugged. 'It's what your father and I do.'

The train journey lasted several hours and was in all respects unremarkable, with the exception of the moment Leonie noted a milk churn had fallen from a waggon by a level crossing.

'Oh,' she said, observing this tragedy. 'That's a shame.'

This high point apart, they continued untroubled, at least externally.

'Where exactly are we going?' asked Leonie quite early on.

'Creslent,' replied Cabal, as if that answered everything.

'I'm not familiar with . . . What was it? Creslent? Where is that?'

'It isn't a town, if that's what you're thinking.' Cabal favoured her with a glimpse over the top of his spectacles. 'Nor yet a village.'

'A hamlet?'

'No.'

They continued in silence for a minute longer, Cabal reading a treatise for light entertainment and Leonie glaring steadily at him the whole time.

'Is it a house?' she asked at last. 'It sounds like it could be a stately home.'

'Yes.'

'Thank you. So where is this house?'

Cabal looked up from his treatise and furnished her with a light frown. 'What makes you think it's a house?'

'You just said it was.'

'No, I agreed that it *sounded* like it could be the name of a stately home. I certainly did not intend you to think that was what it actually was.'

'Cabal,' said Leonie slowly. 'When I said my cream valise was full of ammunition, I was not entirely joking. Do not provoke me.'

'Provoke you? I merely—'

'Creslent. Tell me what and where it is. Do not let a single morsel of other data leave your lips, or this quest of yours may finish in a messy railway murder. I hope I make myself understood.'

Cabal's frown deepened, indicating that, no, she had not, or at least not entirely. 'Messy in what sense?'

'Dumdum rounds. Soft-nosed with an asterisk cut into each and every one of them.'

'I was under the impression legislation had been passed against such munitions? Something about "contrary to the laws of humanity", I believe,' said Cabal. They regarded each other a moment longer. 'I feel sure that you are preparing a barb about me knowing all about being contrary to the laws of humanity.'

'Creslent, Cabal. What is it?'

'Very well, if it will calm your vexatious curiosity. It is an entrance into Hell.'

'Thank you!' said Leonie, not very graciously. 'You could simply have told me that when I first asked.'

Cabal said nothing, but returned to his book with the air of a long-suffering parent.

Presently his reading was once again interrupted by Miss Leonie Barrow pulling down the book in an impertinent manner and forcefully enquiring, an expression of soul-felt shock upon her face, 'An entrance to *where*?'

Creslent turned out to be a service entrance at the rear of a factory that made dinnerware. Cabal, Leonie, and—it being now comfortably after sundown—Horst stood in the lugubrious setting of a narrow English alleyway, cobbled and peopled by dustbins, backed by a low stone wall topped by rusting stanchions threaded by decaying barbed wire. In the field beyond, a solitary goat observed them.

'An entrance to Hell? Really?' Miss Barrow was still not entirely over her surprise.

Cabal did not answer. He was watching the goat as it watched them, and wondering if it were perhaps some sort of sentry.

Horst regarded the building with scarcely greater confidence than

Leonie. 'That reminds me, Johannes. You need more soup bowls. The ones you have are terribly chipped. That's probably not sanitary. Do you think while we're in here, we might pick up some replacements? Leave some money for them, obviously. I mean, we're not thieves, are we? Well, I'm not, at any rate. I'm sure Miss Barrow isn't, either.'

He did not extend this innocence of thievery to his brother, for he knew him too well.

'There are no soup bowls to be had beyond that door,' said Cabal, turning his attention to the steel door upon which local children had scratched doggerel and nicknames.

'Pretty poor crockery factory that doesn't make soup bowls.' Horst had decided he was an authority on dinnerware logistics.

'There isn't a dinnerware factory behind that door, except in a gross physical sense.' Cabal was examining the lock and handle under the light of an electric torch. 'I do keep telling you.'

'Your brother isn't being unreasonable, Cabal,' said Leonie. He paused in the examination to give her a somewhat crusty look. He had noted that she referred to his brother as 'Mr' or sometimes 'Herr Cabal.' He, however, was invariably just 'Cabal.' He wasn't sure whether this was a hooded insult or perhaps a mark of familiarity. In either case, he didn't like it.

'You really are children in the world of the occult, aren't you?'

'I'm a vampire,' said Horst, as if that conferred honorary membership in the World of the Occult, as if it were a friendly society, or perhaps a book club. He said it in such a tone of immoderate enthusiasm—it might have been described as 'perkily'—that any such organisation would likely have blackballed him on principle.

Both Cabal and Leonie opted to ignore the interruption. 'You've never struck me as the practical joking type—'

'I should think not . . .'

'—so I must assume that you are serious in your description of this shabby little door to a plate factory as in fact leading to Hell. What I can't see is why you're so adamant . . .'

And here she paused. Leonie Barrow was no fool, nor was her

father, and nor were the professors who had steered her through her university career. She was a criminologist to the bone, and that instinct and training now triumphed where her natural disbelief had not.

'The graffiti . . .'

'Yes?' said Cabal slowly, already knowing what she would say.

'The children around here must be very well educated.'

'That's one possibility.'

She borrowed Cabal's electric torch without seeking permission to do so and studied the scratches in the metal. Crudely done they might have been, and childish in form, but what was written there was another thing entirely.

'That's Latin. *Omnes relinquite spes o vos intrantes.*' She handed the torch back and stepped away from the door. '*Abandon all hope, O ye who enter here.*'

'Latin . . . hmmm . . .' Horst rubbed his chin. 'The "abandon hope" thingy. I've heard that somewhere before.'

Leonie looked at him oddly. 'You're a very handsome man, Mr Cabal,' she said after a moment.

'Oh!' Horst could scarce hide his delight. 'Why, thank you!'

'I don't suppose you bothered trying very hard at school, did you?'

'Well, no, I mean I . . .' The penny dropped with the psychic *ting* of a coin falling into a very empty vessel. 'Hold on, are you calling me stupid?'

'Of course not,' she said. Horst calmed a little. 'I only implied it.'

'Ah. *Ah.*' Horst turned upon his brother. 'This is your fell influence at work. Insulting people without insulting them. This is you all over.'

'And isn't it heart-warming?' said Cabal in tones sufficiently icy to dismay a mastodon. He was trying to concentrate on picking the lock. 'Might I have a little quiet? This lock is not a physical object in the usual sense. It requires more finesse than one can bring to bear with a bent hairpin.'

'Sorry,' said Horst, and stepped away.

He and Leonie watched Cabal wrestling with the mechanism for some minutes, the only sound being the clicking of the reputedly theoretical lock, Cabal's grunts of exasperation, and his occasional mutterings on the subject of somatic security. 'Like a ritual . . . rule of three . . . second ring defined by bears . . .' And so forth.

In his defence, Horst managed to hold off making inane comments for what was, to him, a herculean period. Eventually, however, he submitted to his natural predilection for inanity.

'Getting anywhere?'

Cabal paused in his work. There was a dangerous quality to his motionlessness that suggested a praying mantis, or perhaps a land mine.

'How do you pick a non-thingy lock, anyway? And did I actually hear you talk about *bears* earlier?'

Cabal rose from the crouch in which he was working and rounded on Horst. 'To address your points in the order in which you brayed them. Firstly, yes, I was getting somewhere, but now that progress has been lost. Thank you.'

'Oops.'

Cabal was advancing on his brother, who wisely was retreating.

'Secondly, one picks a non-physical lock whose apparent physicality is camouflage for the common crowd with intellect, experience, and—very important this—total concentration. My concentration has now been shattered and will probably take several minutes to recover after my doltish brother put a boot through it. Thank you again.'

'"Doltish" is a bit strong . . .'

'And as for *bears*, the simple answer to that is—'

A *click* interrupted him. Both men turned to see Leonie Barrow straightening up before the slowly opening door.

'What?' It took every iota of control Cabal had not to splutter. 'How?'

Miss Barrow held up a bent hairpin. 'I see what you meant about bears, though.' She looked at the growing gap betwixt door and frame and withdrew a little. 'Usually I'm all for ladies before gentlemen.'

'But not tonight,' said Cabal, sliding past her, his gaze never leaving the door. 'Very wise. Horst, come with me.'

'Right behind you, Johannes.'

'I was rather thinking of you going in first.'

'Age before beauty? Although I have a claim on both of those, now I think of it.'

'Supernaturally fast, strong, and resilient before mortal was my thinking.'

Horst was preserving his resources and so did not blur into action. Instead, he went through the door cautiously and slow, the only supernatural ability in play being his senses, brought to a high keenness. To those behind him, he was swallowed into a murky gloom of strange shadows and faltering luminescence. A moment later, they heard him call quietly back to them.

'This is the rummest plate factory I've ever seen.'

Horst's experience of plate factories was probably slight, but despite that, there is an expectation within the mind of anyone entering a plate factory that there should be certain elements present. For example, plates. As Cabal and then Leonie joined him beyond the strange door and its inconstant lock, it became obvious that plates were in short supply there.

'This really isn't the factory.' Miss Barrow's voice was a breath of wonder.

Cabal's brow betrayed fleeting irritation. 'I believe I said that. Repeatedly.'

'Yes, and I didn't believe you, obviously.'

Whereas the exterior of the factory was of a practical brick build, its walls painted white and the specific section that the door let into low-roofed and topped with red tiles, the interior was a wide dome, the walls constructed of exquisitely shaped blocks of basalt, not one of which could have weighed less than a ton, and whose apex was perhaps three times higher than the single storey in which it was supposed to exist.

The dome was supported by five thick columns of black marble, veined with a curious material that was sharp yellow in places but that seemed golden in others. The columns' bases were connected by a great circle of brass inlaid into the floor and, within the circle, the columns were connected to their alternating neighbours by similar lines of metal to form a pentagram. Just visible in the dim light was a low archway behind the column furthest from the door.

'Where does that go?' asked Horst.

'Hell,' replied Cabal. 'I believe I said that, too. *Also* repeatedly.'

Leonie stopped dead in her tracks. This, she could believe down to the very roots of her soul. The thought that one could simply walk through that archway and ultimately end up within the kingdom of Satan filled her with a horror that was as profound as it was existential.

'Why exactly are we here, Cabal?'

'Ah.' Cabal was pacing around the circle, examining it by the light of his torch. 'So you finally take an interest.'

'I thought you were talking figuratively! I kept asking and you kept saying, "An entrance to Hell," so I thought, *Very well, Cabal, have your moment of melodrama now and bathos later when it turns out you're talking about Ipswich or somewhere,* but you meant it. You actually meant it literally. So, I'm sorry for not taking you at your word, but now we're here I have a pressing desire to know *why are we here?*'

'We're not actually going to go to Hell, are we?' Horst had his hands in his pockets and was looking around the chamber like a schoolboy showing polite interest during an educational visit to an antimacassar museum. 'For one thing, it's probably quite a long way. I'd have suggested bringing bicycles if I'd known.'

'We are not. You may calm yourselves on that point.' Cabal had found a small and clearly deliberate break in the circle. He took a piece of chalk from his pocket, knelt by the break, and filled the gap with a drawn line. He rose to continue his survey. Any arcanist creating such a circle would only put a single break in it for convenience's sake. But the circle may not have been laid by such an arcanist, or even a human. There might well be a second, far subtler break in the circle elsewhere, rendering the pentagram deliberately useless and a trap for the unwary. Cabal tried to avoid being amongst the unwary; it was a demographic with a poor life expectancy.

'We are here because it puts us on the other side of the veil between the prosaic world and the Inferno. It has been my experience that crossing that divide by'—he nodded at the door, still ajar—'even a few metres can make all the difference.'

'Difference to what?' Leonie was glad the door was ajar and had positioned herself within easy running distance of it, should needs be.

'To the ease of certain procedures.' Cabal completed his circuit of the pentagram and returned to the chalked link. If there was another break in the circle, it was a microscopic crack, and he really didn't have time to go over every millimetre with a microscope.

'What sort of procedures?' asked Horst. He had unconsciously gravitated closer to Leonie, perhaps because he sensed the ease of the escape route she had adopted and might wish to use it, too, but more likely because, undead or not, he clove to the principle that being close to a pretty girl was infinitely better than not being close to a pretty girl.

'What sort of . . . ? Really, neither of you recognise a summoning circle when you see it?'

'No,' said Horst. 'A summoning? I've read about those. Don't they take ages and you need goats and a knife with a wavy blade and a virgin . . .' Here, he unwisely glanced at Leonie and discovered that it was not only the gaze of the sun that could wither him where he stood.

Cabal was removing his jacket and rolling up his sleeves. 'In the usual run of things, yes, except for the virgin. Never found a use for one yet.'

Horst had learned enough wisdom in the previous ten seconds not to offer any suggestions.

Cabal squared himself towards the centre of the pentagram, took a deep breath, and said, 'Zarenyia!'

His clear tone rang around the chamber for longer than perhaps it should have, and the echo diminished towards the very centre of the great five-pointed star.

'Before you really get started,' said Horst *sotto voce*, 'how long is this likely to drag on? If it's hours, well, you know I have to be mindful of dawn and everything, so just a rough . . .'

Abruptly, the summoning was over. Leonie gasped, Horst said, 'Blimey!' and only Johannes Cabal did not take a step back. He only crossed his arms and, most strangely, smiled.

Strangely for the circle was filled by a monster, a great beast of eight legs and the abdomen of a spider. Where the forebody of an arachnid might have been expected, however, a human torso extended, the upper body of a woman, her skin pale, her hair short and fiery red, her expression warlike. She wore nothing but, slightly unexpectedly, an angora sweater.

'Who dares?' roared the abomination. 'Who dares summon Zarenyia the Merciless from her infernal lair, the webbed caves of many deaths? Which puny mortal . . .'

'Hello,' said Cabal, his smile becoming unnervingly fond.

'Who?' The monster looked upon Cabal.

And then it squealed excitedly, clapped its hands, and capered on the spot, making a noise like a clan of stilt-walkers taking up tap dancing.

'Johannes! Darling! I am *so* sorry about all that "Who dares?" business. I had no idea it was you!' She moved quickly towards Cabal, and Horst was caught between bafflement and the feeling that perhaps he should save his brother from the monster.

He need not have worried. The spider creature apparently became aware of something none of them could perceive, and slowed as she reached the edge of the pentagram. She eyed the air with disappointment.

'A binding circle? Really, sweetheart? I thought we were past that stage.'

'Madam Zarenyia.' Cabal bowed to the creature, and—its smile returning—it curtseyed gracefully back. 'The summoning circle is a mere technicality. I must, however, ask a favour of you before breaking it.'

The monster steepled its fingers before it like an indulgent teacher. 'Fire away, you charmer. You always did know how to get around me.'

Leonie looked at Horst. Horst looked at Leonie. Those looks communicated that they had no words. They looked back at Cabal and the spider monster.

'You have guaranteed my safety already, yes?'

'Of course, and in perpetuity as far as I'm concerned. Unless you betray me or something frightful, in which case I *shall* kill you, but that's not going to happen, is it? We're best pals! No, you're safe with me, darling. Cross my heart.' And here she crossed a point midway up her sternum with a couple of transversal flicks of her fingers. She smiled, and the smile wavered as a thought occurred. 'Well, I *would* cross my heart, but it's back there somewhere,' she indicated the great abdomen, 'and I think it's more of a mass of peristaltic pipes than what you'd call a heart, but the principle's the same.' Her smile returned. ' "Cross my dispersed cardiovascular system and hope to die" doesn't have quite the same ring, does it?'

'That's perfectly acceptable, madam,' said Cabal, 'but on this occasion I am not alone.' He turned and pointed out Horst and Leonie. Somehow both managed smiles, although any list of adjectives used to describe those smiles must needs include 'wan,' 'weak,' and 'insincere.'

'Oh, you brought friends!' The monster leaned her upper body to see them better. 'Well, any friends of Johannes are friends of mine, I would say.' Her gaze settled upon Leonie. 'I say,' she asked of Cabal, 'are you and she lovers?'

'No!' said Leonie sharply, outrage outweighing caution. 'We are not!'

'Ooh, feisty. I like her,' said the monster, talking to Cabal as if discussing a pony. 'How about him, then?' She nodded at Horst. 'Are you and he lovers?'

Even Cabal was taken aback by this. 'Hardly, madam. That's my brother.'

The creature looked at Cabal for some seconds as if expecting further clarification. 'And?' she said when it was not forthcoming.

'I draw the line at incest, quite putting the vexed subject of homosexuality to one side.'

This revelation was greeted by a peal of happy, honest laughter. 'This is why I adore you, Johannes. You're so funny!' She looked at Horst more closely before leaning down towards Cabal to say in a low voice, 'By the way, your brother's a deader. You know that, don't you?'

In doing so, her angora sweater hung loosely before her, and the V-shaped neck loomed open. Horst found himself momentarily transfixed by the sight although for reasons he could not quite remember. The monster glanced upwards and caught his eye. Her smile became coquettish and somewhat predatory. 'Although not nearly as dead as he thinks he is,' she said with the hint of a singsong behind the words.

'Madame Zarenyia,' said Cabal, both unaware of and injurious to the slight mental fugue in which Horst had found himself. Horst blinked; what *had* he been thinking about just then? But Cabal was still speaking. Horst focussed enough to listen.

'Madam Zarenyia, this is my brother, Horst, who—as you so perspicaciously noted—is a deader. A dead man, that is. Specifically, a vampire.'

'Such an interesting family you have, Johannes. Hello, Horst. I hope we can be friends.'

'Madam,' said Horst, and bowed awkwardly.

'And this is Miss Leonie Barrow, criminologist and, for this endeavour at any rate, colleague.'

'Hello, darling.' Zarenyia spent far too long looking at Leonie. It felt to Leonie that she was being undressed and redressed in a variety of inappropriate outfits in the creature's imagination. 'And how did you happen to meet Johannes?'

'He tried to steal my soul,' said Leonie with more force than she had intended.

'Really?' Zarenyia glanced at Cabal and then back at Leonie. 'And they say romance is dead.'

'I'm afraid I shall require the same guarantees of safety that you so graciously extended to me to also apply to Horst and Miss Barrow,' said Cabal, blissfully unaware of the undercurrents travelling around the other occupants of the chamber.

'Of course. With the proviso that I may naturally defend myself and that any betrayal will be met with lovely amounts of retaliation, I hereby promise that I shall not kill, injure, maim, or otherwise cause physical or psychic or magical hurt to Horst Cabal and Leonie Barrow.' Then the monster raised its right hand, index and middle finger raised together, thumb across the ring and middle fingers. She smiled brightly. 'I here so swear. Dib, dib, dib!'

Cabal moved to scrub out the chalk line with his foot.

'*Dib, dib, dib?*' echoed Leonie. 'Are you serious? Cabal, what sort of guarantee?'

Cabal looked back at her, and his expression was severe. 'Madam Zarenyia's dibs are more than good enough for me,' he said, and broke the circle.

'Free!' screamed the monster, drawing itself up to its not inconsiderable full height and raising its arms. Cabal staggered back, stunned. Zarenyia smiled down at him. 'Made you jump! So,' she relaxed down again and rambled out of the circle, clapping her hands together once in satisfaction, 'what's the plan, Johannes? Will there be murder? I do hope so. I *love* murder.'

The chamber was as good a place as anywhere to discuss plans. Further, Cabal had a misgiving that Zarenyia—who occupied a space some five yards across from the tip of one arachnoid foot to the tip of its diametric cousin—might perhaps have a few problems getting out of the very humanly sized door. He vaguely hoped that she might have some sort of trick for managing the door, but that enquiring might force attention upon such a dull matter when he was very much enthused by talking about what he had planned for them all.

It took the best part of half an hour to explain the basic principles of what they would be looking for. (The overarching goal of an underlying principle of life that was called, for the sake of brevity, the 'Fountain of Youth,' was explained to Zarenyia in perhaps thirty seconds. This was largely because she was stupendously uninterested. 'Yes, Fountain of Youth. Very important. Understood. Yes.' She generally only perked up when the subject turned to possible threats and how they might be dealt with. It was plain she already had her strategies worked out for that.)

'I have arranged transportation to the two nearest sites. Once those are investigated, we will each move on to the next site on our lists. We shall then rendezvous at a midpoint convenient for us all and compare notes.'

'We shall?' Leonie cocked her head inquisitively. 'Why doesn't one group go on to the fifth site?'

Cabal looked uncharacteristically sheepish, albeit in an officious manner, like a bureaucrat caught out on the exact wording of subparagraph 27. Leonie read the meaning in that expression with great alacrity.

'Oh, my God,' she breathed.

'Language, darling,' said Zarenyia, legs folded under her in a nightmare of knees.

'You don't know. You don't know where the fifth site is. How can we do this if we don't know where all the threads of this great quest of yours dangle?'

'Miss Barrow has a point.' Horst seemed slightly shamefaced not to be supporting his brother, but only slightly. 'Surely if we miss any of the sites, it's all a bit pointless?'

'The book contains no clues to the fifth site,' said Cabal. He had coloured slightly under all this uncalled-for criticism and was moved to straighten his cravat. 'Only that its location and significance will become plain once the other four have been found. I strongly suspect that the fifth site is of a different sort to the rest.' He looked around their faces. 'I believe it to be where the fountain itself exists.'

'Oh.' Horst nodded. 'That's all right, then.'

'Is it?' Leonie wasn't having any of Cabal's vague hand-waving explanations. 'Is that all right?'

'Yes.' Horst nodded again, albeit a fraction less certainly. 'I expect so. Probably.'

'It is not in the nature of occult tomes to be blazingly transparent, Miss Barrow,' said Cabal. 'We are seeking out the secrets of life itself, not assembling a bookcase. Those secrets are hidden, and hidden for good reason. Can you imagine the state of the world if the Fountain of Youth was signposted so that any Tom, Dick, or Harry could waltz in and help themselves?'

'Happier?' suggested Zarenyia with practised ingenuity.

'It would be chaos. People living forever left, right, and centre, the aged skipping around like new lambs. Think of the impact on the population demographics!'

'Life insurance salesmen would be out of a job,' offered Horst.

But Cabal was not finished on his theme of keeping the wonders of the esoteric world away from the common herd who might do something ghastly and embarrassing, like use them. 'Scavenger hunts would include the Holy Grail! Tourists trooping around the crystal cavern that holds Merlin! Immortality and godlike power bandied around amongst people I wouldn't trust with a freshly sharpened pencil!' He realised he had raised his voice. He coughed and looked away. 'Chaos. It would be chaos.'

'And we don't like chaos,' said Zarenyia firmly. 'It's full of fish, isn't it, Johannes?'

This statement hung in the air for a long moment, partially due to the bafflement of Leonie and Horst, and also by the realisation that Cabal knew exactly what Zarenyia meant by it yet had no intention of elucidating.

'Quite,' was all he said on the subject. 'The book is in the nature of a key to an outer vault, represented by the four locations it describes. Those locations then constitute the key to the final, inner vault. There will be the Fountain of Youth.'

'Delightful.' Zarenyia yawned delicately. 'Now, let us address more important matters; what magnitude of frightfully evil, delightfully expendable enemies shall cross our paths?'

'If we're careful,' said Leonie, giving Zarenyia a guarded look, 'none at all. We can bypass most threats.'

'Oh!' Zarenyia seemed to have a brief attack of the vapours. 'But that will never do! Murders, Johannes! You said there would be murders!'

'I don't know why you're so keen on that,' said Leonie. 'Where there are murders, there are murderers. I thought we were trying to avoid trouble?'

'Not murderers, silly.' Zarenyia fixed Leonie with a fond smile. 'Murderer.' She held her hands out as if accepting applause. 'Me!'

Leonie regarded Zarenyia stonily. 'Cabal . . .'

'Do not trouble yourself, Miss Barrow,' he replied. 'You and Zarenyia shall not be travelling together. I shall be her companion.'

'*Companion*, he calls it,' said the spider-woman, and smirked. It was an expression that actually looked quite good on her. Then, with a clatter of eight armoured legs unfolding in an arachnid bloom beneath her, she rose. 'So I'm with you, and Little Miss Titian with the morals here goes with your brother—is that the plan, Johannes?'

'It is.'

'Perhaps . . .' Zarenyia looked speculatively at Leonie. 'Perhaps I would prefer to travel with her, and you can go with your brother the deader.'

'That is not the plan that I have formulated.' Cabal looked from Zarenyia to Leonie and back. Leonie caught his expression and noted some concern there. That, she felt, was reasonable.

'But she's so *prissy*,' said Zarenyia, and pouted. 'So holier-than-thou.'

'As you're a devil, *everybody* is holier than you, Madam Zarenyia.'

'Oh, you know what I mean.' She flexed her legs, lowering her forebody so she could look Leonie in the face. 'Butter wouldn't melt.'

Leonie made a point of looking Zarenyia in the eye as she spoke, but inwardly she quaked. Yes, a promise to cause her no harm had been made, but weren't devils notorious for finding loopholes? 'If you don't like that, why do you want to travel with me?'

'I didn't say I didn't like you. You just need re-educating a little.' And Zarenyia smiled a smile that promised pleasurable damnations by the wagonload.

They matched stares for several long seconds, but it was Zarenyia who broke eye contact first, though her smile did not waver a jot.

'Oh, you *would*, you know,' she said as she turned away. 'You so very *would*. But not just now. I can wait. Johannes, my sweet. I believe you are to be my travelling companion?'

Cabal looked slightly confused by events, but replied promptly enough, 'That is what I said.'

'Well, let us trot along, then. I adore adventures; let us have one.'

The First Way: JOHANNES CABAL, THE NECROPOLITAN

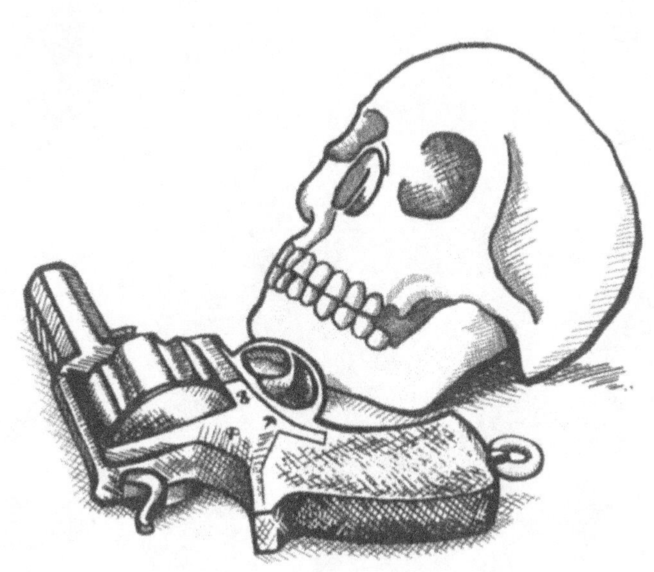

It is traditional to explain, in great detail, the necessary preparations for a lengthy quest of any description. Supplies must be secured, routes decided, contingencies explored, dwarves fed, and so forth. Johannes Cabal, by contrast, bypassed the first largely by the use of finances transferred to banks along the way and the possession of letters of credit and cash in hand for more immediate use, while the second and third hands had already been decided in sufficient depth by Cabal himself without reference to anyone else, thereby forestalling any muddying of the organisational waters by bringing the opinions of others into the affair. As for dwarves, they could feed themselves as far he was concerned; he had no time for them or their interminable songs about gold.

There were, however, a few problems that he was unable to address until they became immediate and unavoidable.

'I don't wish to be the gooseberry who spoils the party,' said

Horst, 'but Miss Zarenyia here is, by and large, a huge spider. I'm not sure they'll let you on a train looking like that, ma'am.'

'Won't they?' Zarenyia was miffed at such impoliteness. 'Well, that's prejudiced and barbaric of them.' She pouted and shook her head in a sharp little motion. 'Does this mean I shall have to pass for human?'

'I fear so,' said Cabal with uncharacteristic sympathy.

'Oh, how utterly loathsome,' she said, and adopted an expression of great concentration.

In juddering degrees, she leaned back so that the tip of the great abdomen touched the stone floor and the legs on her right side drew together, as did the legs on her left. There was no gradual metamorphosis, nor even an instantaneous change, but rather the disquieting air of two figures being there, one far more substantial than the other, formerly the spiderish in the ascendant and then latterly the human, although even that pivotal moment was impossible to judge or even to perceive.

Presently Miss Zarenyia was a fashionably dressed young lady with a small bustle where once she had sported a vast abdomen, a parasol, a hat, and even her hair had lost its gamine effect in favour of red ringlets that tumbled alongside the winsome face of the supernatural serial killer.

'That's how *I* wear my hair,' said Leonie Barrow.

'I know, darling.' The devil was unabashed. 'It's *pretty*.'

Seeing no satisfaction imminent in that quarter, Leonie instead appealed to Cabal, who shrugged, and said, 'It's pretty.'

So the matter was settled.

'The first two points of interest are in Abyssinia and Constantinople. Does anyone have any particular preferences?'

'Well, obviously Horst and Leonie shall go to Constantinople.' Zarenyia said it as a matter of indisputable fact.

'Why?' said Leonie, disputing it.

Zarenyia regarded her as if addressing somebody at a cocktail party who has just been introduced as the village idiot. 'Because Abyssinia is frightfully hot and sunny and so forth, and you're all pale and interesting. You'll fry like a sinner, and furthermore it will bleach that lovely straw colour out of your hair. It cannot be permitted.'

Leonie looked askance at Zarenyia. 'You're pale, too,' she pointed out. 'A redhead.'

'And—important point here that bears remembering—a devil. Not human in any sense that would delight the heart of a doctor. Denizen of Hell and all that? Everything is a warm afternoon to me, from pole to equator.'

Horst considered this. 'Doesn't that get boring?'

'No.' A thought occurred to Zarenyia, and she partially lifted her skirt to show her ankles. She regarded them with dissatisfaction. 'I am sure that you are all thoroughly delighted to be bipedal, but really, you don't know what you are missing out on. So wobbly.' She dropped the hem and looked around. 'So the scorching plains of Abyssinia for Johannes and me, and the louche pleasures of Constantinople for handsome Horst and lovely Leonie, then.'

And so that matter was settled, too.

It is further traditional to explain, in great detail, every footling detail of the trip from here to there. Why this should be is a mystery; one suspects it has something to do with contractual obligations with regard to the number of pages for such stories. Given that it is a novel that you are currently reading and not, for example, a travelogue or a hideously inaccurate biography of Sir Richard Burton, we shall therefore dispense with the travelling beyond the following few points.

It took Johannes Cabal and Zarenyia six days to reach a small township in the northern reaches of the country.

The trip was wholly uneventful, apart from the business with the slave traders. That all worked out well in the end as Zarenyia was given the opportunity to kill a few men, which improved her mood immeasurably, the rolling of the ship and the reduction in the number of legs she sported having combined to put her in a mild dudgeon.

There was also an attempted train robbery, but those happen all the time, so it's hardly worth noting.

It would be remiss not to mention, albeit in passing, the affair with the tomb guardians. And now that it has been mentioned, we may pass on.

Also, a matter of some giant ants, but—given Zarenyia's true form and some chemical ingenuity of Cabal's part—dealing with them was a trivial matter requiring only the inflammation of some five thousand gallons of aviation spirit and the destruction of a dam.

Thus, after six days of restful travel, Cabal and Madam Zarenyia arrived at the small township in the northern reaches of Abyssinia, formerly described by some European observers as being the seat of Emperor Prester John.

This came as a surprise to the Abyssinians, who pointed out that they'd never heard of a 'Prester John,' and that 'John' was a fairly unlikely name for an Abyssinian in any case. Also, that they didn't really have an exact term for 'Emperor' in the European sense, such creatures being surplus to requirements to the people of the region.* Therefore, of the name 'Emperor Prester John,' the first word was redundant and the last unlikely. They didn't know what a 'Prester' might be, either. Nor did the Europeans, but that didn't stop them from dismissing the Abyssinian protests as dilatory, distracting, and irrelevant. Wise heads in Europe had decided that—as it hadn't turned out to be somewhere in Asia after all—then here lay the empire of Prester John, and the locals were too ignorant to have noticed it, or they might possibly be hiding it along with the Ark of the Covenant in a hut somewhere.

'So is it here or isn't it?' asked Zarenyia. She was dressed in a summer frock of beguiling blue, unbesmirched by even a grain of dust, untroubled by any iota of feminine glow. Devils sweat when they want to, but it seemed like a lot of unnecessary work to her.

'I *thought* I had explained this before.' Cabal had, indeed, explained it before, but every explanation had been drawn down con-

---

* Hating to waste the datum, however, they diligently made a note and used it some years later.

versational side roads by Zarenyia not actually caring very much, or they had been distracted by attacking bandits, or giant ants.

'The empire of Prester John never existed *per se*. It is a chimera of a place, lent form by the optimism—they might have characterised it as "faith"—of hundreds of thousands of fools.'

'Christians?'

'I believe I implied that.'

Zarenyia, whose view of humanity was necessarily alloyed by lengthy experience, nodded. 'I see. So, who's this "Percy"?'

At which point the conversation meandered once more.

The locals, wisely, shunned the strangers, although that wisdom was likely a function of a general distrust of a pair of white people, as if white people had ever done anything reprehensible in the continent of Africa. This suited the Caucasians in question admirably, as—in fairness—they comprised of a necromancer and a soul-devouring (albeit well-spoken) devil, and they were up to matters philosophical and bordering on nefarious, as so much philosophy does.

'This is where the African location of Prester John's capital was assumed to be by the gullible of Europe,' said Cabal as they surveyed a small town, bounded by low hills on one side and an arid plain to the other. It did not seem to be much of a seat of anything, least of all government: scrubby trees, utilitarian buildings, bands of bush across the hills so darkly green as to be almost black, and a dusty pale red sand that coloured everything.

'Scenic.' Zarenyia seemed disinterested in the civic aspects of the place; the citizens drew her attention far more strongly. She regarded any passing man with an unwavering stare, the gaze of a praying mantis weighing up her prospects. The men started by walking by, and ended by scurrying out of sight, unsure why they felt so uncomfortable. 'Scrawny creatures, aren't they? Still, a soul's a soul.' She sighed. 'I am making myself *ever* so available, and all I'm getting for my troubles is a lot of frightened looks and scuttling. Haven't they ever seen a gorgeous woman before?'

'Perhaps, perhaps not. But if they have, I suspect that encounter involved blinking.'

'Blinking! I'm such a fool. I keep forgetting to do that.' She slowly closed her eyes and opened them again. 'There, perfect.'

'Perfection indeed, Miss Zarenyia, if only performed approximately twenty times faster.'

'So critical. I do it easily enough when I'm more *myself.* I'm concentrating so hard on not falling over when I'm forced onto two legs, I forget those little details.'

'Blinking.'

'Blinking. Breathing. Bipedal locomotion. That's just repeatedly interrupted falling over, you realise?' She smiled suddenly, her mood mercurial but rarely melancholy for longer than it takes to say 'melancholy'. 'So, onwards! To adventure, excitement, and oodles of delicious murder. How do we progress from this dusty town?'

'This dusty town is our destination, madam. I thought I had impressed that upon you many times during the journey here?'

'Oh, probably. But you do that thing and I get distracted.'

Cabal favoured her with a blink only slightly faster than her own. 'That thing?'

'You know.' He clearly didn't, despite her flapping one hand at him impatiently. 'That thing when you talk.'

Cabal considered. 'When I *explain?*'

'That's it! I just go, "Ooh, another explanation!" and then . . .' She passed the previously flapping hand across her face. Before it arrived, her expression was vibrant and engaged. After it had passed, her face was slack and her eyes rolled up. She held this for a moment before life returned. 'It's like magic! Hmmm.' She looked at him inquisitively. 'Are you *sure* that you're a necromancer? You might be a tediumancer without realising it.'

'Very well,' said Cabal. The very definition of 'a losing proposition' was to try to imbue Zarenyia with any sense of gravity or seriousness. 'No more explanations.'

'Unless I ask. And then make them snappy with lots of hand gestures so I don't suddenly pass out.'

'That is hardly me, madam. You describe an Italian. Nevertheless, I shall be brief. You will have to imagine the hand gestures. This'—and here he indicated the town—'is a mundane location lent arcane significance via—'

And here he was interrupted by Zarenyia's eyes rolling up, her jaw drooping, and a loud, pantomimish snore ratcheting up out of her throat as if she'd swallowed a ripsaw.

'It's a magic gate,' said Cabal.

Zarenyia smiled.

The necromancer and the devil processed through the court of Prester John with great aplomb born of ennui in the former case and a degree of playacting in the latter. Cabal walked steadily, his face stony, disregarding the fabulous sights of the most fabulous court the world had ever known, but that it had never been more than a phantasm of desperation. Before a stern throne of ebony curled around with what seemed to be the tusks of mastodons, Prester John looked down serried rows of lesser kings, plenipotentiaries, lords, and recanted sultans. Cabal ignored them all. Zarenyia waved, and smiled, and complimented people on their hats.

'Well, this doesn't seem so bad,' she said in a stage whisper.

'They cannot hear you,' said Cabal in his usual tones. 'They do not exist. They have never existed.'

'Hush! You'll upset them.'

But Cabal did not upset them, because they were entirely insensate to the presence of the interlopers. It was an endless moment of glory: the greatest Christian emperor—never defeated in war and bane of the infidel Mussulmen—accepted the same envoys, the same gifts, gave the same solemn nods of acknowledgement and acceptance, for all eternity, a gorgeously rendered painting from an improving book for Western children that lived and moved but never progressed.

'Oh,' said Zarenyia. 'Perhaps you won't upset them.' She crossed her eyes and pulled a horrid face in front of an emissary of the tsars. Beneath his fur hat, which must have been uncomfortable in that environment, he did not spare her a look, nor react in any way, or even sweat. She tried patting his face, but the solid flesh flowed around her fingers like motes in a shaft of sunlight and reformed quickly and perfectly. The emissary did not seem aware his cheek and jaw had temporarily been wafted into dust, but carried on as he always had.

'This is nothing,' said Cabal. 'At the always-present risk of boring you, I must emphasise that this is only a gateway. What lies beyond it will be far more solid, more reactive, and infinitely more dangerous.'

'Good-oh!' said Zarenyia.

Cabal opened his ubiquitous Gladstone bag and removed the small tripod with the telescopic legs from which depended the silver plumb upon its silver chain. He set this up beneath the gaze of Zarenyia, who regarded it all with the least possible interest, saving her attention and commentary for the wardrobes of the assembled spectres of those who had never died, having never lived.

Cabal in return ignored her notes upon that man's novel fez with the mechanical mice peeking from it, or that bishop's mitre of golden crystal, or that near-naked slave's natural charms. Around the throne of the emperor, and the subordinate thrones of 7 kings, the ranks of 62 dukes, of 256 counts and marquises, 12 archbishops and 20 bishops, Zarenyia wandered, and none escaped without some comment, her well of observation proving bottomless, her expression boundless, her conclusions pointless, but diverting for all that.

It was only when Cabal produced a syringe that her interest was piqued by the business in hand.

'Oh, narcotics! How very exciting. What will that do to you?'

Cabal regarded the syringe, then her, and decided this was going to become unnecessarily complicated. In this, he was perfectly correct.

'The drug will dull my mind, allowing me to enter the light trance necessary to precipitate the creation of a portal to the first of the pocket realities we must explore.'

'Dull your mind,' repeated Zarenyia, calculation upon her mind. 'A light trance.' She crouched by Cabal and looked him in the eye. 'You only had to ask, darling. You don't have to resort to polluting your pretty little body to manage that.'

Cabal didn't like the way the conversation was going at all. He sought respite in technicality. 'The technique is recognised. Indeed, I have experienced entirely satisfactory effects . . .'

'I'm sure you have, and now it's time for some new satisfactory effects.' She gently knocked the barrel of the syringe to one side with her index finger. 'Now hush and let me take care of you.'

'Madam Zaren—'

She lifted the same finger and placed it to his lips. '*Hush*,' she said with a subtle change of emphasis, taking it from a suggestion to an imperative too compelling to require anything so gross as an exclamation mark.

'—yeeuhhhh . . .' managed Cabal, the last syllables of her name turning to molten butter on his tongue, a process his mind seemed to be emulating. Cabal had, upon his first acquaintance with the devil some years previously, wondered how a woman with eight legs made such an infallible seductress given the prevalence of arachnophobia amongst the common people. He had subsequently seen her practise her wiles, which—although educational in its own way—had not sufficiently clarified why her lovers and victims (a tautology) so signally failed to appreciate that physical congress with a diabolical half-spider monster might not conclude with any sort of happy ending that they could later appreciate.

Now, and accepting the point that she was currently passing for human, he understood all too well. Back in the days when he ran a carnival, one of his hellish crew had belonged to the same order as Zarenyia, and she had carried a troubling air of incipient control around with her, too. On that occasion, however, he had never had the displeasure or otherwise of having that mien exerted upon him.

'There,' said Zarenyia in little more than a whisper. 'There you go. Easy to become stupid for me, isn't it?'

Part of Cabal was outraged by this assertion. It was positing explanations for the effect he was currently experiencing. Pheromones, perhaps. A supernatural hypnogogic agent exuded from her skin, and thence through his lips into his blood. A magical effect. As he considered these, his small internal committee grew smaller and quieter, until there was near silence in his mind. It was blissful.

'Now,' said Zarenyia. She straightened back to a stand and looked down upon him with that habitual, small smile on her lips. 'Now you're all dull, just like you wanted. And no nasty drugs. Say "thank you".'

Cabal made two small grunts that certainly sounded like 'Thank you' when they left the speech centres of his brain, but which seemed to have turned into syntactic porridge on the short run to his larynx, tongue, and lips.

Still, they sufficed. 'You're welcome.' She gestured vaguely at the court of ghosts. 'Now perform your wonderment, Johannes. Take us where we are supposed to be.'

Cabal lowered his eyes to the dusty stone beneath his knees, and his mind twitched in a reflexive, simple way that was far too mundane for him to cogitate in the normal run of affairs. The silver plumb weight swung violently upon its tripod, so violently that first this foot then that lifted. Then the tripod fell over as if kicked, the contraption tumbled onto its side, and the slight musical tinkle it made as metal tapped against metal seemed to raise the curtain upon an entirely new theatre.

The mirage that was the court of Prester John flicked away in that moment as if it were merely a reflection cast upon the glass of a deeper reality. A truer, hidden reality. A terrible reality.

It takes a great deal to frighten a devil, and Zarenyia was frightened. 'Johannes!' she cried. 'What have you done? Look where you have brought us! Pandæmonium!'

Angular plains crouched incipient and frangipane beneath a sky full of everything. If one took a surrealist of the first water, dosed him upon the most efficacious hallucinogens available, then took him to sit in Cthulhu's parlour for an afternoon, and finally gave him art materials to express the resultant inner landscape, it would still have looked like Market Rasen High Street on a wet bank holiday afternoon in comparison to Pandæmonium, and surely this locale was just as pandæmonius as all that?

Yes, but no. It certainly *seemed* like Pandæmonium, Hell's parliament eternally adrift in the spoil heap of the Abyss where Satan dumps his mistakes. But as awareness returned to the briefly enfeebled mind of Johannes Cabal, so did his rationality, and he was able to settle Zarenyia's mind just as easily as she had previously dulled his.

'No. Calm yourself. Pandæmonium possesses no natural ground, only the floors within the building proper. I grant you, there is a superficial similarity, but that is entirely due to the state of the sky, and that in turn is a result of an unfinished creation. It is a cousin of the Abyss, I admit, but it certainly is *not* the Abyss.'

Zarenyia looked around, trying to bring herself back under control. Cabal wondered what had happened since the last time he met her, that the Abyss had gone from a mild concern to a consuming terror.

'You're sure?' She looked at him seeking confirmation as a drowning man reaches for a straw.

'Madam, have I turned into a fish?'

She considered this. 'No,' she said. 'You haven't turned into a fish.'

At her first sight of the insane sky, she had instinctively drawn her head down, shying from the wrath of a cantankerous Lucifer. Now she straightened and looked at him and then the sky with full confidence.

'You're not a fish, so it isn't the Abyss.'

'I feel no chaotic effects upon me, and for that I am grateful and relieved. The fish business is not something I care to repeat.'

'You made an adorable hake.'

'Madam,' Cabal said with great dignity, 'I was a halibut.'*

* The history of Cabal's first acquaintance of the devil Zarenyia and of his brief time as a halibut is described in the story 'A Long Spoon'.

Matters of piscine nomenclature satisfied, the subject moved onto where exactly they had found themselves.

'I understand your concerns, madam. The sky certainly has a certain *abyssal* quality to it, but the rest of the environment is a very different thing.' He looked around the blasted wasteland, a frown forming. 'Very different indeed.'

'That's your "I'm having a clever thought" voice,' observed Zarenyia. 'I know that voice anywhere. What is your clever thought, darling?'

' "Clever" is a very subjective thing—'

'But you think you're terrifically clever, so we'll just take that for read, shall we? What's the thought?'

Cabal gave her a sour look. For an inhuman entity, she was sometimes disconcertingly human in her views and insights. Mind you, they do say that you are what you eat.

'I have seen somewhere like this before.'

'Well, it *is* a graveyard. That's like a social club to a necromancer, surely?'

'Matter of the unsociable natures of necromancers aside, yes, but no. When I say I have seen somewhere—*been* somewhere like this before—I do not speak of generalities. There is a distinct sense of—'

He broke off, staring down the ragged vale. Zarenyia allowed her practised disinterest a pause long enough to say, 'Whatever is the matter, Johannes? You look like you've seen a ghost. Oh!' She matched the direction of his gaze with excitement. 'Is it haunted? Tell me it's haunted!'

Cabal said nothing in reply, however. He started to walk in the direction of whatever had caught his attention, first in a distracted manner, then with determination, and then he started to run, leaving a baffled but increasingly enthused Zarenyia in his wake.

'Is there danger?' she called after him. 'Is it dangerous? Should we make ready? Or something?' He did not reply. 'Good enough for me,' she said to herself, and erupted into legs, and knees, and angora, her previous outfit flittering away into the gaps between realities where she kept her spare clothes. If you should be walking and, suddenly and unaccountably, smell lavender and mothballs, you may just have passed a corner of Zarenyia's intra-dimensional closet.

Resplendent in her natural form and exultant to no longer have to totter around in that ridiculous manner, Zarenyia rose to her not inconsiderable greatest height, shouted, 'I'll save you!' despite there being no obvious threat, and galloped in pursuit of her friend, the funny human Johannes.

She reached him as he stood before a small funereal building of the sort that leads down to a family crypt. Its door swung open. Cabal stood before it as if it were the most horrible thing he had ever seen.

'Stand back!' she cried. 'Let me protect you from this . . . building . . .' She pursed her lips, and added conversationally, 'I'm not sure you're in peril at all.'

Cabal seemed not to hear. He reached out and lifted the door's padlock from where it dangled open on the frame's hasp. It was in far better condition than the mouldering stone it had once been set to protect, a very practical artefact in stainless steel. He looked at it aghast, as if he held his own heart in his hand.

'Padlock,' Zarenyia said informatively.

'It pays'—Cabal spoke in a low, dreadful voice, his thoughts materialising on his lips—'to invest in quality.' He looked up at the lintel above the door. Engraved in the stone was the name DRUIN. 'Oh, gods. What place is this? What have I done in coming here?'

'Oooh.' Zarenyia found the change in Cabal's mood unengaging. 'Angsty. I didn't think you were one of *those* necromancers.'

'You don't understand.' Cabal walked a little way to lean against a table tomb, from where he regarded the crypt building with a strange mixture of disbelief and, just perhaps, fear.

'Bingo! I don't understand. As a word to the wise, I recommend you tell me why this ragged little stone box has put your knickers in a twist. *Please* don't be enigmatic. I've killed people for saying "I'll explain later". Delayed gratification and I are not the best of chums.'

'It's the Druin crypt.'

'I can read.'

'I've been to it twice in my life. The first time I . . .'

He looked unhappily at Zarenyia. She wagged her finger at him, then used the same finger to draw across her throat while she made a horrible cutting noise. 'That's what being enigmatic will do for you. Fess up. What happened?'

'You said you wouldn't harm me.'

'True. But, you know, I'm a devil. We're good at the whole loopholes palaver. I hate doing that usually, but who knows what awful things I may stoop to if provoked by my little pal Johannes being enigmatic and abstruse at me?' She lowered her voice, and the smile vanished. 'Pretty bloody awful things, that's what.'

'I inadvertently abandoned my brother in there.'

'And inadvertently locked the door? This is your brother the vampire, yes?' A thought occurred to her. 'Wait a moment . . . is this *why* he's a vampire?' Cabal did not answer, which was answer enough. She laughed. 'Well, aren't you the loving brother?'

'I had no choice.'

'I'm sure. And the second time was to let him out again? How long did you leave him to stew?'

Cabal muttered something, but Zarenyia's hearing was as supernatural as the rest of her.

'Eight *years?*'

'Yes. I'm not proud of it.'

Zarenyia shrugged. 'I don't care if you are or not. My moral compass is . . .' She considered. 'I'm not at all sure I have one. I'm sure you had your reasons for abandoning your brother to eight years of frustrated vampirism in somebody else's tomb. My main bone of contention is . . . what the Lucifer's cribbage board is it doing here? I thought this wasn't a real place.'

'It isn't.'

'I thought you said these places had been created donkey's years ago as a way of hiding the Fountain of Grails, or whatever it is you think you're going to find.'

'It was.'

'Well, kindly explain to my poor womanly brain why it has a sky like the Abyss and a landscape scattered with *aide-mémoirs* to your family squabbles.' She squatted back on the loom of her legs so their knees rose like the tusks around the throne of Prester John himself. 'Have you the faintest idea what you have got yourself and—I remind you—your poor ill-done-to brother, Horst, the delightful Miss Leonie, and my very own lovely self into? Honestly, Johannes, you're supposed to be the clever one. I'm very disappointed.'

Few things could snap Johannes Cabal back to acerbity with greater rapidity than personal criticism. 'I do not know,' he said slowly and deliberately. 'Yet. This is not how the book presented matters. Yet it was so accurate in other particulars. Therefore, I must conclude that the book's author simply never travelled through into these places—'

'Or deliberately lied?' Zarenyia's eyes went wide at this revelation. Then she smiled broadly, a big, childish grin of delight. 'Oh, I hope the latter! Don't you see what that would mean, darling?'

She looked around the bitter wasteland, the tumbled tombs, the festering sky as if it were the first sight of an empty beach on a summer's bank holiday morning. 'It's a trap!' She clapped her hands, all agog and gleeful. 'So exciting!'

Cabal opined that it could only be a trap if it was impossible to leave the place using the route by which they had entered. This hypothesis, once mooted, was easily tested. They could not leave the place using the route by which they had entered.

Cabal swore volubly at this discovery, which served for a QED under the circumstances.

'This is Ninuka's doing. Possibly.' He glared at the land of graves. Here was the one when he'd been interrupted by a nightwatchman. There was the one where the coffin had been full of bricks, resulting in a complicated few days subsequently. There was the . . . no, he wasn't sure he had ever been in that tomb. Still, it looked familiar. 'Although it seems overly complicated by her lights. How could she have known I would find the book and recognise it for its importance?' He ruminated on this for a moment, disliked the answer that

Ninuka was a great deal cleverer than he had given her credit, and ran that train of thought into a siding where it wouldn't put his self-esteem at quite so much risk.

'So, what to do?' said Zarenyia. She was still delighted about the whole state of affairs, on the understanding that presently a horde of hirelings of their shadowy nemesis (i.e., Lady Ninuka) would turn up and she could kill them all, eventually.

'There is little else we can do, except press on.' Cabal lifted his bag from the unhealthy turf. He was unsure in which direction they should press on to, exactly. Graves, crypts, and tombs scattered the land in every direction, and all looked just as uninviting as one another. As for *that* tomb . . . he looked at it again. He never forgot a tomb, but there was something ineffably evasive about it as it refused to present itself even as he mentally combed the memories of every graveyard, cemetery, burying ground, potter's field, bone orchard, and boot hill he had ever had cause to drive a spade into. It wasn't even that it was a commonplace design: an ancient and weather-aged pagoda some six yards in height, its surfaces plated in slabs of jade. Less a sombre place of rest than a folly or outré statement of the occupant or occupants' worth, a last resting place for somebody of great import—at least in the mind of their estate—to dream away eternity, even as . . .

There must have been some subtle message in the way Cabal stumbled backwards, gazing eye-widened at the pagoda that tipped off Zarenyia to the possibility that all was not well with her comrade.

'Is everything all right?' she asked perspicaciously as Cabal fell over.

Cabal raised a quivering finger to point at the pagoda. 'That . . . *that* . . . I know where I have seen it before . . .'

'It's not yours, is it? Have you had some thrilling foresight of the future and seen yourself carried in state within its emerald walls? Is that it? It is, isn't it?' She considered the building with a critic's eye. 'It's very nice, isn't it? I must confess, Johannes, it's not the sort of place I expected you to end up interred. I was thinking something more along the lines of a ditch.'

'No.' Cabal recovered his feet and a few lamentable fragments of his dignity. 'It isn't mine. But I remember where I've seen it before, and it's impossible that it should be here. Everything else'—he gestured broadly at the tumbling necropolis—'has some personal resonance. This . . . shouldn't even exist. Not here.'

Zarenyia rolled her eyes with impolite incomprehension. 'Sorry, poppet, but I don't have the first and foggiest idea what you are talking about. Why shouldn't it be here if you've seen it in the real world? I say "real world" to be polite, of course. I mean that pit of a world you humans swarm about.'

'It wasn't in the real world.'

Zarenyia showed a modicum of increased interest. 'Hell, then? You've seen it in Hell?'

'I've seen it in the Dreamlands, in the great necropolis of Hlanith. But the stuff of the Dreamlands and of the mundane world are entirely different. This place *cannot* possess both.'

'Copies, perhaps?'

'Not content with taking landmarks from my life, this place contents itself to copy them, too? No. It is the original, impossible though that is. Truly, this is an awful place.'

'Johannes . . .' Zarenyia spoke slowly and suspiciously. 'Are you *frightened?*'

'No,' said Cabal, but he lied.

He had been sarcastic to demons, dismissive to Satan's face, and called Nyarlathotep a little bastard. He had been impolite to cultists, behaved indecorously towards his fellow necromancers, and had once tried—unsuccessfully—to upset a vicar. He had not wavered in any of these endeavours. He was quite capable of feeling fear, he knew, but it was a rare circumstance and rarely—no, never—had he been so existentially threatened as he felt now.

There were rules, laws, principles that governed everything, rules, laws, and principles that controlled every falling raindrop, every whirl of an electron, every frolicking ghost. These laws he understood better than most, and those laws said this place could not be. A pocket universe containing material aspects of the mundane, mortal world was one thing, but it was the presence of an artefact of the Dreamlands in the same place that put it all awry. It was tantamount to an electrical cell having two positives, or a planet failing to generate any gravitational pull; it simply could not happen.

There were, then, principles to which he was not privy, and to which he had never guessed at, and which he did not begin even to understand how he might understand. Not only had he built his house of science upon shifting sands, so had everybody else.

Yes, he was frightened.

'No,' he said. 'Where do you get these absurd ideas?'

'Oh.' She looked at the pagoda and added conversationally, 'Oh, look, the door's opening.'

The door to the jade pagoda was, in fact, a low double door, barely tall enough for the average pall-bearer to pass without crouching. The right hand of the two doors was slowly swinging inwards before them, an inky darkness—uninformative in its totality—being the only thing revealed.

'Do you suppose this is part of the trap, too?' Zarenyia weighed up the possibilities. 'I must say, as traps go it's a little bit lazy, isn't it? Tiny bit short in the bait department. Why would we want to go in there?' She squinted, her inhuman senses apparently able to make something out of the pervading shadow. 'Oh, it's all right, after all. It's not trying to get us to go in. It's letting something out. Much better.'

Something shapeless and dark detached itself from the blackness and covered the ground from the open door to Cabal in a confusion of flutters.

It spoke in a furious voice. 'Cabal!' The voice was human. 'I trusted you!' The voice was female. A hand rose from the tatters and wings of what the better light revealed to be a robe. The hand bore a gleaming, curved dagger.

Cabal stood too astounded to defend himself, so it was as well that Zarenyia was less impressed by the proceedings. She stilted forwards in a shimmer of legs and sent one of them rising in a sharp arc that intercepted the shadowed figure's chest. The figure emitted a loud 'Oof!' of expelled breath and flew back some ten feet to land heavily, the dagger landing safely out of its reach.

The figure tried to rise, but Zarenyia wasn't having that. In a moment she was standing over the attacker, one foot planted firmly, indeed painfully, upon the assailant's midriff. The woman struggled, but Zarenyia wasn't having that, either.

'Now, now, darling,' she chided, 'don't be awkward. Not when I can run you through so very easily. And I have far more interesting plans for you than something as wasteful as a dull old impalement.' Behind her, Zarenyia's spiderly abdomen started to pulse with a salacious anticipation.

'No!' Cabal ran towards spider and fly, waving with both arms as if trying to stop an oncoming train. 'Madam! You must not kill her!'

'Oh, what?' Zarenyia regarded the approaching necromancer with sour disappointment. 'Really? You said I could murder people, Johannes! I must say, this outing is proving a bit shy on souls devoured, if you can bear a little criticism?'

Cabal arrived puffing slightly. 'Madam . . .' He withdrew a notebook while he recovered his breath. 'By my reckoning on this expedition you have so far enjoyed the vital essences of twelve slave traders, five train robbers, and eight cultists of dubious taste—'

'You're telling me . . .'

'—and I therefore must protest that twenty-five victims in no way constitutes "a bit shy" of the opportunities I promised you.'

'Do you have to call them "victims"? It makes it all seem so very sordid.'

'What would you suggest?'

Zarenyia considered. 'Playmates?'

'Victims it is, then.'

'Oh, Johannes.' Zarenyia was pouting unashamedly. 'But they were a bunch of horrid criminals with stinky souls. This girl smells much nicer. Mayn't I just—'

'You may not.' Cabal crossed his arms and looked steadily up at Zarenyia.

'Just a nibble?'

'No.'

'She tried to stab you.' Zarenyia rather spitefully leaned a little more weight on her prisoner, making the pinned woman cry out.

'Lots of people have tried to stab me. It doesn't mean I killed them all.' He took a moment to think about that. 'Actually, that's a bad example. I did kill them all. But I don't want you to kill her.'

'Why ever not?'

'Two reasons. She was communicated to this place during its creation and may be able to offer us vital intelligence about it. And secondly'—he crouched by the prone figure and drew back the ragged black hood to reveal a woman in her mid-twenties, pale of skin, raven black of hair, a stark tiara or crown in deepest ebon upon her brow—'because we are acquainted. Hello, Fräulein Smith. An unexpected pleasure.'

With a little chivvying, Zarenyia finally lifted her foot, and she stood by in a sullen silence as Cabal helped Miss Smith to her feet. Once she was vertical, he left her to recover her dagger and returned it to her, hilt first. 'I forgive your first instinctive reaction to seeing me, Miss Smith; the situation is unusual, and one can easily be forgiven for being a little fraught. I would ask you not to attempt my murder again, however. It would be counterproductive to both of us.'

Miss Smith gave Zarenyia a dirty look, which the devil accepted with a prim smile. 'Did you do this, Cabal? Did you destroy the Dreamlands?'

'I fear you overstate my influence, Miss Smith. If I have inadvertently damaged any of the Dreamlands, it is only your corner of the old cemetery of Hlanith necropolis. Believe you me, I am as astonished by your presence in this place as you are. You are, in the vernacular, collateral damage.'

He was interrupted in his explanations by a mannered cough delivered from on moderately high. 'Ah,' he said, 'but introductions are in order. Miss Smith, allow me to introduce the succubine devil Zarenyia.'

'Don't tell her that right off the wicket,' said Zarenyia pettishly. 'We'll have nothing to talk about.'

'And, Zarenyia, it is my pleasure to introduce you to Miss Smith, former necromantrix and lately the Witch of the Old Cemetery of Hlanith—'

'Ooh, career change,' said Zarenyia with *faux* warmth.

'—with whom I'm sure you'll get on famously.'

Miss Smith regarded the octopodal Zarenyia with cool hostility. 'And you trust a devil, do you, Cabal?'

'I do. We have an understanding. Madam Zarenyia has undertaken not to harm me or my friends.'

'I undertook not to harm you, your toothsome brother, or that handsome lady with the troublesome morals. Not your "friends" in general.'

'True, in which case I must ask you to extend your forbearance to Miss Smith. We are old acquaintances.'

Zarenyia inhaled and sighed out the breath with bored disgust. 'You realise she's another deader, don't you? I'm not quite sure how she's walking around, but that's not the mortal coil she was born into. Although . . . it sort of is. How is that?'

Cabal briefly explained that the body she currently wore was her dreaming form, her actual physical body having been inopportunely hanged by a rampaging mob while she was spiritually elsewhere, and her corpse subsequently used experimentally by another passing necromancer.

'I told you we were old acquaintances,' said Johannes Cabal.

'What a sweet story,' said Zarenyia. 'I welled up at several moments. Very well, darling, very well. I don't much enjoy feeding upon the double dead at the best of times, and you seem nice enough, so yes, consider yourself proof from my devilish wiles.' She solemnly raised the three middle fingers of her right hand, thumb across the little finger and intoned the sacred oath, 'Dib, dib, dib.'

Smith looked quizzically at Cabal. 'What?'

'It's complicated. Just accept the dibbing.'

Miss Smith returned her attention to Zarenyia, and bowed. 'Your dibbing is appreciated, and accepted.'

And so, their fellowship increased by one, they considered whatever to do next.

'This is a deeply arcane situation in which we find ourselves,' said Cabal. 'I hope Horst and Miss Barrow are faring better than we.'

There was an awkward pause, eventually broken by Miss Smith. 'You're just standing there,' she said to Cabal. 'Are you waiting for something?'

Cabal seemed surprised by her comment and then confused. He looked around as if expecting to find an explanation for that confusion written in the air. Finding that an unrewarding avenue of inquiry, he turned back to his companions.

'That was a peculiar sensation. I had a distinct idea that our concerns would be put into abeyance, for a while at least. Yet, no. They are as pressing as they were a moment ago. How very strange.'

'You want strange? I can do you strange,' said Zarenyia, already happy to regard their presence in a mosaic of existential 'graveyards I have known' fragments as perfectly normal. She pointed at the ground a little way ahead of them. 'I think they've got mice.'

A grave lay open, hastily and brutally excavated and the coffin disinterred with vigour rather than care. Bones lay scattered, scraps of meat still adhering to some of them. With the easy lack of repugnance or propriety those who deal regularly with the dead exhibit, Miss Smith took up one of the bones and examined it closely. 'Teeth marks,' she said immediately. 'Ghouls.'

'Oh.' Cabal was thoroughly blasé at the prospect. 'I thought we might be in trouble for a minute. Both Miss Smith and I have had extensive dealings with the ghouls. I doubt we'll have much trouble from them.'

'I cannot agree,' said Miss Smith. 'The ghouls of this place are not like the ones of the necropolis, nor any others I have ever met. Look, Cabal, see how clumsily the grave is opened, how thoughtlessly the traces are scattered.'

It was true; ghouls are fastidious eaters for purposes of self-preservation if nothing else. They eat what they need and no more, and they always tidy up after themselves. They see no profit in drawing attention to themselves, for that way lies outraged humans, and all ghouls really want is a quiet life and moderately gamy meat. This foresightedness has, through generations, become more instinctive than habitual. They would as soon leave blatant clues of their presence as they would boil their heads, leave off breathing, or take up Morris dancing.

'Make up your mind.' Cabal nodded at the gory bone. 'Those are either ghoul teeth marks or they are not.'

'They are, but their behaviour is distinctly inghoulish,' replied Miss Smith, deploying a technical term unique to the profession of necromancy. 'I have always had an easy relationship with them, as you know. But ever since I was brought here . . . I thought they had been transported along with me. I heard them, snickering and glibbering, and was relieved at first. At least I would have allies. But they would not speak. Not only to me, but even to one another. I was forced to take refuge in the pagoda.'

'From the ghouls?' Cabal was aghast; for the ghouls to menace her was equivalent to being threatened by . . . by . . .

The simile foundered in his mind—*nothing* should be less threatening to Miss Smith than ghouls.

'I never saw them clearly, but their outlines were wrong, their voices wrong, everything they did, so very wrong. And'—if she had seemed distressed by her recitation of the shortcomings of these ghouls, it was as nothing to the awful thing she found she must now report—'there's another.' Her voice sank. 'Another witch. I've seen her, with them. The nights here are short, but so are the days. On the first night I was here, I thought I heard something in the distance, so I crept out from the pagoda, and went to see. Johannes, they were having an *orgy*. An actual graveyard orgy.' She looked thoroughly perturbed at the memory. 'It was horrible.'

Zarenyia made a dismissive noise. 'I've been to oodles of orgies. You're just a prude.'

Miss Smith glared at Zarenyia. 'I am *not*.'

Zarenyia lowered her forebody so she could look Miss Smith in the eye, rested her chin in one palm, and smiled a little triumphantly. 'Really? Do tell.'

'I should point out that the orgies Madam Zarenyia attends subsequently fill the obituary columns for weeks afterwards,' offered Cabal.

Zarenyia favoured him with a dirty look, but didn't deny it.

Miss Smith shook her head. 'No, you don't understand. The orgy . . . it was trite. That's why it was horrible. Honestly, I'm a witch who lives in a graveyard. You think I haven't seen orgies before? This one looked like it had been planned by a vicar based on overhearing the sexual fantasies of the choir. It was asinine.'

'I confess I am having trouble imagining an asinine orgy,' said Cabal.

'Oh, I'm not.' Zarenyia crossed her arms and grimaced, a devil of the world. 'I've seen some bloody awful ones. Really, the most fun for the attendees was when I had them. Also their last fun, but that's the price for my favours.'

'A steep price.'

'I've had no complaints.'

Miss Smith interrupted. 'It looked staged, is what I'm trying to say. It was like a novelist's portrayal of a witch's orgy, sporting with monsters. That sort of thing.'

'Never done anything like that yourself, then?' asked Zarenyia with professional interest.

'With ghouls? Eew. No. I mean, they're sweet beasts, but they're a bit . . . eew. If I feel the need for a little companionship, I leave the necropolis and visit the taverns.'

'I feel we are getting off the subject,' said Cabal, thoroughly out of his depth and far from matters he found comfortable. 'Still, we have at least established a distinct oddity in this place. The tombs and graves are real enough, and it even had the option of a real graveyard witch. Yet instead we find a form of playacting in progress. This warrants investigation.'

'Why?' said Zarenyia.

'Because the nature of the place seems to be formed based on those who visit it. Mortal remains, witches, and orgies. These are our concerns, are they not? All are materialised here, and one hopes there is purpose in that, because finding that purpose may be our only way out.'

The trees became weird and eccentric in their growth, the grass a brighter yet more toxic green as they progressed. None of them commented on the matter, but it was apparent to them all that the place of graves was becoming distinctly more melodramatic as they grew closer to the home of the new witch and her cohort of fantastical ghouls, as opposed to the more workaday ghouls with which Cabal was all too familiar.

'What are we intending to do when we find this interloper, anyway?' asked Zarenyia, traipsing lightly across the lurid sod upon her many pointed feet. 'I have to say, I'm a little underwhelmed at the idea of bringing my particular brand of good times to a bunch of corpse-eating doggy boys.'

'I feel the opportunities for murder are still many and alluring, madam.' Cabal was cleaning his blue-glassed spectacles as he walked, and then attended to the hang of his cravat. When the enemy—and enemy they were, he felt sure—were finally encountered, it would be to his advantage to be able to see them properly, and to theirs to be done away with by a man with tidy neckwear, if only from a sense of terminal satisfaction.

'I am *not* devouring the soul of a ghoul. Heavens only knows where they've been, grubby beggars. I don't mind the soul of a double-dyed villain—those are spicy—but I have my limits.'

Cabal, whose own view of ghouls had not been dissimilar until he had endured a brief period of ghouldom himself, decided not to mention any special interest in her views one way or the other. It would only lead to the sort of face-pulling already exhibited by Miss Smith on the same subject, he knew.

'We're almost there,' said Miss Smith, her tone determined

but also betraying apprehension. 'You do have a plan, don't you, Cabal?'

'The immediate plan is entirely one of reconnaissance. You can hardly expect me to evolve some elaborate scheme when the very nature of what we shall face is currently unknown to me.'

'A witch with ghouls. I *did* say.'

'But what sort of witch? There are many. And, I begin to wonder, what sort of ghouls? There should only be one type, but from your description, they would seem different from the usual crowd. I own myself perplexed. I do not enjoy perplexity.'

'Will it be a "reconnaissance in force"?' said Zarenyia, employing the index and middle fingers of each hand to scratch quotation marks into the air.

'Your somatic punctuation dismays me, Madam Zarenyia. If you wish to emphasise speech, may I suggest speaking emphatically.'

'I could do that, yes, but I'm terribly tactile. Anyway, I wished to suggest some irony in the term.'

'By "reconnaissance in force", you actually mean "let's have a look and, if there aren't too many, wade in and kill them", I gather?'

'Ohhhh, darling, I love it when you spot subtext.'

'The spider-woman is purring,' said Miss Smith in an undertone to Cabal.

'Spiders do purr; didn't you know that?' Belatedly Miss Smith realised just how acute the devil's senses were. 'Why, they're just as cute as lickle puddycats.'

Miss Smith quickly and wisely changed the subject. 'Just beyond that rise. That's the witch's home.'

With some difficulty, Cabal managed to talk Zarenyia into adopting a stealthier form. Grumbling, she crushed her aft body down into something more human, although this time she dispensed with the French couture and adopted a green twill suit and walking shoes.

'You look like a Bavarian lesbian,' said Miss Smith, purely as an observation.

Zarenyia was delighted. 'Exactly the effect I was trying for,

Liebling!' She produced an alpine hat with a small orange feather in its band and clapped it on her head. 'Don't I look fiercely practical?' She winked at Miss Smith, who coughed and looked away to hide an unexpected blush.

'Is there anyone you don't flirt with?' Cabal asked as they crept to the top of the rise.

'You, in case you haven't noticed,' she whispered back. 'We're friends, I hope. If you wish to dally in my webbed bower, you need only ask. I shan't be dragging you off there using my usual wiles of saucy suggestiveness. Also magic. Some chemicals, too, but it's all mainly down to how bloody good I am at what I do.'

'You neglected to mention mesmerism,' said Cabal, a little tautly.

'Oh, yes. The 'fluence. Hope you're not still upset about it? It was for the best.'

'True.' Logic could often mollify Cabal. 'It was for the best.'

They reached the ridge line and paused there. Cabal took a small pair of binoculars from his bag. 'I shall go alone. One head on the near horizon may avoid detection where three will not.' Taking it as read that the one head would be his, and ignoring the crabby expressions Miss Smith and Zarenyia were no doubt lavishing upon him as he crawled the last few feet, Cabal crested the hill and looked down upon their new enemies.

The binoculars were hardly necessary; he was looking down a distance of perhaps five feet to where a pack of twenty or so ghouls were creeping up to meet them. The ghoul in the lead saw Cabal appear and grinned at him, its ears standing to attention like those of an inquisitive Dobermann.

'Hello!' said the ghoul.

'Hello,' said Johannes Cabal with a great deal less enthusiasm.

The ghoul pack swarmed over them, but with no obvious intent to hurt them. Instead they were bundled up in a multitude of rubbery arms and borne down the hill in the direction of the new witch's lair.

Cabal gave Zarenyia a hard look as she allowed herself to be captured, but she just gave him a wonderfully happy smile in return and a wink so broad that they probably caught it on the Plateau of Leng that lies in desolation at the edge of everything. One or other of the creatures that frequent that damned place must surely have paused in its performance of horrors and thought, *Did somebody just wink at me?*

Down, down into the vale of the witch they were carried, the colours now the essence of lurid, the great fire before a tomb blazing in jagged tongues, the shadows dancing without nuance or graduation. Cabal looked about himself, his misgivings growing by the second. He had seen artificial realities before, but they had always seemed real within themselves. This was a parody of the real, a clumsy woodcut coloured by a child. He felt they were being carried into a volume of the Brothers Grimm.

Past the bonfire with its blaze of hot, papery flames they were carried in the very dictionary definition of 'triumph' until they arrived before the witch's manse, an extraordinary tomb wrought in obsidian and white marble, crested in red and detailed in green. Statuary of satyrs and nymphs, cherubs and imps were caught in mid-frolic, mid-cavort in the unlikeliest combinations of imagery for a place of the dead. It was not of the real world, but wrought from the fantasies of an addled artist turning his hand to anything that might pay the rent and his exorbitant absinthe bill. It would then be entitled something along the lines of *The Lair of the Witch Queen* and subsequently used as the cover of a magazine for an audience whose imaginations ran hot.

Before the lair of the Witch Queen stood the Queen of Witches herself, less a formal title and more an excuse for fancy dress. And such a fancy dress; she was gorgeously arrayed in a great cloak of black velvet, trimmed in silver, and topped by the sort of excessive high collar that makes the matter of peripheral vision rather moot. Beneath the cloak she wore a dress of crimson silks with a décolletage that owed as much to the arts of structural engineering as couture. She herself was . . . very familiar.

'You!' cried Johannes Cabal.

He was taken aback to realise he had said it in unison with Zarenyia and Miss Smith. They looked at one another with reasonable surprise. Cabal recovered first.

'You know Ninuka?' he demanded of his comrades.

'Ninuka?' said Zarenyia. 'You're wrong. I know Udrolvexa. Has she been calling herself Ninuka, too? That would explain a lot.'

'No,' said Miss Smith, 'that's Tanith James, the hoity bitch. I'd know her anywhere. I gave her that scar myself.'

Cabal and Zarenyia looked as hard as they could, but there was no sign of a scar. Zarenyia raised her eyebrows. 'Well, this is a rum do. We can't all be right, surely? That would be pushing coincidence with some force for my least favourite colleague from the pits of Hell—and you will appreciate that I know some real stinkers—to moonlight as the *bêtes noires* of you two as well?'

Cabal's attention had never left the Witch Queen. 'No. We cannot all be correct, but we can all be wrong.'

The three of them were paraded before her and then secured by the wrists to a trio of great stakes around a fire. The stakes had definitely not been there when Cabal first spied the encampment, but now gave the impression that they had been there for days at least, to judge from the emerald turf grown up around their bases.

'Oooh, bondage!' Zarenyia's smirk was quite unforgivable under the circumstances and unappreciated by either Miss Smith or Cabal.

'Well, well, well,' said the Queen of Witches on settling herself upon her throne of bones, which also definitely had not been there a moment previous.

'Please,' interrupted Cabal.

'You beg for your life very easily,' said the queen, her smirk no more forgivable than Zarenyia's.

'The only begging I was about to make was that you might save us the burden of listening to your villainous monologue, no doubt larded with icy, ringing laughter at dramatically correct intervals.'

The queen looked for a moment as if her temper was going to depart in a huff of 'How dare you?' and threats, but she reined it in, and the triumphant smile returned. 'Do you even know who I am?'

'I believe so. I believe that you are the natural sum of this place. You are the spirit of Nemesis.'

'Tanith James is *not* my nemesis,' whispered Miss Smith.

'You either do her a disservice or think too much of yourself. The Lady Ninuka is undoubtedly mine, at least at a material level. There are certain entities to which I have caused some displeasure and whose powers are undoubtedly greater than Orfilia Ninuka's, but I am not their main focus. She, however, has almost literally moved heaven, earth, and hell to revenge herself upon me. If I meet my death at any near date, there is a good chance it will be at her hands or those of her assigned agents. Search your heart, Miss Smith. You say you scarred this Jones woman; you think she does not hold undying enmity to you?'

Miss Smith started to speak, thought better of what she was about to say, and said, 'But, I'm dead.'

'But, you are also . . . *were* also a necromantrix. This Miss James you mention, what was her discipline?'

Miss Smith considered this, and her face fell, as if being tied to a stake before a bonfire by a clan of comic-book ghouls was insufficient grounds for upset.

'My body was destroyed, though . . .'

'I destroyed it myself.' Cabal said it as if it were a gallant courtesy he had performed upon her mortal remains. In necromantic circles, it actually was. 'But your spirit is extant, and you dwell within the Dreamlands, where you may be destroyed again, and finally, by anyone with a little knowledge and a great deal of animosity. Would that describe Tanith James?'

Miss Smith did not reply. Evidently the description fitted Tanith James to a T.

Cabal returned his attention to the Witch Queen. 'As I was saying. You are the spirit of Nemesis. All three of us have powerful enemies, and you have embodied all of them in however it is that we perceive you. Well, now you have us. What do you intend to do now?'

'Do?' The Witch Queen laughed, and did so in an icy, ringing peal of malevolent amusement. 'Why, destroy you, naturally.'

A stage whisper floated to Cabal from the direction of Zarenyia. 'This is all part of your terribly clever plan, isn't it, Johannes?'

'Alas, no,' he admitted. 'I was not expecting this person to be a material metaphor. It's very disappointing. So, unless my plan was for us all to die in the most embarrassingly asinine way imaginable—and it was not—then no, this is not all part of my terribly clever plan.'

'Asinine,' said the queen. 'What do you mean, asinine?'

'To be brief, madam (for your theatricality wears upon me), you are a conceptual embodiment of undying, personal animus. You currently represent in your uncertain way the three current banes of the lives of two of us, and the afterlife of the third.'

'I know all that, Cabal (for your didacticism wears upon me).'

'*Touché*, I am sure. I promised to be brief, and so I shall. You are a damp squib, madam. A foreshortening of expectations. A bathetic failure. You are Nemesis incarnate, yet you do not hate us. Instead you take the targets of real hatred from real people—'

'And a real devil.'

'Thank you, Madam Zarenyia. And a real devil, and dispose of them mechanically. For all your posturing, you feel no passion. For all your stagecraft, you experience no malefic desire. You take the *raisons d'être* from real people for no real purpose. You are a failure.'

'Yes,' said Zarenyia, taking up the theme and warming to it, 'you're nothing more than a big premature ejaculation. Mind you, where I'm concerned, it's always a bit premature in a sense, if you take my—'

'*Madam*.'

'Sorry,' said the devil. 'Ever so.' She made a gesture as if locking her lips with a key.

'I do not care for your sophistries, necromancer,' said the Queen of Witches. 'You shall die here and now for . . .' She paused, and looked to Zarenyia with puzzlement. 'How did you make that gesture? Your hands are tied.'

Zarenyia lowered both hands, and the hempen bounds swayed in their wake. '*Were* tied, dear heart. If you'd been paying attention you'd have gathered I'm not human; rope bonds are a little insulting. So, past tense. My hands *were* tied. In much the same way your arms *were* attached to your shoulders.'

The Witch Queen looked like she was about to state the obvious, but that was the moment that Zarenyia decided that two legs were bad, eight legs were excellent, and any statements about the current locations of other limbs was lost in the sudden excitement.

'Is *this* your terribly clever plan, darling?' Zarenyia picked up a charging ghoul as she addressed Cabal. 'Bring me along and just depend on me to kill everyone when things get fraught?'

'In essence.'

'I like it.' She upended the ghoul and examined its nether regions. She curled her lip. 'These aren't proper ghouls at all. No genitalia. These are ghouls for maiden aunts. Piff. Boring old option B it is, then.' And so saying, she broke the ghoul upon a raised and chitinous knee, throwing the dying monster aside to turn her attention to its irate colleagues.

Miss Smith caught Cabal's eye. 'Well. This is weird.'

Cabal nodded. 'Coming from a witch whose soul inhabits a cemetery in the Dreamlands, that says a great deal, but I cannot argue with you.' They watched Zarenyia go by, bucking like a wild horse, a ghoul impaled on one leg, and another held by the scruff of the neck being used as a flail to dislodge a third that had leapt upon her back. 'There are certainly elements of the odd about our current situation. Madam! Madam Zarenyia! Perhaps if you freed us, we might be able to help?'

'Busy!' she called back, and she called it happily. Unrestricted violence was as cool water on a warm day to her. 'Gotcha!'

A pair of *faux*-ghoul bodies, entangled and broken, went arcing over the stakes and into the bonfire.

'No hurry.' Cabal dangled listlessly from his bonds. 'I'm sure we'll find some way of amusing ourselves.'

'That's that passive-aggressiveness thing, isn't it?' Zarenyia regarded him with a jaundiced eye. 'I've read about that in my magazines.'

And while Cabal was wrestling with the concept of magazine subscription services that deliver to Hell, and concluding that probably narrowed it down to *The Reader's Digest*, a giant spiderish leg scythed over their heads, slicing off the tops of the stakes and through their bonds in a single action. Necromancer and graveyard witch tumbled to earth in a shower of wood chippings and undignified language.

Cabal climbed to his knees and rubbed circulation back into his wrists while shouting at his rescuer. 'You almost had our hands off, madam!'

'So ungrateful. They'd have grown back.' And so, blissfully unaware of the limitations of cellular regeneration in humans, Zarenyia carried on tearing the ghouls that were not ghouls into lovely, rubbery pieces.*

By the time Cabal had recovered his bag and, more specifically, the Webley pistol of generous calibre that lay within it, there was little point in offering aid. Ghouls lay around in abandonment, some whole, most not, and all quite perfectly dead. Amidst the carnage, Zarenyia stood, scraping one of the vanquished from her leg.

'That was fun. Brief, but energetic.' She cast the corpse aside and performed a little spidery dance of victory. 'I didn't get to kill that Witch Queen character, though. Did you?'

Cabal and Miss Smith shook their heads; neither of them had noticed the queen's escape, either. 'We were hardly afforded the opportunity.'

'Oh.' Zarenyia looked around. 'Bother. I'd say she constitutes a loose end, wouldn't you?'

'She may also be the key to our escaping this place. We must find her, and ideally not kill her.' Cabal gave Zarenyia a significant look. 'At least not until we've extracted any useful information from her.'

It seemed unlikely the spirit of Nemesis could have got very far, and philosophically unlikely that it would seek to go very far from

---

* While the pieces were not especially lovely, it should be borne in mind that at least half the function of these few words is to give the potential narrator of an audio version of this book a doubtful moment.

them in any case. They therefore decided to search the crypts that lay within a small radius of the central structure and, since that radius permitted easy calling to one another, they would split up to do so, the quicker to be done. Agreeing that the immediate act of whosoever found the Nemesis Witch first would be to cry halloo to the others, they split the circle of their search into three sectors and went to work immediately.

Cabal decided to start, rationally enough, at the closest crypt, a prim box of pale sandstone. As he approached it, however, his eye was caught by one lying further away, indeed right at the edge of the search area. He could not say what drew his attention so certainly to this cottage of the dead. It was an unkempt sort of thing, asymmetric with what seemed to be half a flying buttress to the left, the base long crumbled away. The design was of the new Gothik, a style for the pretentious surburbanite. The stone itself was soot-stained, surely snatched from some bourgeois district and dumped here in splendid isolation on the slope between two low hillocks. He did not recognise it at all, yet it seemed very familiar at the same time. Perhaps even comforting.

He walked to it almost in a dream, and his steps fell faster as he approached. This was the place, he was sure. This was where he would have hidden were he to have sought refuge in the curious graveyard, he was sure, but why he *was* sure, he could not say.

The door opened easily under his hand, a well-wrought thing of oak bound in iron strips, and swung noiselessly open. With only the slightest of hesitations, he entered.

The crypt's interior was illuminated by gas mantels, which was a nice change from the usual pitch-darkness or, at best, guttering torches of his experience. Still, what sort of tomb has a gas meter? What sort of corpse can be depended upon to put a shilling in that meter when the lights grow dim?

Low alcoves to the right and directly ahead contained coffins and, unusually, he felt relief that they were whole and he could see no mortal remains. Not that he would take much glee in such a sight, it should be understood, but that corpses in every state from perfectly fresh all the way to mouldering bone and all the intermediate stages of rot and liquescence were so well-known to him as to have rendered him blasé. No, this was not a matter of squeamishness, or at least not of a merely sensual horror.

To the left a ladder leaned against the wall, and by it a grandfather clock, its glass nearly opaque with grime. Yet he could hear the steady tick of the mechanism's escapement within the case. It was, all things considered, a very homely sort of tomb. He could only conclude that the Nemesis Witch had made this place hers and had her ersatz ghouls gather domestic comforts for her, up to and including an interdimensional gas pipe. He bit his lip at this point; either the ghouls were a great deal more ingenious than he had given them credit for, ridiculous cartoon caricatures that they were, or he was not truly understanding what had happened here, what was happening here, what this place meant. He did know, however, that the Nemesis Witch was here, and she was waiting for him at the foot of the steps that opened by the grandfather clock, the steps that led down into the cold, cruel clay.

He did not hesitate to set his foot upon the top step, even though the strong and tried sense of self-preservation that had kept him alive through a hundred circumstances that would reasonably be expected to kill him was warning him, screaming at him that this was a trap that he would not leave unscathed.

Cabal felt the forebodings burst into a dazzling flare of baleful premonition as he took the second step down. Then he took the third. Then the fourth, and the fifth, and so descended into the realm of Nemesis.

The Nemesis Witch, the Queen of Witches, the Red Queen, Lady Misericorde, Lady Ninuka: so many names for one woman. And there she was, waiting for him.

The underground crypt was dry and small, and there was only one corpse there. One end of the chamber was scattered with old household bric-a-brac and faggots of firewood; the other end, accessed through an open arch and up a couple of steps, was clean and empty but for a grave-sized hole dug into the dusty, dry clay. By the grave half sat, half lay Lady Ninuka. She wore something different from her brief appearance as the Nemesis Witch, now gowned in a simple dress the colour of funereal wrappings, grey, white, and a dull cream. It was folded decorously across her legs so that not even an ankle was exposed. She herself looked more purely like Ninuka than earlier, and this Cabal took to be a sure indication that she truly was nothing more than a figment. She was pale and dreadful. She did not smile the smile of an arch-villain when he stood before her. She did not even look at him. She held a bunch of flowers taken from some memorial tribute, and dropped withered petals into the grave, one after another.

'Are you truly the spirit of Nemesis?' asked Cabal. 'I would almost be disappointed if this all turned out to be some scheme of Ninuka's and you are her beneath cadaverous make-up.'

The spirit ignored him. Petals fluttered down.

'Then let us assume that you are not Ninuka.' He spoke to break the silence as much as anything. It weighed upon him. It confined him. 'Let us say that you are something else, either sent to warn me or destroy me; although a warning would be preferable.'

At this her gaze rose to meet his, and he thought he saw some awful thought signed upon her brow, but then she looked pensively aside, and the momentary sympathy was lost.

Nemesis finished plucking every petal from the dead rose stem in her hand, regarded the bare, thorned stick with equanimity, and then dropped it into the grave. She took another rose and started to strip its flower bare.

Johannes Cabal was a remarkably able man in many respects, yet his failings, too, were manifold and equally of note. One such, and one that never worked in his favour yet out of which he seemed incapable of growing, was his remarkable proclivity for growing angry with supernatural entities that could likely render him into ashes, or tear his skeleton from his flesh while he still briefly lived, or slice him thinner than a year's supply of Parma ham in the twinkling of an eye. It was in no sense a survival trait, and yet it endured in his personality.

'When you have quite finished with the deflowering of other people's funerary offerings, perhaps you could answer me? I have travelled a long way to be here, I have travelled with a devil to do so. Which is less unappealing than it sounds, but there's a principle at stake here. I have endured hardships, difficulties, and reversals to find myself in this—and I don't use such a pejorative term lightly—*pantomime* of a synthetic milieu. You think I don't know what this tomb is? What it represents? Exactly who lies in that grave you are so assiduously filling with garden rubbish?'

Nemesis ignored him still. Cabal felt moved to express just what he had been through and his vast disappointment at how things were turning out.

'There were *giant ants!*'

She said nothing, and he had the grace to feel ashamed.

'This must all be for a reason, surely?' He spoke as he climbed the two steps between the halves of the lower crypt. 'Even the most abstruse oracles must speak sooner or later. What am I to take away from this, assuming I can even find a way out of this strange lich field? What am I to deduce from looking into the grave of my . . .'

And here he looked down into the hole, and was silent for a long moment.

'Self,' he finished.

Beneath withered petals and broken rose stems lay the corpse of Johannes Cabal, necromancer. He looked down upon himself with mixed feelings. Presently, the corpse opened an eye and looked up at him.

'Cheer up,' it told him. 'This is just a synthetic milieu.'

Cabal found Miss Smith and Zarenyia some little time later; the former seemed characteristically thoughtful, the latter uncharacteristically so.

'Did you find her, too?' asked Miss Smith.

'I did. It was . . . enlightening, I think.'

'I am immortal,' said Zarenyia suddenly and with emphasis. 'At least as far as ageing goes. Not indestructible, but immortal if all else remains equal. And yet . . .' She seemed almost pained at failing to grasp a comprehension that gambolled just beyond her grasp. 'And yet, life is too short. Darlings, I know I'm a devil and everything, but I've never actually thought of myself as evil. I've put up with the label all this time, but I'm not sure that I care for it now. I want something more.'

'I have unfinished business,' said Miss Smith. 'There's always unfinished business, but . . . this, I can't stay in the Dreamlands.'

Cabal spoke gently. 'Hardly your decision to make.'

'There must be a way. We're necromancers, damn it.'

Cabal nodded. 'I thought this place was a trap. In a sense it is, but there are subtleties here, too. I believe we may now move on. And I really do hope that Miss Barrow and my brother are weathering events at least as well as we. Heavens help them otherwise.'

The Second Way:
LEONIE BARROW, GREAT DETECTIVE

One moment they were at the prophesied place on the outskirts of Constantinople; the next they most certainly weren't.

'So,' said Horst, taking in their abruptly altered surroundings, 'this is the fabled kingdom of Prester John, is it? It's a bit more . . . industrial than I'd imagined. Is it usual to have a deep-cast mine in the middle of a city?'

They were in an unprepossessing urban street, illuminated by gaslights running down either side, one side faced with a long row of small terraced houses of the 'two up, two down' variety, net curtains hanging like cataracts in the blank, dark eyes of their windows. The red brickwork barely showed through the grime of ten thousand chimneys, yet the glass of the windows was clean, the paintwork maintained, and the doorsteps assiduously scrubbed. The phrase 'poor but proud' could not help but occur to the disinterested viewer.

The opposite side of the street was marked by a brick wall some ten feet in height, and looming beyond it were the lift works of two deep-cast mineshafts, the distinctive asymmetric triangle of the structures and the great wheels of the cable runners some fifty feet from the ground more suited to a Welsh valley or a Northern hillside. Behind the buildings was the lowering bulk of a spoil heap, the leavings of the coal extraction process.

'I'll be blunt,' continued Horst. 'It's less mystical than I hoped. There, I said it.'

'You had your mysticism and fabled kingdom just before we got here.' Miss Barrow was far less judgemental about their new surroundings and far more intrigued. 'All that business with the bored man on the throne with the tusks? You recall? No, that was just an overture. *This* is the real point of our journey.'

'If you say so.' Horst stuck his hands in his pockets. 'Don't really see what the idea of the magical shenanigans dumping us by a town-centre coal mining operation is, though.'

'I think that may be the point.'

'The point?'

'The point is we have to find the point.'

Horst sighed and his breath coalesced in the chill air of the night. 'I was rather hoping for something a bit more adventuresome. Bandits. Pirates.' He thought on for a moment. 'Giant ants,' he concluded.

'Adventures are where you find them. Ah. We have company.'

Horst followed her line of sight and saw a police constable of serious demeanour strolling slowly towards them with the steady pace of justice unavoidable. He was wondering how they would explain away their light summer clothes chosen for the Turkish climate when he abruptly realised Miss Barrow was wearing heavy autumnal clothes and, with a shock, that so was he. Miss Barrow examined her gloved hand with only moderate surprise before glancing back at him to check that, yes, he, too, had noticed the change in their circumstances.

'Evening, ma'am,' said the constable as he reached them, 'sir.' He touched the brim of his helmet, but that was the limit of his courtesy as he regarded them with undiluted suspicion.

'Good evening, Constable,' said Miss Barrow. 'A chill one, at that.'

'It is that. Got lost, have you?' This to Horst. 'Long way from the south side here.'

'I suppose we must have. Well, you know how it is; you get talking and the next thing you know, you've wandered miles.' Horst said it with the easy duplicity of a man whose success with women was equalled by his competence at not having seven shades beaten out of him by their attendant fathers, brothers, and occasionally husbands.

'Just so, sir.' The constable had apparently been lied to by better than Horst, which was injurious to the pride of them both. He glanced sideways at Miss Barrow and, remarkably, his brow raised with apparent recognition. 'I . . . might I enquire your name, ma'am?'

Less inured to casual duplicity than Horst, Miss Leonie Barrow blithely supplied it. The result was magical.

'Miss Barrow!' said he, worthy in serge. 'I thought I knew you!' He glanced around the dark houses and nodded. 'Of course. You'll be on the job, won't you?'

Leonie was at quite the loss. Horst glowered on her behalf. 'What are you implying?'

His chivalric wrath was both unnecessary and unnoticed, for the policeman said, 'On a case, of course.'

'A case?' Leonie Barrow considered the words, and the sense of 'rightness' they carried clustered about her on the instant like a cloud of supportive butterflies.

'A case?' She looked at the constable and the look of respect she found there. Not simply the respect any police officer should show an innocent member of the public but rather a professional respect, an *earned* respect.

'A case . . .' On what felt momentarily like impulse but what she realised even during its commission was a grounded and logical suspicion, she opened the reticule that hung upon her arm and looked within. There she found a small but very practical semi-automatic pistol and a business card case. This she opened, took a moment to enjoy the thrill of what she was already sure she would find there, then withdrew a card and handed it to the constable.

Horst, all confusion and frowns and the more adorable for them, shuffled quietly around that he might read the card over the officer's shoulder.

MISS LEONIE BARROW M.PHIL OXON CANTAB
FORENSIC & SECURITY CONSULTANT
PRIVATE DETECTIVE

'Yes,' she said, her smile confident and open. 'Yes, we are on a case.'

It transpired that they were soon to be on another. The constable informed them that Inspector Lament of the Yard required her presence at her earliest convenience. If she could get in touch as soon as possible, he might have need of her proven powers of deduction. She could also bring along her assistant, Horst Cabal, if she must. To this end, the constable accompanied them to the nearest police telephone box to call in.

'Assistant?' Horst was filled with as much outrage as he could manage without making a scene, expressed as a high-pitched whisper. 'How have events conspired to make me your assistant?'

'You have a problem being subordinate to a woman?' said Leonie.

'Not if they're clever, and Johannes seems to think you are.'

That brought Leonie to a dead halt. '*He* said that?'

Horst thought about it to make sure he was definitely talking about the same woman. 'Yes. I'm sure he meant you.' He waved her on to keep up with the policeman. Once they were under way once more, he continued, 'But that's not what I mean. I mean the way he said "assistant." There was a distinct subtext of "comedy sidekick" about it. I'm not sure I care for that.'

'I'm sure you imagined it,' Leonie reassured him while equally sure that he had not. Then she cut off any further utterances of hurt on his part by saying, 'A detective, though. Isn't it wonderful? Just like Sherlock Holmes.'

'Prettier than Sherlock Holmes,' said Horst, the reflexive gallant. 'The trouble is, I think they're expecting you to do some detecting.'

She glanced at him from the corner of her eye. 'And?'

'And you're not. A detective, that is. What are we going to do when they present you with some terrifically complicated case and there isn't a handy butler to point at?'

'What do you think I'm going to do?'

'How should I know? I'm not a detective.'

'No, you're not.'

'Wait . . .' Horst's tone was warning. 'Wait a minute. You cannot seriously be suggesting . . .'

'We are going to look at the case. And then I am going to solve it. Don't you understand, Horst? That's what this place is. It's a test. It's cobbled something together from the real world that touches on what we do, and now we're going to be tested upon how well we do it.'

'Have you ever actually *done* any real detective work before?'

'A little. With your brother along, but a little. And I've done a great deal of studying. Have a little faith in me, would you?'

Horst grimaced. 'And what's my role in all this?'

'You are my faithful assistant, apparently.' This failed to pour any oil on troubled waters. Leonie wondered if said oil was perhaps flammable. It was worth the experiment, so she carelessly and with malice aforethought added, 'And the comedy sidekick.'

Horst began to express outrage at such presumption, but then saw Miss Barrow's smile, and his wrath was punctured. He smiled back, albeit a little dejectedly. 'What if we can't crack the case?'

She had not considered that, but at the instant she did the ramifications became apparent. Somewhere at the end of this was something wonderful, too wonderful to simply be given away or allow second attempts. 'We'll probably be kicked out of here and never permitted to return.'

'Oh, dear. That'll be tough to explain to Johannes. He'll have to have a shot. If we mess it up.'

'I don't think he'll have that option, to be honest.' She looked around at the city about them. 'This quest of his isn't simply about collecting the clues. I'm beginning to see that now.'

'It isn't? I was guaranteed a simple few weeks of clue gathering, dumping them in triumph at Johannes's feet, and then wandering off while he makes sense of them. What makes you think it's not going to work that way?'

'Because this is where I want to be, Horst. Doing what my dad did, if not quite by the same methods. Solving crimes. Setting things right. Making things better. This is tailor-made for me. I don't think this place even existed until I agreed to help your brother. The dice are already cast. There's no going back now. I'm the Great Detective, you're the light relief, and there's a crime to solve.'

They reached the police telephone box a few paces behind the constable, who had already unlocked the small door in the large blue box's side to reach the phone that lay there.

'We have to keep the handset locked away in this neighbourhood; elsewise the kids'll cut the wire, the little buggers.' He blushed. 'Begging your pardon, ma'am.'

To cover his confusion over such saucy language, he made a great show of calling the police switchboard and thence being redirected to the office of Lament of the Yard.

'I have Miss Leonie Barrow for you, sir,' he said with the air of a herald announcing the arrival of an empress before passing the handset to Leonie.

From Horst's perspective the telephone conversation was brief and wilfully enigmatic. Miss Barrow performed a few very serious nods, said, 'I see, Inspector' twice and, 'Yes' four times, and made some notes in a small black book that she produced from her pocket as if she knew exactly how this Platonic ideal of her carried such things. Then, infuriatingly, she said, 'Interesting' in such a way to indicate that it really was terribly interesting and curiosity fairly made Horst squirm.

Then she concluded the call with brusque efficiency and demanded of the constable, 'Where might we find a cab in this area at this hour?'

The constable indulged in a chortle. 'Nowhere, ma'am. Nobody around here can afford a taxi. But the station's not far from here, and we can send you over to wherever the inspector needs you in the area car. Where would that be, ma'am?'

The Alhambra Theatre was a grand venue, of that there was no doubt. A large structure in a far more prosperous section of the city than the terraces by the mines, the theatre faced onto a grand thoroughfare of Roman pretention. The theatre itself would not have disgraced Imperial Rome. A vast portico of pale stone in the neoclassical style, of a scale to make the Glyptothek of Munich seem like a pup tent, topped by a frieze in which Shakespearian characters rubbed shoulders with Euterpe, Calliope, tragic Melpomene, and comedic Thalia.

'That,' said Horst as they stepped from the police car, 'is quite a large theatre.' He smiled at Leonie. 'That was understatement. I've been practising it. Actually, that theatre is absolutely *huge*. I've never seen the like. You could put the Bible on here and have all the characters onstage for the encore, including the five thousand with their fish sandwiches.'

'I'm not sure the Bible specifically mentions fish sandwiches.' Miss Barrow walked by him and started up the steps.

'It hardly needs to, does it? What else are you going to do with fish and bread?' He followed her, considering such exciting theological concepts as he went, and finding solace thereby. After all, how could such a philosophical cove as he be regarded as a humorous sidekick?

At the entrance they were met by a police sergeant who took charge of them and conveyed them hence to the presence of Inspector Lament. Their route took them through the theatre's foyer, a fantasy wrought in marble and red carpet and sweeping staircases that would have given the impression of an opulent ballroom, but for the footling detail that no ballroom was as large, nor did any ballroom of such grandeur usually aspire to selling ice cream in little tubs and cartons of cold drink most safely described as 'orangesque'.

They processed through doors marked as the provenance of *Staff Only* and, subsequent to some windings about narrow corridors whose layouts seemed to have been settled upon using haruspicy, finally and a little unexpectedly, found themselves in the wings and so onto the stage.

'Always wanted to be on the stage,' said Horst. He looked about him. The place was peppered about with strange items of apparatus and *faux*-Oriental decorations, hangings, and lanterns. He was just wondering what sort of play would have such a curious setting when he belatedly realised that a dummy of a man in brightly coloured silken robes sitting slumped in some form of throne was in fact, not a dummy at all. 'Oh, look,' he said, as if spotting an uncommon yet not rare bird during a stroll, 'there's a dead feller.'

This struck him as odd in two respects. Firstly, that even quite outré productions rarely have corpses onstage. This, he reasoned brilliantly, must be the victim of the perfidious crime that he and Leonie Barrow had been summoned to solve. After a moment he revised the thought. This must be the perfidious crime that Leonie Barrow and he had been summoned to solve.

The second odd detail was not one he thought wise to mention in open company. The man seemed to have suffered a chest wound of some description, to judge from the large red stain that disfigured the gorgeous robes. There was a good deal of blood there, and yet Horst—a vampire—had failed to scent it. Usually, the smell of blood glowed in his senses much as the scent of bacon does for so many others. On this occasion, though, he was barely aware of it. Did this mean the blood was fake? Or . . .

He belatedly noticed that he was breathing, and it wasn't purely for purposes of conversation. He tried holding his breath, and it quickly became uncomfortable, so he started breathing again. He thought of blood, and it seemed unappealing.

Leonie noticed his very apparent consternation. 'What is it?' she asked him quietly. 'Whatever is the matter, Mr Cabal?'

'I . . .' He looked at her aghast as he understood the desire that was growing in him. 'Miss Barrow . . . the most extraord . . . I . . .' He looked at her wide-eyed. 'I could absolutely kill a bacon sandwich.'

'There's a cabbies' caff around the corner, son,' said the sergeant. 'Go and get yourself stoked. This looks to be an all-nighter.'

With a muttered apology to Miss Barrow and a promise to be back ever so quickly, Horst bolted back for the wings. She regarded him thoughtfully as he disappeared back into the *Staff Only* corridors, a lust for a bacon roll lending him unerring navigational skills through the labyrinth.

'Loves his bacon, doesn't he, miss?' said the sergeant.

'Only very recently,' she said slowly. 'Usually his tastes are distinctly more rarefied.' She turned her attention to the dead man on the gaudy throne. 'In his absence, perhaps you might tell me why I'm here.'

'Oh?' The inspector cleared his throat with the sardonic air of a man who is used to being outshone by gifted amateurs. 'You can't tell?'

She favoured him with a cool glance, then said, 'Well, all I see is the obvious. A dead man chained upon a throne. He appears to have been shot in the chest by a quarrel presumably launched from the crossbow mounted over there, its trigger pulled by the sand-driven timing mechanism standing by it. Without knowing the specifics of the event, one guesses he is a stage magician whose grand escape from the Throne of Death—or whatever else the publicists might call it—proved rather tardy. Presumably in the normal run of things, he would free himself at the last second? Flinging himself aside as the fatal bolt is shot?' She crouched by the throne, looking at the quarrel's shaft still protruding from the dead man's chest. There was a great deal of blood, considering it was not an open wound. The pressure required to force blood by the shaft offered confirmation to her opinion that the quarrelhead must have penetrated the left side of the heart, causing rapid shock and exsanguination. 'No doctor could have saved him,' she said half to herself. She straightened and addressed Inspector Lament. 'So what makes you think it wasn't simply an accident, Inspector? Conjurers and escapologists have died when things haven't gone as planned before.'

Lament was examining the crossbow, hands clasped behind his back to prevent him inadvertently touching anything. 'True, Miss Barrow. But our man Maleficarus here seemed to think this would be his last performance.'

'He did?' Leonie was just concentrating on pursing her lips and nodding in the most ineffably wise manner she could manage, when her equanimity abruptly shattered. 'Hold on. *What* was his name?'

The inspector made a show of consulting his notebook. 'Maximillian Maleficarus ay kay ay *Maleficarus the Magnificent*. Rather an impressive show from what I've heard, miss. Leastways'—he nodded at the corpse—'I doubt anyone will be forgetting this performance in a hurry.'

'I'm beginning to see what you mean about how this place reflects the people who find it,' said Horst. He was eating the fourth of six bacon rolls he had been carrying on his return, the first of which he'd devoured *en route*. 'Maleficarus? It's an unusual enough name, after all. There can't be that many of them about. Even fewer after Johannes crossed paths with them.* He mentioned running into Maleficarus senior once upon a time, but I don't think it played out like this. Much too mundane for my darling brother. From what I gather, it was all rather more occult.' He illustrated his understanding of 'occult' by waggling his fingers, immediately employing them on the conclusion of this illustration by re-engaging the diminishing stack of bacon rolls.

* The dealings of Johannes Cabal with Maleficarus *père et fils* may be discovered in *Johannes Cabal the Necromancer*, 'Exeunt Demon King,' 'The Ereshkigal Working,' and *The Brothers Cabal*.

'I know about the son, Rufus Maleficarus. Or, at least a little about him. A necromancer, too, wasn't he?'

'Hmmm,' said Horst. 'But he's dead now. Twice. Well, not quite dead. Well, sort of dead. You know how it is with necromancers.'

Leonie Barrow decided not to pursue that subject, which was just as well given the sordid and bloody details of Rufus Maleficarus's varied career as necromancer, Lord of Powers, freestyle bastard, and talking box.

They were talking quietly in a corner of the backstage while waiting for the theatre manager, a Mr Curry, to conclude his statement to the police. Leonie had already told Horst what had happened onstage that evening as witnessed by a full house.

The performance had gone through assorted pieces of legerdemain and illusion and been as well received as every previous performance. Maleficarus the Magnificent was a highly regarded and very popular magician, routinely performing before the crowned heads of Europe, the oligarchs of America, and the general unwashed of everywhere.

So he had arrived at a literal showstopper—the last wonder to be performed before the interval—and, just for once, the show had stopped him. The effect was entitled 'The Throne of Death,' exactly as Miss Barrow had predicted with an accuracy that now perturbed her. It was a little bit of mild *Grand Guignol* suitable for family audiences; *Petit Guignol*, if you will.

Max Maleficarus began by relating a tale to the audience of a mandarin of the mysterious and exotic Orient. A terrible man of profane appetites, he preyed on those he should have governed and thereby made them fear him. The tortures he visited upon them were many and imaginative, and the people were cowed. That all came to an end the day a humble travelling scholar happened into the mandarin's power.

Here Maleficarus was garbed in gorgeous and colourful silks—hardly the clothes of a humble travelling scholar, but in a story littered with factual inaccuracies, it hardly mattered—and the stage around him was decked out in oriental finery. Lanterns and vases were carried in, and banners (sporting fanciful characters that would baffle anyone with even the faintest grounding in sinograms) fluttered down from the full-fly space behind the proscenium.

Throughout the transformation, Maleficarus continued the story, and detailed how the scholar came to loggerheads with the evil mandarin and so was condemned to suffer upon the dreadful Throne of Death. Here, Maleficarus was accosted by stagehands labouring under hastily applied yellow-face make-up and unconvincing wigs bearing black yarn queues.

Struggling—but not too much—he was dragged to the throne and secured upon it, the chains that bound him locked tight with a padlock supplied from a respected member of the audience earlier in the performance, and held by them until that moment. A paper screen bearing a fantastical painting of a Chinese dragon was raised before the throne, hiding the victim from the audience's view.

Now the 'mandarin' began the mechanism of murder. Sand ran from a reservoir onto a balance pan, the spring-loaded mechanism that would trigger the crossbow beneath. When the pan was heavy enough to go past the balance point, it would slam down, and the crossbow would launch its deadly cargo directly at Maleficarus's heart.

Yet, of course, he was never there when it struck. After struggling valiantly against the chain for the minute or so that the balance required to pass equilibrium, Maleficarus would release himself just as the balance pan started its descent, leaping aside as the bolt flew.

Except this time. He had cried out when the mechanism passed the tipping point, a cry he had never made on any of the previous performances. And he remained there, helpless as the pan struck down, the mechanism was triggered, the crossbow released, the quarrel flew, his heart was pierced, and as his blood left him.

'Sounds like an accident to me,' said Horst, and he did so through bacon. On realising the *faux pas* he swallowed and apologised. 'Bacon's the most wonderful thing in the world right now. I don't think coming here just changed our clothes and careers, Miss Barrow. The little voice has gone. Gone altogether.'

'Little voice?'

'In my head. I have a little voice.'

Leonie laughed. 'Your conscience?'

'No.' Horst was emphatic. 'I don't need a little voice to tell me not to do bad things. The little voice I mean is the one that specifically tells me to do bad things.'

'You have an anti-conscience?'

'Hmmm. It came with being a vampire. "Stick your fangs in that un." "Break that un's neck." *All* the time. Such a nag. Anyway, it's shut up. I don't even think I can do the thing with my fangs. Y'know, extend them? Can't seem to do that at all. Blood suddenly seems like a pretty unpleasant thing to be feeding on, and I suddenly have an urge for bacon.'

'You're not a vampire.' Leonie said it with barely a thought. It was so obvious a conclusion. 'Not any more.'

'Exactly. This place, wherever we are, has devampired me somehow.'

She considered this. 'I wonder why.'

'I'm more wondering if it's permanent.' His tone made her look him in the face. There was a longing there, and she understood just how desperately he wanted it to be true. He stirred the nest of paper bags on the small table where they sat, looking for any surviving bacon rolls. 'What if it's permanent?'

Mr Curry was pink and round, startled and baffled, tired and dismayed. 'I really cannot see what I can tell you that I haven't already told the police, madam,' he said, and patted his florid face with a handkerchief redolent of lavender.

'In all eventuality, Mr Curry, nothing. But one never knows.' She smiled and was charming, and Mr Curry was charmed and smiled in return, and throughout all this Miss Barrow wondered when exactly she had become so charming.

'Very well.' He became fatuously ebullient, as an uncle coaxed into opening the biscuit barrel for the children might. 'Very well! Ask your questions, then.'

Leonie's smile hardened just an iota. 'Tell me, why do you think Mr Maleficarus was murdered?'

Curry's smile waned quickly, and he became worried. 'I . . . don't necessarily think . . .'

'I've read your statement already, Mr Curry. You're very cagey about it, and I can understand that. It looks like a tragic accident, and that's probably exactly what it is. Best to get things sorted out and get your theatre's name out of the news as quickly as possible. Despite what some think, I doubt many people come to see a death-defying act in the hope that the performer will die. The thrill of coming close is enough.' She spread her hands in a conciliatory manner. 'I am simply a consultant the police have on retainer. We all want this dealt with quickly for a plethora of reasons. So, in your own time . . .'

Curry cast his gaze about his office, seeking alternatives. He sighed upon finding none, and said, 'He told me. Straight to my face. "Lemuel," he said, "I am not peaceful in my own mind that all will go well this evening." He said that. I asked him what he meant, but he seemed to think he'd already said too much and became as silent as a clam. And then this happens. It was as if'—he leaned forwards, opening his eyes too wide for propriety—'it was a premonition.'

'It was suicide,' said Horst with undue cheerfulness. 'Bit of a melodramatic way to do it, in front of a packed house and all, but all he had to do was twiddle his thumbs and wait for the crossbow to do its business.' He noted Leonie Barrow's somewhat acidic expression and changed tack with the natural assurance of the saloon bar Lothario that he had once been. 'Or he was just off his game for some reason. Touch of dyspepsia, not feeling right in himself, frets about things, and—when it comes time to do the miraculous escape—he just can't concentrate. "Did I pay the newsagent for this week? Did I turn the gas off? Did I do this? Did I do that? Oops, out of time." *Twang!* Dead.' Horst smiled self-indulgently and awaited the applause for his masterful piece of deduction. When it didn't come, he said, 'Or it was an accident. It could always just have been one of those things, I suppose.'

'So, to enumerate,' Leonie counted off the points on her fingers, 'it was murder. It was suicide. It was an accident. It was an act of God.' She regarded him with dry aspect. 'These are your conclusions?'

'Yes.' His smile wavered as he thought about them. 'Doesn't actually narrow things down much, does it?'

'Deduction means to take away the things that are not so. Whatever is left is the truth. It's like chipping away from a block of marble until a statue is left.'

Horst considered this. 'That's very poetic, Miss Barrow, but—'

'For heaven's sake, call me "Leonie." '

'Oh! Thank you. Yes, where was I? That's very poetic, Leonie, but there are all kinds of statues you might get out of a block of marble.'

'An artist might argue there's only one, and so I stand by the simile. There are all kinds of statues you might make, but only one of them is the truth. All the rest are failures or, worse yet, miscarriages of justice. We must be careful with our chisels, Horst.'

'Yes, we must. Indeed we must.' He shook his head. 'I have no idea what you mean by that.'

'For the moment, we have more potential witnesses to interview. Firstly, the closest witness.'

'And who is that?'

'Maleficarus's assistant, one Athena la Morte.'

'L'amour?' Horst asked, sensitive to the possibilities of love.

'La Morte,' Leonie corrected him, sensitive to the ubiquity of death.

Athena la Morte—born Pansy Kett—was discovered in her changing room, where the police had put her until such time as they decided what to do next. Horst knocked and entered first, and so discovered Miss la Morte in the process of repairing her make-up. Leonie noted that her eyes were puffy, and when Athena blew into the handkerchief Horst offered her, there was little evidence that the sniffling was histrionic.

Even in such a dismayed state, she was clearly a very attractive woman in her mid-twenties, dark hair still clipped back as it had been when she had worn it beneath a wig and headpiece that evening as a concubine of the wicked mandarin. Beneath her candlewick dressing gown in an unflattering shade of pale terracotta could be seen the historically inaccurate but still very fetching *cheongsam* she had worn as her costume.

'Trick?' she said to Horst's inquiry. 'There was no trick. That was an honest piece of escapology. Every evening, every matinee Max had to crack a padlock he hadn't seen before. And he did it. Max is a genius.' She faltered. 'Was.'

'Why the paper screen, then?' asked Miss Barrow, sitting by la Morte. Horst had made a beeline to take that chair, but a warning glance from the Great Detective had stopped him in his tracks, and now he was standing, forced to be sympathetic from a safe distance. Safe for Miss la Morte, that was. Since discovering that in this curious city that never was and probably never would be, he was fully human and prey to human wonts and desires, Horst had recalled which of those wonts and desires were his personal favourites and was looking to exercise them before the presumably inevitable return to vampirism. So far he had successfully sated his desire for bacon by dint of it being reasonably simple to address. Higher on his list was another desire that Miss Barrow seemed intent on thwarting at every turn.

Athena smiled ruefully. 'What's honest escapology to a performer isn't really the same to the punters. They think you should be able to pick a lock without tools. Course, no one can do that. So, Max has . . . had . . . lock picks concealed. The screen was so the audience couldn't see they were hidden in the arms of the throne, or how he used them.' She looked hopelessly from face to face. 'I can't understand it. The lock was a bog-standard Schumann. Whoever brings in the lock has to give written assurance that the lock is new and hasn't been tampered with in any way. It's closed and unlocked a few times in Max's sight so he's satisfied nobody's trying to be clever by altering the mechanism. His life depends on it being an honest feat of skill. He could do a Schumann in his sleep. I just don't understand what went wrong. Except . . .' She frowned. 'I'm not sure.

I'm onstage, obviously, and half of my job is to distract the audience. Nothing is unrehearsed. I always know what I'm supposed to be doing, but . . . maybe my timing was off.'

Leonie was making notes. 'Off in what way?'

'I could have sworn the crossbow shot before it was supposed to. Not by much—only a second or two—but that might have been enough.' She shook her head. 'I'm making something out of nothing. The timing was *never* quite predictable. You'd think a sand clock would be accurate to a second when it doesn't have to run very long, wouldn't you?'

'Yes.' Leonie underlined something. 'Yes, I would. Who's responsible for the apparatus? The police mentioned an engineer?'

'Engineer . . . yes, I suppose you could call him that. That's Max's son. I haven't even seen him since this happened. The police seem to be keen on keeping everyone apart.'

'That's good practise, Miss la Morte. People's memories are less reliable than you might think. If a couple of witnesses compare notes completely innocently before statements are taken, they can influence one another. Something one of them thought he saw becomes something they both definitely saw.'

'Yes, I can imagine that.' La Morte gestured at her costume. 'A lot of a stage illusionist's job is making people think they saw something that they didn't.'

Leonie wasn't entirely listening. She had noticed Horst's expression had become uncharacteristically serious. 'Horst?'

'Miss la Morte,' he asked. 'This son of Mr Maleficarus, what is his name?'

'Rufus,' she replied. 'His name is Rufus Maleficarus.'

'He's the killer,' said Horst with certainty as they went to interview the son of the deceased. 'As sure as night follows day, he's the killer.'

'This isn't our world,' Leonie reminded him. 'He might be a wonderful and loving son here.'

'No. Rufus Maleficarus is a stinker of the first water. His stink is strong enough to travel across the spheres. Every Rufus Maleficarus in every possible world is an utter stinker, too.' He nodded with certainty. 'You'll see. I bet he'll be wearing plus fours, the blackguard.'

He was not wearing plus fours, although that didn't stop Horst from scowling at him. Leonie had never met him in the flesh, and Horst had only seen his corpse, and that a riffle away from this reality. But Horst had heard of the history of Rufus Maleficarus in forensic and unalloyed detail from his brother, and drawn from that the only possible conclusion: Rufus Maleficarus was a stinker. Further, he had seen the result of Maleficarian magic himself in a conflict that had claimed the lives of people he had liked, and who had deserved more than to be snuffed out by this, the most preposterous of magicians. Johannes had explained that Maleficarus was not entirely responsible, at least at a metaphysical level, for these specific deaths. Given that he was, however, also undeniably responsible for scores of deaths in a cack-handed scheme that almost resulted in the global extermination of humanity, that footling mitigation was very small beer indeed.

This iteration of Rufus Maleficarus wore brown warehouse overalls and suede, soft-soled shoes, the better to travel unheard around the near-stage areas while a performance was in progress. He was red-haired and clean shaven, a man barely into his twenties. He was not nearly as ursine as the version Horst was more familiar with, but his frame was large, and it seemed likely he would grow thus in the next few years. He was also surly, which was unendearing.

'I've already spoken to the police. I didn't see anything, and I wasn't anywhere near the stage when it happened. Why can't I go?'

'You don't seem very heartbroken about your father's death,' said Horst. Leonie gave him a warning look, but he was at pains to ignore it. 'In fact, you just seem irritated by it.'

'We all die sometime. Magicians get killed doing their acts sometimes. It happens. Not often, but it happens. Bullet catches, water escapes, even a guillotine illusion once, I heard.' He smiled, a twisted cynical line across his face. 'Audience certainly got their money's worth that night. My dad was very good, but he risked his life every time he sat on that throne. We all knew it. It's the life.' He cast his hand around the understage area where he apparently held domain. It seemed to have been at least partially converted into use as a workshop, judging from the workbench, the pots of paint, tools, spools of wire, board, and even welding gear propped up in the corner.

'What do you think went wrong?' asked Leonie, heading Horst off at the interrogatory pass.

Rufus turned his mouth down in professional consideration, the sort of expression a plumber displays just before he says the dripping tap means a new boiler is required. 'He was slowing down. It was obvious. Every year it took him longer to do the same old things. He shouldn't have been using such risky *prestige* at his age. Lost his fire. He was all about going off to the Far East a few years ago, learn some new stuff from them. But that looked too much like work, so he didn't bother. Just carried on with the same old card tricks and nonsense. He'd have been pulling rabbits out of hats at children's parties in a few years, the way he was going on.'

He took a long breath and blew it out. 'This might be the best thing that ever happened to him. Magicians who get killed by their acts get a sort of immortality. The name of Maleficarus will live on, now.'

Leonie looked up from her notebook. 'You really don't sound very fond of your father.'

'Fond?' Rufus scratched his nose. 'Not really the kind of man you get fond of. If he'd done what he said he would, gone east, I'd have been proud of him, you know? Do something a bit different. A new direction. But no, that was too much bother.'

'Where exactly were you when the incident occurred?'

'Incident?' He laughed without humour. 'I was checking the props for after the interval, staging them to go into the wings.'

'You were in the wings?'

'No, not at that point. I was under the stage. I spend most of my waking hours under the bloody stage.' He half laughed at his choice of words. 'I'm used to hearing screams from the audience when the crossbow shoots. Then there's laughter and applause. Not tonight, though. Not tonight.'

'I've changed my mind about Rufus Maleficarus,' Horst said as they walked back to the stage. 'He's *too* obvious. I've read detective stories. I know how this works.'

'This isn't a detective story.' Though she was loath to admit it, Leonie couldn't help thinking Rufus was a little too overtly unlikable to be the villain of the piece.

'But it *is*. This isn't real life. You're not really the world's greatest detective or whatever you're supposed to be, and I'm not the light relief.' He pulled a face. 'Except I am, aren't I? Obsessed with bacon rolls and the fairer sex all of a sudden, to comic effect.'

'I thought I was going to have to extract you from Miss la Morte's cleavage with a crowbar.'

'You exaggerate. I made a point of looking at her face once a minute or so. You must admit, though, she's a very handsome creature.'

'If you like that sort of thing, I suppose she is.' She chased a half thought that had occurred to her during the questioning. 'Doesn't something strike you as a little *off* about her, though?'

'Off? She seemed very sincere.'

'That's not what I mean. Maximillian's act seems very staid in many respects; enough to disgust his son, certainly. Yet he has an assistant whose wardrobe seems to run strongly to black, crimson, and silver, who is stage-named for the goddess of wisdom and prudent warfare in addition to death, and whose role on that stage is to play the villainess as much as anything. None of that strikes you as odd?'

Horst shrugged. 'You see all sorts of acts, all sorts of themes in the theatre.'

'What I mean is how it seems to be two halves of different acts glued together. She simply isn't the sort of assistant I would expect for somebody whose performance is so very much of the old school of gentleman illusionists. She belongs to a more current generation.'

* * *

They arrived at the stage to find Lament overseeing the work of the police photographer. Overseeing, in this case, comprised mainly of standing to one side and smoking a pipe.

'Done your detectin', then, Miss Barrow?' he said with what Leonie recognised with a small tickle of pleasure was a fond irony. She had only just met Lament, but in this world their acquaintance was apparently well formed, and mutually respectful.

'Not nearly, Inspector. The incident has interesting aspects.'

Lament's face, already as dour as a bloodhound receiving bad news, fell further. 'Oh, Lord. It doesn't, does it? I thought we could just chalk this up to a terrible accident and go home.'

'That might yet be the true state of affairs. I'm just curious about some details.'

'Such as?'

'Well, to whom Miss la Morte is betrothed. That would be a beginning.'

Horst almost jumped. 'What? What makes you—'

Leonie touched her bare ring finger. 'She clearly and habitually wears a ring; the mark on her finger is obvious. Equally obviously, she doesn't wear it for performances. It makes her more interesting and therefore more distracting for male members of the audience if she appears unattached, and a ring is all too apparent when caught in the limelight. I glanced over her dressing table and saw it there, an engagement rather than a wedding ring. I didn't feel it was the right time to enquire directly of her, so I left it until now. Who is her fiancé, Inspector?'

Lament didn't even need to resort to his notebook, but simply nodded at the throne. 'The deceased.'

Leonie cocked her head. 'Really?'

'You seem surprised.'

'A little. Presumably becoming his assistant is how they met in the first place?'

'I would think so, miss.'

She bit her lip and looked up into the shadows above the stage beyond the grid. 'One would think so. Indeed one would.' She slapped Horst in the chest with the back of her hand. 'Come on, faithful sidekick. I need to ask more questions of Miss la Morte.'

Horst's shoulders sagged at the suggestion. 'Do you need me to come along? Her changing room's not *that* close to the stage.'

She looked him in the eye as she moved a step to present her back to Lament and, when she was sure she had his undivided attention, said, 'Cleavage' in an undertone.

'Lead on, my captain. I shall follow you to the ends of the earth,' he said, suddenly motivated.

He was to be a little disappointed, however, as—by the time they returned—Miss la Morte had changed out of her stage clothes and was wearing an altogether soberer ensemble suitable for returning to her digs.

'Engaged? Why, yes. To Max. But how is that relevant?'

Leonie Barrow was candid. 'I have no idea. I am simply trying to form a full image of everybody and how they relate to one another. How did you meet Max Maleficarus?'

'Rufus introduced us. His father was encouraging Rufus to spread his wings, to go out and put his own act together. Rufus is a very capable magician himself, you know.'

'That was my understanding,' said Leonie, with a modicum of irony. 'What happened to those plans?'

La Morte looked uncomfortable. 'Max did. I did. We . . . we just got on very well, and all of a sudden Rufus's act didn't seem so pressing. Max needed a new assistant, and . . . it just seemed the obvious thing to do.'

'And how did Rufus take this?'

'He was confused about what was happening at first. Then he was angry. My God, he was angry. But he took a little time off, cooled down, and came back. He said perhaps it was as well he didn't go solo just yet. He wanted to work on his act a little more first, in any case.'

'I see. Purely as a matter of curiosity, what sort of act was Rufus working towards? Something a little more dramatic than his father?'

'Dramatic?' La Morte laughed uncertainly. 'Max's act was dramatic enough. You should have seen him when the time was almost up and he struggled madly on the throne just to gee the audience up. Always made it out. Always.' She looked bleakly into nowhere.

'Of course. I meant in tone. Something a little darker, perhaps?'

Miss la Morte smiled awkwardly. 'Oh. I see. This is to do with my stage name?'

Leonie shrugged and smiled. Horst noticed it wasn't the warmest of smiles. There was something of frozen mercury and razor blades about it.

'Roofy . . . Rufus thinks that stage magic has to keep moving on if it isn't to stagnate. People want sensation. Why not give it to them?'

'What was Max's view of that?'

'That change is inevitable, but that reaching for it too soon looks desperate, not challenging. The audience can smell desperation. He thought that Rufus was onto something, but its time had not quite come yet.' She looked from Leonie to Horst and back, her need to emphasise her sincerity palpable. 'Max was entirely supportive of Rufus. Always has been. He loved his son.'

They found a quiet corner in which to compare notes. Horst's were mainly pictures of goats. 'They're the only animal I can draw,' he said. 'But, really, there's little to detect here, isn't there? We still don't have the faintest hint that this isn't what it looks like—a terrible accident. I agree the *ménage* between father, son, and beautiful assistant is a tad . . . unusual, but that doesn't mean the old man simply didn't have some wretched luck.'

'There are five possible explanations for what happened on the stage tonight,' said Leonie Barrow. 'Firstly, it is just as you say. Max Maleficarus simply didn't manage to undo the padlock in time for whatever reason. His concentration was off, he fumbled the lock pick, the apparatus malfunctioned and shot too soon, or a dozen other possibilities.

'Secondly, that it was suicide. That he deliberately sat there and waited for the sand to tip the balance.

'Thirdly, that Miss la Morte engineered his death.

'Fourthly, that Rufus did. I'm considering that they were in cahoots as part and parcel of those possibilities.'

'Cahoots,' said Horst for no other reason than the word felt nice in his mouth.

'And finally, that Max Maleficarus was done to death by person or persons unknown to us at present.'

'That sounds thorough. Which do you favour?'

'I don't know. If we're not sure of motive, or even if there ever was a motive, it's hard to bring anything to the perpetrator's door. Method, perhaps. If it was murder and a method is detectable, then that might give us an idea as to the killer's identity.'

'You're frightfully good at this,' said Horst. 'You sound just like a real detective.'

'While we're here, I *am* a real detective. Try to remember that, Horst.'

'And I'm the slightly dim sidekick. I know, I know. I didn't mean it as an insult. More, you know . . . a compliment. You are good at this, Leonie.'

'If I find out what happened on that stage tonight, then I'll agree. Until then, this is all playacting. Come on, let's do what I should have done right at the beginning and study the crime scene properly. Sherlock Holmes would be furious with me. I cannot theorise without data, and I'm a fool to try.'

The photographer had finished his work, and the police were on the point of removing the body by the time Leonie and Horst returned.

'Might I crave your indulgence for just a few minutes, Inspector?' Leonie applied the hapless expression and joined hands suggestive yet not precisely analogous to an attitude of prayer, a combination that worked well on older men in her experience. Her father, any rate. As a ploy it seemed to have definite puissance, for paternal relays almost audibly clicked home in Inspector Lament's head, and he nodded indulgently.

'Ten minutes and no more, Miss Barrow. We're all keen to wrap this one up for the evening.'

Leonie thanked him and went straight to business. She examined the body, the quarrel still thrust through the dead man's heart, the chains and padlock, the lock pick grasped in the cold fingers. Then she briefly looked over the paper screen pierced by the bolt and the marks on its reverse side that showed it had been repaired after the previous few times it had been penetrated.

Lament consulted his notebook. 'They replace it after about eight performances on average.'

'Eight? Why eight?'

'That's a week's worth. One evening performance a day, matinees on Wednesday and Saturday. No performances on a Sunday, obviously.'

'Eight a week.' She checked her pocket diary and found that it was full of notes she had no memory of making; entries made by the historical version of her that this playhouse of a reality had made for the real her, referring to other people, places, cases. It seemed she was quite busy and quite successful. It made her feel both a fraud and anxious not to let herself down, in several manners of speaking. She swiftly counted the repaired tears and counted seven. This tallied with her diary; it was Saturday evening. Somewhere in that fake city, fake newspapermen were writing up a fake story for fake people to read in the morning.

Faithfully followed by Horst, who was developing craning curiously to one side and rising on the balls of his feet to a minor art form, Miss Barrow next went to inspect the actual engine of death.

It was, she had to admit, a very competently wrought piece of engineering. Behind all the fanciful direction lurked a device of brilliant simplicity built to a very high standard. Everything about it demonstrated forethought, from the steep angles of the sand reservoir to prevent clumping to the precision bearings on the balance itself, all built into a steel frame that would not admit warping or any other cause for imprecision that might result in the sort of terrible accident that had occurred that evening.

'This is the dead man's design?' asked Leonie, sprawling unladylike upon her back to inspect the device's underside.

'It was, miss.'

There was silence for a moment, and the assembled company of men looked just about everywhere but at the pair of lady's ankles so indecorously exposed as Miss Barrow lay beneath the device like a mechanic beneath a car. Finally, her voice wafted out. 'And he built it?'

'No. The son, Rufus, is the engineer. He built it.'

Leonie climbed back to her feet and dusted herself off. 'He knows his job. I can't see anything obviously wrong. Or any way it might be influenced.'

She turned her attention to the contents of the scale. It seemed at first her interest would be as brief as her other investigations had, perforce, to be, yet this time she hesitated.

She took a pinch of sand and sprinkled it along one of the prop's horizontal struts. Then she reached into her jacket pocket and withdrew—with, to Horst's eye, evident delight—a magnifying glass. This she used to examine the grains for a few seconds.

Lament came over, his indulgent air giving way to professional interest. 'Have you found something, miss?'

'Possibly.' She squinted at the sand through the glass for a few moments more. 'Horst!'

'At your service!'

'Would you fetch a fire bucket for me, please?'

Nonplussed yet obliging, Horst trotted off into the wings. Presently he re-emerged carrying a battered bucket upon which was helpfully painted the word FIRE.

'Thank you.' Leonie took a pinch of sand from it and sprinkled it a little further along the same strut. She then spent the next minute examining first one sample and then the other without saying a word, causing her audience inexpressible frustration.

Finally, she stepped away, offering her magnifying glass to the inspector. 'Take a look, Lament. Tell me what you see.'

Perplexed, the inspector spent a few moments looking at them. 'Two samples of sand, miss. Quite different. One is very fine and pale, beige, I suppose you'd call it, and the other has larger grains and more of a red colour to it.'

'And that's all?'

'Well, it would be easier if you'd kept the samples further apart, miss. They've become a bit mixed up with one another.'

'Take another look.'

Conscious of his subordinates' eyes upon him, Inspector Lament's patience was wearing thin. 'There's nothing else of note. Just that . . .' He started to say something extraordinarily salty, remembered there was a lady present, and turned a fierce pejorative into a short collection of nonsense syllables. 'I'm a fool! The samples aren't mixed up at all. Well, not by you. The sample from the fire bucket has none of the finer grains, but the sample from the balance is riddled with coarse sand. How is that? *Why* is that?'

For her answer, Leonie probed into the fallen sand on the balance and, pinched neatly between thumb and forefinger, produced a cigarette butt. Horst glanced into the fire bucket; the surface was specked with similar fag ends.

'I would suggest that you find a clumsy stagehand, Inspector. Occam's razor always suggests we should look for incompetence, accidents, and pure rotten luck before assuming conspiracy. I think Maleficarus the Magnificent may very well have been done in by the former.'

The body had finally been removed while further enquiries had been made. Finally, the unwitting culprit was discovered; a stagehand called Jacobey who was neither more nor less clumsy than any of his fellows, but neither was he immune to the confoundments of wretched luck. A young man and eager to make a fist of it in the theatre, he had been dismayed that, in stowing away the crossbow device after the previous evening's performance, he had caught the well-built but ungainly frame on a corner and succeeded in spilling much of the sand from the scale pan.

Being of a practical mind, he had gathered up as much as he could in a dustpan and put it into an empty bucket he had secured for the job. A good quantity of the sand, however, was lost between the boards, and he was momentarily baffled as to where he might make up the shortfall. Then he remembered the fire buckets that so many of the staff used as convenient ashtrays and sought one out. The sand hadn't looked *exactly* the same, but after some stirring, the two types seemed to mix well enough, and he was sure that, thanks to his quick thinking, there would be no trouble.

Then Maleficarus the Magnificent had ended up dead, and Jacobey had decided this was the ideal opportunity not to tell anyone about it, because 'Manslaughter' can look very bad on a *curriculum vitæ*.

'I'm awfully dense, I'm sure,' said Horst in the heavy tone of somebody who knows it is his role to be awfully dense and to make the protagonist look terribly clever, but that doesn't mean he has to like it, 'but why would mixing the sand change anything?'

'You're close to the money already,' said Leonie. 'It's all about density. You saw that machine; it's a precision piece of engineering. *Any* change in the way it's operated could affect how long Maleficarus had to perform his escape. The rough sand added to the fine sand the apparatus had been calibrated for was enough to alter the density of the mixture. It made it trigger a little early; not very long, but quickly enough to catch Maleficarus by surprise.'

'Oh.' Horst seemed a little underwhelmed. 'I'm a little underwhelmed,' he said, confirming it. 'What about all this backstage drama and jealousy and Rufus being such an utter arse that he couldn't possibly have done it?'

'He didn't do it.'

'I know, but it shouldn't just have been down to one silly ass of a stagehand, should it?'

Leonie shook her head. 'Aren't you even slightly impressed that I solved this?'

'Of course I am. You're terribly clever. I've never said you're not. Just I was hoping for a little more *Sturm und Drang*, you know? At the very least, a bit of a "You may be wondering why I've called you all here today" moment. I'm not disappointed that you solved all this, just that what you solved turned out to be a silly accident. That boy won't get in trouble, will he?'

'Not from the police. There was no reasonable way he could have known what would happen. His career at the Alhambra might be over, though.' She tightened her lips. 'You're right. It is a bit underwhelming. I wonder if that's the lesson this place is supposed to teach us.'

'Perhaps. I still don't understand why we're in such a peculiar place, anyway.'

They had left the theatre and were walking along the great thoroughfare. In the east, the sky was growing light. At a newsstand, they bought an early edition of the local Sunday paper.

'The *Sepulchre Sentinel?*' said Leonie. 'This city's called Sepulchre?'

Horst wasn't very concerned by that, instead focussing on the headline, DEATH ON THE STAGE—POLICE CALLED AS FAMOUS MAGICIAN AND ESCAPOLOGIST DIES IN GROTESQUE INCIDENT.

Inside, the story sailed around the edges of whether the death was accidental or deliberate, but it was clear the reporter was hoping against hope that it was murder by some thrillingly obscure method.

'Bad luck, old son,' muttered Horst. 'You're going to be as disappointed as the rest of us when Lament does his press announcement.' He suddenly became more animated. 'It could still be murder, you know! What if friend Jacobey knew full well what changing the sand would do?'

Miss Barrow blew out a breath into the chill air. She was wondering at what point they would be allowed to move on from the sinister city of Sepulchre. She had assumed it would be dependent on solving the case, but that did not seem to be so. Perhaps she would have to solve more than one?

'It's not impossible, but it seems very unlikely,' she said. 'Jacobey had a good character and apparently wouldn't say "Boo!" to a goose. What would his motive be?'

'He might be a hireling?' said Horst, but his enthusiasm for the idea was foundering.

'From what I saw of the backstage people, there are half a dozen more reliable and more corruptible hands I would have chosen before Jacobey for that job. No, it seems off. I'm sure he didn't do it deliberately.'

'If you say so, o Great Detective. I suppose you must be right. If it's all just brought down to the laws of physics like that, it doesn't allow for much uncertainty.' No answer came. He turned to find Leonie deeply pensive, inured in a brown study. 'Why the morbs, leader?'

'I should go back. Insist Lament actually have those sand samples tested for density. What you just said about physics, you're right. I've been insufficiently scientific.'

'That rough sand's obviously heavier, though.'

'"Obviously" doesn't butter science's parsnips, Horst. "Obviously" means you're taking things on faith. Everything should be tested and . . .' She fell silent.

As the silence extended uncomfortably, Horst watched her with growing consternation. Her eyes were half-shut and the fingertips of her right hand twitched as if she were enumerating things in her mind.

'I know what that is,' he said slowly. 'I've seen Johannes do something similar. You're cogitating, aren't you?'

She made an irked noise at least as much hiss as shush at him, and he fell silent.

Her eyes opened, and she looked angrily at Horst. Then he saw her anger was directed elsewhere. 'You were right,' she said.

'I was? Hurrah!'

'Then you were wrong.'

'One out of two isn't bad.'

'Possibly right and wrong. I've been so muddle-headed. We need to get back to the theatre before Inspector Lament lets everyone go.'

'It wasn't an accident?'

'I don't know yet, but I suspect not.'

'You don't know? Why? What do you think killed Maleficarus?'

'If I'm right . . .' She was already walking quickly back towards the theatre. 'If I'm right, science killed the magician.'

Miss Leonie Barrow was all business and no chat when she secured re-admittance to the building. 'I'm sorry,' she told Lament, 'but I may have been premature when I suggested the case was solved. If I could beg your indulgence for just a few minutes longer?'

Inspector Lament's patience, apparently a plentiful commodity where she was concerned in the usual run of things, was nevertheless beginning to run dry. 'Miss Barrow. We have been here all night. The sun is very nearly up. We are all tired. Could this perhaps wait?'

Perhaps it could, but Miss Barrow was subject to an ineffable sense that it should not. The sun was rising; it seemed relevant to the presence of Horst and herself that she should be done before the sun finished doing so, a simple rightness to the time. She did not doubt this feeling; for all her reliance upon the scientific method, she was wise enough to know when science—known science, at least—was insufficient to comprehend every possible circumstance. She had personal experience of that which chafed at the boundaries of the known, and did not presume to test it when she was so utterly beyond those boundaries herself.

'No,' she said with certainty. 'We should resolve this matter immediately, if at all possible.'

'I thought it was already,' said Lament under his breath, but did not argue further and had everyone of note in the matter brought to the stage prior to finally being released.

On reaching the stage she made her way directly to the crossbow device. The stage around it occupied her interest for the moment. 'Mr Curry. These marks upon the stage. They seem semi-permanent. What might be their function?'

Mr Curry seemed at least as dismayed as Lament that the investigation was conspiring to still keep him from his bed even after he had been assured that all was settled. 'They're for the scene shifters, the stagehands. So they know exactly where to put the properties.'

'Close enough isn't good enough, then?'

'Heavens, no!' He chortled at such naivety. 'They are employed commonly enough even in the most undemanding of sitting room comedies, never mind a magician's act. Things must be placed exactly so. Lines of sight and placement of props are of paramount importance.'

'Good, good.' Why exactly it was 'Good, good' she didn't care to share at this juncture. Instead she said to Horst, 'What keeps that flower in your lapel?'

Horst wasn't sure he had heard aright and raised his eyebrows. 'I beg your pardon?'

'Do you use a pin?'

'Well, yes. They tend to . . .'

'May I have it, please?' She held out her hand, and when he didn't immediately oblige her, she beckoned for it impatiently. Beginning to wonder if somehow Johannes had possessed the woman, he handed it over. She examined it briefly, muttered, 'Good, good' to herself once more, and then vanished beneath the machine again.

There were quiet sounds of tinkering for a second, and then she emerged, started to hand the pin back, thought better of it, and put it in her own lapel while assuring Horst she would return it shortly, and then demanded a balance or scale of some sort. Mr Curry sent off his stage manager to recover the scales used in a production of *The Merchant of Venice* the previous year, and everyone stood around in a slightly baffled silence while they were fetched, with the exception of Miss Barrow, who spent the time striding around the stage and alternately examining things with her magnifying glass, and glaring at Curry, Rufus Maleficarus, and Athena la Morte.

When the scales arrived, Miss Barrow wasted no time in measuring identical volumes of sand out from the fire bucket, and from the crossbow device. She snorted with something like disgust at the results, and turned to face her audience.

'You may,' she said without a hint of irony, 'be wondering why I have called you here tonight.'

Horst was suddenly filled with great admiration for Miss Barrow, and a desire for popcorn.

'I am guilty of wasting a lot of time, and I must ask you to forgive me for that. I have been . . . distracted recently. My focus was poor, and it has taken me far too long to understand what has been going on here. Strictly, I ask forgiveness from all but one of you. That person has been furnished with a few extra hours of liberty due to my lack of diligence, and he . . . or she . . . should not forgive me, but thank me for that time. Now, to facts.

'The sand. The sand that killed him. It didn't, and if I had thought about it more carefully at the time, that should have been obvious to me without even having to weigh it. I made a silly assumption—that the coarse sand must have a greater density than the fine sand and so it tripped the crossbow that much earlier. That cannot be so. If we assume that the rock that is the source of the sands has a similar density, then the finer stuff will—if anything—have the higher density. Smaller particles and smoother grains means smaller air gaps between those grains. This is borne out by the simple weighing you just saw, but even then the difference is minuscule. Even extrapolating to the larger bulk of sand used in the device, we are only looking at an ounce or two.'

'But in an escape timed to the second, even that small difference . . .' Lament paused, thinking it through. 'Of course, even if it made a small difference, it would have been in favour of the deceased. He would have had an extra second or two, not less.'

'Exactly. And there is a further factor. The adulterated sand had already failed to kill him once. Why would it suddenly do so this evening?'

'The matinee performance!' Mr Curry was pleased to join the deductionary clique. 'Of course! Why didn't the effect go wrong yesterday afternoon if the sand was of such concern?'

'Yes.' Miss Barrow's gaze darted from face to face. 'The sand had nothing to do with the tragedy. There was no accident.'

'Then what is it, Leonie? That is . . . Miss Barrow?' asked Horst.

'Murder or suicide?' He somehow prevented himself from commenting further that, obviously, murder would be far more thrilling, so that had his vote.

She spat the word out. 'Murder.'

Horst strangled down the very nearly overwhelming impulse to clap his hands with glee while shouting, 'Huzzah!'

Inspector Lament looked at the candidates for the crime. 'You're suggesting the apparatus was tampered with, I take it?'

'It was.'

'Then that puts Rufus in the clear. He wasn't anywhere near the apparatus, there's no trapdoor or anything in a position to allow him to tamper with it, it's subsequently been checked and found to be operating exactly as it should, and this is the closest he's been permitted since his father's death, so he has had no opportunity to remove any traces of sabotage.'

'That is correct in all but two details, Inspector. He was able to get very close to it during the performance. About'—she held up a hand with thumb and index a couple of inches apart—'yay close. Indeed, his proximity was vital for the illusion to work in all those other performances.'

'It wasn't an illusion.' Miss la Morte was adamant. 'You don't understand. It was an escape, done by skill alone.'

'That was the illusion. Max was undoubtedly very practised and highly competent. But he was also slowing down, and he knew it. You said it yourself, ma'am. You never knew exactly how long the escape would take. It was always more or less the same period, but with a few seconds' variation. If the scale was so accurate, how was even that much possible? And how did Max always seem to know exactly when the pan was going to fall and trigger the crossbow?'

'He . . .' La Morte's voice wavered, unsure as she replayed events in her head and found her rationalisation of events now fell short. 'He could see the pan starting to fall.'

'I think the only time he saw the pan fall unexpectedly was tonight. Previously, he always knew exactly when it would drop.'

Lament went to stand by the Throne of Death and regarded it

curiously. 'How? He couldn't trigger it himself. There is absolutely no connection between the throne and the mechanism.'

'There is. And tonight that connection killed him.' She looked at Rufus Maleficarus. 'Didn't you, Rufus?'

'You're fishing,' he said evenly. 'You're throwing dirt and seeing if anyone reacts.'

'Not at all. I said the inspector was wrong on two details. The first was that you were very close. You were directly beneath the stage, after all. The second was that you left no trace of your involvement.' Miss Leonie Barrow took the pin from her lapel. 'But you did.'

Before the gathering, she walked a few steps to the crossbow mechanism. She held the pin up for them all to see, and then she brought it close to the metal pan of the balance mechanism. With a sharp *click* whose significance far outweighed its volume, the pin snapped from her hand and stuck to the metal.

'It's a magnet!' said Horst.

'It's magnetised,' she corrected him. 'The result of its many, many exposures to an electromagnet. One built by his son and used at every performance to trigger the balance at the exact moment his father signalled him to use it.'

'The struggle.' La Morte spoke as in a reverie. 'He'd struggle, slam his feet down just as he freed himself. It was a *signal?*'

All eyes were on Rufus Maleficarus. He shrugged. 'Nice theory. How do you intend proving it?'

'These gentleman,' Leonie said, nodding at the police officers, 'and I shall be going through your understage workshop in close detail, looking for a suitable bar and the length of wire you undoubtedly spent the time waiting to be interviewed putting back onto a spool. But you know what wire's like; it never quite smooths out perfectly. I should think it will be painfully obvious. Of course, we were never supposed to know what it was we were looking for, were we?'

'You can't prove a thing.' Rufus seemed bored now.

In contrast, Miss la Morte was growing more passionately upset by the second. 'Why didn't I know about this? I was in the act! Why was I never told?'

Leonie shrugged. 'Only Rufus can tell you that now. I would guess it was because Max was trying to impress you. A middle-aged man pulling off an escape eight times a week that would terrify younger men. He probably meant to tell you at some point early on, but it became more difficult with every week that went by. After a while he began to fear that if he told you the one great death-defying moment of the show was as illusionary as all the rest, he would lose your respect. That there was still risk wasn't enough. He would rather face a crossbow quarrel than disappoint you.'

'Oh, God. Max. You stupid, stupid man.' She began to weep in exhausted, hopeless little gasps.

'Stupid's right,' muttered Rufus. He looked around, jagged little reckonings showing in his eyes. 'If he'd stuck to his word, none of this would have happened. Well done, Miss Barrow. You deserve your reputation. I thought you were as big a fraud as my father at first, but I have to admit this late rally of yours . . . I'm impressed. Well, don't you want to know why I did it?'

'I know why you did it, and you just filled in the last detail. Your father fronted your act and reduced you to a backstage engineer while he got the plaudits. This was only intended to be for a brief while, wasn't it? A season or two? Then there'd be some grand publicity about the father passing on the mantle, and you were to take over and he would become the engineer or perhaps just retire. But then things became complicated. He fell in love with Miss la Morte and, rather more unexpectedly, she fell in love with him. Now he had a new lease on life. Now a season or two wasn't enough.'

'I have plans, you know.' Rufus shook his head. '*Had* plans. Such plans. A new form of magical theatre. More risky, more risqué. My father took them all and made them the same as everything else out there. Bland. Predictable. He took Athena away and turned her into another pouting assistant. Some faint shadows of what I had planned, but becoming safer with every performance. He'd have had you in ostrich feathers and sequins by the end of the season, Athena! Just another showgirl!' He calmed and looked at Lament. He curled his lip. 'I was angry. I lost concentration. My finger slipped,

and I activated the magnet too early. Just a little too early. It was an accident.'

'No, it wasn't,' said Leonie Barrow.

He turned his surly leer upon her. 'Prove it.'

'The sun.' Horst watched it rise above the busy skyline of municipalia and industry, the cold rays of a new day throwing golden light into soot-stained streets. He held his hand up to bathe it in the brightness, delighting in how it felt good and how it didn't feel of violent combustion. 'Is this a gift? Is this some way this place is saying, "You play a blinding silly ass, Horst. Kudos to you, old man"?'

There was no immediate reply. He looked over to find Leonie Barrow cross-armed and furrow-browed. 'For somebody who just solved a pretty tricky crime, you're looking a bit woeful, glorious leader.'

She looked at him and did not so much shake off the reverie as crawl disconsolately from it. 'I failed, though, didn't I? Rufus is right; nothing can be proved beyond what I demonstrated and what he confessed to. If the police try him for murder, it will all come down to how good the barristers are and just how arrogant he is in front of the jury.'

'Ah, the British jury. Stout yeomen all.'

'Exactly. A bigger bunch of nincompoops it's hard to imagine. Yet if they let him off with manslaughter instead, who can blame them? There's nothing to suggest premeditation. If he decided even a minute beforehand to kill his father, it's murder. If he triggered the thing on the spot in a paroxysm of rage, it's manslaughter. If he fumbled and did so while distracted, it's accidental. Only Rufus knows the truth, and his truth will get him off with the lightest charge. The jury will have little choice.'

'That's the law.'

'It is. Doesn't feel much like justice, though, does it?' She watched as the sun melted the hoarfrost from along the ridge of a nearby wall. 'Perhaps that's what this was all about? I don't know. I wonder if we're supposed to move on now, or if we're stuck in Sepulchre for a while.'

Horst shook his head. 'I have no idea. I just know I've missed the sun. Also,' he said, flexing his hand, 'I sort of miss being a vampire. I'm feeling very mortal all of a sudden. Weaker. More vulnerable. Not sure I like that.'

'It's what you once were. You'll get back into the swing of it, I'm sure.'

'Yes, but . . . you know Johannes is saying he thinks he might be able to cure the vampirism. I was all 'Yes! Wonderful!' about it at the time, but this is making me wonder.' He looked to Leonie, troubled and sincere. 'Before, I was nothing. Not really. I was charming, I suppose, and I like to think I was witty, but so were any number of other fellows. But after what happened to me, things changed. I became special. Unique even. Not that I'm the only vampire, but I doubt you'd find another quite like me.'

Miss Barrow nodded; it seemed a likely truth.

'I helped save the world. That's something, isn't it? But old Horst couldn't have done it. He'd have been dead in the first five minutes. Properly dead.' He shielded his eyes to look into the dawn. 'I miss the sun, but perhaps that's a sacrifice I should make. What do you think?'

She half laughed. 'Why are you asking me?'

'Because you're the Great Detective.' She started to laugh again, but then saw there wasn't a glimmer of a smile on his face and the laugh died. 'Or at least *a* great detective.'

'You mean that, don't you?' She said it with some wonderment and perhaps even a little gratitude.

'I do. Johannes is intelligent, but you're clever.'

'He'd have figured out what was going on with the balance faster.'

'Probably, but that's because he would have focussed on the balance and barely spoken to anyone else. He'd have found the method, but he would have been very slow finding the motive, if he found it at all.'

'The Great Detective. It's sweet of you to say that.' She pecked him on the cheek to his mild astonishment. 'Is that you being honest or charming?'

'Occasionally I have the opportunity to be both,' he said.

They watched the sun rise over Sepulchre.

The Third Way: ZARENYIA, PRINCESS OF HELL

The land of the infinite cemetery sloped downward and so they descended the gentle gradient—the necromancer, the witch, and the devil. They spoke little and all proved curiously unobservant as the dank earth gave out to sand beneath their feet, a fine pale powder moderated with larger, dark red grains that glistered like wet blood and made the landscape revealed before them sparkle and shimmer. Johannes Cabal reflexively deployed his spectacles of blue glass, Miss Smith squinted, and Zarenyia hummed 'By Jingo' for lack of any other outlet for her customary garrulousness.

As the soil became sand, the tombs and crypts of the benighted place grew larger and windows made an appearance in their structures, so that by degrees they became houses and then mansions and palaces, and so the grey-blue sky became the dull maroon of a persistent headache.

Then . . . a tic of perception, and all three of the travellers realised the subtle changes wrought around them in an instant. They drew to a halt and looked about them in differing degrees of nonchalance.

Miss Smith uttered an oath to make porters and fishwives blush. Cabal grimaced and made reference to the loss of beloved verisimilitude. Zarenyia crossed her arms across her chest and declared she had been to this place before, but, 'It's changed. It shouldn't look like this. Why are the manses ruined? Why is everything derelict? Where is everyone?'

'Where are we, exactly?' It was Cabal who spoke, although he was already reasonably sure he knew the answer.

'Why, it's Hell, dear heart,' replied Zarenyia, surprised at such apparent naivety. 'Isn't it obvious?'

'Why should this be any more Hell than that cemetery was my necropolis?' said Miss Smith. Cabal raised his eyebrows to Zarenyia as if to say, *Why indeed?* For her part, Zarenyia had the faintest impression that the humans were ganging up on her, and she did not care for the experience in the slightest.

She sniffed and pointed at a great building constructed largely of rusted iron and bloodshot tachylyte, the massive blocky structure of the former, the aggressive ornamentation of the latter. The place was not, to coin a phrase, in fine fettle. The fifty-yard-long spears that once formed a close cage around the mansion had fallen away in a tumble of linearities, giving the place the air of a game of spillikins abandoned by Titans.

'That's Balberith's palace. Stabby, isn't it? But look at the state of it! Yes, he may be all about murder and argumentation and suchlike, but he's *frightfully* house-proud. What has happened here?'

Cabal regarded the ruin with equanimity. Over to the right he saw another glorious mansion brought low perhaps by violence or merely time. A once-glorious thing of cherry-red and white marble, it stood skewed as if Gog and Magog had leaned heavily upon its eaves. Statuary of a licentious sort lay scattered about, brokenly wanton. 'That would be the house of Lilith?'

'Oh, she'll be livid when she sees her place in that state,' Zarenyia confirmed, albeit not without a very distinct lamina of *schadenfreude*. 'Ah, me. *Quel dommage*.'

'You're smirking.'

'I know.'

Any further badinage was quelled by the sight of dust, a plume like dried blood, growing on the near horizon. 'Something's coming,' said Cabal.

'You say that as if it's a bad thing,' replied Zarenyia, never shy of the opportunity to deploy a *double entendre*, or a *single entendre*, or occasionally just to chat about penises and orgasms with forensic specificity.

'How to characterise our situation? I am unpopular with Satan, you are exiled from the rings of Hell without good cause, and Miss Smith'—he glanced at her, and she returned it with an expression of expectant curiosity—'Miss Smith is . . . I don't know, but I do not think much of her chances when confronted by a herd of intemperate demons, either, nonetheless.'

'I may be very dangerous, for all you know, Cabal,' said Miss Smith. 'They may run screaming from my magic.'

'Might they?'

'They might. Or, they may not.' She looked back in the direction from which they had come, but the last signs of the great cemetery had faded like a verbal contract. 'Is it too late to start running?'

'Run? From a hullabaloo? Never!' Zarenyia turned to face the approaching welcoming party. 'Unless they're terrifically dangerous. Run like the wind in that case.' She noticed Cabal looking at her lower body. 'Oh, darling, not now! What an awful time for you to take an interest! Hullabaloo!'

'I was just wondering if this would be a good time for you to assume your arachnid form, madam. Helpful for both combat or flight, assuming one or the other proves necessary.'

'Really? That's the only reason you were looking at my skirt?' Zarenyia was visibly dismayed. When she spoke again, it was with some disappointment in her voice. 'I'll pop out the other limbs at the right moment. Element of surprise and all that. Speaking of which, have you brought your wand with you?'

'Wand?' Miss Smith was shocked, wands being for mountebanks, hedge wizards, and even necropolis witches, not scientifically minded necromancers.

'I have not,' said Cabal, a little quickly. 'I had no reason to do so. There is little stuff of chaos around here upon which a wand might work.'

'Oh, that's a shame.' Zarenyia spoke past Cabal to Miss Smith. 'He cuts such a fine figure with his little stick in his hand, waving it around.'

Cabal may have blushed. Under the light of that hellish vault it was hard to tell. 'Ladies! Pray pay attention to—'

The demons arrived.

Cabal regarded them with freezing disdain. 'What do you monstrosities want?'

They were unedifying creatures, true, but at least there were only two of them. One was a herpetologist's worst nightmare; an otherwise interesting bipedal lizard that had suffered some sort of terrible internal tumour. The cancer had grown and spread until it filled the reptile's body, misshaping it, wrecking its symmetry, making it grossly rounded, grotesquely distended in its limbs, given it a bubbled, cyst-racked skin, insanely mismatched eyes, a bad haircut, a small moustache, its breath disagreeable, its diction regrettable.

'Oh, he called us "monstronities", De'eniroth, didja 'ear 'im?' it said.

The second demon was taller, thinner, and generally less tumorous. This ended the list of its charms. It took the form of a great, stringy maggot, some ten feet long, that bent in a loose S shape, the lowest straight furnished with an indeterminate number of little legs that propelled it along upon a carpet of fairy steps. The upper body bore a pair of arms that would have given a tyrannosaurus an unaccustomed *frisson* of superiority in the upper-arms department, white ropes of ganglion and muscle that ended with tiny clutching hands that, for the demon's sake, one hoped were more practical than they appeared. The demon had no head per se, but only a gullet within which rings of teeth spun slowly and wetly counterwise to their neighbours. If it had eyes, they were not evident. Perched high upon the corpse-pale brow immediately above the gaping maw was a brown trilby of the sort preferred by bookies.

'Hur-hur. "Monstronities". Hur,' it said.

Cabal somehow held his temper. He disliked being toyed with at the best of times, and this particular circumstance was trying his patience badly. He would have suspected the hand (or tentacle, or waving tendril of materialised thought) of Nyarlathotep behind this but for the lack of a characteristic atmosphere of trifling sadism. No, this place—like its predecessor—was nothing but a morality tale wrought in broad strokes and bright colours.

'And what are you called?' he asked the first demon. 'De'zeel or something similar?'

The cancerous lizard looked at him with evident astonishment. Then, rallying its limited powers of dissimulation, it said, 'No.'

The maggot frowned, which was as unappealing as it sounds. 'Isn't it, De'zeel? Why did you tell me it was, then?'

While the lizard flapped its angular arms at the maggot and the maggot whipped its ropey limbs in defence, Miss Smith said in a voice that betokened both wonderment and disdain, 'You *know* these things?'

Cabal shrugged the shrug of a man of substance discovered by his fashionable friends in the company of the family he's been trying to disown since his teen years. 'In a manner of speaking. This is an echo of my past. If the men involved had died and gone to Hell as they so richly deserved, then these are very likely the demons their souls might eventually have become.'

Miss Smith took a moment to absorb this information. 'The human versions of them aren't dead yet? In the real world, I mean. They still live?'

'Oh, no,' said Cabal, snorting a little at such credulity. 'I killed them myself.'

It says little for the company of necromancers and, indeed, devils, that neither Miss Smith nor Zarenyia saw anything at all unusual or reprehensible in the statement.

'Then, why couldn't these actually *be* the demons created from their damned souls?'

'Because their souls are still bottled up in their bodies. I needed some cheap labour . . . *free* labour . . . and they were handy and disagreeable. I had my pistol and reagents handy, so why not? I think it turned out to everyone's satisfaction.' His audience regarded him with suspicion. Cabal elucidated. 'They got to drive a train. They'd never have done that were they still alive.'

Both Miss Smith and Zarenyia nodded with agreement; it was all perfectly reasonable, after all.

De'zeel stopped thrashing at De'eniroth, and both demons turned their attention upon the intruders.

'We are guardians of this 'ole flank of 'Ell,' said De'zeel, gesturing grandly over the glittering dunes. 'Hidennfy yerselves, or we are hempowered by the Prince of 'Ell'—here he turned a jaundiced eye upon the party, jaundiced, sclerotic, bloodshot, and home to several bacterial conditions of which conjunctivitis was the very least—'to do yer.'

'Do our what?' asked Zarenyia with professional interest.

'Kill us,' said Miss Smith.

Zarenyia wilted, this being the latest of her recent disappointments. Then she perked up. 'Oh, wait. You're *threatening* us?' Her smile returned, a delightful expression filled with spring sunshine, heartfelt joy, and the imminence of wholesale slaughter.

'Control yourself, madam,' said Cabal. He turned to the demons, aware of and ignoring Zarenyia mimicking him behind his back. 'You are to conduct us to the presence of His Infernal Majesty.' He said it as if arranging an appointment to have the carpet shampooed. 'What we have to discuss is for the ears of Satan only.'

De'eniroth gave the impression of blinking stupidly, despite the absence of obvious eyes. ''Oo?'

'Satan,' repeated Cabal, the word slowed with caution. 'The Prince of Hell you just mentioned. He's called Satan. That's what he's called.' He looked from one idiot demon to the other and back again. 'Lucifer? He's called that sometimes. The Prince of Lies?' Still no response. 'What sort of demons are you if you don't even know the name of your employer?'

'Lucy-furr . . .' The sound of De'zeel's thought processes were almost audible, and would have seemed much like fracturing ice and old clockwork if they were. 'I know that name.' Suddenly he clicked his fingers, making a noise like crushing a louse the size of a tangerine in the process. 'I do! That was the old boss.' He grinned, and several tooth splinters oozed out on a string of drool. ' 'E's gorn now. We've got a new bloke.'

'What? How can there be a "new bloke"?' demanded Cabal. 'This isn't some sort of corporation, subject to hostile takeovers. Even Hell isn't *that* evil. The whole point of Hell is that it is and has always been Lucifer's domain! What exactly is supposed to have happened to him? Revolution? Coup? An assassin angel came down from on high with a blessed elephant rifle? *What?*'

'He retired.' This said the lizard demon, and no more.

Cabal gawped, not something he was inclined towards in the usual run of things. 'He did *what?*'

'Retired. Said 'e'd 'ad enough, an' chucked it in.' De'zeel regarded the dumbstruck expressions of the humans (well, two out of three wasn't bad) with pleasure. 'Said the joke wos over an' 'e wos done. Orft he went. Prob'ly got a cottage now. Cottages is nice.'

'The joke?' Cabal thought back, and then wondered how close an analogue this place was to the reality. Was this an echo of the true current state of Hell? If so had he, Cabal, inadvertently been instrumental in causing the greatest theological upset in . . . well . . . *ever?* It was a matter of the most monumental import. The opportunities were immense. New alliances could be forged, new paths opened. The vistas of potential research blooming before him, no matter what the outcome of the current expedition, were breathtaking. With Satan off looking after the roses around the door of his retirement cottage (Cabal guessed it would be in either Dis, Tartarus, or Essex; probably Essex), Cabal would be free to make overtures to the new management.

'So,' he said, 'who is the new Prince of Hell?'

De'zeel and De'eniroth both huffed out their chests, made complex yet underwhelming salutes of obeisance to their ruler, and chorused, 'His Infernal Majesty, Ratuth Slabuth!'

'Shit,' said Cabal.

'Not a friend, darling?' said Zarenyia. 'Really, you should try being nice sometimes. I gather we're back to Plan A?' Without waiting for a reply she turned her attention to the demons and managed a smile no human could have managed in the face of the worst that both the vertebrate and invertebrate worlds could produce. 'Hello, you sweet things. Quick question—do you both have anything that might equate to sexual organs?' They seemed surprised by this tack and looked foolishly at her, a look much practised. 'I mean, more or less. Just enough for a girl to . . .' They still seemed very blank. She sighed. 'You know what? Never mind answering. I'll conduct an examination of my own. You just lie back and think of Gehenna.'

And so saying, Zarenyia shed her earthly form. Her extra legs erupted from her lower torso as she reared up, suddenly towering over the startled demons. Her abdomen seemed to swell out of nowhere, her clothes shredded into mist, and she stood triumphant and clearly outclassing De'zeel and De'eniroth in every conceivable category, a queen in chitin and angora.

Her smile was ravenous and vicious, the smile of a shark. 'I am Zarenyia! Devil of the outer darkness where even demons fear to tread! I am the smiling death, the final embrace, the killing kiss! I bring the shuddering finality to my enemies! Unbeholden to the thrones of Hell, you have no defence from me, pit spawn!' Her smile became a little more Women's Institute. 'So, I'd just pucker up and enjoy it, if I were you.' She pointed at De'zeel, who stood rooted to the spot, his unlovely eyes wide with awe. 'You first, poppet. You probably have more to work with. As for you'—she turned her attention to De'eniroth—'just stay put until it's your turn. No running away, or I'll just have to run after you, and that will make me grumpy.' Her smile hardened. 'You don't want to see me grumpy, believe you me.'

The demons looked at her in silence and then, very unexpectedly, fell to their knees. Or at least De'zeel fell to his knees. The situation was less clear-cut with De'eniroth, but he seemed to sink a little lower, and he curled his body around a little more so there was more on the lower side of the S of his body.

'Mistress Zarenyia!' they cried. 'We must take you to the prince immediat'ly!'

'Eh?' said Zarenyia. 'What?'

'Your comin' 'as been foretold, it 'as!' said De'zeel. 'You are most respectfully invited to the court of the new Great Satan his own self, Ratuth Slabuth!'

Zarenyia rested back on her haunches slightly in the manner of a toast rack being gently bent back, the better to regard the grovelling demons. Her brow harboured much in the way of suspicions. 'Johannes, are these fellows committing some heinous and cunning ruse upon me?'

Cabal was as taken aback as she. 'If they are anything like their mundane counterparts, they are severely lacking the wit for any scheme much more complicated than putting on their shoes.'

'They're not wearing shoes. The maggoty one would need several dozen little baby pairs, by the looks of him.'

'I was talking metaphorically, madam. My point is, no, I doubt this is a scheme. Or, at least, not one they have evolved.'

Zarenyia digested this, then addressed the demons. 'If I go with you, what happens to my travelling companions?'

De'eniroth and De'zeel looked at one another. 'Dunno,' said De'zeel after a short, wordless conversation with his colleague that largely consisted of shrugs. Maggots do not shrug convincingly. 'But it's really important you come wiv us, Mistress Zarenyia. 'Is Infernal Majesty is really, really keen to see you.'

'What do you think, darlings?' asked Zarenyia of her companions. 'I mean, when all is said and done, this *isn't* Hell. It's more like improvisational theatre.'

'That is no improvement,' said Cabal.

'Philistine. You know what I mean.'

Cabal nodded. 'I do. There is a story to work out here, and running away from it will not resolve matters. Very well; we shall act in this play, though no one has seen fit to offer us a script.'

'That's the spirit! I'm rather enjoying all this, to be honest. We're having fun, and I've met some of your friends and your brother, all of whom seem *absolutely* delicious.' Here she favoured Miss Smith with a smile that left the necromantrix slightly breathless.

Zarenyia turned back to the demons, her smile now a beacon of complaisance. 'Lead on, my sweets.' They started to do so, but she stopped them. 'One tiny proviso. Should it transpire that this is all some overture to a tedious trap of one sort or another . . .' In a movement so rapid it blurred the thick air, she flipped De'eniroth onto his side and trapped one of his multitude of legs in a joint close to the end of her right foreleg. With no discernible effort and ignoring the agonised squeals of the demon, she scissored the limb off. She raised the miserable piece of flesh, speared on the leg's tip. She was not smiling at all now. 'I shall destroy you both in ways your fetid little minds could not conceive if you were a thousand times cleverer than you are. Which is to say, of roughly average intelligence. Johannes, tell them; do I follow through with my warnings?'

'She does,' he replied, a witness to one such event.

'There.' She flung the wiggling limb off into the distance, and she smiled brightly. 'Now, let's go and see the new boss, shall we?'

As they progressed in the wake of the demons De'eniroth and De'zeel—poor additions to an already displeasing vista—there was a muttered conference between the members of the mismatched little expedition.

'Awful mess, isn't it?' Zarenyia indicated with a nod a palace that seemed to be in the progress of rotting. Tubules dangled haplessly in the fevered air, and ichor oozed from spiracles running in vague lines along the building—if *building* it truly was, and *growth* if it was not—pooling in lazy grey-green rivulets of filth. 'That's Beelzebub's place.'

Miss Smith followed the nod. 'Horrendous.'

Zarenyia cocked her head, considering the architecture. 'Actually, that's an improvement. But it's still not supposed to look like that. What has happened here? It looks like a battlefield.'

'You!' said Cabal of the demons. The misshapen lizard looked back over its shoulder. 'Why are the mansions of the princes in ruins? What has happened in Hell?'

'Lucifer's doin', ain't it?' rasped De'zeel. 'When 'e pigged off to take up watercolours or whatever 'e 'ad planned, 'e didn't say 'oo was to take over, did 'e? Only left a constitutional crisis in 'is wake, selfish bugger. Owin' to us not 'avin' a constitution, 'part from the *Abandon 'Ope* thing, and that's more like a advisory.'

'No succession? What happened then?'

De'zeel pointed at the ruination of Hell. 'Civil war, innit? "By the sword divided." In ta lots of lickle bits, often as not.'

'And, of all the Princes of Hell, Ratuth Slabuth came out on top?' Cabal was having trouble with this idea. 'Beelzebub, Lilith, Asmodeus, they ended up as also-rans, their mansions and palaces in ruins, and a ridiculous non-entity like Ratuth Slabuth gets the basalt throne?' He shook his head. 'He wasn't even a prince! The last time I saw him, he was a corporal.'

De'zeel shrugged, an action that made his head bob upon the line of his shoulders like a dead pig in a cesspool. 'Politics, innit? S'always politics.' It was an analysis both cynical and sadly irrefutable.

Cabal gave up; these demons were clearly next to useless as sources of information, or most things. Instead he expressed his exasperation to Zarenyia and Smith. 'Ridiculous. How could Lucifer just leave things in such a state?' But his mind was already moving ahead and, if he was right about Lucifer, this had never been more than a sideshow to him in any case. He could have abandoned Hell just as easily as he abandoned any of his multitude of faces.

'Who is Ratuth Slabuth?' asked Miss Smith. 'You seem to know a lot about him. I've never heard of him before.'

'Used to be one of Lucifer's generals,' supplied Zarenyia, pleased to gossip. 'For reasons I could never understand. Good at the bureaucracy, I suppose, and there was a period when Lucifer was very bureaucratically inclined. Pettifogging little brute, dotting and crossing his way up the ranks. I recall talk of him even being raised to a princedom.'

'What happened?'

'Blessed if I know, and as I find being blessed uncomfortable you may be sure I don't. All of a sudden he was spectacularly out of favour and all his generalship and hopes of becoming an infernal prince up in smoke, which is a cleverer way of putting it than I realised when I started the sentence. As to why, it's a bit of a mystery.'

Cabal could have explained the primary reason for Ratuth Slabuth's fall from—and one uses the term advisedly—grace with great clarity, but it seemed a little like boasting, so he did not. Besides, if he was going to be making the new Satan's reacquaintance shortly, he was sure Ratuth would be unlikely to have forgotten him and there would probably be some gloating.

The structure of Hell seemed to have changed somewhat in Cabal's absence, but then he reminded himself—as he forced himself to do every few minutes—that this was not actually Hell exactly, the demons were not exactly demons, and the Ratuth Slabuth they would soon encounter was not exactly Ratuth Slabuth, former general of Hell, patronising snob, and proud tenant of the upper cantons of the enormous population spread across multiple realities, all of whom counted Johannes Cabal as an enemy.

In any case, his experiences of Hell's physical organisation to date did not tally at all with the scenery through which they now travelled. Previously it had all been tunnels and chambers, lava outfalls, stalactites, and stalagmites. The open red desert beneath the light of a burning, curdled moon that could be no true satellite was all new to him, nor did he recall this particular manifestation in any of his reading. The gibbous, flaming moon in particular gave him some grounds for concern, an echo of events that sounded loud and insistent and that boded no good if his fears were in any wise grounded. Unable to do very much about it, he contented himself with pointedly ignoring it on the off chance it was possible in this place to 'cut' supernatural astronomical bodies, and thereby send them home in high dudgeon to sob their hearts out in a suitably vast boudoir.

The experiment didn't seem to be working thus far, but that was little enough reason to give it up just yet. Or ever.

The plain littered with the ruins of former diabolical grandeur gave way to a slow rocky incline that abruptly gave way to reveal that they were on the edge of a vast shallow crater as if torn out by a large though insubstantial asteroid, perhaps made of marshmallow, the wreckage of which was subsequently devoured by many ants over an extended period. It could just as easily have been an ancient volcanic caldera, but that offered fewer possibilities for marshmallow-orientated simile.

In the centre of the crater—whatever its origin—the land rose again as a spike of dark rock. The three of them paused in their progress to look at that wondrous structure. Striking thousands of feet up from the base of the crater stood the needle worked at every point into colonnades and balconies, arches and embrasures, and an embarrassment of columns, with finials and plinths of all manner of design where columns might reasonably go and pilasters where they couldn't.

'That,' said Miss Smith, 'is the stupidest wedding cake I have ever seen.'

In the red-hued shadows cast by the burning moon and its lazy glow that licked across the vault of what passed for Hell's sky, a city had gathered around the base of the needle, a humdrum ramshackle sort of place made from abrogated sins and cardboard boxes, corrugated iron and obsolescent dread.

'Your new Satan's building efforts seem very polarised,' said Cabal. 'Who lives in the needle? Where "live" is a very relative term.'

'That's 'is Infernal Majesty's palace.'

'*All* of it?'

The demon De'zeel nodded.

'What has become of the princes?' demanded Zarenyia. 'Where are Asmodeus and his crowd? They can't be living in those ruins we passed, can they?'

''Is 'Igh Sataness says pride is what put us down 'ere, so nobody gets nuffink wivout working for it. 'E gets the big 'ouse 'cos 'e worked 'ardest. Obvious, innit? He came up from the ranks, got busted down, came up again. So . . .' The lizard pointed at the needle, so impressive in some ways, so utterly ludicrous in others.

'Why all the columns?' asked Miss Smith.

''E likes columns.'

'E did indeed. Cabal once more had the impression that this slippery realm that used the legend of Prester John as its shingle was trying to say something again, but he was not sure what it was. Perhaps it did not matter. It seemed to Cabal that, unappealing an idea that it was, he would perhaps be wisest not to treat these experiences as a puzzle box, or at least not quite yet. Surely, he thought, not all the pieces were yet in play, and what of Horst and Miss Barrow? Might they have made discoveries of their own? All the points of data—or at least a decent majority of them—were required before he might bring himself to profitably theorise. In the meantime . . .

'Is that Leviathan?' said Zarenyia suddenly.

What had at first appeared to be a municipal hall covered with broken-down cardboard packing boxes joined with wire was now revealed to be a huge creature under a blanket of broken-down cardboard packing boxes joined with wire. The entity's vast cetaceous face looked mournfully down at them as they passed. By its front left flipper and hopelessly dwarfed by its bulk was a small sign, also written on rough brown cardboard. *Please Help*, it read. *Unable to Work Due to a Persistent Medical Condition*.

'Don't *look* at 'im!' protested De'zeel when he noticed where their attention lay. 'You'll only encourage 'im.'

''E's a mangledinker, in't 'e, De'zeel?' said De'eniroth, spending long seconds over each syllable and still getting them wrong.

'A malingerer! Yus! That 'e is!'

Filled with righteous indignation, the demons marched (we must assume De'eniroth was marching, but really it was very hard to tell; certainly his many leg-like undulipodia assumed quite a martial rhythm in their movement) past the redundant Prince of Hell. Miss Smith looked back, and saw a tear sufficient to fill a pond run down Leviathan's cheek.

'They're a cruel lot around here, aren't they?' she whispered to Cabal.

'It *is* Hell. A reasonable facsimile of it, at least.'

She accepted the point, but added, 'I wasn't expecting it to be quite so petty. Something more grandiose. But they seem to be content to practise the little sins of neglect that we see every day on the streets of any metropolis.'

Cabal looked at her askance. 'You expected better?'

'Yes. It's silly, but I was. Selfishness is the real root of all evil, but I thought we would see it grown here into extraordinary forms. Instead we have poverty and beggary while the powerful live up in the grand house and ignore it, as do their lickspittles. This is no more Hell than is London.'

'Well . . .' began Cabal, but the thought was lost as they arrived at the needle's gatehouse.

The grand reception to the needle was situated within a huge blockhouse sufficient to contain the Royal Albert Hall, should it ever be stolen and require a place to hide it. Nor is 'blockhouse' an entirely undeserved description. Yes, it had columns—many columns—and buttresses and crenellations and all manner of other architectural details that most architects spend a lifetime keeping out of the same building at the same time for fear of causing some sort of aesthetic overload. Yes, it was grand and impressive. Yes, it was all of these things and yet it still felt very, very military in nature. It was a barracks for hordes of demons who—the expedition noted as De'eniroth and De'zeel greeted and were greeted in return—were of the same mind as their guides; that is, very little mind for anything at all but an easy life. These were the ranks of the easily persuaded, those of weathercock loyalties and a finger or other useful appendage kept permanently moistened for the speedy discovery of which way the wind blew.

It was hardly surprising that Hell had an embarrassment of such treacherous riches; it was, after all, a land of opportunities for the disloyal and inconstant, and reliable unreliability is a sort of constancy in itself. What was perhaps a little more surprising was that they had thrown over any number of other opportunities to turn their coats in favour of hitching the flickering lanterns of their fidelity to a minor player such as Ratuth Slabuth. Yes, he had once been one of Lucifer's generals, but more by dint of his accountancy and organisational skills. As unlikely successions went, it was of an order with Attila the Hun being usurped by his tailor.

However he had managed to worm his way to the top of the pile, it was plain his was not a popular government. Lucifer had managed affairs using a sort of *laissez-faire* style that verged on not caring at all, enforced with occasional and terrible displays of merciless force against detractors and troublemakers. Lucifer had few rules and allowed Hell to more or less run itself, which, given how easily the minds of many of his subjects ran to chaos and turmoil, was possibly wise. If he had demonstrated any great genius for the position at all, it had been knowing the right demon for the right job, and in keeping the unaligned devils out of the main part of Hell so they might not sow resentment by the simple fact of their being.

It had been light-touch management carried to its extreme, but given that Hell's basic function was to be beastly to the souls of the damned and given that being beastly was very much a default position for the majority of demons, it had worked well enough. Even Lucifer's later adoption of cribbage and macramé to the horrors of the pit had worked surprisingly well. The truth of it was that an eternity of very much anything becomes torture after a while.

Ratuth Slabuth, in contrast, was the micro-manager from Hell in all senses. He had somehow engineered a coup (and probably done so using a lot of diagrams and a ream of graph paper) and rationalised the operations of Hell. It was probably far more efficient, but it was also hugely disruptive to creatures that enjoyed their own brands of huge disruption and didn't care for Ratuth's paginated, verified, and cross-checked version in the slightest. Hence the blockhouse.

Cabal had noted no other entrance visible in the cleared area around the needle's base and this did not surprise him. The needle was obviously a military structure predicated primarily on defence, and castles do not usually have a preponderance of entrances. Ratuth Slabuth was plainly not a popular ruler, and revolution threatened his reign of error.

There was considerable surliness on the part of the guardian demon in the reception blockhouse, although this was as likely due to the presence of De'eniroth and De'zeel as anything else; it seemed they garnered little respect amongst their peers. That offhandedness vanished on the instant that De'zeel announced—with sufficient dropped aspirates to power a family of Cockneys for six months—that the lady with all the legs was none other than Mistress Zarenyia, Devil of the Outer Darkness and Casual Severer of Limbs.

As had been the case with De'eniroth and De'zeel, this was all that was required to turn demons that looked like huge tripedal rhinoceroses crossed with praying mantises, armoured in pitted iron and carrying swords the size of windmill sails, into oleaginous waiters on discovering a crown prince with generous tipping habits has taken a table in their section. Cabal and Miss Smith tried not to look too embarrassed by all the inexpert fawning going on. Zarenyia, however, was very much in her element.

'Boys, boys, boys!' she laughed, in this case a mild admonition rather than a declaration of her diet. 'Don't crowd a girl. Such *rude* boys. It may come to spankings if you carry on like this much longer.'

'Sorry, miss,' muttered the largest of the behemoths, somehow managing to blush through eighteen inches of armour plate. 'We're just really excited to see you.'

'She gets that a lot,' said Cabal, but no one was paying him any attention at all.

The behemoth was still talking. 'Satan ordered your presence weeks ago, and will be very happy that you are here.'

'Weeks ago? But, poppet, even I didn't know I'd be here weeks ago.'

The behemoth frowned, causing some of its skull armour to bend such was the puissance of even its facial muscles. 'No, Mistress

Zarenyia, we are surprised to find you here. Satan sent search parties to the outer darkness.'

'He did?' Cabal noticed even Zarenyia's natural ebullience faltered in the face of this intelligence. 'That's very . . . satanic of him. You must have lost a lot of demons doing that.'

The behemoth shrugged. It was like watching a hillock during a highly localised seismic event. 'All of them. But you're here now, so that doesn't matter! Huzzah!'

Zarenyia cast an uncertain sideways glance at Cabal. 'Yippee,' she said.

As they progressed onward through the gatehouse and into the needle proper, so the entourage grew. Cabal was unsurprised to see that De'eniroth and De'zeel were now merely hangers-on, despite protesting their pivotal role in events to anyone who would listen, but no one would. He was more surprised and, it must be said, faintly insulted to discover that he was also very much on the edge of the spotlight. If he had been asked to explain why he, Johannes Cabal, necromancer, freelance sociopath, and lurker in the shadows, was so put out by the lack of attention being put his way, he would have laughed an abrupt, unconvincing laugh and said he was perfectly content not to be the centre of attention. It really would have been a terrifically unconvincing laugh, however, and the questioner would have to be a gullible muggins of the most credulous sort to accept it as anything but the dissembling of a peeved man. It was probably not envy nearly so much as a sense of a perturbation in the rightness of things. He, after all, was Johannes Cabal, and he had gone to pains to make himself unpopular in Hell, albeit as a side effect of other endeavours. Yet here was Zarenyia, a devil and therefore inimical to the hierarchies of Hell, being fawned over as if she were a successful young actress who had wandered into the Society of Roués.

His increasingly vile mood was not improved by the prospect of traipsing up the thousands of steps necessary to attain the tip of the needle, where Ratuth Slabuth no doubt maintained his throne room. That this burden was removed from him gave him no joy, however.

The very centre of the needle was hollow, an immensely deep shaft that started wide and narrowed in similarity to the angles of the outer wall. Running in a dizzying helix up the side of the shaft was exactly the staircase Cabal had anticipated and feared. He noted it did not seem to have a handrail, another of Hell's grotesque Health & Safety failings. He did not savour the thought of climbing it in the slightest.

He decided to start with the rhetorical, thereby giving himself the opportunity to wax wrathful subsequently. After gaining the attention of the lead behemoth with some difficulty, he gestured up into the great spiral of stairs that wound up into the gloom above. 'Do you honestly expect us to walk all the way up those steps?' he demanded.

The behemoth looked at him as if he were an idiot, which, coming from something that looked not quite as intellectual as a side of beef in a helmet, felt understandably insulting.

'No,' it said, and the tone it took in no way alleviated the sense of insult. 'You'll fly.'

'Fly?' Now it was Cabal's turn to treat his interlocutor as a dimwit. 'Do I look like I have wings?'

'No,' agreed the behemoth, 'but *she* does.'

'She?' was all Cabal had time to say before a pair of arms snaked around him beneath his armpits.

'Relax, and let me take care of *everything*,' whispered a female voice in his ear that bore distinct similarities of timbre to certain of Zarenyia's utterances. Usually the ones just before she fed.

Abruptly, he was airborne. His startled yelp drew the attention of Zarenyia herself, whose face hardened immediately when she took in Cabal's very tactile new friend.

'Don't you *dare*,' she said, and her voice was cold enough to coalesce carbon dioxide snow from the air. Cabal thought for a strange moment she was talking to him, but then the voice by his ear said, 'Don't worry, *Mistress* Zarenyia. I shan't break him.' And so saying, Cabal found himself borne up into the sulphured atmosphere of the needle shaft.

'That woman had wings,' said Miss Smith, more to assure herself she was not delusional than as a useful statement of fact.

'Succubus,' said Zarenyia, her face thunderous. 'I'll give her "Shan't break him". Get aboard!'

'Aboard?' said Miss Smith, vainly looking about for a train, or a steamboat, or possibly a balloon. She was still looking when one of the devil's forelimbs grasped her around the midriff and all but threw her onto Zarenyia's back, where the great curved spiderlike abdomen joined the distinctly humanlike torso.

'Hang on,' said Zarenyia, and leapt to the nearby curve of the staircase. Miss Smith grunted at the impact, but barely had time to draw breath before Zarenyia set off in hot pursuit of the hapless necromancer.

She did not, however, charge up the staircase. Instead, she headed straight up the wall, the tips of the great armoured legs somehow adhering to a surface that was not merely sheer, but that angled in some degrees past the vertical. Miss Smith suddenly found herself in dire straits; angora is not the easiest material upon which to gain a grip and she was forced to find the bare skin of Zarenyia's midriff.

'What *are* you doing back there?' said the devil, not censoriously.

Miss Smith could only make a startled squeal for an answer, for Zarenyia was now entirely inverted beneath the next turn of the staircase and Miss Smith's grip slid further up. She was sure that if she didn't fall to her doom, she would instead simply die of embarrassment. She prided herself on an outgoing sort of personality open to new experiences. Inadvertently touching up a spider-devil, however, was nowhere to be found on her to-do list.

'I'm sorry!' she managed to blurt as Zarenyia flipped around the staircase's edge and brought them both the right way up once more. 'I'm so very sorry! I didn't mean . . .'

'I know you didn't, but it's sweet of you to apologise. The fault is mine, though. I keep forgetting humans can't just stick to things like a normal person. We need a different strategy if we're to keep you safe.' She looked about her on the level of the needle onto which they had emerged. 'This way!' she cried as if Miss Smith had any say in the matter, and set off at a canter towards a double door built into a shallow archway.

'What's through here?' she gasped out, clinging on for second life and only soul.

Zarenyia's canter broke into a gallop. 'No idea. Let's find out, shall we?'

The doors were as massive as anything else in that dizzying tower, a construction of such Brobdingnagian scale as to make Cyclopes suck their teeth and say it was a bit much for their taste. Yet the foot-thick wood shivered under the impact of single-minded devil legs and smashed open to allow the passage of Zarenyia and her dismayed passenger. Nor was she the only dismayed one there; they were in one of Hell's many halls of records wherein sins were tabulated, tallied, assimilated, and, where applicable, marked with a gold star for a job well done. All the minor paper-shuffling was performed by a positive legion of administrative imps and several score were currently present, mainly engaged in throwing armfuls of carefully ordered documents into the air while scattering from the devil's headlong passage, all while squealing in the time-honoured manner of the swine of Gadarene.

Zarenyia honoured their presence in as far as she halloed, 'Stand clear! Make a hole! Get out of the way, you frightful little vermin!' ahead of her, but she neither moderated her heading nor her speed by so much as a jot. Filing cabinets were flung aside, imps were accidentally speared on arachnoid legs, desks were overturned in the charge. The noise was cacophonous, the chaos wholesale.

Miss Smith realised that she was enjoying herself.

Even when she realised Zarenyia's course was taking them directly towards a wide bay window that looked out across the shanty town outside, and the blood sand plain within, she was not affrighted. Instead she tightened her grip, narrowed her eyes, and trusted to her new and unusual companion.

For her part, Zarenyia slowed a little as her spinneret and hind legs got busy. Under her abdomen they delivered to her a length of twined silk—still sticky—and this Zarenyia took by the ends in her human hands and swung the centre up and over both their heads in the manner of a skipping rope. The silk caught Miss Smith in the small of the back, and then she was drawn close as Zarenyia pulled on it with a modicum of her inhuman strength. Once she was forcibly spooned against Zarenyia's back, the devil quickly knotted it around her own waist.

'There,' she said over her shoulder. 'That will keep you much safer. Feel free to hang on with your arms, though. I shan't be troubled by it, truly. I don't really have a concept of over-familiarity, you see.'

Miss Smith could see, and embraced Zarenyia tightly. Devil and witch grinned fiercely at one another.

'That's the spirit,' said Zarenyia. 'We're having such fun together!' And then she jumped out of the window.

The imps of Satan's needle were long inured to odd noises; permanent residents of Hell get used to almost anything. There was, however, an unfamiliarity in the pace, magnitude, and variety of odd noises they were experiencing that day. The ones who happened to look from the windows stood the best chance of seeing exactly what was causing all the fuss.

Galloping up the side of the needle came a spider-devil of the succubine variety, laughing uproariously, and upon her back rode a woman in black wearing an ebon crown, joyfully whooping and using such profane language that the imps simply had nowhere to look. Up and up they raced, wrecking gargoyles* and smashing windows as they went. It was all probably accidental. Probably. Debris, laughter, and salty invectives were left in their wake, and the imps could only assume a hen party was in progress.

Finally, they attained the top of the needle, or very nearly the top in any case. It was clear that the needle's tip was given over to a tall throne room with open verandas about it upon which Satan and his senior management could look down upon the lesser evils. These had

* Hell gets little rainfall, and the blood sand plain none at all, so it will be understood that 'gargoyle' in the architectural sense is not the one used here.

banister rails upon them, the safety of those who frequented such elevated heights obviously deemed much more important than those beneath them in both social and physical terms.

Upon one such rail, a silken cord as thick as a man's thumb yet strong enough to garrotte Mount Eiger suddenly wrapped and gripped. Upon the other end of the cord swung upwards and into view Zarenyia and Miss Smith, Zarenyia's legs rapidly working as she drew the cord back to her. They swung up past the horizontal, and had attained the veranda before they had time to fall back. The cord detached, and they thundered into the presence of Satan with rather less than a 'by your leave'.

They got there moments after Cabal, whom they discovered staggering around in a state of great agitation, his face grey, and dangerously close to hyperventilation. Zarenyia's delight vanished at the sight of him. She snapped the cord binding Miss Smith to her in a single furious spasm.

'Get down, darling,' she said. 'Things are going to get messy.'

'We'll take them all on.' Miss Smith glowered at the shocked ranks of hellish aristocracy arrayed thereabouts.

'A sweet thought, but I'm only interested in one presently. And she is *mine*.'

Cabal was walking in roughly their direction, but his legs were weak beneath him, and the line of his walk was desultory and wandering. He pointed back at the succubus who had carried him to the needle's apex.

'That . . . *woman* . . . took liberties. With . . . with . . .' Cabal, for once, found himself unable to express his feelings. 'All the way up the . . . up here . . . she touched . . . she *did* . . .'

'Hush, hush, sweetness.' Zarenyia had, in the many years of her existence, destroyed many lives, devoured many souls. She was sure she was inured to suffering, having been the author of so much of it herself. Yet from somewhere in her, the sweet tones she had so often employed as a weapon were here used softly and with sympathy and, for once, without simulation. 'You don't have to say anything. I know exactly what she did.'

For hadn't she done much the same herself a thousand times?

She glared at the recalcitrant succubus, a creature of opulent form and licentious lines dressed in something that looked like she had made it herself from a borrowed spool of red satin ribbon, and returned the spool almost untouched. 'I said—and I mark it quite clearly—*don't you dare*. It seems you dared.'

The succubus smirked. It was a salacious smirk. 'I said I wouldn't break him. He's still alive, isn't he?'

Presently, the succubus sailed out into the brimstone sky, before arcing gracelessly (with a lot of limb thrashing and screaming due to a sudden lack of wings) downwards, and ploughing through the ceiling of a lean-to containing a dishevelled long-legged owl wearing a crown made from stained parchment. Stolas, formerly a Prince of Hell and commander of no less than twenty-six demoniacal legions, was not handling unemployment well. He watched the succubus groaning in the shallow crater she had made upon impact.

'Ugh,' said the succubus, rather less alluring for the moment.

'I used to be somebody, you know,' said Stolas. The succubus didn't say anything to that so he prodded her a few times with a talon until she groaned again. Accepting this as sufficient to count as a dialogue, he continued, 'I don't get many visitors.'

Zarenyia flung the succubus's wings, torn out by the roots, over the balcony edge and watched them flutter down into the shadowed mass of the shantytown. '*Frightful* rudeness,' she said, turned in a clatter of chitinous footfalls, and clicked her way indoors.

In the midst of the great council of Satan rose a throne, albeit a sensibly sized one, with a small table by it and, in the opposite arm, what appeared to be a horizontal loop of stone in which a goblet sat. The throne's occupant took up the goblet, took a sip or two while it considered these new persons, and then returned the goblet to the loop where, sensibly, it couldn't be knocked over. This was a very sensible sort of Satan.

'I feel reasonably sure I know to whom I speak,' he said, for his voice was that of a male, even if his body was a mass of strange angled bones and struts that both gave a topological hint of terrible ontological truths that would shred the intellect from any who might try to broach them whilst also resembling homemade Christmas decorative chain made by folding and plaiting paper until one forgets where one is up to and accidentally creates a topological hint of terrible ontological truths that would shred the intellect from any who might try to broach them, much as happened with Aunt Julie.* This non-Euclidean (of course it was non-Euclidean) mass was topped with a horse's skull, and the skull wore a helmet of Greco-Roman design and splendid aspect, all gold and silver with a crest of horsehair that swayed so beautifully with every movement of the skull beneath it that psychic impressions of it might settle into the dreams of advertising copywriters and inspire the most extravagant claims for shampoos.

This was Ratuth Slabuth.

'*Reasonably* sure, but I should ask. May I know who you three are?'

Zarenyia was still in a mood and not prepared to take nonsense from anyone, least of all a horse's skull perched upon a mathematical conundrum. 'You know full well, Slabuth, but if you insist. I am Zarenyia, devil of the shadowed tunnels, succubine of the first name of the Blinded Dodecateuch, corruptor of passions, eater of souls, and really rather put out by your poor minion control.'

Before Ratuth Slabuth could say anything, Miss Smith—still all awash with endorphins both from her heady ride up the needle as well as proximity to Zarenyia and the intoxicating effect such intimacy with a succubine tended to have upon humans—said in a loud and penetrating voice, 'I am the Witch Queen of the Necropolis!' She looked around with satisfaction at the gawping sea of demoniacal faces ranged upon her. 'You fuckers,' she concluded, still smiling.

'I see,' said Ratuth Slabuth. He made a note in a book and placed

* Poor, poor Aunt Julie, who, after the goose but before the pudding, looked up at the accidentally wrought intra-dimensional decoration, got as far as saying, 'That's rather a topological hint of terrible ontolo—' whereupon an event of exquisite horror occurred. Nobody fancied pudding after that.

it on the occasional table by his throne. He looked at Johannes Cabal. 'And you, sir?'

Cabal had been half bent over, still racked with the assorted shocks his rapid ascent had provided him. At Ratuth Slabuth's words, however, he froze for several seconds, then slowly stood straight, bringing his gaze to bear upon his interrogator.

'You . . .' Words again failed him for a time, but he rallied, focussed, drew breath, and tried again. 'You . . . jest.'

The horse skull gazed at him, perhaps even through him. 'I do? How odd. I am not generally known for my jocularity. But the nature of whatever it is that you think amusing is unclear to me, so I shall ask again; who are you?'

Cabal glared back, the recent indignities visited upon his person momentarily forgotten in the face of this new one visited upon his pride. He knew this was not the real Ratuth Slabuth, but felt impelled to answer it as if it were. Rationally, he reassured himself that this was necessary to permit them to work their way through whatever challenges this place might impose. Heavens forfend he have any emotional reasons.

'How quickly they forget.' Cabal said it as if to himself, and larded it with a surfeit of nuance. 'You really don't remember me, Corporal Ragtag Slyboots?'

There was a sharp intake of breath from the watching horde, which expressed amongst the bone demons as mournful toots as if upon ocarinas.

'Ragtag Sly . . . *Slyboots?*' The new Satan looked down upon the dishevelled human with astonishment. Then he astonished the dishevelled human by laughing. It wasn't even the classical 'Nyahahahaha!' laugh beloved of those who are about to dump their unloved interlocutors into an acid tank, or shoot them, or kick them off a convenient cliff. It was—apparently—the honest laughter of a jolly uncle on being caught in some harmless practical joke sprung by his infant niece. 'Hohohohohoho!' he went, thereby upsetting Cabal, who had rather been hoping for the 'Nyahahahaha!' variety as proof that the barb had struck home.

'I haven't been called Ragtag Slyboots in some time,' said Ratuth Slabuth, wiping figurative tears of mirth from his vacant eye sockets. When his mirth had subsided (accompanied by the plaintive toots of bone demons letting their breaths out), he continued. 'Ah, Cabal, isn't it? Yes, I remember you. All that business with the Carnival of Discord? That *was* you, wasn't it?'

'Yes,' said Johannes Cabal, a necromancer of very little infamy indeed, it seemed. 'That was me. You were a general, and then Lucifer reduced you to the ranks, because of me. Because of *me*.'

The reaction when it came was not quite the one anticipated.

'Mr Cabal,' said Satan, 'thank you so very much. I owe everything to you.'

Cabal's vocabulary clattered to an empty halt. 'Eh?'

'Let me tell you how it happened.' Ratuth rose grandly from his throne and for one profoundly awful moment, Cabal thought he was going to sing.

'When Lucifer hied himself off to wherever it was he hied himself off to,' said Ratuth, 'as you might imagine, things became rather fraught in his absence. All the Princes and, indeed, the Princesses of Hell—as an aside, does anyone know why the princesses are called princes, too? No? I don't suppose it matters really—were instantly forming little alliances and backstabbing one another, and doing the sorts of things demon lords and ladies are supposed to do. Have you ever noticed that such things are ultimately unhelpful for society as a whole? All that energy and resources expended in internecine squabbling. Silly, isn't it? One would think entities of great antiquity would pick up a few ideas about common cause and cooperation, but no. Conspiracies and backstabbing, backstabbing and conspiracies. All of which they predicted, counter-plotted against, which was taken into account, spawning counter-counterplans, ridiculously complex *matryoshkas* of concentric schemes, all constructed to conceal the innermost goals that were so compromised by that point that they had the overall effect of tying shoelaces together. Mountains of effort for molehills of effect. Laughable.

'So I simply left them to it. As you so correctly point out, I was a mere nothing, a spear-carrier. Why would they concern themselves with me? Asmodeus, Mephistopheles, all my former colleagues, my brother generals, my lords and ladies . . . suddenly I was of no more worth than one of the flies buzzing around Beelzebub's arse.

'And that was perfect.'

'Even a Prince of Hell has only so much time, so much energy to expend, and they burnt it all in a magnificent bonfire of their vanity. Demons, you will understand, have a great deal of vanity; it was a conflagration. And when it was all over, they had employed every trick, squandered every favour, cast away every precious asset, and every back was heavy with knives. That was all. Otherwise, things were much the same. Pointless.

'This is Hell's trouble in a nutshell. Everyone is so busy being evil, they forget to get anything done. Not me; while the princes and the dukes and all the rest of them were wasting their time, I was putting together my own little army. It didn't have to be large, and it wasn't. All it had to be was coherent, disciplined, and determined.'

Ratuth Slabuth gestured out towards the horizon, dark as clotted blood. 'This is what I wrought. I found the high and mighty resting after their exertions, and I cast them down. Again. One would think after being kicked out of Heaven, they would take steps to ensure some degree of job security, but I can only assume that they were under the impression that they could fall no further.

'I proved them wrong. I threw them out of their palaces, dissolved what was left of their legions, cast them into the gutter, and I have taken precautions to ensure that they never rise from it again. They made mistakes, and Hell is not a very forgiving place.'

Cabal was in an argumentative humour. 'But you yourself rose from the ranks twice. Isn't it a flagrant hypocrisy to deny the same opportunity to others?'

Ratuth Slabuth looked at him quizzically. 'You do realise that I'm Satan, don't you? Hypocrisy really is part of the job.'

To this Cabal had no answer, and he fell into a truculent silence.

'So, you're not cross with dear Johannes, then?' asked Zarenyia.

'My dear lady, he is my unwitting benefactor. Of course I was angry at the time, but things worked out so splendidly, how could I possibly remain so? All's well that ends well, after all. I am Satan, my position is unassailable and will remain so because I will not take my eyes from any potential enemies.'

'You should thank me, then.' Cabal was still in combative mood.

'I think the operative word in my previous utterances was "unwitting", Johannes, old stick. One cannot be thanked for causing an accident, no matter how beneficial that accident later turns out to be. No, I think my gratitude will be confined to simply not having you thrown into a sulphur pit for all eternity. That's quite nice of me under the circumstances, isn't it?'

Cabal found himself suddenly nostalgic for Lucifer.

Ratuth Slabuth continued, 'Now, a small matter of bureaucracy. The demons of Hell all belong to a well-defined and rigid hierarchy. I have recently had to redefine it for reasons that must be obvious . . .' He produced from the impossible angles of his body a green folder bound in black ribbon. 'I have diagrams here, if anyone is interested? No? Well, in any case, the term "devil" is applied to those infernal entities that are not subordinate to this system. Being at the top myself, I am therefore the only resident of Hell that may call myself "devil", a distinction that gives rise to the popular if technically inaccurate term "*The* Devil".' His equine skull somehow managed to smile at all those there present, even managing the nuances required to make it plain that it was an insincere, managerial sort of smile.

'It complicates matters, however'—the skull turned to regard Zarenyia—'when an unaligned devil without a portfolio wanders from the outer darkness into Hell proper. Rather makes a mess of the nomenclature.'

'Lawks,' said Zarenyia. 'How inconvenient. Poor nomenclature.' She bent her neck towards Cabal and whispered *sotto voce*, 'What's a nomenclature?'

'Therefore some sort of accommodation must be reached, and a note made for any such future situations. Can you believe that the previous administration simply skated over matters such as these? Lucifer trusted to *laissez-faire* decisions and unregulated improvisations, if you can credit such a thing.'

'Gosh,' said Cabal innocently, 'he really was evil.'

'Well, quite,' agreed the new Satan. 'But it's one thing to spread venality, corruption, and despair in the mortal realm, quite another to have shoddy bookkeeping in one's own domain. Whatever was he thinking?' He sighed. 'In any event, we must normalise Mistress Zarenyia's classification while she is within the borders of Hell proper. If you would follow me, madam?'

And, so saying, Satan sloped off like a mid-level functionary, a somewhat bemused Zarenyia following along. Cabal and Miss Smith were left alone with a lot of seemingly embarrassed demons.

'Is he like this all the time?' Cabal demanded of them. There was no vocalised reply, but a few surreptitious nods gave the answer all the same. Cabal spread his hands to his audience in supplication. 'I am so sorry. This was impossible to foresee.' The demons nodded ruefully.

'So what's this about really, darling?' Ratuth Slabuth and Zarenyia had retired to a side room of modest dimensions, being only mildly gargantuan in scale. Beneath a gleaming dome of stone, within the marbling of which the faces of the damned seemed to writhe, Satan settled himself into one of his comfy thrones with the throw cushions, and Zarenyia settled herself upon a bed of leather pillows, lovingly wrought from the skins of used-car salesmen. 'I have wandered the highways and avenues of Hell on many occasions without halt or hindrance. I find it hard to believe you really wish me and those like to carry passports in future.'

'You are very perceptive, Mistress Zarenyia.' He settled his sharp angles more comfortably into his throne, making some of its more sensate members emit muffled screams. 'You are quite right, of course. I have brought you here by means of a small ruse. Naturally, there are no concerns regarding your status here; I long since devised a deviltry clause, right from the first of my hierarchical analysis green papers. I mean, really. What sort of Satan wouldn't?' He smirked bonily. 'Apart from my predecessor, obviously. No, no. I wanted to take you aside for another matter entirely.'

Given her nature, Zarenyia wondered if Satan was proposing what she thought he might be proposing. It quickly became apparent that, no, he wasn't. She felt an uncharacteristic degree of relief at this. She didn't care much for Ratuth Slabuth's personality, and his physical form presented a few challenges, too.

'The thing is, Hell is large and complicated. Then there's the whole business with the mortal world. One thing I have learned in my sojourn thus far, much to my chagrin, is that one has to delegate. I envy the other chap his omnipresence, omnipotence, omni-this, and omni-that. It would make the administration all so very much easier. Alas, it is all too much for my humble self.' He seemed to be one of those entities that took great pride in his humbleness.

'You have a small army of arse-kissers out there,' said Zarenyia sweetly. 'Form a cabinet.'

'Oh, nothing would be easier,' said Ratuth Slabuth, but without enthusiasm. 'We are never short of sycophants in Hell. Competence, however, is a rarer commodity. The princes, for all their self-regard, were a necessary part of the apparatus of damnation. I brought them low because they presented a threat to the long-term stability of the realm and of my new regime. Their ability was never in question.'

Zarenyia realised with a small shock where this was going, but said nothing, expressed nothing. She had not survived as long as she had by being naive, no matter how she might behave.

'I need new princes,' said Satan slowly, regarding her through narrowed eye sockets. 'New princesses.'

'That you can trust?'

His laugh was sudden and, by his lights, honest. 'Good heavens far, far above, no! Trust is as rare as a devil's tears here. I don't expect it, nor set much store by those who profess it. No, common interest is a far more reliable bond. For example, I am thinking my first appointee should be primarily concerned with the mortal realm. I would need someone whose *curriculum vitæ* involves a great deal of interaction with humans, somebody who can pass amongst them undetected, sowing sin in his . . . or her . . . or possibly its wake. I need a personable demon. A people demon.'

There seemed little point in pretending she didn't know what he was getting at, so she said, 'You are fond of operative words, Satan. I think the one there is *demon*. I am a devil.'

'Through choice?'

'Yes.'

'I can understand and respect that, but the fealty of a Princess of Hell weighs far less heavily than that of a common lemure. You would be a free agent for most of your time. The occasional conclave to decide this or that, but otherwise footloose and fancy-free to do as thou wilt. Common purpose, you see? Your natural inclinations lie in the same direction as my needs for a new and senior demon.'

Zarenyia rose from the pillows and walked up and down before the throne, hands behind her back, ruminating on Satan's words. 'You're tempting me,' she said at last.

Ratuth Slabuth shrugged, the angles of his form rattling at the gesture. 'Again, rather part of my job. Just think of it, my dear: no hiding in the outer darkness any longer; all the souls you can eat, just providing rather more actually reach Hell; and you shall never have to be summoned to manifest again, as the ability to do so at will is a gift of the position. Oh, and of course a palace constructed to your design and furnished to your every whim. Really, what else can I offer you? Doesn't every girl want to be a princess?'

Zarenyia did not answer, but only continued to pace back and forth. Not so long before, she might have told this new Satan, thank you, but no. She liked the outer darkness. She liked being her own creature. She liked being a devil.

Now she realised things had changed, and it was Johannes Cabal that changed them. He had needed somebody with her very specific skills and asked her along for an adventure. A real, actual adventure, and it had changed her. When it was all over and they had said their goodbyes, she had found the shadows and darkness of Hell's borderlands no longer inviting, but only dull. She had hung in her web and reminisced, reliving events over and over. The cobwebs blew gently in the sulphur-heavy air there around her, and she watched them with something new gnawing at her: ennui. There in the endless twilight she waited and waited for the slight spiritual tug that told her that she was being summoned back to the mortal world. She waited and waited, and she waited in vain. If not Cabal, then somebody. Just *somebody*. She wouldn't even devour them, not necessarily. Perhaps they could go on an adventure, she and this faceless, putative mortal, who always seems to wear a black suit and speak with a German accent. She had been delirious with joy when the summons finally came, although she had taken pains to conceal the extent of her pleasure on arrival. Really, darling—a girl has to maintain some mystique.

'May I ask how long this offer is open?' she said.

'How long?' He seemed surprised. 'You're still not convinced?'

'It's a splendid one, and don't think for a moment that I am not terribly tempted. Merely that I'm a tiny bit busy at present. On an adventure and everything, you see.' She didn't feel it necessary to add that Ratuth himself was nothing but a facsimile of the real thing, as were all the demons, as was this 'Hell', and that any offer made here was therefore moot, to put it mildly. It seemed rude to bring something like that up.

'Ah, yes. Cabal's little fool's errand.'

'Oh, you know about that, do you?' Zarenyia thought it very metaphysical of a fictitious rendering of a real entity to be aware of the circumstances that had brought it about, and therefore unattractive.

I do hope he isn't going to break the fourth wall, she thought, or at least, generated inhuman cerebral processes that equate to a human mind thinking words much like that. *If the dreadful oik starts whinging on about how ghastly it is to be fictional, I may very well scream.*

'The Fountain of Youth? Yes, of course. You wouldn't be aware of it of course, but every time some mortal or another invokes the Five Ways, it impinges on Hell, often at a very inconvenient time. Happily on this occasion, it brought you to me. Who says nice things don't happen to embodiments of elemental evil?'

'I'm sorry, sweetheart, I fear that we may be talking at cross purposes. I have no idea what this "Five Ways" of yours is. Johannes has got himself a little book. I forget the name—somebody's diary, I think—but I am sure it isn't called *Five Ways*.'

'Oh, my dear lady, no. We are talking entirely of the same thing or, strictly speaking, things. The *Five Ways* is a whim of my predecessor. It exists in different times and places, and goes by different names and appearances, but it always promises much. Nor does it lie.'

Zarenyia wondered how she might delicately raise the business of Ratuth Slabuth being a temporary copy of the real thing, and was struggling to find a way. Then she remembered that she was a devil and therefore permitted to behave very badly when circumstances called for it. This was a dispensation she greatly valued; it had made her feel quite good about herself during mass murders and when leaving dinner parties early, the latter usually because she had murdered everyone there. It was good to be a devil.

'The thing is, darling—and pardon my bluntness—but Johannes's little magic book seems to create false versions of aspects of the world and its abutting worlds, just long enough to make their point. I wouldn't raise the matter except you seem to be quite keen to do so yourself. The meat of it is that we are here *because* of the book, therefore, the inescapable conclusion is . . .' She shrugged, spreading her hands apologetically. That didn't seem quite enough considering she'd just implied that Satan was a storybook character to his face, so she raised her spiderish forelegs and made an apologetic gesture with those, too.

Ratuth Slabuth confounded all that by laughing. 'Oh, now I begin to understand your wariness. You believe me to be just part of the fiction of the Five Ways. No. Hell is the birthplace of the Five Ways, and represents one of its trials.'

Zarenyia's eyes widened. 'So, you're saying—'

'Yes. But don't trust to my word. To be frank, you would be foolish to. Use your senses. Reach out and taste this world, this Hell.'

Zarenyia gave Ratuth Slabuth a wryly suspicious eye, but did as he suggested. Creatures of the under- and overworlds have certain senses denied to mere mortals for the simple reason that mere mortals would never need them and, should they ever develop them, madness would shortly overwhelm them as they became aware of the superficiality of mundane existence, the great depths that undermine it, and the great heights that overarch it. Zarenyia reached out and found threads of happenstance and need, the weave of interactivities, the fabric of reality. She could smell that it ran threadbare out in the desert behind her towards the end of the endless cemetery, but here it flowed as it did anywhere, uneven as a web woven by a drunken spider.

'Ah,' said Zarenyia. 'Unless my senses deceive me, this really is Hell.'

'Just so,' said Ratuth Slabuth with monumental complacency.

'Lucifer has truly abdicated his role as Satan?'

'I believe I said as much, yes.'

'And you're the new Satan with all Lucifer's powers devolved to you?'

'I would term it "unto you" as a more elegant phrasing, but yes.'

Zarenyia was feeling uncharacteristically overwhelmed. 'The offer is real.'

'A Princess of Hell. Indeed. I am entirely in earnest.'

Zarenyia, needing time to absorb that the offer—breathtaking enough even when she hadn't believed this reality—was genuine, changed the subject, albeit to one in which she was keenly interested. 'This Five Ways, what exactly is it?'

'Just one of Lucifer's whims, and let me tell you, there'll be far fewer of those sorts of shenanigans henceforth. Focus on core business, that's the ticket.'

'If Lucifer devised it, then why does it follow through on its promises?'

'Because no one really wants what they think they do. Briefly, the Five Ways manifests in different ways depending upon the culture it broaches. It always offers the moon, however; sometimes literally. It will draw in five individuals, and they will be challenged in five ways, hence the nervously brilliant name of the thing. At the end of it, assuming they haven't died or been driven mad or just become distracted along the way, they will receive their hearts' desire. These boons will, naturally, destroy them, as is the way with achieved ultimate goals.' Ratuth Slabuth fluttered a tangent dismissively. 'I'm convinced he was just at a loose end when he came up with it. Seems like make-work, doesn't it?'

Zarenyia was totting up names in her head: herself, Miss Barrow, Miss Smith, and the brothers Cabal. Five.

'Oh, bother,' she said. 'I like to think of myself as quite the wily one, but I appear to have gone galumphing into a trap like an utter *ingénue*. It's quite damaging to the old self-image, I must say.'

'Hardly a trap, dear lady. You can walk out of it at any time, and now you know what it is, you have no reason not to.'

'No. I suppose not.' She turned her attention to Satan. 'In which case, to business. A princess, you say?'

'Princess, palace, and power. All yours for the asking.'

'Well, then. I suppose, allowing for the usual caveats about how if the deal isn't what it appears to be, I reserve the right to get violently cross about it, I accept. I just need to get Johannes and Miss Smith along the way, and then you shall have my full attention.'

'Ah, yes.' Satan settled himself more comfortably upon his throne. 'In Miss Smith I have no interest. She may return to her precious necropolis in the Dreamlands with my blessings, for whatever they are worth. Very little, I would guess.' He coughed slightly, an affected noise that rattled his vertices. 'Johannes Cabal is, however, a different matter. He will have to be dealt with.'

Zarenyia showed no emotion, but she felt it. 'You gave the impression that all was forgiven and forgotten, viz. Johannes.'

'Yes, I did. Those were lies. Fathering them is expected of me these days. Be assured, Mistress Zarenyia, I am in no wise done with that necromancer. He was the author of my humiliation, he conspired against me and brought me low simply for doing my job.'

'Which was . . . ?'

'Trying to engineer his destruction. He is a very awkward and recalcitrant man, you know? But I was never anything but professional in my dealings with him.' Ratuth Slabuth . . . *Satan* rose from his throne, and the awful geometry of his form unfolded until he towered, massive and emanating malevolence. 'But he humiliated me, made me look a fool in front of Lucifer, and that was all that was required.'

Zarenyia weighed this, and thought it sounded like grapes of the sourest vine. 'You mentioned something about sulphur pits, earlier . . .'

'Molten sulphur, yes. But, no. Entirely insufficient. I have much better torments lined up for him.'

Zarenyia sighed. 'Darling, I think I've been involved in enough innuendo-laden conversations to know where this is going, but I shall have to disappoint you. I cannot destroy him for you.'

'Eh?' said Satan.

'I have given my bond not to harm him nor any of his merry crew.' She neglected to explain that this did not technically extend to the late addition of Miss Smith, but she liked the necromantrix and did not care to give Ratuth Slabuth any options there. Nor did she feel the need to clarify that the giving of her bond had involved saying 'dib' a lot.

To her concealed dismay, he seemed to take this philosophically. 'Of course. I anticipated something of the sort. Why else would he travel with a whimsically inclined killer? So, he trusts you?'

'Yes. I think so.' Another lie of omission; she was fairly sure she trusted him, too; an unusual sensation for a devil.

'Excellent!' He rubbed together a couple of extruded extremities that he used for handling things. 'Then that is all that is necessary. You will not harm him—a bond is unbreakable, after all—but you shall be vital to his downfall. The passion of Johannes Cabal shall begin with his betrayal . . .' He regarded Zarenyia through empty sockets darker than the most corrupt thought, and the bone of the skull creaked as he smirked. 'Princess Zarenyia of the Ninth Circle.'

It was enough to turn a girl's head. Power, privilege, and as many murders as she cared to commit, which was quite a few. It might pall eventually—things usually do—but she would have a glorious few millennia reaching such a state.

And yet she found herself testing the Hell around her at first from a sense of disbelief and then as a reflex. It passed every sniff and touch she gave it, psychically and otherwise, but she knew it would. Rationally, she was as positive as she had ever been about anything that this was truly Hell, and that Ratuth Slabuth's promise to her was his bond. All she had to do was betray Johannes Cabal.

She knew she wouldn't be hurting him directly; her own promises to him precluded that. Not hurting him physically, at least. Thinking back, she had failed to extend her bond to cover allowing him to come to harm by the hands, claws, and writhing thorned tentacles of others or any other such bit of petty weaselry. It had never occurred to her to do so at the time. After all, she was a solitary creature, spending decades at a time in the web-shrouded caverns of the outer darkness. She knew no one to connive with, no fellow devil with whom to conspire.

Then along came Johannes Cabal, and there had been fun and murders galore. The best time she'd had in . . . well, *forever*. And then he'd gone again, and she was by herself once more in the long silence. Not even a postcard. Funny how he only got in touch when he wanted something. Typical man. Typical human.

It would be a small betrayal, really. She would simply lead him up the garden path as she had with so many of his species, and then leave him there to dry. Alone and undefended while Ratuth Slabuth did whatever it was he planned to do. She hadn't asked. She had no desire to know. There would be a brief unpleasantness for Cabal that would last no longer than eternity, and she meantime would be Princess Zarenyia. It was sad, but you can't make an omelette without damning a few souls to everlasting torment. It was a fact of life.

Yes, existence was full of hard decisions that would sting for a while, but one just had to think in the long term. The very, *very* long term. She stiffened her resolve. A brief moment of pain, and then everything would be all right.

* * *

'Hello, darlings!' said Zarenyia as she breezed back into Satan's throne room, a shambling, scuttling sound in her wake assuring her that Ratuth Slabuth was following. 'Forms signed, *bona fides* authenticated. You will be delighted to hear that I am now declared a legal visitor to the scenic heart of Hell. Hooray for me!'

'Finally.' Cabal looked up sourly from the table where he, Miss Smith, and the demons De'eniroth and De'zeel were engaged in a game of cards under the eyes, antennae, and other sensory organs of the hellish horde there gathered. He flung down his hand of cards and rose, removing his jacket from the back of his chair as he did so. 'I lost interest in this ridiculous game somewhere during the initial deal.'

There was another of those idiosyncratic sharp intakes of breath from the audience of demons; they took their cribbage very seriously.

'His Lord Satan here'—Zarenyia carelessly jerked her thumb over her shoulder in Ratuth Slabuth's direction—'has been an absolute doll. I believe we now know where we should be going to next.'

Miss Smith unfurled a jet-black parasol and placed it upon her shoulder to ward off the rays of a non-existent sun. 'Excellent. We should be moving on, really.' She nodded politely. 'Thanks, Satan. Lovely Hell you have here, but time is pressing, I should think.'

'And where precisely is it that Ragtag Slyboots here thinks we should be going?' said Cabal, having apparently lost at the card table any vague sense of diplomacy he may once have enjoyed.

'Still trying to bait me, eh, Cabal?' said Satan, and chuckled. 'I really don't have the luxury to indulge in such pettiness these days, I am afraid. I wish I *could* indulge you, but simply too busy. You understand, I'm sure?'

'Not really,' said Cabal. 'You being in charge of Hell is tantamount to a second undermanager at a Pompeiian olive orchard being given responsibility for the Roman Empire. You are a small sort of demon, Ragtag. You were over-promoted once and it didn't end well. I don't see it going swimmingly for you or your charges this time, either.'

'We shall see, shall we?' said Ratuth Slabuth, and chuckled again. He gave the air of being very pleased with himself. 'But I haven't answered your question. In the centre of the Ninth Circle, below the now disused throne of the old Satan (I really can't be bothered with all that lava and so forth, and as for a basalt throne, whatever was he thinking of? Terribly uncomfortable, believe you me), there is a tunnel that leads down to his original stronghold, the Ivory Citadel. It is a place secreted away and forgotten by almost all. There, all and every destined time and inevitable place may be reached. There, Fate itself awaits.'

'That sounds like a powerful sort of location,' said Cabal, his suspicion evident. 'Very useful in a variety of ways, I would think. Why, then, is it secreted away and forgotten?'

This time Satan did not chuckle, but the jaw of the horse's skull he used for a head curved into a deeply satisfied smile. 'Because who truly wishes to confront their fate, of course?'

When Johannes Cabal had undertaken to find the truth at the heart of *The One True Account of Presbyter Johannes by His Own Hand*, he had at no point imagined that it would involve leading a procession of demons through the ruins of the Ninth Circle to the great shattered edifice that had once been the palace of Lucifer, before he decided to resign and seek opportunities elsewhere. Yet here he was, striding alongside the shambling disgrace of planar geometry Ratuth Slabuth that—in the real Hell—would be a resolute foe, accompanied by Zarenyia the succubine spider-devil and the dead and dismantled (yet looking very good on it, considering) Miss Smith the necromantrix. In their wake walked, shuffled, and oozed a horde of demons, who seemed to be along out of curiosity as much as representing any sort of court for the second Satan.

The former throne room was a very different place than Cabal remembered it. Then it had been heated and underlit by a vast pool of lava, the throne of Satan rising massively in the centre of a peninsula thrust out into the deadly lake. Without an army of imps equipped with pokers, however, the lava's surface had been permitted to cool and was now a ruffled field of grey stone, liquid caught and frozen forever in flows and wavelets.

Cabal considered the physical organisation of Hell as he understood it, and now saw the significance of this place. It had begun to dawn upon him how he had misinterpreted the geography of Hell as they approached Lucifer's palace and he could see that it rose up limitlessly above the surrounding plains until it was lost from sight in the crimson gloom. When he had come here on previous occasions, he had descended directly through the rings via the palace itself—a spindle in the midst of endless open spaces, its base here in the Ninth Circle, its zenith forming the gatehouse to Hell in the middle of the Desert of Limbo.

It seemed that perhaps not even the Ninth Circle was truly the palace's foundation; if what Ratuth Slabuth had told Zarenyia was true, then below it was a place that extended the spindle's ability to touch every circle of Hell out into all else. To Cabal's mind there was a *rightness* about this. So much in the occult followed "as above, so below", then here, of all places, should contain the archetype of the principle.

'This way!' said Ratuth Slabuth, leading the conga of the damned across the isthmus towards the empty throne. He seemed to be enjoying himself. 'Almost there!'

They followed him counterclockwise around the great stump of the basalt throne, massive and inspiring of awe even when vacated. Even Cabal felt his spirits depressed in its presence. The last time he had seen it, it was occupied, and the occupant had not been friendly. Some ghost of that animosity hung around and coloured his thoughts a morose shade of dark blue stabbed through with arterial red.

He was not displeased that Ratuth Slabuth did not pause to offer a guided tour, but instead brought them smartly to a broad crevasse some ten yards wide at the rear of the throne's base. The crevasse gave out into a rough tunnel and, from somewhere out of sight beyond the twists in the path, a milky glow dimly emanated. Though the lava had long since solidified, there was still a steady warmth emanating from the frozen lake. Despite this, the breeze that blew up from the place beneath was chilly and, in some way Cabal could not quantify, disturbing. It smelled of bad decisions and unforeseen eventualities. He did not care for it at all.

'This is it, then?' he asked of Ratuth Slabuth, or Satan.

'It is, indeed, yes.' Satan seemed enormously pleased with the outing. Cabal half expected him to reach into some intra-dimensional space in his ribs and produce a picnic hamper.

Cabal looked down into the tunnel. 'The Ivory Citadel is just down there?'

'It is, yes. Your fate awaits you, Johannes. I do so hope that you enjoy it.'

Cabal did not truly understand how it was that he finally understood, but there was a pressing certainty that had grown so heavily upon him as they had made their way there, it rendered him soul-weary and saddened.

'It isn't really the next step in our journey at all, is it?'

'Ah, now, then.' Satan looked up at the roughly hewn vault of the great audience chamber as he weighed his words. 'Yes, and no. It's not *exactly* what you wanted, but it's certainly the next step. Indeed, it is the last step.' He shook his head in a slow mockery of sadness. 'Alas.'

'The Ivory Citadel doesn't exist.' Cabal looked at the horde of demons arranged in a loose arc around them, hedging them in and preventing any easy escape. At ground level, at least, but if one's party included somebody who was very good at running up walls . . .

He slid a glance at Zarenyia to prime her to be ready to act. She, however, was looking the other way. His glance turned into more of a glare, but still she seemed to be finding all sorts of things interesting with the sole exception of the imminent emergency at hand. Cabal would like to have hissed or gently side-kicked one her legs to draw her attention, but there was Satan, beaming at him with awful unctuousness.

'Doesn't exist? Of course it exists!' Satan laughed at the wonderful joke he was playing. 'I was entirely honest about it . . . up to a point. The point being that the citadel leads anywhere. Rather, it specifically leads nowhere. There is nothing within those pale walls but the final death, the utter extinction, the snuffing out of every vital essence.'

Cabal swallowed. 'The final death is a myth. Something always survives. Even when Madam Zarenyia here devours a soul, there are leavings.' He looked urgently at her, hoping that by mentioning her name he would finally attract her attention. But no, she was still finding her sudden interest in diabolical vulcanology supremely absorbing. With a growing sense that he had been handily outmanoeuvred, he plunged on. 'There is always something left. The soul is a very resilient thing.'

'So it is, it takes a great deal to destroy every last little peck of one. And, guess what, Johannes? The Ivory Citadel is just the place to make it happen.'

'You're going to kill us? Just like that?' Miss Smith was understandably upset at the revelation. 'I'm not even properly alive and you're going to kill me?'

Satan seesawed his head from side to side while he considered. 'Your destruction isn't vital, but really, my dear, you are *such* an aberration. I cannot help but think that the cosmos would be a tidier place without you. So, yes. You're going to die. Permanently. Sorry.'

'Madam Zarenyia,' said Cabal in a taut undertone. 'I think we should be making a sharp exit at about this time.'

She seemed to ignore him yet again, but this time she turned, her legs cascading back and forth as she did so until she was facing the tunnel. 'Yes, darling.' Her voice was strange and faraway, as if she was thinking of something else entirely. 'I think you should. Run along now, you and Miss Smith.'

Cabal looked around. It wasn't immediately obvious where exactly they should run; the cordon of demons was tight and unbroken. He looked up at Zarenyia and saw she was looking him in the eye, and her face was sad. She nodded towards the tunnel. 'Off you pop, Johannes, there's a dear. Take Miss Smith with you, and good luck.'

Perhaps Hell is seismically active, for Cabal felt the ground shift beneath his feet, or perhaps he didn't. His legs grew weak. His stomach squirmed. 'Madam Zarenyia, you can't mean . . .'

'Her Highness, the Princess Zarenyia.' Satan unfolded his Jacob's ladder of a body and grew huge and hateful. The horse's skull leered down from beneath the glimmering Roman helmet, reflecting a dim orange glow as the lake around them grew hotter and hotter. 'Show a little respect, Cabal. You are in the presence of royalty.'

'Zarenyia, please . . .' Cabal realised that for the first time he was honestly, truly pleading for his life. All the times he had not deigned to do so, because of all those other times he had gone into danger with contingency plans already in place or he had seen a flaw in the deathtrap, an oversight in the ambush. This was the first time the noose was around his neck, and the contingency plan was drawing it tight. He searched for something, *anything* that might bring her back to his side.

'You . . . you *dibbed.*'

'Her Highness's promise was not to hurt you, I understand?' said Satan. 'Well, she shan't. The citadel needs no help to do its work. Or, of course, you could try to make a run for it here. I would be fascinated to see how many steps you manage. Just think, Cabal, it was in this very chamber that you humiliated me. And now this happens.' Beyond the demons, the surface of the lake cracked and lava slipped through, the solid surface breaking up as ice floes do in the arctic spring. Satan looked around with palpable satisfaction. 'Now I shall have good memories of the place. Quite cosy, actually. I may move my court here. Tradition is a fine thing, isn't it?'

'Hurry along, Johannes,' said Zarenyia. Her smile was false and her eyes tortured. 'Go on. Don't want to keep the old Ivory Citadel waiting now, do you?' Her synthetic gaiety cracked in her throat.

'We trusted you,' said Miss Smith. She pointed at Cabal. '*He* trusted you, and he doesn't trust anyone. How could you?'

'Ha ha ha ha, foolish mortal.' They were just words drawn from a penny dreadful, as impersonal as a motto in a Christmas cracker. Zarenyia's eyes darted to the tunnel. 'Go meet your fate. Go *on*!'

Her eyes met Cabal's, and he understood. 'Very well,' he said quietly. He turned to face Satan. 'You win, Ragtag Slyboots.'

'*Must* you call me that? It seems very petty at this juncture.'

'It's your true name. Before all your airs and graces. Call yourself Ratuth Slabuth or even Satan, but you're still the same milk-souring non-entity you ever were beneath it all. You have been lucky, not clever. At least I shall finally be shot of you. Yes, you win. Congratulations.' He held out his arm to Miss Smith. 'Shall we? Our fate is sealed. We may at least go to it with dignity.'

Miss Smith removed her crown and tossed it at Zarenyia's feet. 'You'll need to look the part, *princess*,' she said. Then she took Cabal's proffered arm and, like a couple promenading in the park on a Sunday afternoon, they entered the tunnel.

Zarenyia said nothing, but she took up the crown as if it were precious to her, and carefully donned it.

Satan watched them go with enormous satisfaction, soured only by a lack of polite grovelling on Cabal's part. That would have been enjoyable, but one cannot have everything. Still, at least he had the pleasure of watching the infuriating mortal go to his oh-so-richly-deserved final deserts. Miss Smith was blameless in the affair, but Satan being Satan, collateral damage was a perk rather than a liability. There they went, disappearing into shadows, betrayed and doomed. Lovely. And here was his new Princess of Hell, watching them go. She could have cackled a bit more as she rubbed Cabal's nose in it and generally enjoyed her act of wickedness more demonstratively, but that would come in time, he was sure. Perhaps he should run a course on the correct deportment of senior demons.

Indeed, Princess Zarenyia was watching them go with no apparent emotion at all. That would never do. Demons are built of passion, after all. She should be showing something. Satan turned his full attention upon her, and felt for the first time a slowly wiggling qualm in his consciousness. Something was not right here.

'Your Highness.' His voice was low with suspicion. 'We should be going. I shall order that the tunnel be sealed permanently.'

Then Zarenyia turned to him, looked him in the eye sockets with an insouciant smile, and said, 'You do that, poppet.'

Suspicion crystallised into certainty. He growled with sudden anger. 'What have you done?'

Out in the lava lake, the last floating stone floe rolled and sank beneath the glowing surface.

'Me? Oh, nothing. Nothing at all. Just done a betrayal, like you said I should.'

'What are you saying, devil? That you have betrayed *me*?'

The lava started to glow a cherry pink, and the heat in the chamber became stifling as Hell itself responded in kind to Satan's growing fury.

'Only sort of, darling.' The smile remained broad, but her eyes narrowed. 'You might call it a sin of omission.'

Miss Smith was disgruntled by the speed with which Johannes Cabal sought annihilation. As soon as a twist in the tunnel hid them from the view of the collected demons, he had quickened his gait from a sober 'man walking to the gallows' pace to a 'if we don't get a move on, we shall miss our train' semi-trot.

'I am not so very keen to see the Ivory Citadel, Cabal. If you want to rush off there, be my guest, but I plan to take my time.'

For his reply, Cabal pulled her down behind a boulder. For her reply, she belaboured him with her parasol. 'I am very much *not* in the mood,' she said as she rained blows upon his head and shoulders. 'You should have asked earlier. Nicely. Over dinner.'

'Madam.' Cabal sounded pained, if not necessarily physically. 'You may belabour me with your parasol later at your leisure. At this instant, however, I would appreciate it if you desist.'

Miss Smith desisted. 'Then why are we hiding behind a boulder? You heard that house of cards with the skull and a hat; they're going to seal off the tunnel. There's no going back.'

Ruminating upon just how much of his life seemed to consist of explaining to women why they were hiding behind things, Cabal reached into his jacket and drew the little Senzan pistol from its holster. 'Do you know how to use a gun?'

She accepted the weapon with distrust. 'Of course I don't. I'm a witch these days. It's all wands and fell powers.'

'I am not sure your "fell powers" will work in this environment, but I am confident bullets will. They are of my own design and will have some effect even upon demons. They may not kill demons, but

I guarantee it will be very upsetting to them, all the same. The device is simple; release the safety catch thus, aim along the top of the weapon much like pointing, squeeze the trigger. Repeat until some sort of resolution occurs.'

Miss Smith glanced dubiously at him. 'And while I'm irritating demons, what will you be doing?'

'Irritating them alongside you.' He opened his Gladstone bag and withdrew from its depths the bulky form of a Webley .577 revolver.

Her dubious expression darkened. 'Why do I get the girly little gun?'

He handed her the revolver. She weighed it against the semi-automatic for a moment and then handed the Webley back. 'Unwieldy, isn't it? Very well, so you have your artillery piece and I have my *bijou* little demon-botherer. Is there a plan, or is this just a tantrum that involves firearms?'

'To be candid, I do not know for a certainty. The plan, if it exists, is not mine.'

'Then whose?' Miss Smith popped her head up to peer over the boulder and up the tunnel. 'Zarenyia? Didn't she just betray us?'

'I do not know that, either. It certainly looked like a betrayal. I suspect not of us, however.'

Satan, previously Ratuth Slabuth, née Ragtag Slyboots, was prone to a certain footling administrative wiliness that, in a poor light, might be construed for cunning. He liked to flatter himself that his coup had been a masterpiece of patient scheming and that his was the triumph of that quiet man, but the truth was he had been lucky. He lacked for the killing instinct that had promoted the previous Satan's cabinet of princes and generals to positions of power, but his own position with that group had always been that of a reliable factotum, not of a trusted confidante. When he had been given a simple task of elementary perfidiousness to perform, he had failed in it and been demoted to the non-commissioned ranks for it. He had hated Cabal for the humiliation, but then it is the habit of small men—and demons—to blame others for their failings.

These failings were multitudinous, and it truly was only a matter of time (and little time at that) before some imp or minor devilkin with an ounce of nous overturned the order once more. One such failing was a general heedlessness, an incipient lack of sagacity that coloured, or rather failed to colour, his every action. If there was a princedom available for complacency, Ratuth Slabuth would surely have risen to it long ago.

In this particular case he had failed to do what Zarenyia had been doing whenever she had a moment since learning that this Hell was indeed *the* Hell; she had been testing the bounds of its reality. It struck her as reasonable that, since the Five Ways had brought them there via an entrance woven at the continuum of its reality and what we may laughingly call our own reality, that it would also provide an exit when necessary. She had not been able to detect it, only tasting the decaying weft that briefly connected Hell to the endless cemetery and was now too fragile to return across.

Then, as this penny-ante Satan she so roundly loathed had smugly laid out his silly master plan to destroy Cabal utterly, she had felt the glimmering formation of the hoped-for exit. It had come from Satan's mouth, born on glowing threads of eventuality and recourse; it had risen from the plan of Lucifer's tower that he showed her; it had grown in the air like the scent of nearby water. The Ivory Citadel. Perhaps most of the time it was indeed the home to the final death, but—for a short engagement only—its place would be taken by the path through the Five Ways.

So she had played along, she had fooled Satan, and the most depressing part of it all was that it had been so easy. He really wasn't up to the job.

'You're really not up to this job, are you?' Zarenyia laughed. She would be destroyed soon, she knew, but better this than rotting of boredom in a palace, burdened by a meaningless title bestowed by a fool. She nodded at the encroaching crescent of demons. 'You can do much better than this idiot, you know. I am only amazed that he's lasted this long. Any of you could do a better job. Well, not *you* exactly, darling—sorry to raise your hopes.' A demon with the face of a rhinoceros, the intellect of a rhinoceros, and the ego of a shy virgin, stood crushed. 'But the rest of you with a few wits about you. You would make a far better Satan.' She nodded directly at one of them illustratively as she spoke, a thing like a wilful rag doll made from spite and gingham that, incidentally, smelled of aniseed. Zarenyia's attention moved on, so she did not see the diminutive demon nod slowly. Mimble Scummyskirts liked the sound of that.

Ratuth Slabuth—he truly did not deserve the title of Satan—withdrew his own senses. He had felt the edge of his domain where it tended into the dreadful negative of the Ivory Citadel fade into something else. The Five Ways. It could only be the Five Ways.

'Why?' he roared, his anger raising the inferno about them. The lava bubbled. 'I offered you everything! Why would you throw everything away for that . . . that *shit*, Cabal?'

'Language, sweetheart. And, here's a pointer for the future, should you have one. Tempting people involves offering them something that they actually want. I never really knew what I wanted, you see. I thought I would be happy with adventures and murder, and in no way am I deprecating them—adventures and murder are super fun. But I found something else. My funny little friend. I know humans live so briefly, and it should not concern me when that span is shortened further still. But you, Ragtag Slyboots . . . I was not about to betray my friend, my only friend, for the likes of you. So.' She smiled brightly, but her eyes were sad, her remaining time brief. 'Why don't you take your palace and your pretty pink princess tiara, and stick them up your non-Euclidean arse?'

She turned and fled.

Zarenyia had little enough of a plan, and what she had consisted of 'Fight until they kill me; give Johannes and the chippy little thing with the parasol time to escape.' It was elegant in its simplicity, and modest in its aims, unburdened as it was with anything approaching an exit strategy. She would fight in the tunnel to limit the number of challengers who might engage her at once, and she was fairly confident that she would last a few minutes at least. She would also have the tactical advantage of experience; she did a lot of hunting in the tunnels of the outer darkness—mainly of demons who had become lost at the furthest marches of Hell—and had a few tricks up her angora sleeves.

Her rapid retreat had caught Ratuth Slabuth—she really couldn't think of that nincompoop as Satan a second longer—on the hop, but now she heard him roaring orders that substituted bluster for authority. If nothing else, she thought she might have fatally undermined His Satanship. It would have happened sooner or later in any case, but now she felt sure it would happen a great deal sooner. If Satan couldn't be relied upon to successfully deal with a couple of mortals, really, what was he good for?

Fifty yards into the tunnel, she found a useful narrowing and skittered to a halt, performing a full turn as she did so. The pack leaders of the pursuing party were not far behind, but they were small and fleet rather than large and dangerous. She speared the first on a foreleg, tossed its convulsing body into the air with a careless flick, and batted it down the tunnel at its fellows with her other foreleg, forcing them to scatter or be knocked over.

In the breath the attack allowed her, she ran up the wall, trailing silk, and then allowed herself to fall from the ceiling. It was an ugly way to build a web, but she doubted they would afford her the time to do a proper job. She was fighting under disadvantages greater than merely numbers. She was a weaver of traps of assorted forms, and the close press of the enemy prevented her from doing so. Further, her succubine abilities were of little use when confronted by so many. Ideally, she'd ask them to queue up and take a ticket while she dealt with them one by one—male, female, indeterminate, or anywhere else on the spectrum, she was confident of popping just about anyone and anything's cork in the most terminal of ways. Demons, however, were appallingly uncouth, and this Satan was no gentleman.

A scurvy of imps ran at her with spears, trying to overwhelm her with numbers, but she raised the bladed barbs along the ridges of her legs and scythed them down as easily as wheat in a field, the kind of bad-smelling wheat that bleeds all over the place and complains bitterly about being harvested.

The entrée completed, the main course arrived. Zarenyia faced them with more evident confidence than she felt. She was beginning to think that lasting even a few minutes might turn out to be optimistic, for here came Grith demons, hollow-eyed spectres of misery, bearing broadswords. These were not cannon fodder by any means; Ratuth Slabuth did not care to wear her down first. Fine, she decided. If he didn't mind losing a few elite troops simply because he was in a foul dudgeon, that would count against him, too, when the butcher's bill was reckoned up. She would be very dead by then, but you can't have everything.

The first ran at her, sword trailing in both hands, ready to swing. She saw another start its run almost immediately and saw their reputation was deserved. This was no hasty attack, but rather a practised team manoeuvre. While she was dealing with the first, the second or third would already be killing her. Very well, she would just have to spoil their party piece.

She moved to engage the first of the Grith, but instead of fighting it, she suddenly changed course and ran up the wall past it. It swung to follow her, and so didn't realise the attack was coming from the side. Zarenyia was still trailing silk. It caught the Grith under the armpit, and it barely had time to realise the sticky cable had snagged it when Zarenyia released her end and the Grith was yanked off its feet and off towards where she had begun the frame of her apparently unsuccessful web.

Its fellows did not hesitate at all as their comrade vanished off into the gloom with a despairing cry, but Zarenyia had not expected them to. They would already be moving to a secondary plan, and this, too, she would have to outwit. She flipped forwards and landed behind the two remaining Grith, ready to fight. One she smashed aside with a hard flick of her No. 3 Port leg. The other came at her, sword back to swing. Zarenyia feinted right, then swung back and left, the tip of the demon blade only just missing the threads of her angora sweater. She moved forwards hard, grabbing the Grith's sword hand with her own and swinging it in a half circle so they were facing the same direction. It struggled to no avail; the demon was strong, but the devil was stronger. It was held helplessly, its sword pointing uselessly down the tunnel.

'Now, now, poppet,' she whispered in its pointy ear, 'I like my boys to lead with their weapons. Now, show me how you use it.'

Out of the gloom swung a frantic shape, the first of the Grith to attack and still fixed firmly to the end of the silk line. Neither it nor the one Zarenyia held had even half a moment to react before the first swung directly onto the second's sword, the night-black blade easily piercing it to emerge in a welter of innards from its back. The sword's tines caught on its victim's ribs. Zarenyia released the Grith and let it swing away clinging to the corpse of its comrade. Now its rhythm was broken, it would be easy meat in a moment. In the meantime, however, she had the third to . . .

The third had recovered more quickly than she had allowed. To a round of guttural cries and whinnying shrieks of delight from the rest of the demons, the third Grith landed on Zarenyia's back. She spun, kicking like Sleipnir in a mood, but the demon grabbed her hair close to the roots with its free hand and hung on.

'No hair pulling, you dirty little bastard! Ow!' Then she felt the blade touch her throat and realised she was not going to even last a few minutes. It saddened her; she'd hoped her last stand might have been something legendary, but she'd been in literary disagreements with higher body counts. It was very disappointing.

There was a sharp little sound and the blade swung away from her throat. She braced for the blow, wondering a little why the Grith didn't simply draw the edge across her throat, then she wondered what cunning ruse the Grith intended by falling from her back, and then she wondered how one gets Grith brains out of angora.

Miss Smith watched the tumbling body with some satisfaction. 'You're right,' she said to Cabal. 'It seems easy enough. I wonder if that was a fluke, though.' She turned and shot the second Grith from the swinging corpse of the first as it tried to free its sword. 'No. No fluke.'

Zarenyia was, by turns, delighted and horrified. 'You're back! You idiots! *Run!*'

'I shall not, madam. Miss Smith may, if she cares to, but speaking for myself'—here he paused to put a .577-calibre hole in the face of a belligerent cacodemon—'I do not care to abandon one of the very few entities in whose presence I am content.'

'Kill them!' cried Ratuth Slabuth, borrowing his imperatives from *The Big Black Book of Obvious Utterances for Megalomaniacs*. 'Kill them all!'

His horde of demons surged forwards, driven less by obedience to—as far as Satans went—the lesser of two evils, and more by a general appetite for violence.

'There's no point in us all dying,' said Zarenyia, backing once more into the throat of the tunnel to limit the attackers' options.

'There's no point in any of us dying,' said Cabal. 'There's no need to cover our backs. An orderly fighting retreat will take us out of here.'

'Just out of interest, do you have very many more bullets for these guns, Cabal?' Miss Smith's own pistol ran dry as she spoke, the slide locking in the rear position to tell her she was in trouble.

'Ammunition. Of course. Here.' Cabal tossed her an extra magazine, realising as he did so that her pre-skirmish briefing could have been more detailed.

'What do I do with this?' she said, brandishing the caught magazine and confirming his realisation.

'Release the empty box, slide in the new one sharply until it engages, release the slide catch, and that should chamber the next round ready to fire.'

The explanation was short, clear, cogent, and entirely wasted on anyone who didn't know what a slide catch was.

The demons pressed close. Cabal revised his tactics. 'When I said, "Orderly fighting retreat," perhaps I meant we should just run with the utmost urgency. Starting about now.'

He quickly swapped his Webley for Miss Smith's semiautomatic, although he was a little dismayed that she took this as permission to start firing with it in a two-handed grip.

'Jumps around a lot more, doesn't it?' she said, shattering the sternum of an onyx demon into shards and splinters. 'Must feel very bad for your wrists if you shoot it for very long.'

Cabal didn't trust himself to reply; he wasn't used to casual acquaintances playing with his Webley. He focussed on returning the Senzan pistol to firing condition as quickly as he could that he might recover his pistol. They once more swapped weapons.

'I used all your bullets,' said Miss Smith, without the grace to say so apologetically. She returned to plinking demons.

Lips pursed, Cabal emptied the brass casings from the revolver and stoically thumbed in fresh rounds. All around, the demons pressed closer yet, and he felt the balance of probabilities swing firmly away from simply running away being a viable strategy and towards them all dying in a tunnel in Hell.

He checked his pocket and discovered only a handful of rounds left. There were more in his bag, but he doubted he would have the opportunity to recover them. He would expend the rounds he had, then he would draw his sword cane, and perhaps pink a couple of the distressingly large and muscular-looking creatures that were working their way forwards through the press. Then he would be torn limb from limb. Not exactly how he had hoped the expedition would end, but there were never any guarantees. Zarenyia looked back at him as she dismantled some lesser creatures and she smiled. Miss Smith had run out of bullets again and seemed to be attempting to call down damnation upon the horde with her witchcraft, but—as Cabal had feared—it was of little use in a place where all were damned already. That avenue proving unfruitful, Miss Smith started smiting about her with her parasol, her expression furious and her language unsavoury. Cabal smiled a small smile, too. At least he would die in good company.

At which point it may be instructive to see what was happening more or less at the same time elsewhere.

The dogs were a surprise. As Miss Leonie Barrow, the Great Detective, and her faithful sidekick, inveterate foil, and slightly dim comic relief, Herr Horst Cabal, strolled through the streets of Sepulchre, they found themselves passing one of the mighty metropolis's great necropolises. The city apparently housed five of them, spread equidistantly around the outer suburbs. Some were grander than others, some more aesthetic. This particular one was the Leosh Street Municipal Cemetery, a bleak sort of place arranged around an imposing if hideous neo-Gothic chapel of rest that stood tall in the centre of the grounds.

Despite it being barely dawn, the gate stood unlocked and swinging in a slight breeze. That in itself was enough to draw Miss Barrow's attention. The sudden appearance of perhaps twenty mutts and strays of the parish rushing towards the entrance from all directions, squeezing through the gap offered by the unsecured gate to run at full pelt towards the chapel, was another.

Horst was just saying, 'Well, they seem in a hurry,' when the clear sound of a shot rang through the chill air to them. Then another, and another.

'The game's afoot!' cried Horst, and then he made a mild cry of pain as Miss Barrow punched his upper arm.

'*I* say that, Horst. You just follow me around, stating the obvious. Come on!' She gripped the lap of her skirt, lifted it far enough to give her feet clearance, and was off while Horst was still formulating an unobvious reply. He gave up quickly—it transpired she was right—and followed her lead.

'Why are the dogs running towards the shooting? Are they gun dogs?' Inwardly he cursed himself for saying the obvious thing. The dogs were all manner of breeds and mongrels, as a moment's attention would have told him.

'They didn't all emerge from the same point. They've come from all over. That's interesting in itself,' called Miss Barrow over her shoulder.

What was also interesting was that the dogs were all gathering at a short set of descending stone steps in the chapel's shadow that seemed to lead down to its cellar. The dogs were wildly enthusiastic at the prospect of whatever lay behind the door at the base of the steps and danced around yapping happily and wagging their tails at the approach of Leonie and Horst.

'They seem friendly enough, don't they?' Horst patted the head of a red setter. It skittered away from his touch, but did not seem otherwise put out by his attention. It made a short run down the steps at the door and then bounced back, looking at Horst expectantly. 'What do you suppose is in there? Some sort of sausage hoard or something?'

'I have no idea, but it may be meat of another kind.' She was about to elucidate when the sound of another shot stopped her words. The shot was close, yet far away, oddly attenuated, as if it were the memory of a sound. Whatever it was, it plainly emanated from the far side of the door. Deciding that further discussion was a waste of time and breath when the answer was only the turn of a handle away, she crouched by the padlock that secured the door.

'What a piece of rubbish.' She was confident that, as a master detective, she would have lock picks stored away in her cuff, just so, and just so she did. She didn't need to force the skill to use the picks into being; her father had shown her the knack one summer when she grew bored of pressing flowers and painting watercolours. 'This padlock might as well be made of soap for all the good it is.' She applied pressure through the torsion pick and set to work with the hook. 'It's an insult,' she muttered. Five seconds' work and the shackle sprang free. She threw it dismissively to one side. 'It pays to invest in quality, you cheapskates.'

'What did you say?' Horst suddenly had the oddest feeling that things were a little awry. Not necessarily threateningly so, but just wrong in some respect. 'I have the strangest feeling.'

'*Déjà vu?*' Miss Barrow released the hasp on the door.

'That, yes, but what's that thing when you realise a pug has grown to the size of a Shetland pony in the last thirty seconds?'

Leonie hesitated, her hand on the handle. 'A delusion? Whatever are you talking about, Horst?' She turned and saw a pug the size of a Shetland pony at the edge of the pack of dogs. Nor was it the only noticeable member of the group. The red setter Horst had tried to pet was now up upon its hind legs. Its hair seemed to be retracting into its body. 'Oh,' she said at the sight, a little faintly. 'That's unusual.'

Beside her an Alsatian had also reared up. It nodded urgently at the still closed door. 'Quickly,' it said in tones liquid and guttural by turns. 'We must hurry.'

'This is all becoming remarkably *Alice in Wonderland* all of a sudden.' Horst looked around him as the pack transformed *en masse* into things that were like bipedal dogs, but were not dogs. He looked at Miss Barrow, at something of a loss. 'I suppose you'd better open the door for them.'

Deciding that doing what the hairless rubbery dog-men wanted was probably a better stratagem than not doing what the hairless rubbery dog-men wanted, she turned the handle and swung the door in. She was not able to see what lay beyond for a moment because the dog-men ran past her in a flowing torrent of grey flesh the colour of cold clay. When they had gone by, only the one who had been an Alsatian for a while hung back. 'Come on,' it said in those strange tones. It ran through the door, paused to beckon Horst and Leonie to follow. 'The matter is urgent!' Then it was gone, down into the depths beneath the chapel.

'That is an odd sort of cellar,' said Horst. He climbed down the steps to join Leonie. Together they peered into the gloom. There was no cellar there, or any sort of chamber at all. Instead, the door opened into a tunnel some ten or so feet wide, roughly hewn into what looked like igneous rock. It ran off at a slight downwards angle, gently curving to the left.

'A door into adventure,' said Leonie.

'It doesn't have to be so literal about it. After you.'

'On this occasion, I shall throw your chivalry in your face, Mr Cabal. After you.'

The demons were thinning, but this was less good news than one might hope, as it allowed the larger abominations at the rear of the crush to move forwards. The battle had slowed to a straight exchange of blows between the sides coloured by the certainty that the demons must prevail by simple weight of numbers. To all present, the battle no longer truly felt like a battle, but merely a stubborn avoidance of the inevitable.

Even the sound of combat had become desultory, with demons not actually engaged standing mostly silent apart from the occasional supportive whoop when one of theirs fought well and, far more frequently, a sympathetic groan when a disengaged limb or new corpse hit the ground.

For her part, Zarenyia wasn't enjoying matters much, either. Her usual method of dispatch was more intimate than a skirmish in a tunnel really allowed for and, while she wasn't averse to numbers, she preferred them scattered around a bedchamber. At her sides, the humans fought well enough, but they were only humans and weariness was setting in. Miss Smith had abandoned her black parasol in the demonic eye socket in which she had placed it, and taken up a dropped halberd that she wielded with more enthusiasm than skill. Cabal had some practise with his sword-cane, but as the scale of the antagonists grew, it became of diminishing utility. The minute when the defence of their position was no longer tenable was upon them, and they could only congratulate themselves that it had not happened sooner.

Then Johannes Cabal said, 'I hear glibbering,' Miss Smith responded, 'About fucking time,' and then they were attacked from behind. Except they weren't. The fleet rubbery forms—sometimes like men, sometimes like hounds, sometimes upon four legs, sometimes upon two—flowed past them like water past stones in a stream bed and onto the demons in a second. The battle took a new complexion as the demon horde found itself abruptly facing a ghoul pack.

'What is the meaning of this?' roared Ratuth Slabuth from the executive director's position at the back. Nobody had the leisure to tell him, so he continued, 'Ghouls! This is Hell! You have no right to be here! Begone!'

The ghouls replied to this as they fought and tore and bit at the demons. 'The Witch Queen of the Necropolis called us. Johannes Cabal whose fate is entwined with ours needs us. And you're just an interim Satan until they get somebody who knows what they're doing, anyway, so . . .'

And here, the precise terminology became terrifically rude, for ghoulish glibber is a language flexible and satisfying when it comes to invective, and English may only hint at it.

Then something blurred by and struck a Vinz demon forcefully enough to disengage its whipcord neck and multiple legs from it spherical body.

'Hullo,' said Horst. 'How is everyone? Look, Leonie! I've gone all vampirey again!' This he demonstrated by tearing the arm from a nearby antagonist and then beating it over the head with the flopping limb.

'How lovely for you.' Miss Barrow checked her cuff and was disappointed if not surprised to discover that not only had her lock picks disappeared, but even the concealed pocket in which they had been stored had vanished, too. It seemed that her time as the Great Detective was over, and that realisation sent a pang through her. Oddly the pang centred on her shoulder and she realised that there was an unaccustomed weight there. She looked and found a khaki strap running over it that had certainly not been there a minute or so previously. A moment's examination revealed it to be a sling, and in looking down her body to see what it was attached to, she made certain other discoveries.

'I have a shotgun,' she said, and brought the feisty-looking 12-bore pump-action weapon up to examine it with awe at its sudden appearance, wonder at its grim boding, and some undeniable glee as to its immediate utility. 'And trousers.' She had only ever worn trousers when helping in the garden or in the garage on her father's car. They were not something she was used to wearing in polite company, which—she realised—entirely let out her current company.

She considered the shotgun, pushing up the dark, broad-brimmed, and shallow-crowned hat that had also added itself to her wardrobe without permission as she did so. Despite never having held such a device before, she felt inspired to take a firm hold of the forestock grip and pull it back. The weapon made a satisfying sound of steel-on-steel, and something very similar and just as satisfying as she pushed the forestock back to its forward position. The shotgun seemed to become palpably more dangerous in her hands by that simple act. She had used double-barrelled shotguns of lower bore when shooting clay pigeons on a couple of occasions, and knew to shoulder firmly, address her target (a spiny beast that was harassing one of the ghouls unforgivably), release the safety catch with her thumb, and squeeze the trigger. She knew it, but was surprised by how reflexive it all felt to her. Even the greater recoil of the 12-bore over that which she had previously experienced seemed familiar.

The spiny demon went all head over heels and viscera a-tangle as the cloud of pellets caught it in the midriff and ended its harassing days permanently. The roar of the gun was overwhelming in the close quarters, and the battle seemed to pause for just a moment. In that moment, Miss Barrow introduced another cartridge into the chamber to the accompaniment of the lovely positive mechanical sounds, and felt quite wonderful doing it.

'Run, Ratuth Slabuth,' said Johannes Cabal. He was not at all sure that the fight was turning, but it was a moment of optimism for his side, and he thought it reasonable that it might be matched by a moment of pessimism for the other. Perhaps a little persuasion might cause their morale to crumble. 'Just let us go and no more of your creatures need be destroyed.'

The creatures in question seemed to think this was a good idea, and looked to their leader. It was a vain hope on their part. Ratuth Slabuth drew himself up as much as the tunnel ceiling would allow and snarled, the bone of his face curling and creaking to accommodate the flexions of his hatred.

'Never! You die here, Cabal!'

'Which one?' said Horst, unhelpfully.

The attack was renewed, but the timbre of it had changed. Now the demons fought defensively, and were no longer trying to get past Zarenyia, only to avoid being cut or smashed or otherwise having a bad day. Leonie only had to aim her shotgun for the demon in her sights to disengage from combat and scurry back, seeking cover. She rested her finger outside the trigger guard and re-engaged the safety catch without drawing attention to doing so. She could see the enemy wavering.

'You lot,' she called. 'We're not interested in you. Leave now and we will let you go.'

The demon assault instantly failed. Ratuth Slabuth was rendered speechless with disbelief and rage as his troops ran past him and back out of the tunnel. Some of the larger ones who could not avoid his eye at least had the courtesy to look embarrassed about it.

'Well, well. Just you and us now, Ratuth Slabuth.'

The arch-demon turned from watching his force slither away like draining cess and turned the full force of his regard upon Cabal and his company.

'Five of you,' he grated in a voice of rusted iron and lockjaw. 'You are the company of the Five Ways?'

'Indeed,' said Horst with insouciant bravado. 'We might well be.' He whispered from the side of his mouth to his brother, 'Are we?'

'I believe we are,' Cabal told Ratuth Slabuth and, in passing, his brother.

'Who's the scaffolding with a cow skull on it?' put in Horst as a supplemental question.

'*Cow* skull?' Great was the wrath of Ratuth Slabuth.

'That?' Cabal pulled a face as if smelling something unpleasant. 'That's what passes for Satan these days.'

The clearing of the lines of battle cast the conflict into a new light. The ghouls did not mind spoiling the plans of man and monster alike, but they preferred to do so from the shadows. Having a bit of a barney with a bunch of demons was all fun and games, but when the guv'nor got involved, it was time for a prudent withdrawal. They crept back and, making excuses to Miss Smith about the hour, the venue, and just-remembered dental appointments, into the shadows they once more faded. The sound of glibbering diminished with the rapid patter of ghoulish feet.

Leonie Barrow looked at the shotgun in her hands. It did not seem such a panacea for demonic problems any longer. 'We should be going, I think. That would seem to be a wise course of action.'

'Johannes, be a sweetheart and accompany the ladies back along the tunnel, would you?' said Zarenyia. She manoeuvred slightly, bringing herself to face Ratuth Slabuth squarely. 'Horst, you seem usefully dangerous. You stay with me.'

'We can fight,' said Miss Smith, waving her halberd in a manner potentially injurious to friend and foe alike.

'We can.' Miss Barrow regarded her shotgun, and then the curiously geometrical Satan doubtfully. 'But I don't think we would do much good. Trust the spider-lady. Let's go.'

The three backed away slowly until they were firmly disengaged from the scene of combat. Then—Miss Smith pausing to drop the halberd and take up her poor, misused parasol—they turned and ran.

'Think we can take him, sweet Horst?'

'No idea,' said Horst as he settled into a boxer's stance. 'We can give it a jolly good try, though.'

Ratuth Slabuth viewed him with disgusted disbelief. 'Are you seriously intending to fight Satan using Marquess of Queensbury rules?' he demanded.

'I don't see why not.' Horst experimentally shuffled his feet and tried dodging and weaving. 'We're both gentlemen, aren't we?'

'I . . .' Ratuth Slabuth had to think about that. 'I suppose I'm meant to be. I didn't realise that extended to engaging in fisticuffs with fops.'

Horst stopped dodging and weaving on the instant. 'Steady on now.' He waved an admonishing finger in Ratuth Slabuth's face. 'I'm sorry about the cow skull comment, but that was an honest mistake. I'm not a veterinarian, you know. But that's no excuse for casual name-calling, I'm sure.'

'You're quite right. I was speaking out of . . . Where's that wretched spider-devil gone?'

It was a minor feat for a large spider/human hybrid woman with a sunny disposition to disappear in such a small area, but a major one for anyone claiming to be the devil of devils to have lost sight of her. It was not a state of affairs that lasted long, however.

Zarenyia landed on Ratuth Slabuth's back with a cry of, 'Peep bo!' and swathed his skull (of a horse, for specificity's sake) in silk before leaping clear. Ratuth Slabuth roared in maleficent rage and struck after the direction he gauged her to be in, overbalanced, and fell lengthways down the tunnel. Lying thus, his head was brought closer to the ground than was usual for him. Something else unusual for him was being punched a resounding blow in the face, strong enough to dislocate his jaw.

'A hit!' Horst danced pugilistically around the prone body of Satan. 'A very palpable hit!'*

'Time to go.' Zarenyia plucked Horst up and threw him onto her back.

'I punched Satan!' Horst was all a-bubble with boyish enthusiasm, she noted. She also noted that he embraced her about the midriff to prevent himself falling off with far more willingness than his brother had ever shown.

'Yes, you did, darling, and I'm sure we're all enormously proud of you. But now, you see, Satan is coming after us, and I fear he will be in a frightful bate.'

'Yes, true. Still, *pow!*' Enthusiasm worked out, Horst sobered a little at the proposition of a cross Satan being terribly Satanic on his person. 'We should leave.' Zarenyia hardly needed the suggestion; they were already galloping headlong down the tunnel back in the direction from which Horst and Leonie Barrow had first appeared.

'There's a whole city back there,' Horst told her as they clattered along in hasty escape.

'I know. The Ivory Citadel.'

'The Ivory what? No, no, it's called Sepulchre.'

'It is the place of final death. To go there is to be snuffed out of the now, then, and forevermore.'

'It wasn't *that* bad.'

Behind them, Horst became aware of a curious noise. It put him in mind of a rake drawn over gravel combined with the sense of imminent arrival one gets on the platform of an underground station upon the London Tube when the train is still just out of sight.

---

* This constituted most of the Shakespeare that Horst actually knew to be Shakespeare.

'Can you hear that?'

Zarenyia did not trouble to look back. 'A frightful bate,' she said under her breath, and pushed herself harder.

She ran as quickly as she dared for some seconds, which was a very decent speed under the circumstances. She did, however, wonder where the others had got to. The tunnel did not split and so offered no alternative routes, yet—based on past experience—she should certainly have run down three blundering humans by now. Then again, the tunnel should have been heading downwards, but it was clearly rising.

'This isn't right. The Ivory Citadel is beneath Satan's throne. We shouldn't be heading upwards. We'll end up in lava at this rate.'

'No, this is right,' said Horst. 'This is the way we came, and it sloped down for us the whole way.'

'Sepulchre, you said?'

'Yes. A great big industrial city. I think it's in the North. Odd I haven't heard of it before.'

Zarenyia was confident that the reason he hadn't heard of it was not because his usual concerns rested squarely in the contents of dresses. She reached out her senses and perceived at once that the tunnel through which they travelled had not existed ten minutes before, and would not exist ten minutes hence.

'We're in the Five Ways. We can still escape!'

'What is this Five Ways thing people keep going on about? Well, I say "people", but I suppose I mean Satan, and now you. So, what is this Five Ways thing devils keep going on about?'

She ignored him—she was sure his brother would be delighted to explain things to Leonie and him in inordinate detail later—and concentrated on not thinking about the inconstancy of the floor upon which she ran. She had to believe more strongly in it than the real tunnel, or she would end up on the wrong one and find herself with Horst trapped between a fatal location and a batey Satan.

Horst looked back and, ignorant of the importance of believing the lie in such circumstances, said, 'How queer. The tunnel behind us is sort of falling apart.'

And it was, but not in drifts of rock dust and plummeting stalactites. There was a peculiar tearing occurring in Horst's perception of the tunnel, and two nearly identical tunnels were becoming separated. Oddly, there was also a sense of the living rock being torn open into a cavern as the tunnels grew apart. He felt he could almost see through the tunnel walls, and no sooner had that thought occurred to him than it was true.

Beneath her feet, Zarenyia saw the tunnel floor become translucent. Some two hundred feet or so below them, she could see the real path running like an open road directly to a great castle of domes and minarets, all the colour of old bone. The sight of it filled her with a fear she had never felt before. 'Stop thinking!' she snapped at Horst. 'You're wrecking the illusion!'

'I can't help thinking!' It was an admission he had never had cause to make before.

'Oh, for crying out loud.' Zarenyia took Horst's hands and moved them further up, a sovereign cure for men thinking, in her experience.

'Oh. I . . . Oh, my goodness,' he said, thoroughly distracted. Beneath her feet, the way grew more solid.

It was an improvement, but not a resolution. The false if preferable path was still merely a thing of whims and fancy, and as fragile as a dream. Behind them it sheered away from the real path like a split twig, and crumbling into nothing from the sheer point to the tip at, presumably, Sepulchre. And also behind them, on came Ratuth Slabuth.

He was prone and his angles were extended so that he gave the impression of nothing quite so much as the living skeleton of a great snake over a yard wide and thirty long. Tatters of silk hung from his skull where they had been torn free of his eye sockets, and his jaw hung at an uncomfortable angle, clacking rhythmically like a loose door to the beat of his run. On his lower surfaces a multitude of limbs created for the purpose scooted him along at distressing speed, yet the sense was still ophidian rather than of a hideous millipede (though there were certainly elements of that, too). His very-nearly-feet things on the end of his will-do-for-legs things slid and tripped at the edge of the fracturing realities, but he was faster to the line of transition if only by a whisker, and more and more of his forebody was gaining the relative safety of the Sepulchrean tunnel.

Johannes Cabal, Miss Smith, and Miss Leonie Barrow had paused in the tunnel ahead, the door to the outside world—or rather, *an* outside world—just ahead of them.

Miss Barrow eyed it with suspicion. 'I left that door open.'

Miss Smith joined her. 'The ghouls shut it, perhaps?'

'They didn't strike me as very tidy creatures.'

Miss Smith nodded. 'They're not. Astonishingly messy eaters.' The two women went on to make sure the door was actually unlocked while Cabal hung back. He was pleased to see Madam Zarenyia appear around a bend in the tunnel at full flight, Horst clinging to her by an unorthodox and inappropriate manner. Cabal's lips thinned; there would be words presently. Then his peevish expression gave way to wide-eyed surprise. He had never for one instant thought that Ratuth Slabuth would press the pursuit without his demons. What could have provoked him into . . . Cabal noticed that the horse skull's jaw was sadly askew. He sighed. Just perfect.

Behind him he heard Leonie Barrow call to him, 'The door's locked!' Then to Miss Smith, 'This doesn't make sense. It was padlocked on the other side when we came in, but this time it's the door's own mortise lock. The ghouls couldn't have done it.'

'Can you get through?' shouted Cabal.

'I can pick it . . . damn it! My picks have gone.'

'Use mine.'

He started to reach inside his jacket for the small leather case containing his own set of lock picks when Miss Barrow said, 'No time,' and immediately followed the statement with a discharge at point-blank range of a 12-bore cartridge into the door frame where the lock's bolt shot home. Miss Smith squealed and giggled with girlish delight at such havoc.

'Yes, that did it. Ready when you are, Cabal.'

Zarenyia was almost with them. She would need a moment to shed her passenger—possibly two moments, as he seemed very happy where he was—and metamorphose into a fully human form, or she would never be able to negotiate the doorway ahead.

Then Ratuth Slabuth stretched like the most malevolent jack-in-the-box imaginable* and, extending forelimbs made from rage and set squares, snagged Zarenyia's hindmost legs. She went sprawling, Horst being thrown forwards in a clumsy somersault while bearing an expression at least as disappointed as it was surprised.

Behind him, Ratuth Slabuth felt the tunnel fading away, the conceptual space of a cavern joining the true and apparent tunnels forming in its stead, a great aching space lit from below by the milky light of the Ivory Citadel.

'I am Satan!' The loose jaw clacked hideously and a rage beyond sanity twisted the empty eye sockets into parodies of expression. 'You are naught but dust! You *shall* be dust!'

His rear body sagged into the chasm opening beneath them, his aftmost limbs scrambling uselessly to gain tread. He tried to pull himself clear of the growing nothingness, but only succeeded in dragging Zarenyia closer to the precipice.

Zarenyia looked back and glanced downwards. The citadel seemed to be reaching up for them all. She tried kicking back at Ratuth Slabuth, but his grip on her hindmost legs was too secure, and her No. 3 legs on either side insufficiently strong and too awkwardly placed to get in any decent blows.

'What are you doing, you maniac?' she shouted at him. 'That place will destroy us all!'

If Ratuth Slabuth heard her, he did not react to her words. 'Worked my way up from corporal!' he bellowed. 'Twice!'

More of the tunnel floor faded away; two-thirds of Ratuth Slabuth's long body now hung over certain doom. Zarenyia felt herself sliding inexorably downwards. She saw Cabal run forwards

---

* Given the designs of many jack-in-the-boxes, the author appreciates that it may take some moments before the reader is able to imagine something more malevolent still. That is perfectly understandable. The reader should take his or her time. The author can have a cup of tea while he waits.

offering a hand, as if a mere mortal could hope to drag two such huge creatures back by himself. That, however, was not his plan.

'A line, madam! A line! Cast me a line of your silk!'

This at least her No. 3 limbs were a match for. She exuded silk from the spinnerets at the end of her abdomen and fed the line forwards to her human hands. 'Careful! The tip is very sticky!' She cast the line and Horst blurred across to intercept it, catching it neatly behind the adhesive end. The brothers Cabal drew the line up towards the door. They didn't get so very far before too much of the tunnel faded, and Ratuth Slabuth fell into space, dragging Zarenyia after him. Horst threw the end of the silk at the tunnel floor and it anchored there instantly, which was as well, for a small part of a second later it came under a great impulse as it took the weight of two warring devils.

Horst looked at the approaching precipice. It did not seem so very far from the line's anchor point. 'Johannes? Bright ideas? Quickly?'

Cabal nodded at the silk. 'That was my bright idea. It's up to Madam Zarenyia now. We have done all that we can.'

Over the Ivory Citadel, Zarenyia and the second Satan struggled. Ratuth Slabuth made to climb over her to reach the line and safety, but she fought him back with her other legs, and he ended up back where he had started, dangling from her aft legs. Zarenyia kicked and struggled, but he refused to let go. She wished fervently that he had genitals; she could generally be very persuasive when genitals were involved and, as a last resort, she could always have kicked him in them. Alas, he was utterly asexual both physically and behaviourally. It was all most vexing.

Above her the tunnel to safety was flaking away into pieces that dissolved the moment after they were formed. She knew the Cabals would not have been able to anchor the line very much further along. Her time was short. Extreme measures were called for.

She looked down. 'I think I shall just have to do without you.'

'What?' Ratuth Slabuth glared up at her. 'I am Satan incarnate! You will not cast me aside easily, traitor!'

'I wasn't talking to you, you dull creature.' She flexed her No. 3

legs and their bladed edges extended. Ratuth Slabuth had already dodged their attentions earlier and knew himself to be out of range where he was, clinging onto her No. 4 legs below their last joints and gripping hard enough to prevent them showing their own blades. He looked up past them to see Zarenyia grow dewy-eyed. 'Bye, gals. I'll miss you.'

Without a second's further hesitation, the No. 3 legs hooked over the hindmost limbs close to where they joined what would have been the cephalothorax, if she had been a true spider rather than an infernal representation of one that carried its brain in the head of a humanlike superstructure. The legs closed sharply, scissoring through their neighbours. The rear limbs fell away, Ratuth Slabuth still clutching them hopelessly.

It would be nice to report that he said something clever, telling, or even poignant at this point, but all he managed was 'Nooooooooooooooooooo!' all the way down, predictable to the end.

He fell into a courtyard in the citadel. There was a brief milky miasma as of a fog rising and falling in a matter of five seconds or so. And then the Ivory Citadel was just as it had been a moment before, empty and enigmatic, the colour of old bone. No ghosts wandered its corridors, for ghosts were far too alive for it to tolerate.

So perished Ratuth Slabuth, also known as Ragtag Slyboots, also known as Satan (albeit briefly).

Johannes and Horst Cabal watched with growing dismay the failing edge of the tunnel creeping towards them and, more immediately, the end of Zarenyia's lifeline. They were relieved when her hand appeared, gripping at the edge, but then it vanished as the edge faded into flakes of never-being. They both rushed forwards and took up the slack on the line, heaving like bargemen upon the Volga. A great spiderish leg appeared, followed by her upper body, and then more legs swung over and gripped. Cabal's relief was attenuated when he saw how uncharacteristically pale and exhausted she appeared. He and his brother helped her over the precipice and into—at least momentarily—safety. Cabal saw she was looking rather more insectoid than arachnid all of a sudden, and was appalled to see the ugly stumps of her rear legs, dribbling ichor from the almost surgical cuts through the patella analogues.

'Madam!' His concern was unaffected. 'What happened to your legs?'

Zarenyia smiled weakly. 'The Devil took the hindmost.'

Another tranche of tunnel crumbled away behind them. 'You must transform into human form, madam, and do so immediately! The door is too narrow!'

'Not so sure I can, after all that. Sorry, darlings, I'm quite pooped. Think I might even be dying. Wouldn't that be an anticlimax after seeing off that Ratuth wotsit-uth?'

At the door, Cabal could see Miss Smith and Leonie Barrow waiting, the door held open. Beyond it was a swirling gloom. It didn't look very appetising, but it was surely better than a graceless plummet to the Ivory Citadel and eternal extinction.

'Zarenyia.' Cabal leaned close to her and spoke in an urgent undertone into her ear. 'Please. You must focus. Just for a few seconds. We can save you, but you must help us.'

She laughed a soundless little laugh. 'Look at you, sweetness. If I didn't know better, I'd say you cared.'

Cabal said nothing. The silence drew Zarenyia's attention more than words could. Then she closed her eyes and grimaced with concentration. The transformation was difficult and nowhere near as elegant as the ones she had previously demonstrated, but it did the job. Even while she was still partially arachnid, her skirt still sporting the six legs and her dress itself simple and unassuming for lack of will or strength for anything more grand, Johannes and Horst Cabal were lifting her up with her arms draped over their necks and making the best speed they could for the exit.

It was barely fast enough. Cabal was the last through the door and, as he lifted his trailing foot from the tunnel floor for the last time, he felt it give way beneath him like thin ice. Then he was through and, with no human agency, the door slammed shut behind them.

The Fourth Way: HORST CABAL, LORD OF THE DEAD

The darkness swirled about them like liquid, flowed, and finally began to ebb.

'Welcome to Sepulchre!' said Horst, and favoured them all with a showman's bow, as if he had built the place in his lunch hour.

'Sepulchre?' Cabal looked about them through the thinning coils of darkness. 'It looks remarkably like London.'

'It is quite grand in places, true. Miss Barrow and I were at a huge theatre, quite as large as anything in London. Larger.'

'I see. And this Sepulchre of yours also contains its own Nelson's Column?'

'Oh, I doubt it. That would be silly.' He looked up. 'Oh!' A reasonable exclamation from somebody who had just been successfully stalked by 169 feet of granite and bronze. They were undeniably in Trafalgar Square.

Putting the impermanence of their path from his mind for the moment, Cabal crouched by Zarenyia. Her transformation was complete, but she was plainly sorely weakened by her recent travails.

'I've hardly eaten since we started on this quest of yours, Johannes,' she said as he propped her back against the stone wall of the strange little cylindrical police box from which they had emerged. 'You promised murders.' She said it with a mannered pout, but the import behind it was plain.

Cabal nodded, rose to his feet, and looked around. It was a public place; there *must* be somebody expendable around. It was then that he realised something was very wrong with London, which is to say, in addition to all its more usual flaws.

'Where is everybody?' They seemed to be at the tail end of the day, and the overcast sky was darkening. There was no conceivable reason that one of the metropolis's busiest junctions should be entirely devoid of any living people. On the nearby roadway at the junction with the Strand stood a horse-drawn tram, unattended. Cabal took a few steps to examine it more closely, and saw whitened bones lying between the traces.

'I suspect . . .' He looked around at the darkened buildings. None showed the signs of extended neglect, but there was something undeniably unkempt about the scene for all that. 'I suspect that we are not safe in the open. We should seek shelter as soon as possible. The Five Ways are working at full effect once more now that we have left Hell, and we know nothing of this place.'

'It looks like London,' said Horst.

'Apart from that it looks like London. Thank you, Horst. I know I can always depend upon you to state the blindingly obvious.'

'It's a talent.' Horst looked at the sky. 'I'll tell you something else that's a talent. Knowing just how likely the sun is to do me a mischief. I don't know what's up behind those clouds, but it isn't the sun.'

'Of course not. It's merely a representation of the sun, in much the same way this is only a representation of London, and this Sepulchre place was only the representation of some sort of materialised metaphor.'

Leonie Barrow and Miss Smith were helping Zarenyia to her feet. 'And that was a false Hell we just escaped from?' said Leonie.

'No. No, that was the real Hell.'

'Real?' She paled. 'And . . . that was actually Satan?'

'I really punched Satan.' Horst was considering getting himself an engraved pewter mug to commemorate the fact.

'And I really killed him,' said Zarenyia. She sounded faint. 'That will either make me a lot of friends, or a lot of enemies.'

None of them missed the waver in her voice. Horst nodded at a long building in the neoclassical style running across the north side of the square, fronted by a central columned portico flanked by two lesser examples, and topped by a short tower and dome. 'National Gallery?'

'It will do while we plan our next move. Help me with Madam Zarenyia.'

Moving as quickly as they might, the party headed northward to the gallery and entered through the front door, which needed only mild persuasion of the flat-footed kick sort to open.

They found a quiet corner in the surprisingly shallow building, and paused to ascertain their exact situation in as far as they might. Miss Barrow was still trying to take in why her clothes had changed and why she was armed with a shotgun and, she discovered to her consternation, a bayonet in her pack and a short, wide, flat knife in a boot scabbard.

'In the Dreamlands,' said Miss Smith, 'one arrives garbed in the manner one sees oneself.'

'I have never wanted to go around dressed like a scruffy bandit,' said Leonie. She did not admit that, now it had been thrust upon her, she really didn't mind it so much, either.

'This is not the same mechanism as the Dreamlands, Miss Smith. There it was an expression of passion. Here it is a function of, for want of a better term, drama. We are involved in a thespian game of uncertain rules with a hidden goal.'

Cabal spoke absently; Zarenyia seemed to be sinking into unconsciousness. If she did so fully and could not be roused, he was uncertain how they might feed her should they find a suitable source of sustenance. He revised the thought. How *he* would feed her should *he* find a suitable source of sustenance. It was hard to imagine the moralistic Miss Leonie Barrow resisting the urge to lecture him on the sanctity of life, no matter how sybaritically pleasant the sacrifice to Zarenyia's survival might find it. Usually, Cabal would simply have sneered in Miss Barrow's face, but these days she had a very large shotgun and the will to use it. He decided that under the circumstances, some discretion and artfulness would be necessary.

Miss Smith seemed very sensible and unlikely to be upset by it, and Horst was a vampire himself, after all, although he limited himself to blood and not the irresistible draining of souls and certain other bodily fluids. That said, if he'd been offered the option of something similar when he was first turned, Cabal was reasonably sure he would have accepted with alacrity. That said, he couldn't depend on both being stoic about him feeding a sapient being to Zarenyia. They might get all principled at an awkward moment. No, this was simply something he would have to attend to by himself.

'The area should be reconnoitred,' he said, neglecting to mention what he would be reconnoitring for. He replenished the load in his Webley (noting in passing that the empty space in the ammunition box had been filled with new rounds), and set off towards the exit as if that was all settled, then.

'I agree,' said Miss Smith. 'I'll go with you.'

This gave Cabal pause. 'You will?'

'Yes. Oh, and you might as well have this back.' She passed him the Senzan pistol. 'It's all full of bullets again. So is this.' She handed over the spare magazine. He examined it briefly and found it was indeed fully laden with live ammunition.

'If you are to go with me,' he said, gently introducing the subtext, 'which is by no means a certainty . . . oughtn't you to keep the weapon?'

'I don't need it.' She beamed at him, reached into her dress pocket, and produced a wand. Glimmering, twisted, and black, it looked like a stout twig recovered from an oil slick. It also, he realised, had an air of the crown she had worn in the boundless burying ground and Hell. Then he saw the crown in question was once again in evidence upon her brow, apparently recovered from Zarenyia.

'I didn't realise you had a wand.'

'Neither did I. I just found it in the wand pocket in my dress.'

Cabal had had cause to wear trousers with such a specially sewn accessory in the past and this point did not require clarification. 'You have a wand pocket in your skirt? Very foresighted of you.'

'No.' She smiled as if she and a very shaky progression of cause and effect had conspired to snare him in such an error. 'I like to think I look ahead, but the pocket and the wand are none of my doing.' She slashed the air experimentally with the black thorn. The air seemed to distort the light travelling through it in a halo at its tip, like the meniscus of water dimpled beneath the foot of a pond skater. The edge of the dimple seethed with momentary darkness, causing Cabal to step back.

'You should be careful, madam. Wands have a nasty habit of going off at inopportune times.'

'You're telling me,' muttered Zarenyia, drifting at the edge of consciousness. 'Johannes has one, you know. Terribly clever with it. He got me my sweater. Lots of fish. So many fish.' Her voice faded into sub-vocalised semi-words.

Everybody looked at Cabal.

'She seems very impressed with your wand, Cabal.' Leonie Barrow stood arms crossed, head cocked, and eyebrow raised.

Miss Smith made no bones about it and smirked nakedly. 'Tell you what, let me play with yours and you can play with mine.' She inadvisedly gave her wand a last little wave before sliding it back into its pocket.

'Like school all over again, isn't it?' said Horst. 'Girls teasing you and you standing there with a face like thunder.'

'Shut up,' said Cabal.

'As you wish, although the cat's out of the bag on that score now.

Anyway, what I was going to say was, "Yes, good plan. I'll go with you, too."'

Cabal let out a sigh. This was very typical of his life; he would evolve a simple plan and it would fail at the first hurdle thanks to people taking an ungratifying interest in his affairs.

'Am I to understand that nobody thinks I can conduct a brief reconnoitre of the area and so everyone wishes to come along to oversee me? I'm sure three of us will obviously make a fraction of the noise of one. If only there were another twenty of us; we would pass silent and invisible.'

Horst wrinkled his infuriatingly handsome countenance with unfamiliar thought. 'Does it really work like that? I was sure it would go the other way.'

As was so often the case, Cabal was not sure if his brother was sincere or playing the goat. Rather than wander into that bogland, he changed the subject. 'What about Madam Zarenyia?'

Miss Barrow looked down on the semi-comatose devil where they had bedded her on a bench. 'I'll stay with her. I have a ridiculously large gun and more blades than Sheffield. I'll watch over her and guard her.'

'There, that's sorted out, then,' said Horst. 'A map would be handy, wouldn't it? There'll be offices and a decent chance one of them will have a London street map. I'll go and have a look.' He paused at the door and looked back at his brother with an agreeably self-satisfied look upon his face. 'See that? I had a good idea. It does happen.'

Miss Smith went to help him search the offices more quickly, leaving Cabal alone with Leonie Barrow and Zarenyia for a moment.

He coughed a little awkwardly. 'It's good of you to watch over her, Miss Barrow.'

'It's the human thing to do, Cabal. I must admit, when you talked me into this, I was not expecting to end up babysitting a monster.'

'You once called me a monster.'

'I did. And you are.' She looked at Zarenyia. 'It seems some monsters are people, too.'

'Oodles of fish,' mumbled Zarenyia in her dreaming.

'In any case, thank you.' Cabal nodded curtly and walked away.

He paused as Leonie spoke. 'You like her, don't you?'

He didn't answer for some moments, because he did not have the answer to hand. 'Yes, I do.' He reached the door, paused, and looked back at Leonie. She waited for him to speak, but he did not. Instead, he gave another nod and was gone into the gloom.

Leonie settled herself on the end of the bench and looked over her sleeping charge. 'If my dad could only see me now,' she said in an undertone. She settled the shotgun across her lap. 'He'd be bloody furious.'

Cabal's little party of three—three times larger than he really wanted—headed out of the darkened gallery some little time later, clutching the only map they could find; a somewhat fatuous document intended for tourists showing the more famous landmarks towering over the surrounding city, and the myriad smaller streets off the main byways were notable for their absence. They concluded it would have to do until they found better, and decided to loot a newsagent as and when they happened across one. Horst said he hoped it was one that sold sweets as he would like some Victory V lozenges, and would leave a sixpence on the counter for them even though the proprietors were likely as dead as the rest of the city. Then his brother reminded him that he was dead himself, and a vampire, and that Victory Vs were not really an option for somebody of his situation. Horst accepted this, although it made him sad, and he spoke little subsequently, focusing instead on trying to recall exactly what a pleasant sensation it was to suck a Victory V.

Then Miss Smith mentioned that she preferred Fisherman's Friends herself, at which Cabal commented that this did not surprise him at all, Miss Smith fell into an aggrieved silence of her own, leaving Cabal to enjoy the subsequent quietude, untroubled by people airing opinions that did not tally with his own and that were therefore merely noise.

If they had been communicating, perhaps they would not have become separated. A little quiet chatter is useful simply as a way of keeping a group coherent, and without it, neither Johannes Cabal or Miss Smith noticed when Horst thought he saw something down a side street off the Charing Cross Road and went to investigate without troubling to mention it to his companions. By the time Cabal glanced back and saw Miss Smith in his wake and no other, Horst had already been gone for more than two minutes, although Cabal had no way of knowing that.

'Well, don't ask me,' said Miss Smith when Cabal gave vent to his understandably hypocritical complaint that she should have kept an eye on Horst. 'If you're not your brother's keeper, then I'm damn'd* sure I'm not, either.'

'He could be anywhere.' He looked up and down the road, but it was empty but for the debris of a sudden and indeterminate apocalypse. They had passed many abandoned carts and omnibuses, the skeletons of horses and a few humans. Too few humans. Cabal racked his mind, trying to think what might distract Horst sufficiently for him to wander off like this. 'We're not near Hamleys toy shop, are we?'

Miss Smith, a Londoner before her unfortunate discorporation and exile to the Dreamlands, shook her head. 'That's right over there.' She pointed roughly westwards. 'We haven't been near it at all.'

'We might have found him playing with a train set there. As it is, I am at a loss. We shall have to retrace our steps.'

As they started southwards, Miss Smith said, 'What do you think happened to London? Where is everyone?'

'I cannot begin to guess. The lack of human remains suggests some sort of evacuation, but it must have occurred very quickly. You notice all the horse skeletons are still in harness? They were abandoned where they stood, and they starved there, unable to find food because they were blocked in and unable to pull their loads out of the stationary traffic. After a while they grew weak, and we see the results.'

Miss Smith looked at the bones of a dray horse, but couldn't quite bring herself to say, 'Poor thing.' Its resemblance to a recent acquain-

---

* She actually used a stronger term than 'damn'd', but the author is a delicate creature and declines to say 'fuck' too much.

tance of horrid memory was simply too marked. She contented herself with a shake of the head. 'We're not going to find your brother like this. He was definitely still with us when we were this far south, but we've looked down every side street along the way, and there's no sign of him. He seems able to look after himself; we shall carry on looking around and go back in half an hour or so. He'll be waiting for us, I'm sure he will.'

'Probably.' The streets were growing gloomy by painfully slow degrees. It seemed this particular toy theatre of a world loved its dusks too much to let them fly by. 'Very well. Let us strike north until we reach Tottenham Court Road, thence westward and south until we reach Trafalgar Square once more via Soho and Leicester Square. It will be dark by then.' He looked around at where the bluing sky limned the rooftops and ridges. 'Or not. This is a curious sort of day.'

Now that Horst was no longer—by strict definition of dictionary, anatomy manual, or holy book of choice—a human being, his senses functioned in new and exciting ways. They were not simply sharper, although that was much of it. They functioned differently, and his awareness was now a more complicated place. He could smell a faint but not unpleasant acrid smell from Zarenyia, for example, that no human should exude in much the same way that Miss Smith's scents were exotic, speaking of some unimaginably distant place, yet were attenuated by her unusual status of conditional vitality while still distinctly those of a mortal woman. He could hear the very faint sighs his brother gave when he glanced at Miss Barrow while he thought no one else was looking. He could see the blush just too controlled to show on Leonie Barrow's skin when his brother passed by, or when Zarenyia said something risqué. The invisible blush was there much of the time, to be honest.

That much was acuity, but Horst's vision was also honed to be that of a predator and thus very sensitive to motion. Something moving in an otherwise static environment appeared to him as a brilliant glowing smear of movement against a still-life painting. He had seen such a smear as he glanced down a narrow way by one of the many theatres along Charing Cross Road. Acting without the benefit of thought—an ability that was nothing to do with his vampiric state—he walked down what would have been an alley but for the impressive architecture flanking it.

'Hullo?' he called ahead. If he had been merely human, he would not have been quite so open in his approach, but being a monster of sorts gave him all manner of unexpected edges in disagreements of the punching and stabbing sort. If a human rounded the corner with murder in their heart and a cricket bat, carving knife, cavalry sabre, or revolver in their hand, he was confident he could outmanoeuvre them and render them unarmed at the cost of no more than possibly accidentally breaking their arm, depending on the force necessary to dissuade them, or possibly tear off a couple of fingers if they got in the way.

No raging maniac or frightened citizen turned the corner in response to his call, so he rounded it himself and found them waiting there. 'Oh, dear,' he said.

It was a girl, or had been a girl of perhaps eight or nine years of age. Whatever age it had been, it was hers permanently now, for she was plainly dead.

'Hullo there,' said Horst, crouching so as not to cut quite such an imposing figure. 'My name's Horst. Who are you, then?'

The ghost blinked at him through eyes that were just dark smudges on a grey face. 'You can see me?' Her accent was of the East End, which was in keeping with the cheap linen dress she wore that had seen better days even before it became the garb of a little dead girl.

'Yes, I can. Why? Is that unusual?'

'They can't see us, the livers'—she pronounced it as the bird of Liverpool, *Lye-ver*—'not normal, they can't. I follow 'em about sometimes, but they just say stuff like "Gettin' cold, ain't it?" an' "I fink somebody jus' walked on me grave" an' that. They never sees me, though, or 'ears me, or nuthin'.' She managed to communicate suspicion by scrunching up the darkness that was once her eyes. 'You is a liver, ain't ya?'

Horst shrugged. 'I don't think I am, technically. Look.' He bared his teeth and pointed at them illustratively as he extended them.

'Lumme,' she said. 'You're a leech, int' ya?'

He put his fangs away. 'I've been called that. I prefer "vampire" to "leech", and "Horst" to "vampire".'

The girl did not seem overly astonished to be in the company of a self-confessed vampire. 'Me name's Minty.' She curtseyed.

Horst rose and bowed low. 'I'm delighted to make your acquaintance, Miss Minty.'

The ghost giggled. 'You're silly.'

'I've been called that as well.' He looked to the sky. 'I think night has more or less arrived. Would I be right in thinking we should be off the streets?'

Minty sniffed. 'S'pose. You still got flesh, you could get 'urt.'

'But not you?'

She shook her head. 'Nuffin' 'urts me no more. I'm past pain now.' She nodded with the certainty of the young, a state now set in amber. 'That's good, innit?'

'It's a silver lining, true.' He didn't feel it necessary or diplomatic to point out the darkness of the cloud that bore that lining. He looked around for a bolthole. 'There's a tea shop over there. We can . . .'

'There's a pub over there,' said Minty with far more emphasis, and headed to an alehouse on the corner, just across the way. 'Me mum didn't 'old wiv me goin' in pubs,' she explained as Horst tested the door and found it unlocked. ' 'Cept to get me dad for 'is dinner. But me mum din't drink, not at all.'

'Really?' Horst was hardly listening to her, instead attuning his senses to the new environment. It was musty, and there was the distant smell of old decay from the direction of the taproom, so after he had ushered Minty in and closed the door after her, he settled in the saloon.

'So, Minty. I am a stranger here.'

'You talk funny. I've 'eard sailors wot talk like you. Are you a Kraut or somethin'?'

'I was born in Germany, yes. But I grew up in England, and I'm naturalised now.' The blank eyes were blanker than usual. 'That means I am English now, even if I sound like a—'

'Kraut.'

'A German, yes. What I mean, though, is that I'm not very clear on why London is dead. How did this happen?'

'Yer a leech. 'Ow can you not know?'

'I didn't become a le . . . a vampire here. I do understand you, don't I? You're saying lots of people here became vampires?'

'An' ghosties an' ghoulies an' deaders an' ravens an' stuff.'

'Ghouls?' The ghouls that had helped them in the battle with Ratuth Slabuth had simply seemed to vanish after the retreat. Johannes had told him after his own encounter with the ghouls in the Dreamlands that they had paths into their warrens everywhere, invisible to anything but their eyes. That may be so; as already mentioned, Horst's senses were well beyond the norm, yet he had seen no other turnings from the tunnel that had brought them here. Then again, from the few pithy comments his brother had made about something called 'the Five Ways', that may well have been because they weren't supposed to see them. All this was a living dream, all of dead London, and even the ghost of a little girl standing blinking patiently at him in the saloon of an abandoned pub. He was still Horst, though, and he felt sorry for Minty, though she was no more real than a character in a book.

'It were the curse, weren't it?' she said, he hoped, rhetorically. 'The ravens flew away from the tower an' we was all cursed and died.' For illustration, she gripped her throat and made a horribly death-rattling sound. 'Ecchhhhhhhhh . . . I sounded just like that when I went, I did. Glad to go, too. Been coughin' up blood all night an' it were really tirin'.' She stopped throttling herself and grinned. Horst could see a gap in her teeth where a new one was growing in. 'I don't get tired no more. An' I can go in pubs an' nobody cares.'

Horst had distantly heard of some legend associated with the ravens at the Tower of London. 'Doesn't that legend say that if the ravens die out or leave, the crown falls and Britain with it?'

'Yus. The crown fell off of the Queen's 'ed when she was doin' a thing in Westminster. The ravens 'ad gorn, and there was a right fuss, but the Queen said it was all'—Minty adopted a highly pitched posh voice, apparently the tone of royalty—'*it is all soupy-stitious nonsense. We will just get some more ravens, won't we? Yeah.* So she was talking to all the genklemen at Parliament an' she 'ad 'er crown on. *It gives me great pleasure to launch this Parliament and all what sail in it. Oooh, I've come over all funny.*' Minty gripped her throat. '*Ecchhhhhhhhhhhh . . .* Fell down the steps, an' her crown fell orft, and then the genklemen went *Ecchhhhhhhhh . . .* an' everybody died. An' some of 'em came back as monsters an' that. An' the 'ole city was dead after a couple of days an' I'm a ghost.' She shrugged. 'Wish I'd got to be a leech. Could still touch stuff, then. Wish I could do that.' She looked at her hands, as grey and undefined as mist with smudges for fingers. 'This ain't fair, bein' a ghosty.'

'Being a vampire isn't all fun and games, either, I have to tell you. Being dead generally isn't a wonderful experience. That's assuming you know about it at all. Do you have anyone to talk to usually? Any ghosty friends?'

She shook her head. 'Not many as died ended up as ghosties. I sees 'em about sometimes, but I stays away. Some of 'em 'ave gone a bit mad, all wailin' an' carryin' on. People wiv bodies can't 'urt me, but maybe *they* can. Don't wanna risk it, do I?' She looked speculatively at Horst. ' 'Ave you got any leech friends?'

'No. I'm here in London with family and acquaintances; they're a mixed lot but none of them are vampires. In fact, I was walking up towards Tottenham Court Road with my brother and his friend when I saw you. I hope they'll be all right.' He nodded with reasonably justified certainty. 'They'll be fine.'

'Are they livers? Alive, I means? Town's dangerous for livers 'less they're in a big gang. They might get in trouble.'

Horst gave a rueful smile. 'I'd be astonished if they didn't. I'm not so very worried, though. The lady is apparently technically dead but somehow alive. And she's a witch.'

'A witch?' Minty's eye smudges grew big. 'Is your bruvva a wizard or summat?'

'No. Well, yes, but don't call him that. Yes, he's a sort of wizard, and worse.'

'Worse?' Minty said it breathlessly. In a city of horrors, it took quite a lot to impress her these days, but Horst was managing it.

'Uh-huh. He's a *scientist.*'

Zarenyia was not edifying to look upon as she slept, if it was indeed sleep as mortals know it. She had stopped breathing a little while before. As soon as Leonie Barrow had noticed, she had attempted to restart the cycle on inhalations and exhalations so beloved of aerobic organisms. She had some first aid training, and so attempted the kiss of life. This did not prove a success as a medical technique, although it had an unexpected corollary in that Miss Barrow found herself unexpectedly overcome and had to sit down for a while with a silly smile upon her face and unexpected vistas in her mind.

Zarenyia began breathing again, but only long enough to murmur, 'Naughty girl,' before stopping again. Leonie belatedly realised that drawing breath was merely a habit for the devil, and useful for talking, but otherwise an affectation. Her colour remained good, and the pulse in her neck still showed as regular but perhaps weaker than it ought to be.

Unable to make herself useful as a nurse, Leonie instead busied herself by checking the security of the gallery. It was well locked up, by and large, but there was nothing that could be done for the shattered lock in the main door, or to make the tall windows that flanked it any less breakable. She paused by one of the windows and looked out across Trafalgar Square. She had been through the real thing several times in her life, and it had never been anything but furiously busy, full of tourists taking in the sights and Londoners cursing them for it. Seeing it entirely devoid of life and, worse yet, likely to remain so but for she and her companions was one of the most remarkable sights of her life. Well, that and the last night of the Brothers Cabal Carnival. And the business with the *Princess Hortense.* Actually, she had to concede that she had seen several very remarkable sights in her life, and every instance had been to do with Johannes Cabal in some capacity. The sights had never been enjoyable, true, but they were undeniably remarkable.

It was also curious how the city seemed to illuminate itself. There may well have been a brilliant full moon in the heavens, but it was impossible to tell through the thick, high cloud that choked the sky from horizon to horizon. The buildings themselves seemed illuminated by a deep midnight blue projected from an unseen source. It reminded her of how stage sets were artfully illuminated in the theatre when a nocturnal scene was called for. That in turn reminded her of her small triumph in the sadly non-existent city of Sepulchre. She missed the place, with its remarkable architecture, its sense of having been thrown together to be interesting rather than functional, and best of all its endemic crime problem. She had a feeling that even the lowliest crook there was capable of committing apparently impossible crimes that required the ratiocinations of a great detective. The Great Detective. She smiled to herself: that had felt good; she couldn't deny it. If only the real world could be so obliging. Fewer knocks to the head with a cudgel and more arcane poisons from the Mysterious Orient. That would make her very happy.

She looked up at the sound of a cry from the square. A man was running across the paving stones as a jackrabbit runs from the hounds. A moment later the hounds arrived. A gang of six men were pursuing the first in a group that turned into a skirmish line as they harried him towards the base of the column. They were laughing and view-holloaing at one another like public schoolboys as they cut off their prey's retreat and closed the noose around him. Leonie did not like the way this was developing at all. She picked up the shotgun from where she had left it leaning by the window and considered it. It held five cartridges. She would have to get closer to stand a decent chance of scoring solid hits, and there was no guarantee that she would hit with every shell. It seemed unlikely that she would have a chance to reload. And what if they were carrying firearms, too?

As she calculated the odds, time was running out for the hunted man. She opened the door a crack and was able to hear the confrontation across the strangely still night air.

'I never dun nuffin' to you!' The man was garbling in terror. 'Leave me alone! Ain't there 'orrors enough in this place?'

'Oh, my God, Rupert, did you hear that?' One of the pursuers was somehow managing to drawl even while recovering his breath. 'A double negative and a dropped aspirate. Killing him would be a mercy to the Queen's English.'

'Queen's dead, old boy,' said another. 'Well, *sort* of dead, at any rate.'

Leonie suddenly recognised the easy resort to cries of 'Tally-ho!' and 'Yoiks!' These were City gents, gone feral.

'I know a way out of the city!' said the trapped man. 'I can lead you out, like!'

'Lead us out?' More laughter. 'Why would we want to leave London? Have you seen the rest of the country? Absolutely ghastly; full of people who can't enunciate properly. No, no, no. Simply won't do. We're happy here. We know where there are some absolutely splendid wine cellars, and we can do as we like.'

'One thing, though.' The circle was tightening on the man. 'Laying in provender can be a tad trying. One grows bored of rats, even in a delicate sauce.'

'Hence,' said another, 'our embrace of anthropophagy.'

'Anfro-po-wot?'

'Cannibalism, you stupid man.' They fell upon him.

They took no time at all to kill him, but they did not do so very elegantly. 'Oh, steady on,' she heard one say. 'Careful with the claret. Oh, Charles, you ass, it's all over my trousers now.'

'Do stop complaining, Gideon. We're due a trip to Savile Row, anyway. We'll see what's on the peg.'

'Speaking of wine, what shall we have with this creature when it's cooked? I rather wish we could catch more pigeons. I'm getting tired of red with every meal.'

Leonie had no idea what came over her. The sensible thing would simply be to lie low, let them gather up their kill, and leave. The sensible thing would be to avoid any sort of contact. The sensible thing was to accept that she couldn't help the man now, and attempting to avenge him would not resurrect him even if she succeeded.

The sensible thing could go hang. Besides, there were other considerations, other lives in the balance that night.

She leaned the shotgun by the far side of the door frame, took off her hat to loosen her hair and display it over her shoulders. She replaced the hat and took a couple of deep breaths while she steadied herself for the stupidly dangerous thing she was about to do. Then she opened the door and crossed the short distance to the stone rail of the raised portico overlooking the square. She made herself as noticeable as she could, but the men were too busy dressing their victim for transport to glance in her direction. Exasperated by how much trouble it was to bring unwanted attention these days, she gave what she guessed a girlish cry of horror might sound like.

The men looked up. For an endless moment it was as if she had somehow turned them to stone by her unexpected appearance. Then one found enough impulse to shout, 'A filly!' which inspired another to cry, 'I say!' another, 'Tally-ho!' and suddenly it was like a Saturday evening in a restaurant visited by an Oxford University dining club.

Leonie gave throat to another squeal of feminine weakness at the sight of the six charging in her direction, and ran back indoors hoping against hope that she shouldn't have done the sensible thing, after all.

Her plan was simple in the extreme, and she hoped her pursuers were simple enough to play along. She shot the lower bolt on the door home; apparently when the gallery had been abandoned, the last curator had used the front door and so secured only the lock. The bolts had not been used and so had not been destroyed when Horst made his forceful entrance. Against six men, the solitary bolt wouldn't last long, but it wouldn't need to. She took the distinctive hat from her head and skimmed it across the floor to the eastern side, appeared briefly at the eastern window, ran off in that direction once she was sure they'd glimpsed her. Then she ducked under the window and headed west, snatching up her shotgun from where it leaned upon the door frame just as the handle was tried. She slid under the western window, and ran pell-mell off into the shadows of the west wing to hide. There she waited, her shotgun cocked and ready to shoot if they showed the discourtesy to find her.

She was barely in cover when the door took a battering and the bolt failed under an enthusiastic shoulder ram. The men poured in through the doorway in a moment and looked eastward, the direction they had glimpsed her moving. Lying in the gallery doorway was her hat, lost in her panicked flight from ungentlemanly frightfulness. Shouting, 'Come on, girlie! We just want to say hello!' (although the ribald laughter at this implied saying hello was probably not their priority), the foremost led the others in that direction. Soon, Leonie heard the cry of discovery.

'She's fainted,' said one.

'Could've sworn she was a blonde,' muttered another.

'However shall we wake her up?' said a third. There was more laughter.

'I think I know how!' said the first. There was more laughter, much of the same note as the previous laughter, detached from humour and latched onto cruelty with a rusty needle.

In her hiding place, Leonie felt assured enough to re-engage her gun's safety catch, which for that particular weapon meant lowering the hammer to half cock to immobilise the trigger. 'I bet you do,' she said to herself, and settled down to wait.

The brief search of the area to the north of Trafalgar Square had turned up little but more signs of an historical terror of a few months before, followed by a period of intermittent beastliness between the survivors of the catastrophe and something predatory that was presumably instrumental in that catastrophe. Cabal and Miss Smith looked at the surprisingly rare tattered corpses and held informed little chats about likely causes that would have horrified anyone in polite society. As it was, everyone in polite society seemed to have been done to death, so that was only a fleeting concern for them.

They rejoined Charing Cross Road along Bear Street and were soon back in Trafalgar Square. Cabal looked around for a moment and, seeing nothing untoward, was set to return to the Gallery. Miss

Smith, however, stopped him and pointed towards the column. Around the base, dark shapes moved.

'What are those?' said Cabal. He moved a little closer, taking the Webley from his bag as he did so. 'Crows? At *night?*'

'Not crows.' Miss Smith walked past him towards the creatures. 'Those are ravens.'

The large birds ignored the two during their approach but for suspicious sideways glances as they gorged themselves on something. Cabal didn't like the behaviour of the birds at all. He had some experiences with wilful corvids (although coupling the term 'wilful' to any member of the crow family might be considered tautology), and these examples seemed unusually self-assured.

When they were close enough to see it was a human body the birds were feeding upon, Cabal swore and ran forwards, shooing the ravens away. They refused to leave, spreading their wings and jumping at him and pecking. It took Miss Smith's intervention—wand drawn—to make them back away. Indeed, they did it easily at her behest. She said, 'Shoo,' and they shooed to a few feet away.

Cabal knelt by the body to examine it. 'Ach. It is a man. I feared it might be Miss Barrow. Hard to make out scale with those birds in the way, although this unfortunate was not tall.'

'Did the ravens kill him?' Miss Smith gave the unkindness a hard look. The ravens did their best to look innocent of all charges, but failed despite actually being innocent.

'I do not believe so. There seem to be stab wounds, and the corpse is partially disembowelled.' He frowned and looked up at Miss Smith. '*Post-mortem*. If I didn't know better, I would suggest the body was in the process of being field-dressed, as a hunter does with a deer.'

'That's not the kind of attention we've seen given to the other corpses that we found.'

'Men did this, and something distracted them away from their kill.'

'The gallery.'

Both of them ran in a cautious trot north to the steps of the National Gallery, weapons in hand and at the ready.

* * *

Cabal and Miss Smith discovered the freshly damaged main door and entered expecting all manner of trouble. What they actually discovered was Leonie Barrow sitting on the edge of a bench in the foyer, her shotgun across her lap and her hat in her hands, looking aghast into the eastern galleries. They followed her gaze and saw immediately what was so absorbing her interest.

'They deserved it,' Leonie said faintly. 'They deserved it and worse. Just . . . I'm going to have to live with myself for sending them in there.'

The galleries were very different from how they had appeared when Cabal had led the expedition out. Now they were loomed in loose, floating skeins of fine black silk that billowed and flowed under the slightest breeze. Notable were cocoons of approximately man size dangling in the complex catacomb of web. With a solid *tack-tack-tack* of long, hard, pointed feet on long, hard, pointed legs making an awful mess of the flooring, Zarenyia stepped forwards from the shadows once more in demi-spider form, wreathed in smiles and sporting all eight legs. She turned a little to show off the rearmost.

'Look!' she said with childish delight. 'I've got new ones. I feel like a new woman!'

'How did this happen?' Cabal's eyes flicked between Miss Barrow and Zarenyia, uncertain whom to address, but it was Zarenyia who answered.

'Sweet Leonie got me some chaps to eat! Rough beasts they were, well-spoken but with vile manners. Still, they were all full of unrequited lusts.' She smiled darkly and her voice lowered. 'Easy meat.'

' "Some chaps"?' echoed Cabal. 'There's a body out in the square. Is that—'

'They murdered him, Cabal.' Leonie looked sickened and pale. 'They were going to eat him. Not monsters, not like your normal fare. The sort of men you might see on the train and think nothing of. They were going to eat a fellow human being. And they thought it was funny.' She put on her hat and got to her feet. 'I don't regret what I did. It's just . . . the sounds. I could hear them dying. Not sure I'll ever forget that.'

She turned and walked away. Zarenyia's happiness faltered. 'Darling, it wasn't painful for them. It's a super way to go, really and truly. Look, I'll show you their faces, they all died smiling! Admittedly, some of that's the effect of being the teeniest bit desiccated, but most of it's sincere, really it is!'

'They knew they were dying,' said Leonie over her shoulder. 'They were terrified. All the physical pleasure in the world couldn't hide that.' She went through the doorway to the western galleries and was lost from their sight.

Zarenyia made a step to follow her, but Cabal stopped her. 'Not now, Madam Zarenyia. I believe Fräulein Barrow would appreciate a little time to herself.'

Zarenyia looked down at him with incomprehension, perhaps even distress. 'I don't understand why she is so upset, darling. She was the one who brought them to me. What did she expect to happen?'

'Exactly what did happen. What is necessary is not always pleasant. You must be patient with Miss Barrow; she has a conscience, and they can be troublesome. I have one that is nowhere nearly as evolved as hers and, believe me, it is a dreadful nuisance.'

'A conscience?' Zarenyia looked off in the direction Leonie Barrow had gone. 'I've heard of those.'

Horst the vampire and Minty the ghost walked into Trafalgar Square a quarter of an hour later. Horst had offered to hold her hand, but she was too insubstantial for that to be in any sense practical, so instead he allowed his hand to hang open at his side, and she gripped it. He could feel a tiny hint of pressure and of a coldness across his palm when she did so, but no more than that. At least it was a gesture of trust, although in truth neither could have done a thing to harm the other even if they had wished it. Sometimes gestures carry a necessary weight that can be borne by nothing else.

Horst was talking. 'So there are survivors? Living ones, I mean?'

Minty nodded. 'Livers, yeah. But they're not nice. Anyone wiv any brains would've left for the country, what wiv everyfin' that were 'appenin'. Some people jus' don't wanna go, though. They 'ung around and fought each uvva instead. London's a mess. Like 'Ell, it is?'

'I was in Hell just recently, as it happens,' said Horst conversationally. He looked at the louring buildings and the debris-cluttered streets as they lay beneath a malevolent sky. 'Hell was rather nicer. And there are vampires like me?' Minty nodded. 'Anything else I should know about?'

'The deaders.'

'Well, *we're* dead, if I was to play the pedant.'

She shook her head emphatically. 'Not like us. Proper deaders. Dead people wot walk about.'

Horst's spirits sank. 'Zombies?'

'Dunno. Most people just called 'em deaders, while there were people still around to call stuff things.'

They had arrived at the steps leading up to the National Gallery's entrance. 'Well, here we are,' said Horst. 'My friends are inside. You're welcome to accompany me, but I can't guarantee that they'll be able to see you as I can.'

'S'all right. Used to livers not bein' able to see me.'

'The other thing is some of my friends are a little bit unusual. In fact, it's easier to say some of my friends are usual, as they are in minority.' Minty squinted at him. 'Look, just don't be surprised or frightened by anything you see. They're good people. No, that's not true. One of them is a good person, and the others are a bit unusual, and not necessarily exactly what you might call "good", per se, but . . .' He looked at her. She was still squinting at him. 'They're all right, I think I mean to say. Come along if you want to meet them.'

She didn't say she did, but neither did she leave his side. The tiny hint of coldness remained across his palm.

They walked in and found everyone had decamped from the gallery's east wing to its west. A glance to the east demonstrated why.

'Are those *bodies?*' he asked of his brother.

'They are indeed. We do not have the capital to ourselves, and what survivors there are will not be winning any prizes for hospitality.' Cabal looked at how his brother was standing, particularly at the odd way his left arm hung away from his body. 'Why are you standing like. that?'

Without waiting for a reply, he took up his ubiquitous Gladstone bag, sorted through its contents, and withdrew a spectacle case. From this he took a pair of glasses with amber lenses. He put them on and peered at Horst's left hand and the space beside it.

'Hello, young lady,' he said. 'I see my brother has made a friend.'

'Lumme,' said Minty. 'He's a liver, but he can see me!'

'I can see you, but I cannot hear you,' said Cabal. 'These spectacles only enhance my eyesight, rendering certain unusual wavelengths into visible light. If we are to talk, it must be through the medium of my brother.'

'Oh, goody,' said Horst. 'Now I'm a medium.'

'Better than being a poor. You should savour the promotion.'

They were interrupted by Miss Smith entering. 'You're back, Horst!' she said, stating the obvious. Then she looked at Minty, and crouched down to her height. 'And a sweet little girl. What's your name, darling?'

Minty blinked, her dark smudge eyes narrowing to lines and then open again. 'Minty,' she said, finding herself at something of a loss.

'Minty! What a lovely name.'

'But . . . you're a liver, too, miss. An' you don't 'ave no magic specs. 'Ow is it that you can see me?'

'Magic specs?' Miss Smith looked to Cabal, who was bracing himself for the inevitable slight. 'Magic specs are for amateurs. I don't need them.' She leaned closer to Minty and whispered, 'I'm a witch.'

'Lumme,' said Minty again.

A clatter of arachnoid feet announced the arrival of Zarenyia. She clapped with pleasure at seeing Horst, who was no less delighted to see her back on her feet—all of them—even if the sources of the sustenance necessary for this remarkable recovery were hanging swathed in webbing behind him. 'Zarenyia! You're up and about!'

'And you're back, Horst.' She swivelled her head inquisitively to regard Minty. 'And you have a ghostly girl with you. Hello, poppet. My name's Zarenyia. I am simply delighted to meet you. What's your name?'

'Minty,' said Minty again. 'Pardon me asking, missus, but what are you?'

'What am I? Oh, isn't she a delight? I'm a devil, sweetheart.'

'Wot? You're the Devil?'

'A devil. There are quite a few of us. But no, not *the* Devil at all, although the job is going begging if you want a change in career.'

At which point Leonie Barrow stepped from the western doorway. 'Why is everyone talking to Horst's left hand?' she wanted to know.

'Lumme,' said Minty.

'Livers an' deaders' an' leechers an' ghosties an'—'

Johannes Cabal sighed. 'Yes, thank you, Horst. While Miss Barrow and I appreciate the relay service, taking such pains over the impersonation of the girl is really not necessary. Please use your own diction.'

Horst paused and looked off to one side where Cabal could see the ghost (and Leonie couldn't) as if listening. Cabal could see her lips moving with a certain emphasis. Horst nodded and reported, 'Minty says it was a brilliant impersonation and I should carry on using it.'

Minty's expression clouded indignantly.

'I can lip read a little, Horst, and what I caught was—and you'll forgive me any tonal inaccuracies, I'm sure—*That don't sound nuffink like me.*'

Minty nodded once with righteousness, crossed her arms, and glared at Horst.

He conceded with poor grace. 'Very well, but you're missing a fine performance. To recap, the city contains some roving gangs of thugs much like those that made the acquaintance of Zarenyia, vampires, ghosts, zombies—'

Minty's mouth moved, and Horst stopped abruptly. He looked at her, and frowned.

'What was that?' said Cabal. 'I made out two syllables, but I have no idea what the word was.'

Minty said it again to Horst, and then to Cabal with a serious nod at the end. It was nice to be the centre of attention for once, and taken seriously, to boot. She seemed intent on wringing every moment out of the situation that she might.

'I caught it that time, I think. Horst, did she say "soldiers"?'

'Soldiers, Minty? There are really soldiers here? What are they doing? Fighting the zombies. The deaders, that is?'

'A bit. Most o' the time they're huntin' down the leeches.'

Cabal considered this intelligence when it was passed onto him. 'That is unexpected. I would have thought the zombies a greater threat. Certainly a more numerous one. Ask her how they destroy the vampires.'

When she was asked, she looked at Horst as if he were an idiot. He weathered it easily, inured from long exposure. 'I din't say they was killin' the leeches. They talks wiv 'em. Give 'em bits of paper like them notices what they sticks on walls, too.'

'Notices? The army is handing out pieces of paper to vampires? I know the British have a reputation for politeness, but surely that doesn't extend to issuing vampires with cease-and-desist notices?'

Horst listened as Minty spoke and relayed her words immediately. 'She didn't say they were British, either.'

'What?' Cabal rose to his feet. 'She's sure?'

Minty was sure. She'd seen enough British soldiers and sailors in her neighbourhood to recognise the uniforms. The soldiers running around London wore different uniforms entirely; a dark grey 'wiv red bits,' said Minty, tapping her shoulders.

Cabal's expression grew astonished, but the astonishment was being eaten away by a growing dismay.

'Dark grey with red epaulets?' Horst shrugged. 'Who's that, then? The French? It would be typical of the French to take advantage of things if Britain is all of a mess like this, wouldn't it?'

'It isn't the French.' Cabal's voice was a harsh whisper.

'Cabal!' Leonie had taken position by the window to make sure they suffered no more incursions that night. 'Over here!'

There was a dull droning sound from outside, growing louder and very occasionally marked with a sharp cracking sound. They all crowded around the windows to look out and then, following Leonie Barrow's cue, up.

In the sky over Trafalgar Square, a great airborne vessel flew by at a stately pace. A huge, vaguely rectangular lozenge with four great flat mechanical housings mounted on pylons that thrust out of the port and starboard sides, fore and aft. Gun ports showed clearly over the hull, studding it regularly.

'I'm not mistaken, am I, Cabal?' Leonie's whisper was as strained as Cabal's. 'That is what I think it is?'

'It's an aeroship!' Horst's voice was, by contrast, full of enthusiasm. 'An aeroship! I've never seen one so close! Well, there was the *Catullus*, but that was an aeroboat, really. That thing is huge! Gosh!'

'It's not just an aeroship, Horst. Yes, I am very much afraid that you are right, Miss Barrow. It is the *Princess Hortense*, of unhappy memory.'

They allowed the *Princess Hortense*, or whatever it was called in this splinter of reality, to move on. The reason for its slow flight was clear now; it was monitoring the city. Once a searchlight stabbed into the metropolitan darkness and was followed a few seconds later by a rattle of machine-gun fire. They watched the tracer-laden stream of bullets lash an area near Horse Guards Parade. The searchlight scanned around a little after the fire ceased, then settled and tightened. Another burst of fire, and the searchlight was extinguished. The aeroship turned eastwards and travelled on following the line of the Thames until it was lost to their sight.

'Mirkarvia,' said Cabal. 'Again. And yet . . .' He looked at their little party, his gaze settling on each in turn until it reached Miss Smith, upon whom it tarried. 'I begin to see it.'

'See what, brother?' asked Horst.

'The pattern. I have been guilty of developing an incomplete and untested thesis; trusting to it simply because we have been pushed reluctantly and at speed between pillar and post from the instant we set foot upon these Five Ways to which Ratuth Slabuth alluded. I suspect I have allowed myself to fall under a misapprehension because of a pleasing coincidence.'

'Right,' said Horst. 'Of course. I see.'

'You do?'

Horst shook his head.

'You never start to surprise me, Horst. I am not prepared to postulate at present—'

Horst nodded, supportive of the decision. 'Good. There are ladies and a child present.'

'—as to the basis of my suspicion. I would prefer more facts, although the few I have to hand already certainly point in a suggestive fashion.'

Zarenyia smiled blandly as if daring anyone to make an obvious comment. When no one did, she said, 'So we're off on an adventure again, are we? Fact hunting, and derring-do, and ideally killing a few people. Proper people. These "deaders" Minty talks about will be soulless already, and where's the nutritional value in that?'

'You just . . . *had* half a dozen. You want more?' Leonie looked at the spider-devil with horror.

Zarenyia managed a contrite expression. 'I'm afraid so, dear heart. I used a lot of the . . . ah, *essence* I took from those frightful men in growing back my legs and generally improving the state of my health. To be blunt, I'm still famished.' There was an awkward silence. 'Have I mentioned how much I like your hat? It looks lovely on you.'

'What exactly are we looking for, Johannes?' asked Miss Smith. 'And, while I'm asking questions, why that very hard look you gave me earlier? Don't you trust me all of a sudden?'

'I value common cause over trust usually. But, in your case, you have my trust, too. You shouldn't place too much significance upon my eye happening to linger upon you. Just something that occurred to me, and thinking of how we met in the great cemetery was the stimulus that started that particular train of thought.'

'So there you go,' said Zarenyia brightly. 'Dear Johannes looked at you and was all stimulated. Happens to me simply all of the time.'

'Not quite what I—'

'Hush. Ladies like to be flattered.'

Dear Johannes settled into an exasperated silence for a moment before remembering he'd been asked two questions.

'To answer your first question, we must find some of these soldiers. We need to know what they know.'

'Stalking soldiers. This sounds dangerous,' said Leonie.

Zarenyia smiled a not entirely pleasant smile. 'Which is what makes it fun.'

If there is any better scout for moving through a city occupied by monsters and foreign troops than a ghost of a former citizen who is lent near invisibility by the former attribute and familiarity of the locale by the latter, they must be few in number. Certainly Minty—finding herself treated far more respectfully in death than she ever was in life—took on the role with enthusiasm and the sober mien of the young when graced with a vital undertaking. The rest of the party moved slowly, watching side streets, windows, and the sky in case the aeroship or another like it might return. It was this last consideration that had been used to dissuade Zarenyia from taking to the rooftops; if the crew of the aeroship had grown used to spotting and attacking individuals on the street from a height of perhaps two hundred feet, they were unlikely to have any trouble at all spotting a large spiderish woman skipping along the tops of the buildings.

The plan was to find and investigate the area where the aeroship had opened fire, the reasoning being that there was only so much that could be done from the air, and that survivors would have sought refuge off the street as soon as the firing began. This would necessitate the deployment of ground troops to clear the surrounding buildings and declare the area secure. Cabal's group would get there first with any luck and be waiting for the soldiers by the time they arrived. Assuming that troops were following in the aeroship's slow progress, then they would be heading west to east. Cabal's group would be approaching from the north, and arriving at the same time as a platoon or two of Mirkarvian soldiers did not seem very advantageous. Therefore, they determined to move slowly enough that they would get there second, but not so slowly that the troops would have moved on by the time they had arrived.

'There's an art to an ambush,' said Zarenyia, and nobody else felt confident enough about it to argue.

Her instincts were reliable, as was only reasonable given that she was—quite apart from being thoroughly charming and a very pleasant conversationalist—an ancient supernatural predator. Horse Guards Parade had definitely seen better days. The ubiquitous abandoned carts, cabs, and carriages dotted the area, the skeletons of the horses still in more traces than not. A hansom cab lay on its side, shattered by heavy machine-gun fire, leaving the naked wood exposed beneath the glossy black paint. By it a body lay, and around the body two men crouched, checking it, while a cordon of soldiers armed with repeating rifles in tactically sound positions protected the area. Cabal and his party would have blundered straight into the guards if Minty hadn't turned a corner and run into one, and then directly through him. The soldier shuddered as if a chill breeze had caught him, but otherwise did not react.

Minty took in the state of affairs in the parade, and then trotted back to report, this time taking the time to go around the soldier.

'There's about twelve blokes wiv big guns,' Minty demonstrated by stretching her arms, 'an' a couple of blokes wiv little guns. Those two are 'avin' a look at a deader. A proper dead deader. I fink that aeroship done for it. It was all full of 'oles and ever so 'orrible.' This, she said gleefully.

Cabal ruminated. 'The Mirkarvian Army models itself on the Prussian, perhaps unsurprisingly. Twelve would be a *Gruppe*, with a couple of officers along. Five of us versus over a dozen soldiers. I am not sure that I like those odds.'

'You're right, Johannes.' Horst started counting off points on his fingers. 'We have a devil, we have a vampire, we have a witch, we have two heavily armed civilians, we have total surprise—' He looked to his side as if listening. '—yes, a splendid point. We have a ghost. Those hapless swine with the rifles are the ones in trouble, Johannes.'

Cabal considered, and then reconsidered. 'Perhaps you're right. Very well. A quick plan to isolate and neutralise them, bearing in mind that we must keep at least one alive to interrogate.'

Everyone nodded, with one exception. Cabal sighed heavily; he now realised that the opportunity to plan had already gone. 'Where is Madam Zarenyia?' he asked, but expected no useful reply.

Private Trizlo was scanning the area to the west of Horse Guards Parade when he happened to notice that Private Ulchir was not at his position. He hadn't liked the look of the buildings when they were directed there by the aeroship's searchlight; too many places for things to hide. People, and worse than people. Every member of his *Zug* said out loud that the billet was an easy one, if boring. Every member was lying; he heard the sleeping whimpers and moans of men in nightmares. This city may have been conquered before a single Mirkarvian set foot on British soil, but there was nothing easy about the job they had to do. The capital had to be cleared; cleansed of every surviving Briton and every one of the monsters the strike against the city had created. It was an ugly way to make war, but the British had started it by refusing to give Mirkarvia *carte blanche* to do as it wished in its region. They should just have minded their own business when first Senza and then Poloruss fell. With all the troops these conquests brought into the Mirkarvian Empire and the powers Her Majesty possessed, it was a foregone conclusion what would happen. It wasn't Mirkarvia's fault it had. Destiny is like that.

Still, this wasn't good soldiering. It was little more than hunting vermin, but some of the vermin could bite back. Every *Zug* had bad stories about clearances that had gone wrong. Sometimes they even lost people.

Trizlo looked around the clutter of pale stone buildings on either side of Whitehall. They could hide a dinosaur in this place, never mind a wight or a leech. Where the hell had Ulchir gone? This was just typical of him; wandering off without letting anyone know. He looked to Corporal Hesk to offer an exasperated glare. But Hesk was out of position, too.

Hesk wanted to make sergeant, and so he was by the book. He would have to have a damn good reason before he would leave his post. What was going on here? The lieutenant and the medic were still searching around the shattered hansom cab. He hated to jump past reporting to his NCO, but Trizlo didn't see what choice he had.

He opened his mouth to draw breath to call to the lieutenant, but got no further. Out of nowhere, a man in a stylishly cut suit appeared before him. 'Good evening,' said the man, who doffed his hat, and then punched Trizlo unconscious before he could respond. Trizlo was caught as he fell and whisked out of sight. The Mirkarvian cordon continued to thin, minute by minute, by sundry means.

By the time Lieutenant Skir and Medical Officer Borus finished their examination, their protective detail had entirely vanished.

'Where is everyone?' said Skir. His hand went straight to his holster, only to find it empty. 'My gun!'

Borus gaped at his commanding officer's empty holster for a moment before remembering himself and going for his own gun. It, too, was absent. They looked around them in rising horror as they realised the desperate straits in which they found themselves. In doing so, they found that they were not quite alone.

'Gentlemen,' said the man in the black suit and, inexplicably given the evening light, tinted glasses that seemed to bear amber lenses. 'Your men are gone. Some are probably still breathing, but that can be altered very easily. If you value the remaining lives of those under your command, you would do well to mark my words carefully and answer immediately and truthfully any questions I might put to you.'

'Who are you?' demanded Skir.

'A bad start, Lieutenant,' said the man. Skir noticed a distinct German accent. 'You are surrounded, and I have your men. Well, most of them. A few eggs were broken in the making of this omelette. In short, you don't ask questions for the duration of this encounter, only answer them. To demonstrate the principle, I shall start with an easy question. That question is, "Do you understand?"'

Skir bridled, but swallowed his wrath. 'I do.'

'Good. Then here come the more complicated ones, beginning with . . . why is the Mirkarvian military in London at all?'

A much-depleted *Gruppe* made its way through the deserted streets of London. The only survivors from their run-in with a nest of wights—'deaders' was altogether too prosaic a term for the Mirkarvian military, and 'zombies' smacked of exoticism—they now numbered only three: the lieutenant, the medical officer, and one soldier, as well as two prisoners, both women. Of these two women, one was a tall redhead possessed of a subtle beauty almost supernatural in its intimation. She was dressed perfectly in a fashionable dress, seemed to regard being arrested by the occupation force as a very jolly sort of day out, and kept having to be reminded to keep her hands on her head. The other prisoner was shorter, hair as black as midnight, with a very pale complexion. She was dressed like a fashionable widow, and carried a battered black lace parasol in one hand while keeping the other hand on the back of her head in an apparent faint nod to prisoner protocols. The soldier keeping an eye on them had his hat pulled down hard, the peak hiding his face. He carried a non-issue pump-action shotgun, and his uniform was not a very good fit. Of the officers, the medic seemed happy with his lot, but the lieutenant was thin-lipped and tended to scowl at his fellow officer's comments rather than answering them.

They were heading west by southwest long the Mall; St James's Park would have been the shorter and certainly more scenic route under normal circumstance, but in that unnatural night it was home to strange noises and movements in the undergrowth or, at least, stranger than is usual even for St James's Park. Thus, they progressed up the Mall towards Buckingham Palace, late residence of Her Majesty before her unfortunate incident.

As they approached, it was plain that it was not much of a residence these days, nor anything else but a burnt-out and exploded ruin. A wrathfulness had been practised upon it, and little was still habitable, the northern corner being the only major exception—now converted into a barracks to judge from all the soldierly activity occurring there. The new Queen of England and Wales, Scotland, the entirety of Ireland, all the little islands, and anything else she liked the look of had never intended to stay in as dull a heap as Buckingham Palace, and so she had had it reduced. It was a nice situation, however, and an enjoyable view, so she had taken up residence *en site*.

Johannes Cabal adjusted the stolen cap of his stolen uniform* and looked along the length of the Mall at the Red Queen's present address. Above the blackened ruin of Buckingham Palace floated an aeroship, held in position by tethering cables running from great blocks of concrete emplaced around the palace grounds. The aeroship itself hovered perhaps eighty feet from the ground, and no obvious way of gaining entrance was visible.

'Like a spider in her web,' said Horst—the profoundly unconvincing medical officer—as the party halted to take in this new development.

'Hardly,' said Zarenyia. 'She has style, though, this arch-enemy of yours.'

'It's sort of like the *Catullus*,' continued Horst. 'Her aeroyacht. Just much bigger.'

It certainly didn't look much like the blunt weapon represented by the vessel they had seen earlier. This ship had a distinct prow, and the lethal air of a raptor about it; a great steel hawk had settled upon the capital of its enemy and eaten—if not the heart—at least a kidney from the fresh corpse of a nation.

'How on earth are we supposed to get aboard that?' said Miss Barrow from beneath her ill-fitting cap.

The plan Cabal had evolved involved nothing more complicated than getting by a checkpoint or two using their stolen uniforms and documents, but the unusual stationing of the Queen's residence made that course seem naive and likely to end in a spectacular defeat that would doubtless take many of Orfilia Ninuka's troops with them, but not Her Imperial Majesty herself.

* The concerned reader is doubtless fretting over the fate of Lieutenant Skir and the surviving members of his *Gruppe*. Feel free to carry on doing so.

'I can get up one of those cables easily,' said Zarenyia. 'Easy-peasy. I'll need all my legs out, but spiders and threads tend to get on rather well.'

'And can you carry us all with you?'

Zarenyia thought about it. 'No,' she said. 'I suppose that's important, isn't it?'

'It is. Still, your ability to climb aboard quickly and, one hopes, unnoticed gives an extra sinew to any new plan we might hatch. As it is, I think we should turn off this road as soon as possible, and . . . damn it.'

An army truck was pulling away from the eastern end of Constitution Hill and clearly manoeuvring to enter the Mall. There was every likelihood that they would be questioned if spotted, and a fight within eyeshot of the hostile barracks situated in the surviving northern corner of the palace would probably not end well for them.

They were closer to the park side of the road, and Cabal led them into the trees without hesitation. The foliage closed behind them, and a few moments later the lorry rumbled by. It did not check its speed at all as it passed. It seemed that they had been unobserved.

Horst looked around the unnatural gloom of the park. 'Minty says the park is full of nasty things.'

'It certainly is now. I pity the zombie that crosses our path.'

Buoyed up by the bravado engendered by such—not unreasonable—thoughts, they pressed into the darkness.

Cabal's opinion of their chances of passing through doom-haunted St James's Park unmolested turned out to be entirely reasonable and not the piece of bravado it may have seemed. There were indeed creatures and entities lurking in the shadowed places that would have done a common or garden gang of humans to death or thereabouts in a twinkling. But the senses of the uncanny can perceive the uncanny, and—while the flickering spirit of a young girl might not have given them great pause—the presence of something cheerfully devilish, something engagingly vampirical, something stoically witchy, and something peevishly necromantic proposed more pain than gain for any predatory observers. Even the sole figure untouched by strange energies carried a bloody big shotgun. The dangerous forces within the park decided there were easier ways to amuse themselves than mixing it up with this particular covey, nor did any of the Mirkarvian troops stationed at the ruins of the palace notice five figures surreptitiously cross the bridge over the park lake.

They emerged from the park at the eastern end of Birdcage Walk and made their way towards the river. The Palace of Westminster was hardly in any better state than Buckingham Palace. The body of the structure looked to have been bombed, and the northern clock face of St Stephen's Tower was bisected at a jagged angle a few degrees from the vertical where the tower's top had been shorn away as if by a blow from a giant's axe. The remains of the great bell Big Ben lay in shattered curves at the tower's base in Bridge Street. Only the southern end of the complex where the House of Lords lay was relatively untouched. It seemed the bomb-aimer's mark had been the tower; this had been the surgical destruction of a symbol.

Horst looked to the south and frowned. 'There's something going on here.' His voice was uncharacteristically serious. 'Can't you feel it?'

Cabal went to stand by him, removing his cap as he did. He did not care to be in military uniform of any kind, but chafed at the sheer showiness of grey. He felt like a fashion model. 'What sort of thing do you mean?'

Minty drifted by. 'You don't wanna go in there. It's all full of leeches. That's where they 'ide. The soldiers don't know it, though, 'cos the leeches are really careful 'bout bein' seen around 'ere.' Having delivered this report, she drifted away again.

'How many?' called Horst after her.

'Loads,' she replied, enigmatic and unhelpful.

When Cabal was apprised of this intelligence, he grew thoughtful. 'We haven't run into any of the supernatural horrors spawned by Ninuka's assault with the exception of the girl—'

'Oi!' said an otherworldly voice possessed of outrage and poor diction.

'—but perhaps we should make the acquaintance of a few.'

Horst regarded him quizzically. 'I'm waiting for the wisdom of that idea to come to me, but it's taking its time. Why would we wish to pay a house call upon a bunch of vampires? They're not all as couth as me, you know.'

'I'm rather hoping that they're not.'

Leonie Barrow pushed her cap back on her head. She didn't like the uniform nearly as much as the adventuress outfit with which this reality had seen fit to gift her on leaving Sepulchre. 'Is this another of those ideas of yours that only seems to be insane, Cabal, but that when put into operation actually turns out to be suicidal?'

'You really *do* know my brother, don't you?' said Horst.

'Only too well, and I have the scars to prove it.'

'Oh?' said Horst with unfeigned interest. 'Where?'

Cabal grimaced. 'Largely psychological, Horst.' Ignoring his brother's expression of disappointment, Cabal turned and pointed at the dark building that had once housed the lords and bishops whose great wisdom and imagination had never been anything but an unparallelled boon to the empire. 'That hall is apparently home to a horde of bloodsucking leeches that have been forced to maintain a very low profile due to the proximity of the centre of Mirkarvian power in the British Isles, or whatever Ninuka calls them these days. I doubt they enjoy that. Let us test that theory.'

'And if you're wrong?' said Leonie.

'Then we fight our way out and think of something else, assuming the first part of that sentence comes to pass.' He nodded at her shotgun. 'I would have thought that would make you happy, Miss Barrow. You have barely had a chance to use that ostentatious weapon yet.'

'I am not fond of guns, Cabal.'

'As you say. May I ask a favour of you? I should like to examine one of those cartridges, please.'

As taken aback by his politeness as anything else, Leonie slid a black-and-blue-banded cartridge from her belt and handed it to him.

'Thank you,' he said as he studied it closely. His switchblade snapped open in his hand. Using a low nearby wall as a workbench,

Cabal quickly worked the cartridge's crimp open and spilt out the contents into his palm. He swirled the pellets around with the tip of his forefinger 'Interesting. Observe: silver, undoubtedly blessed; Lengian metal; grains of rock salt; lead. This cartridge is intended to wound anything, no matter how resistant the target usually is against mundane weapons. Here . . .' He dumped the shot and opened case into Leonie's cupped hands. 'Thank you.'

Leaving her to wonder what to do with the gutted cartridge, Cabal brushed off his hands and said, 'From what I have observed, and as I have previously stated, the greatest concentration of pure threat to be found in this blasted metropolis is us. Madam Zarenyia, what is your view of vampires?'

'Your brother's nice,' she said, offhandedly picking twigs from her bustle, 'but the rest can go hang. Awful boors. All fangs and tuppenny-ha'penny mesmerism. They're not even very good at it.'

'Excuse me.' Horst was somewhat offended despite the disclaimer. 'I happen to think I am rather good at it.'

'Sweetness.' She said it like a not entirely sympathetic aunt breaking the news about Father Christmas to a wide-eyed nephew. 'You aren't. No vampires are. You only think you are because humans have such silly, feeble brains. Really, anyone can mesmerise a human.' She looked around. 'Ah, me. I fear I have upset the whole company one way or another.'

'So you would feel no compunction in destroying vampires if they prove difficult?' Cabal dragged Zarenyia back to the topic at hand, a chore that accompanied most conversations with her.

'Oh, yes. Bit soulless and bland, but they pop nicely if you poke them hard enough.'

'Thank you. Miss Smith, have you any experience of them?'

'Not directly, but I know what they're vulnerable to.' She drew her wand and smirked a smirk sufficiently wicked to grace a witch of any persuasion.

'Excellent. Horst, how do—'

'Yes, yes, I'll cheerfully smash any vampire into pulp if it gets us out of here. Can we crack on, please, Johannes?'

Undaunted, Cabal addressed the group as a whole. 'Splendid. I think my faith in our general level of threat is well placed. Let us visit the lords in their den.' And he smiled a smile that echoed Miss Smith's in that it was entirely sincere and entirely forbidding.

After being largely destroyed by fire in 1834, the Palace of Westminster was rebuilt throughout the middle decades of the nineteenth century. The resulting building in the perpendicular Gothic revival style is notoriously labyrinthine, giving the impression at least internally of a building that evolved rather than being designed. It was to the advantage of the exploring party, again with Minty the helpful ghost leading the way, that unfriendly Mirkarvian bombs had simplified the matter of reaching the chamber of the House of Lords tremendously. Whereas it would once have involved a degree of aimless wandering of corridors, it was now merely a matter of climbing over a great mound of rubble that had once been the offices of the parliamentary leaders and the chief whips, over further rubble that had previously constituted the Moses Room used for Grand Committees, and finally through the inward slope of rubble that used to be the northern and western walls of the peers' lobby.

This brought them to the very door of the House of Lords. Pausing only to check firearms and wand, they entered.

Formerly, the chamber was of great pomp, some eighty feet long by forty-five wide, the five ranks of benches on either side covered in expensive red leather, the sovereign's throne down at the southern end—used only at the state opening of Parliament yet representing the symbolic presence of the monarch for the rest of the parliamentary year—the Woolsack before it upon which the Lord Chancellor sat, and the Judges' Woolsack before it.

Being pressed into service as a nest for a bunch of itinerant bloodsuckers had done nothing for its aesthetics at all, however. On every bench sprawled dishevelled bodies beneath windows inexpertly painted out in black. On the Woolsacks, even on the throne, were limp vampire bodies from every walk of life, creed, and colour. When Ninuka had unleashed her strange curse upon the capital, it had plainly been indiscriminate and random in its workings. Here vampire broker lay by vampire sweep, vampire debutante by vampire waitress.

'I once visited the Houses of Parliament with my dad,' whispered Leonie Barrow to Zarenyia. 'We stopped here and watched for a while in the public gallery'—she pointed—'just up there.'

'This must be quite a change, darling.'

'Actually, less than you might think.'

Cabal coughed, loudly and in a mannered fashion. A couple of vampires raised their heads and looked at him blearily. It was very disappointing of them. He had gone in there expecting at least a degree of trouble and instead found something like a club around dawn on New Year's Day.

Coughing made a couple of them blink, but it was all going far too slowly for Cabal. 'Ladies and gentlemen,' he bellowed, picked up a chunk of plaster debris, and threw it at the nearest vampire.

It struck the creature with a satisfying thud, and the predator of men and lord of nocturnal terrors so targeted said, 'Owwwww . . .' in a whiny nasal voice and rubbed his plaster-smirched hair slowly. 'What you go and do that for, eh? That hurt.'

'What a shower,' said Zarenyia. Her clear tones penetrated to every corner without necessitating the raising of her voice a single decibel. 'What an absolute shower.'

'You'd better be careful just what you say,' said a gent of the City, rising with some difficulty from a bench, and recovering a battered top hat from the floor. He donned it with great dignity. 'Do you realise where you are?'

'We were given to understand this was a hotbed of vampiric activity,' said Cabal. 'We were misled, and have discovered only a flophouse for the haemovorous community. It does one's heart good to see that the mere collapse of Britain has not resulted in any lowering of standards.'

'Who are you, and why do you come here, mortal?' The voice came from the throne. The City gent looked fearfully to it, and sat down quickly, his deference clear.

The man on the throne uncurled slowly and rose to stand before it. Possessed of height, looks, and an aristocratic air, he, at least, filled the role of vampire better than any of the other wretched creatures thereabouts. His suit was rumpled from lying in it, but was obviously his own tailored possession before the great collapse, and hung well upon him. He emanated an air of authority that flowed over the horde around him and brought them to heel.

Cabal did not give a tinker's cuss.

'You there,' he said, waving a finger in the vampire's direction. 'Are you the one to talk to? I am Johannes Cabal. Who are you?'

'Cabal. A foreign-sounding name belonging to a cove with a foreign-sounding accent. A Mirkarvian, perhaps?'

'I am neither Mirkarvian nor do I hold that state of thugs and blowhards in any degree of respect. My accent is Hessian, but I hold a British passport.'*

'Then you should bow before me. I am the King of England.' The vampire gave a mocking half bow.

'He's a bit irritating, isn't he?' said Zarenyia in a *sotto voce* whisper that would have filled the Colosseum. 'Can we kill him now?'

' 'E's a snotty geezer,' agreed Minty.

The vampire narrowed his eyes at them, but held his temper. 'I do not boast emptily. I am, as far as can be ascertained, the highest-ranking noble in line to the throne still extant. Therefore, I am the King.'

Cabal slowly drew in a deep breath, and then let it out just as slowly. He wanted no possibility that his exasperation was not painfully obvious to all present. 'I notice you say "extant". Most would say "alive". I think being alive is probably regarded as quite important to a smooth succession, wouldn't you?'

'These are strange times.'

'They are indeed. And about to get stranger. But you still have the advantage of me, sir. What is your name?'

---

* As indeed he did, and it was notable for being his only real passport, unlike the eight others that were all under assumed names and various nationalities.

'I am Lord Varney of Clemsy, baronet—'

Any further quoting of *Debrett's* was interrupted by an unseemly nasal outburst of mirth. Horst found himself the centre of attention. ' "Varney"? Really? And you're a vampire? Varney the Vampire? That is, without a breath of intentional irony, your name?'

'You find that amusing?' Varney clearly didn't.

'Well, no. Sorry. It's your name and I suppose . . .' Horst started laughing again. 'I'm sorry, truly. It's ridiculous. Your name, that is. Please don't tell me your first name's "Vincent" or I may split my sides. Actually, please tell me it is; I could do with a good laugh. It's been a bit grim recently.'

'My name is not—'

'It's a tonic to run into somebody as ridiculous as you. I should thank you.'

'My name is *not*—'

' "Vincent Varney the Vampire." That would be tremendous, wouldn't it? You could get top of the bill in the music hall with a name like that. What a turn.'

'*Enough!*' The murmurings that had been growing by the waking nest grew quiet. The noble chamber was silent, but for Horst giggling. 'I will not be mocked, certainly not by the likes of you.'

Horst's giggling slowed. 'The likes of me? What likes would that be, exactly?' Varney said nothing. Horst nodded. 'Let me ask you the same thing, but back to front. What exactly are the likes of you? Look at you, in your expensive yet tasteless suit, sprawling around on a stolen throne and proclaiming yourself the King of England. You want to know how big your realm is, Your Majesty?' Horst held out his arms to indicate the chamber. 'Here. This is it. All of it. Outside this room the country is held by a real monarch. The Red Queen herself, Orfilia Ninuka. A very nasty piece of work, but you cannot fault her for energy and will. She has taken Britain and, I would guess, several other places along the way westward from Mirkarvia. It's because of her that the Queen is dead, so long live King Vincent Varney the Vampire in his huge kingdom of one room.'

There was a tense silence. Every vampire in the place was awake and watching now. 'My name,' said Varney slowly and with the sort of exquisite menace that only comes with fangs, 'is not Vincent.'

Horst wasn't playing any more. Cabal watched him from the corner of his eye; sometimes his brother almost sank beneath the surface of the monster he had become. It was a rare enough event, but every time it happened the effect was more noticeable, the capacity for violence closer to the surface.

Horst spoke. 'I don't care. I really have no interest in your name any longer. You were vaguely funny for a while, but now I think I am done with you. We came here with the intention of rallying the vampires against the invaders. After all, you were all born Britons, were you not? A force of you sent in at the right time and the right place could do wonders in reversing this poor country's fortunes. But that would be an effort. So Lord Muck over there has you avoiding the Mirkarvians so as not to rock the boat. They know you're here; you do realise that? How could they not?' He reached inside his uniform tunic and pulled out a map. He held it up for the company to see. 'This is a military map. A *Mirkarvian* military map. Here on the House of Lords it says, *Leech Nest: Avoid. Low threat.*' He threw the map on the chamber floor. '"Low threat." There must be three or four dozen vampires in here, and they regard you as slightly less of a worry than a wasps' nest. Because they know, they know that you are terrified to touch them, so you feed off other survivors. As far as they're concerned, you're an actual asset to their invasion. Proud Britons all.' He took a step forwards, and spat on the floor. 'Your Majesty.'

Varney simply disappeared. There was a sense of speed that excelled the ability of the human eye to discern movement, a disturbance in the air and in the dust and debris on the chamber floor travelling in a straight line from where Varney had been towards where Horst stood.

A hair's breadth of a second after Varney vanished, so did Horst. Before merely human reactions were sufficient to draw breath in surprise at these phenomena, Varney reappeared in mid-air two-thirds of the way from the southern to the northern wall, tumbling helplessly and at high speed as if launched from a siege engine especially designed for propelling mid-ranking nobles in the least dignified way possible. He crashed into the Table of the House whereupon the clerks once did their work, and shattered it as it half turned over from the massive impact.

Varney climbed back to his feet from the hardwood ruin and stared with disbelief back down the chamber floor. There stood Horst with one foot out. He glanced down at his extended foot and shrugged. 'Childish, I know, but I just couldn't resist.'

'You . . . you're a vampire?' This obviously hadn't occurred to Varney before. He glanced over his shoulder at Cabal and the women, and they all smiled at him not at all reassuringly.

'I am,' said Horst, 'and I have been for some time now. Longer than you, certainly. Look, Vince, we came here to have you all join in the fight against the forces of a darkness much darker than anything you can wheel out, not to humiliate you. If that's what it takes, though, well . . .' He cocked his head to regard Varney. 'Actually, in your case, I'd regard that as a bonus.'

Varney became aware of how very bad an impact capable of smashing a heavy piece of furniture into quite small pieces could be for one's clothes. His suit was in sad array, and flesh showed at several points. His dignity was already undermined, his honour sullied, his authority questioned. His vision bloomed into red rage.

The charge did not surprise Horst, but the fury-inflamed energy and speed of it did, and he did not dance aside quite as easily as he had planned. In fact, he did not dance aside at all; Varney hit him hard in a bull's rush of a charge—head down and legs pumping—and blew the breath from him as he was carried halfway down the chamber. He was thrown clear at the end of it and would have been delighted to have been gifted with a second to recover. Varney was not of a generous mind that moment, however, and a scything blow speaking more a back alley than the boxing ring hit Horst hard in the right cheek. It lifted and threw him some ten or twelve feet, hitting the Woolsack backwards and rolling over it to land in an ungainly crouch. He looked up in time to see Varney already running for him, so he grabbed the nearest heavy object—the Woolsack itself—and threw it one-handed. It had barely left him before it struck Varney and so was still possessed of a good deal of kinetic energy, which it communicated to Varney by knocking him flat.

He rolled free before Horst could press his advantage and snatched up an impromptu weapon of his own. Horst frowned at him. 'Isn't that the Speaker's mace?'

It was, indeed, the mace of the Chamber, and another symbol of royal assent for the activities that were carried on therein. It was also a large, heavy piece of metal that, although heavily ornamented, was still at heart a weapon of the most brutal sort.

'You don't think it's a bit, y'know, uncouth to run around using the Speaker's mace as . . . well, a mace, now I stop to think of it. Still . . . tradition and all that. You wouldn't . . .'

Varney would, and did. He hissed in a manner so feral it would surely have disappointed his old house master, and leapt at Horst, swinging the mace in a powerful arc. Horst had better things to do than stand around waiting for it; he turned, ran at the front row of benches, jumped at them, landed on the near edge with his leading foot, twisted to face Varney once more, and extended that leading leg hard. He sailed over Varney's head in a parabola so stylish one would have thought he'd been practising such a move, rather than the reality of vampiric reactions, strength, and reading far too many swashbuckling romances.

Varney had over-extended himself grievously in the mace swing, and even his great strength was subject to the laws of physics, thus he could only watch his prey somersault with maddening ease over him if he wanted to keep the mace. This he was keen to do; the mace was still a deadly weapon for all its political symbolism, and a thoroughly pounded vampire is as unhappy a creature as a thoroughly pounded human.

Maintaining possession of it therefore came with the downside of the infuriating German vampire in the stolen Mirkarvian medical officer's uniform flipping insouciantly over Varney's head, having the temerity to wink at him as he did so, and then finally adding injury to insult by punching him with sickening force as he did so.

The blow would have broken a mortal man's neck as certainly as hitting him in the face with a girder. Varney's head snapped around, and he forgot all about Horst Cabal for a moment as he blinked away stars and comets. Horst came to rest on the western side of the floor, and braced to attack once more.

The City gent leapt to his feet and then dithered in a posture of possible attack, caught on the cusp of wanting to help Varney and not wishing to do it alone. He vacillated heroically there, looking significantly at his neighbours. With evident reluctance, the chamber began to rise.

As has been intimated earlier, the sound of a pump-action shotgun being—as the Americans put it—'racked', which is to say the action being pumped to place a shell in the chamber and simultaneously cocked, is distinctive and carries an ineffable menace even to those who have never heard it before. Indeed, some suggest that there is such inherent threat in the sound that it alone may prevent a confrontation before it even begins. It certainly provided a pause for thought amidst the vampiric spectators within the House of Lords.

As one, they looked to the source of the sound and discovered Leonie Barrow thumbing a fresh cartridge into the space opened up in her gun's tube magazine by the action of chambering its predecessor.

'These cartridges contain lead, silver, salt, Lengian metal, and are blessed. I'm sure there's something in there that will sting.'

The gent sneered a little uncertainly. 'You would have no chance to reload. We would tear you to pieces before you could.'

'Ah, the old misapprehension.' Cabal drew two pistols, the Webley in his right hand, the Senzan semi-automatic in his left. 'It is not about destroying all of you, just some. The point, of course, being, who wishes to try their luck first? First in, first blown to ashes.' He looked at the vampires. 'No? Nobody wishes to be first?'

'Only two of you are armed.'

'Three.' Miss Smith drew her wand and wagged it at the City gent. Disconcertingly, its tip seemed to leave scratches in the reality of that world that re-formed a moment after the wand had passed; the overall effect was of a malign sparkler.

The attention of the vampires shifted to Zarenyia at the back of the group. 'Me? Oh, I don't have any guns or wands or anything like that, I'm afraid, darlings.' In a sudden explosion of movement and impossible dimensions, she grew to her full diabolical proportions, her spider legs arched, and, with a *snik!* of moving plates, the blades appeared along her legs. 'Despite which, I am quite confident that I will make little puddles of jam out of the majority of you, should you wish to test me.'

Cabal nodded to the fight. 'If any of you intervene against my brother, we shall intervene against you.'

The City gent seemed almost to deflate, whatever loyalty he felt to Varney seeping out of him like sour air. He sat down.

Varney and Horst, weapons temporarily forgotten, were wrestling in the middle of the floor. Both stood with mouths agape and fangs bared, each with hands jammed under his opponent's chin to keep those fangs away. Horst changed tactics first, apparently wilting and half dragging Varney down with him, but then immediately changing his grip, seizing Varney by the belt and waistcoat, heaving him up over his head, and then throwing him towards the northern end where Cabal and the others waited.

Varney came to earth amidst the ruins of the Table of the House. It was nowhere near as hard a collision as the previous time, however, and he landed well.

As he rose, Cabal standing behind him pursed his lips, considered the pragmatic approach to the situation, and began to raise his revolver. A hand caught his and he found Leonie Barrow looking him in the eye and shaking her head very seriously.

'No. This has to be won fair and square or they won't follow us. No interventions *means* no interventions.'

Cabal breathed in heavily through his nostrils, but lowered his gun hand on the exhalation. 'You are correct, Miss Barrow. If the Varney creature kills Horst, however, I shall destroy him regardless of consequence. He is my brother, after all.'

Leonie fought down an ill-mannered and undiplomatic smirk; no matter how amusing or even—very occasionally—touching she found Cabal's clumsy forays into a meadow of emotion he had once steadfastly denied, this was a serious business, and she had no desire to diminish it. Well, perhaps a small desire. 'I didn't know you cared,' she allowed herself.

Cabal watched the fight rage around the chamber for a few seconds. 'Neither did I.'

Any faint pretences towards civilised conduct had long since been lost in the duel. Both combatants had reserves that they could burn at will, and part of the struggle that was not obvious to the Cabal party was victory might well hinge on whoever could husband his resources most successfully. This looked likely to be Horst; Varney was the newer vampire and had faced few challenges during his existence in that unhallowed state. He lacked experience, was led by his dignity and pride, which drew him into anger, and so to overreaching himself.

Which wasn't to say he couldn't provide surprises. The centre of the chamber was now scattered with overturned chairs, disembowelled Woolsacks, and the remains of the great Table of the House, which was looking less like it had ever been a table every time one or other of the fighters was thrown into or through it. It was in this shattered ruin that Varney made his move.

The coup began innocently enough, with Varney pulled from the ground by his ankle, swung around in several energetic circles much as a Scotsman throwing the hammer at the Highland Games, to be released at the moment of greatest impetus to arc gracelessly some twenty feet into the sad remnants of the great table. Horst took a deep breath, more from exasperation than necessity, and ran over to continue the debate there. As he arrived, however, matters took a new complexion. Varney, burning the last of his already scant reserves, emerged from the debris like a rocket with a strong sense of entitlement, straight at Horst. In his right hand he carried a sharp length of broken wood, perhaps eighteen inches in length. With a cry of anticipation, the vampires arose, not one of them so ignorant of their new unlives that they could not recognise an extemporised stake when they saw it.

Varney struck hard at Horst's chest as he ran headlong onto the weapon. Horst saw it too late to evade bodily, but early enough to throw up his left arm to ward it off. The timing was off, the execution sloppy, but the end effect successful, albeit at the cost of a stake thrust through his forearm.

Horst pulled away from Varney, who held on hard to the stake and pulled it from the great wound it had caused. Horst looked with utter horror at the gaping wound through four layers of cloth, his arm, and the radius. He screamed. 'This jacket is *borrowed*!'

Varney smiled, offered him the address of his tailor, and struck again. This time, however, Horst was waiting. During the momentary break for smirking and the declamation of *bon mots*, he had burnt some of his own reserves, which were sadly depleted but still in much better supply than Varney's. When Varney belatedly pressed his attack, Horst was ready.

As the stake lanced towards his deliberately unguarded heart, Horst jerked up his damaged forearm to strike the underside of Varney's hand. Deflected upwards, Varney's wrist slapped into the palm of Horst's right hand where it was grabbed and held tightly.

Horst was just debating whether to break Varney's arm or merely dislocate it when a small voice said in his mind, *Let me handle this*. It was a small voice he had not heard for some weeks, but he had not been placed under these sorts of pressures for some weeks, either. It was a small voice with which he had thought he had made his peace. He realised that he had managed no such thing. It had simply lain in abeyance, waiting. It was the voice of the monster he might become, if he permitted it. If he was weak. If he allowed it.

When he wrenched Varney's arm down, so placing the point of the stake over Varney's own heart, it was to the horror of them both. Horst felt the muscles move in his right arm, but he had no control over them. Something hot and atavistic flowed in the thin vampiric blood there, something that was not him. Almost faster than even his own accelerated senses could perceive, he released Varney's arm—poor, stupid, sluggish Varney—drew back his right arm, his hand opening, and then struck forwards with sickening, superhuman force, the palm striking the dull end of the stake. It shot forwards like the action of a pneumatic poleaxe, and like a well-applied pole-axe, it killed well-nigh instantly.

Varney's eyes widened. He gasped. He crumbled away into dust and beetles that skittered away into the crevices of the hall. The stake tumbled to the floor, dusted with remnants of aristocrat as light as talcum.

There, said the little voice. *All done.* Horst sobbed and stepped away.

Once, not so very long ago, Johannes Cabal would have congratulated his brother on an elegant and surgical removal of the obstructive Lord Varney, and moved on to the next item on the agenda. This was not quite the same Johannes Cabal, though. He walked to his brother's side, placed a gentle arm on his shoulder, and said, 'Come away, Horst. There is little point in dwelling upon it.'

'I didn't mean to do it.' Even by vampire standards, Horst was pale. 'I don't know how that happened.'

'He came at you with intent to kill. You had no choice.'

Horst looked at him sharply. 'I *always* have a choice.'

'I suspect this isn't the time to go into the logic of the event, but I'm afraid I must. There was clearly no alternative. My Lord Varney's personality was very easy to read; even if you had defeated him and shown him mercy, he would never have accepted losing his position of authority. He would have been a thorn in our side at every turn. It would not have surprised me in the slightest if he had run off to Ninuka to warn her of our presence and intentions. He would have preferred to work for the woman who crushed his country, such was his vanity, his pride. I repeat—you had no choice.'

The anger faded from Horst's eyes. 'You're not helping, you know.'

Cabal lowered his voice a little, but in the quietness wherein all listened, all heard. 'I know what you're battling with, Horst. I know it frightens you. If I succeed'—he looked at Miss Barrow, Miss Smith, Madam Zarenyia—'if we succeed, I have great hopes it is a burden that may be lifted from you. The prize is inestimable, but these trials placed before it are unavoidable. I am sorry.'

'At least you didn't try to tell me that he was never a real person, so I shouldn't care.'

Cabal shrugged. 'These splinters are self-contained, and we are merely contingent upon them. All is as if it were always so. I do not understand the mechanism; perhaps they truly were always so and are sifted to find one that fits our requirements. If the trial of the Five Ways really was the invention of the first Satan, then anything is possible. He was a creature of quite literally unimaginable power. Anything is possible.'

Cabal stepped away from Horst and addressed the chamber. 'Varney is dead. Destroyed, and good riddance. You have a simple choice: either accept our leadership and stand once more for your country and principles, or regretfully we shall have to destroy you all. I believe there are rules of fealty that run through your . . . subspecies. Do you pledge loyalty to us, or will there have to be more violence here?'

The City gent rose to his feet. He seemed calmer and more reassured now that the surprise of the battle was over. 'We are patriots here, I think, and yes, we are compelled by laws of fealty that draws us by the sinew, even against the will. I believe I speak for us all, then, when I say, we shall *not* follow you, sir.'

Cabal's shoulders drooped. 'After all this and we have to have another fight? This is very inconvenient.'

'You will permit me to finish, sir. We shall not follow you, but *you*'—and here he pointed at Horst—'we shall follow to the ends of this miserable, blighted earth. We are at your disposal, my Lord Horst, I think you said your name is?'

'Lord?' Horst put up his hands and shook his head with evident dismay. 'No, no, no. I am no lord.'

'You are, sir. You are Lord of the Dead, and your word is our law.'

Horst looked around as the vampires rose to pay obeisance to him. He looked aghast. 'The Lord of the Dead?' He looked at Cabal. 'That was what Ninuka wanted me to be. Her general of the undead. I can't, Johannes. I cannot.'

'You must. This is a game, and those are the rules. We have each been tested and awarded laurels that we have or have not enjoyed. Now it is your turn.'

'*Great Detective*,' said Leonie Barrow. It sounded like a moan. 'Oh, I've been an idiot. Of course. Now it makes sense. I thought they were very swift to hand out the superlatives.'

'My own future is misted, and I do not think I exactly fitted the bill in the great necropolis.' Cabal took his brother by the arm and led him back to the group. 'I may not have triumphed precisely, but I finished far from being a failure, and that apparently sufficed. Besides, I think that experience was telling me something else.'

'But, Johannes, sweetness,' Zarenyia was considering his words, 'I was offered a principality of Hell as my very own, and I turned it down.'

'Surely you see that this was the test? Giving in to temptation is easy. Resisting it for the sake of others, there lies the triumph.'

'And I became the Witch Queen,' said Miss Smith. She shook her head. 'But that was almost by accident. How is that a trial?'

Cabal lowered his head and was silent for a long moment. When presently he raised it again, his expression was somber and perhaps even sad. 'Miss Smith. You are not part of this undertaking. I am sorry, but the trials were never meant for you.'

She flinched as if he had spat in her face. 'What? But this Five Ways thing . . . there are five of us. What are you talking about? Of course I'm part of it.'

'You were drawn into it by forces of association, specifically your association with me. Your necropolis in the Dreamlands is part of my life and experiences now, but—unusually—one that comes with an occupant. Your presence in the unfolding events is the merest accident.'

'But there are *five* of us.'

'There are, but you are not the fifth point of the pentagram of forces that circle around the prize. She lies less than a mile away, over the ruin of Buckingham Palace.'

Cabal looked at his comrades. 'We find ourselves drawn into a trap. Ninuka meant for me to find *The One True Account of Presbyter Johannes by His Own Hand*. Ever was she the student of human nature. Even mine; a thought that distresses me in a variety of ways.'

'She read you like a book, Cabal.'

'I believe I intimated as much just this moment, Miss Barrow.'

'Played you for a fool.'

Cabal's face darkened, but it was no more than the truth. 'We have unwittingly performed a great and dangerous ritual for her, and now she enters it at the end with overwhelming forces at her command with the intention of claiming the prize for herself.'

'Overwhelming, you say?' Zarenyia gave an insouciant toss of her hair.

'Superior, then—at least numerically. Now, however, we have shocking troops.' He gestured at the vampires. 'My mistake. *Shock* troops.' He studied Horst's stolen uniform, now sadly the worse for wear thanks to repeated journeys through furniture. 'We shall have to find you something more fitting for the coming battle. A general's uniform, perhaps. Or perhaps there's still something ermine-trimmed in the cloakroom here suitable for a lord.'

'Do shut up, Johannes.'

'To think that we would one day have a peer in the family. I am quite filled with emotion.'

And so, bickering, they settled down to plan the assault on the floating palace of the Red Queen, Orfilia Ninuka.

The Fifth Way:
RUBRUM IMPERATRIX

General Klaus Fischer did not enjoy the daily briefings he was obliged to supply Her Majesty. She rarely gave the slightest impression that she was listening; more than once she had been reading while he supplied the gloss overviews of the vast number of reports that were submitted, analysed, and rendered from mere information into valuable intelligence. He would say that he was wasting his time for the vanity of a woman who liked to pretend that she maintained a finger upon the pulse of the incorporation of the British Isles. (It was always an 'incorporation', according to all documentation and newspapers, never something as crude and uncalled for as an 'invasion'. After all, Britain no longer had a functional government, or anything approaching one. It was now green and pleasant real estate, available for whosoever had the means to take it.) He would say that, but for her unnerving ability to look up from her book and ask a deep question based on the meanings between the lines, or to demand that new data be ascertained and brought to her as soon as was humanly possible.

The general was a lifelong warrior and had been the right hand of Count Marechal, the Queen's late and—by her at any rate—lamented father. Marechal had been an ambitious man, and his plans to pincer Senza, the hated northern neighbour of Mirkarvia, with an unexpected airborne assault from the loathsome but useful allied state of Katamenia might well have worked. Fischer had been left to damp down the remains of one of Mirkarvia's occasional little outbreaks of civil disobedience while Marechal travelled to Katamenia to make sure the assault was properly prepared.

The plan never reached fruition, and Marechal returned as an urn full of ashes in the arms of what had turned out to be the count's greatest creation—his daughter. General Fischer did not enjoy the briefings because he, a broad-shouldered man standing six feet and two inches in his stockinged feet, was afraid of Orfilia Ninuka.

She had once merely been wilful, but now she was a monster. Nobody called her mad, for she was possessed of vanity and vengefulness. Nobody called her mad, for she maintained a diffuse and effective secret police that, with the abetment of eavesdroppers, informants, and even the occasional loyal citizen, seemed to know every unguarded word. Nobody called her mad but for she herself, and surely a touchstone for true insanity was that the lunatic does not realise his or her state?

Nobody called her mad, for was she not the Red Queen who dealt in blood and abomination? Did she not hold a small army of Katamenian cut-throats in her thrall, who would die for her as eagerly as they would kill? Was she not a necromantrix, so that even death was no release for those who died in her prisons and interrogation cells and the awful glass oubliettes in which humans were observed in their faltering mortalities even as an insect may be left to die in a test tube?

With the fall of Senza, the Mirkarvian military gained easy access to Western Europe in general and the Mediterranean in particular. The fleet of warships and troopships culled from the vanquished surface navies of Senza and Poloruss sailed out towards the Atlantic. Commentators and terribly clever civil servants concluded that this was merely the new regime showing off. After all, with no clear lines of logistics it seemed incredible that there might be a brutally military point to all this. As is so often the case with commentators and terribly clever civil servants, they had failed to understand with exactly whom they were dealing.

The surface ships, after all, were not the only examples of useful materiel that had fallen into Mirkarvian hands. Poloruss's aerofleet was justly famous. Indeed, a new flagship was midway through being fitted out prior to its commissioning voyage, when disaster struck the country. Whatever it was going to be called hardly mattered to anyone except military historians; what it was called now and its new function were far more important: the *Rubrum Imperatrix*, personal ship and mobile palace for the Red Queen herself.

From this flying aerie, Queen Orfilia had headed a shadowy fleet over misty northern climes and through clouded skies, unseen and unsuspected. No storms or bad weather troubled the fleet, nor did the cloud ever break to betray it to ground-based observers. Meteorologists would regard this as an unusual combination, but perhaps Her Majesty simply had the luck of the Devil on her side.

In any case, she and her ships arrived over the grey skies of Britain just as the surface fleet passed through the Strait of Gibraltar and, under the curious eyes of the Spanish and then the Portuguese, turned to the north.

By the time the invasion fleet arrived at the English south coast, the war—an inaccurate term, but 'slaughter' seems overly emotive—was already over. Ninuka had rained hell and damnation down upon London, cursing the metropolis using magics only whispered of since the days of the Assyrians, who had wisely never used them.

The *Rubrum Imperatrix* remained in London while the rest of the fleet dispersed to bring havoc down upon a country abruptly decapitated. Scattered battles and last-ditch defensive engagements still raged, but it was only a matter of time. Orfilia Ninuka sat in her study and gave orders as easily as she might once have offered chitchat at a *soirée*. She didn't seem very much like the sort of person who might have *soireés* any more.

Fischer watched in silence as Ninuka now took up the gloss of incoming reports and read down the list, wafting herself slowly with a Chinese fan in her off hand. She paced languidly about her study-cum–throne room, once the intended day office of a flag admiral. She walked by the two great panes of thick glass joined at the prow line by a supporting girder. She would insist on doing this, parading around where anyone might see her. The glass would stop anything short of a close range shot from an elephant rifle, but such weapons and those with the skill and will to use them might very well be out there in this wounded city caught in a never-ending cycle of dusk, night, dawn, and then dusk again.

'I see nothing of London itself here, General.' Ninuka spoke suddenly, breaking him from his reverie. 'Is there no new intelligence? No news?'

The general thought for a moment before speaking. 'Your Majesty, may I be so impertinent as to ask why you remain so interested in this place? It may have been interesting enough before our arrival, but now it feels like taking residence in the rotting skull of a dead empire. The rest of the country is not yet pacified, whereas London is, if anything, overly so.' He saw the tightening of her jaw that had led directly to the deaths of good men before his very eyes and hastened to explain himself. 'I do not criticise, ma'am. I only seek to clarify my understanding of your strategy.'

'My strategy.' The idea seemed to amuse her. 'Ah, General, if I told you exactly the point of all this you would not give it a moment's credence. Worse, you would think me mad even if you were sensible enough to keep that thought to yourself. I will tell you this much; the pivotal act that this entire invasion was predicated upon shall occur in this city, and it will happen soon. You are a career soldier, Klaus. I know you have been wondering what possible goal can there be in bringing down an imperial power that has never shown our country anything but polite disinterest, a country that is so far from the fatherland that holding the territory would be next to impossible, especially with the army already stretched in our new Senzan and Polorussian conquests. Well, it was never about gaining territory. The Irish and French can fight over it when we leave. Oh, yes.' She smiled at the general's inability to hide his surprise. 'We are not staying longer than necessary. If you must have political reasons for us being here, perhaps it was to create instability in the perceived world order from which we may profit, or perhaps it was simply to demonstrate the invincibility of our forces and our fearlessness to engage. Perhaps it is all about fear.'

The smile faded. She looked out into the lacerated corpse of dead London. 'Tell yourself what you like. It is my will that we are here.' She dropped the sheaf of unpinned reports to the floor, where they scattered. Doing his best to maintain some dignity, General Fischer gathered them up. 'Now tell *me*, what has happened in London in the last twenty-four hours?'

'I shall find out immediately.' He strode to the pearl-handled electrical voice pipe and cranked the handle. 'This is General Fischer. Bring me all patrol and intelligence reports submitted for the London area—'

'Central London. I am only interested in central London.'

'Correction, specifically central London in the last twenty-four hours. Deliver them to the queen's study immediately. No, not 'in an hour', *now*, damn you, or do you want to explain your testudinal slowness to Her Majesty yourself? I thought not. Get on with it!'

The reports arrived hastily crammed into a file box twenty minutes later in the hands of a pale and sweating adjutant who dared not look at Ninuka as he handed it over to Fischer. For her part, she amused herself by crossing her arms and staring at the young officer until he backed out of her presence, bowing and saluting and ultimately falling over when he was exiting the room.

She laughed at that, and there was a startling innocence that startled the general. Then it was gone, and she was holding out her hand. 'First report.'

He followed her around the room as she studied report after report, rarely doing more than briefly scanning the first page before dropping it to the floor and holding out her hand for the next. Back and forth they promenaded, a thickening spillage of intelligence in their wake. Then she stopped so abruptly that he almost walked into her.

'What's this?'

He took it from her and quickly read it. 'The National Gallery. Foot patrol discovered six male corpses, drained of bodily fluids . . . Surely *nosferatu*, Majesty?'

'Read on.'

He did so. 'Webs? Some sort of giant spider? I can only guess it is one of your . . . one of the abominations the curse visited upon the city.'

'No, General. I am very aware of what my curse visited upon London, and giant spiders were not invited.' She put the report on her desk, an impressive white structure trimmed with gold, and yet largely constructed from board and aluminium to keep its weight down, presenting an air of *faux* solidity due to a thick desktop and bolts holding it to the deck. 'The next report now.' He handed it over and they continued their short, repetitive walk punctuated by littering.

Fischer was not surprised by her second halt as they were at the bottom of the box. All that remained was a short handwritten memo apologising to Her Gracious Imperial Majesty, but a patrol shadowing one of the aeroship sweeps was overdue and therefore its report was not available. Her eyes narrowed, and she looked off to one side. 'They were supposed to be cleaning up after the MIAS *Lammasu*. They last exchanged signals'—she went to the window and pointed—'just down there. I saw the *Lammasu* open fire just beyond the perimeter. But that was hours ago.' She looked into the darkness again. Fischer could see little more than their own reflections in the glass, but Queen Orfilia's gaze seemed to drive out deep into the city's decaying heart. Perhaps it was. 'Where are you?' Fischer thought she was talking to him for a moment, but she was only thinking out loud. But those thoughts confused him. 'Why are you taking so long? Hardly the first time you barged into my home.' She noticed the general watching her in the glass and smiled at him. 'I am expecting visitors, General. Four of them. They will attempt entry to this vessel, and they may even succeed. Do not underestimate the ingenuity of their leader.'

'I will double the guard and put them on a high state of alert immediately, Your Majesty!'

'No, you will not. I want them alive—ideally—but I want them in my grasp. Particularly their leader; a pale man with blond hair who habitually wears black. Oh, and he will almost certainly have a leech with him, a rather handsome man with light brown hair. You may have to destroy him; equip the men accordingly. As for the other two, I cannot guess. They are of lesser importance in any case.'

'How do you—' began Fischer, but he saw her smile fade instantly and the question faltered to an untidy death in his throat. 'Yes, Your Majesty. It will be done.'

He hurried from her presence, propelled by urgency and relief at being dismissed.

She hardly cared. She placed a hand on the glass and looked out once more, seeing the corpses, the chaos, and the gutted city for what they were—stage props for a final confrontation. She would keep Johannes Cabal alive only as long as she was sure that she might need him. Once that time was gone, she would be happy to kill him herself. Her father's pistol was in the drawer of her desk, awaiting the moment of revenge.

She saw the reflection of her father's funerary urn in its place in a case mounted safely upon the wall where she could see it as she worked. 'Good girl.' She could hear his voice in her imagination, or perhaps the urn spoke. It hardly mattered which.

Cabal was out there. Soon he would be hers, the game would be over, and she would have the prize. She whispered to the night, 'My will be done.'

'Isn't this the same plan as we had before?' Zarenyia was down to two legs again and resenting the loss, temporary though it was.

'Not quite.' The remnants of the Mirkarvian patrol were now represented by only the lieutenant and a single private who walked with a slight hunch in an attempt to hide his possession of a bust. The borrowed medical officer's uniform was in too poor a state to go without drawing attention long before the plan required it, so Horst had returned for his own clothes, and seemed the happier for it. He was not with their little pretence of two soldiers bringing in a brace of prisoners. Instead he was off trying his best to be a general of the undead and Lord of the Dead without bursting into either tears or laughter. 'Now,' said Johannes Cabal, 'we have a reserve force.'

'Doesn't that make us the main force?' Miss Smith had cheered up a little on finding an umbrella shop that she had looted of a nicer black lace parasol than its predecessor, which was showing signs of combat fatigue. 'Johannes, there are four of us. What sort of main force consists of four people, three women and a man. Well, two women, something fairly like a woman, and a man?'

'Are you being cheeky, darling?' Zarenyia smiled delightedly at Miss Smith. 'I love it when people are cheeky with me. Sometimes I don't even kill them for it. Usually, but not always.'

'Dibs, madam,' said Cabal, trying to bring the ribaldry under control before things became any stranger than they already were. 'You gave dibs to ensure the safety of the whole party.'

'Technically, not for Smithy here,' Zarenyia pointed out, 'but don't worry. I was just teasing.' She leaned her head towards Miss Smith and whispered, 'I'm sure you love being teased, don't you?'

Miss Smith looked straight ahead and did so with a notably fixed expression. 'I'm not even sure why I'm here any more. If Ninuka really is the fifth part of this . . . what would you call it? A ritual? Then what business is it of mine? I'm risking my life for nothing here.'

'Your situation is complicated, I admit,' said Cabal, 'but if you require some degree of self-interest, then your isolation from the Dreamlands is surely sufficient. If you stay with us, things may improve for you. If you do not, they will surely deteriorate.'

'Thanks, Cabal. Knew I could depend on you to bolster morale and supply pep. You've really put a new spring in my step.'

Her step remained resolutely unspringy.

They were closing on a checkpoint set up some hundred yards from the end of the Mall where it bifurcated into Constitution Hill and Spur Road when a complication arose. Horst suddenly halted as if hearing a loud sound, looked over to his right, and said in horror, 'Minty!'

'What?' Cabal looked to the space where he assumed the child to be. 'What's amiss?'

'She's burning!'

And, to those that could see her, she was indeed aflame. She struggled back, vaporous wisps of cold blue fire wrapping around her. To those who could hear her, she was screaming, high-pitched and terrified.

'It 'urts! It 'urts!' She was sobbing. When all sensation has been annulled and is merely a memory, it seemed unusually cruel that its return should be of such a violent flavour.

Horst danced around in an agony of his own, seeing her, hearing her, yet unable to help directly. 'Get on the floor! Roll around! Put it out!'

She tried, but the flame would not be diminished by such a mundane trick. She rolled hopelessly around, her screams shrill and unending, but the immolation continued regardless.

Until the flames suddenly winked out.

Cabal looked at Horst's astonished expression, the moment marked by the cessation of his dance of anxiety. 'What has happened? Is the girl . . . ?' He almost said 'dead', but hesitated for reasons of accuracy as much as tact.

'They went out,' said Horst. 'They just . . . went out.'

Minty climbed back to her feet and examined her hands that, moments before, had been burning like dry sticks. To her obvious confusion, they were unmarked. 'I was all on fire, I was,' she said. 'All alight like a Chrissmus tree.'

'She's unharmed, Johannes. What happened?'

Cabal thought about it for a moment, and then said, 'Ask her to walk towards the palace slowly, with one hand extended. If anything happens, she should step back immediately.'

Horst turned to relay the command, but Minty was already doing it, shying away from her own pointing index finger as if it was made of dynamite. That was perhaps not such a bad simile, as—a few cautious palaceward shuffles later—it exploded.

'Ahhhhhhhhhh!' screamed Minty, with permissible dismay. She fell backwards, and the finger was instantly extinguished and rendered unmarked. This Horst dutifully relayed to Cabal.

'The area is warded,' he replied. 'Difficult to extend against the corporeal, but against an ethereal entity such as a ghost, easy enough to cover a substantial area if you have the resources.'

'Ninuka fears ghosts?' said Leonie. 'But why?'

'Not ghosts. Miss Minty's discomfort is a corollary effect. The warding is doubtless to prevent certain arcane forms of surveillance, scrying and the like.'

'She doesn't want to be spied upon?'

'Yes. But, in all modesty, the number of persons within the ruins of London that might be expected to carry out such a practise would reasonably be considered as none. Not a one.'

'This is for you?'

'For *us*. Yes.'

They moved on shortly afterwards, leaving Minty in their wake. Horst looked back more than once, seeing her standing alone at the edge of the warded area, daring to come no closer, yet loath to walk away. She started to once, but dithered and came back. She watched them until they were lost from sight.

They approached the checkpoint. 'Let me do the talking,' said Cabal, as if anyone else was keen to. 'I can do a passable Mirkarvian accent.'

'I can do a perfect one,' said Zarenyia, 'but nobody let me dress up as a soldier.'

'You would call the sentry a "poppet", and that would be the end of the subterfuge.'

'True, I probably would, but that might not be such a disaster as you suppose. That's the thing with terribly manly men, darling: I bet they get up to all sorts of shenanigans after lights out in the barracks. Just imagine.'

'I would rather not.'

'Oh, go on.' After a moment she added absently, off in a fancy of her own, 'Baby oil . . .'

They reached the checkpoint, and it took a herculean effort by Cabal to address the sergeant there as 'Sergeant' and not 'poppet'. He had been preparing a detailed explanation of why he was reporting to the wrong outpost, why his patrol was so sadly depleted, and how he had come into possession of civilian prisoners, but the sergeant was uninterested, simply pointing the way to the remains of Buckingham Palace's northern corner for full debriefing. Thus, relieved at getting past the first trial of what threatened to be quite a gauntlet of them, yet dismayed that his rehearsed answers would go unheard, at least for the moment, they moved on.

'We're in trouble,' muttered Leonie Barrow.

'We're in the ruins of a monster-haunted London occupied by Mirkarvian troops. You've only just noticed that means trouble?' said Cabal.

'Guard duty is for privates. One of the privileges of being a non-commissioned officer is delegating jobs like that to squaddies. I come from a family with a lot of police and a lot of armed services people in it. Believe me, I know.'

'So why was a sergeant in sole command of a checkpoint?' said Miss Smith.

'Exactly. Unless the job was not just to be watching it, but watching for who comes through it and not making a mess of it when somebody specific approaches. Is there any way Ninuka might be expecting us, Cabal?'

'Of course she's expecting us. I confess I was not expecting her attentiveness to be quite so prescient. You are right, Miss Barrow. We are probably detected.'

'Phew!' Zarenyia sighed a melodramatic sigh of relief. 'Oh, good.

I do so hate all this shilly-shallying. May I get all leggy and start killing people now?'

'You may not, madam, but that time is drawing close.'

She nodded sagely. 'Deferred gratification. I've heard about that. So this is what it feels like. Hmmmm.' She considered this new sensation. 'It's slightly irritating.'

They continued in silence for a few seconds more before she added the observation, 'Oh, and by the bye, there are gentlemen with guns very quietly forming a cordon around us. I do believe they think they're trapping us.'

Cabal took in their immediate surroundings; there was no cover to speak of, which was of course the intention of their imminent ambushers. 'The time for you to produce six more legs and proceed to spread dismay amongst our enemies is almost upon us, Madam Zarenyia. Bear in mind that your transformation will have a profound effect upon their morale—'

'Makes a change from affecting morals . . .'

'—so wait for the apposite moment. And, here we go . . .'

A major was walking out from the barracks, a squad of four men, rifles unslung, at his back. He himself had his pistol drawn and ready. 'Halt there! You, in the uniform. Remove your cap.'

'Nobody ever says "please",' said Cabal, which was hypocritical of him. He did, however, remove his cap.

The officer regarded Cabal's exposed hair for a long moment as if reading the future in it. Finally, he said, 'You are Johannes Cabal?'

'I am, yes. How do you do?' He tossed the cap to the side, the time for dissimulation plainly passed.

The officer was looking at the rest of the party. 'We were told there would be another man with you.' He nodded at Miss Barrow. 'Is that him? What is funny?' For Zarenyia could not repress a small laugh.

'Hardly, darling,' she said, and Cabal was irked to note her Mirkarvian accent really was perfect. Then in equally perfect English, she said, 'Show him, Leonie.'

'I can speak Mirkarvian, you know,' she said, but took off her own cap and shook her hair loose.

'I don't doubt it. You look like you'd be terribly clever with your tongue.'

'Just don't react,' suggested Miss Smith to Leonie. 'She stops doing that if she can't get a reaction.'

'You are no doubt thinking of my brother,' said Cabal to the officer. 'Regretfully, he is not with us.' This was technically true. 'No doubt that intelligence was handed down from Orfilia Ninuka herself, and now you are in the awkward position of knowing that she is fallible. I wouldn't mention that to her, if I were you.'

The major was hardly listening. He had visibly relaxed at Cabal's truthful yet misleading statement about Horst and was now looking at the women with curiosity. 'So . . . none of you are vampires.'

'Bloodsuckers?' said Zarenyia. 'No, no, no. I can assure you that none of us feed on blood.' This, again, was technically true, although it did not exactly answer the question, for there are vampires, and there are vampires.

His briefing being incomplete, the major failed to ask about any potential witches or devils amongst their number. 'You will disarm immediately, or you will be shot.'

'Ooh,' said Zarenyia, 'you're forthright. I like that. We should get to know one another, Major.'

'Keep your blandishments to yourself, whore.'

Zarenyia's smile did not waver in the slightest. If anything, it grew broader, although there was a hint of hardening in her eyes. 'I've known lots of whores, darling, and generally found their company better than that of, say, soldiers. I suspect, however, that you meant it as an insult. So, yes—you and I are definitely going to have a little time together.'

Leonie was unslinging her rifle with slow, unthreatening movements and laying it upon the ground, before stepping away from it with her hands held up in clear view. Cabal was far less considerate of the nerves of the ring of conscripts around him, undoing his uniform belt, and tossing it and the holstered pistol upon it to one side. He held his hands away from his sides, but that was the closest he intended to come to putting them up. 'Now what, Major? You and your men seem to have us at a disadvantage.'

Addressing his subordinates, the major shouted, 'I want every one of these prisoners shackled and searched. Jump to it!'

Four soldiers ran forwards, chains and manacles clanking in their hands. 'Oh, for heaven's sake, does Ninuka really believe that one man and three women present such a huge threat, Major? You're behaving like a lot of frightened mice.'

The barb stung, but the major replied with minimal snarling, 'My orders are explicit, Cabal. You are, to quote them, "not to be underestimated". I have no intention of disobeying them simply based on my unflattering impressions of you.'

Cabal shook his head. 'Still as obedient an army of marionettes as ever you were. Very well. Carry on.' He held out his hands for cuffing. As he did so, he gave Zarenyia what he hoped was a significant look. He needn't have worried; if there was one thing she was particularly attuned to, it was significant looks.

She turned to the major. 'Look, sweetness, ever since I embarked on this little adventure with Johannes here, people have been falling over themselves to put me in one or another form of bondage. Normally, I'd be delighted to oblige, but I'm afraid I have plans for this evening so, if it's not too inconvenient, perhaps you'd be a darling and call off your little boys? They can take their chains and whatnots with them, and we can all be friends. How does that sound?'

The major regarded her coldly. 'Shackle that one first. And gag her incessantly yakking mouth while you are about it.'

'My. You certainly have a way with the ladies.' Zarenyia did not smile at all as she said it.

'I would advise you not to aggravate Madam Zarenyia, Major,' said Cabal.

The major laughed. 'Or else what, exactly?'

'Well, that would be the difference between a swift, pleasurable death and a slow, agonising one. Those really are your only choices now.'

The major nodded, and Cabal was felled from behind by a rifle butt to the kidneys. Zarenyia watched him writhe on the floor for a moment, her face expressionless. She turned her head to look at the major. 'Slow and agonising it is, then,' she said.

The sudden transition of the very attractive yet somehow unsettling lady into a huge spider-woman was not something any of the conscripts had covered in basic training. A bladed leg swiped at the man who had struck down Cabal. The soldier screamed as most of him fell one way, the remainder of him falling silently the other. Of the eleven surviving men, seven swore, two squealed less manfully than they would previously have believed possible, five rifles were dropped, and three pairs of underwear filled.

The major was built of slightly sterner stuff. Admittedly, he gawped at first, and his jaw flopped open and shut as he tried to take in what was happening. Then he remembered the pistol in his hand and brought it up to fire.

It's quite possible, indeed likely, that the bullet would have done Zarenyia little or no damage if it had actually hit her. She was not in the mood to give him the chance, however. She leapt forwards as a wolf spider does upon its prey, landed just short of him, and, as he was staggering back from her, she scythed his gun hand off at the elbow using the extruded blades upon her left foreleg.

'Staunch that, darling. I don't want you dying before I kill you properly,' she told him with a smile that froze his heart. Then she was gone in another jump to land amidst the troops. There were shouts. She struck one man who was raising his rifle to his shoulder upon the head, and her leg did not stop travelling until it was down past his sternum. Leaving the dead man as a lazily drawn Y spilling offal before his legs failed, she turned upon the others, and the shouts became screams.

Leonie Barrow grabbed Cabal's uniform tunic by the scruff and dragged him by main force into the area shielded by Zarenyia's armoured bulk. He grunted with annoyance at the imposition, but the pain was too great for him to find his feet with any hope of maintaining them, so he used his hands to help pull himself across the cracked paving slabs.

To his other side, Miss Smith had produced her wand and was crouched with her free arm crooked to support her wand hand as if she were target shooting. A soldier some thirty feet away moved sideways to shoot past her, perhaps at Zarenyia, perhaps at Cabal. Miss Smith did not give him the chance; glass sparks and malenginuity spat in a spray of lethal intent from the wand's tip. It did not strike the soldier, who jumped back from it the instant he saw the woman in black was not merely waving a stick around. The jet struck the ground before him, and for one brief, joyful moment, he thought she had missed and that the advantage was his. The muzzle of his rife swung over to glare at her. She had not missed. The pavement, doused in strange energies, buckled and rose to form a great, concrete hand, articulated at the slab edges. The private barely had time to realise all was not well when the slab hand slapped him flat as an unsqueamish man might a cockroach. Across the back of the now inanimate hand splinters of concrete flew up like champagne bubbles as the dead man's name and epitaph appeared. She had enjoyed the novelty of the self-engraving tombstones in the Endless Cemetery and was keen to adopt it as a signature upon her works henceforth.

For her part, Leonie Barrow snatched up her dropped rifle, wrapped the sling around her shoulder to stabilise it, worked the bolt to put a 7.62mm round into the chamber, and sighted at the backs of the more sensible Mirkarvian troops, which is to say the ones that were running away. As she discarded targets as low threats and—English as ever—a strong desire not to shoot a man in the back if it could be helped, she swung the rifle back and forth, acquiring and discarding, acquiring and discarding, until she found a man in her sights who had taken partial cover behind a lamp standard from where he was drawing a bead upon Zarenyia. Leonie aimed low, and fired. The bullet took him in the thigh, and he fell over sideways, glanced fearfully at her as she worked the bolt once more, and then half ran, half hopped away from her, leaving his rifle behind. She began looking for a new target, acquire and discard, acquire and discard.

Cabal looked around him, breathing deeply as the pain in his back slowly subsided and the desire to vomit with it. He was in the middle of a protective cordon, and the thought struck him that just how had he ended up in a situation in the space of a handful of years wherein three people were prepared to fight to defend him when once, not so long ago, being surrounded by people with weapons and the will to use them would invariably have been a very bad thing. Perhaps, he concluded, it was because he had a soul now. Perhaps—and it was a very peculiar thought that caused him a little discomfort—he had friends now. A little discomfort, but not nearly as much as the pleasure that the idea brought him.

There was little time to feel warm and wanted for something other than capital crimes, however. From the direction of the impromptu barracks building an inhuman wail grew via a slow crescendo into an ululating climax that threatened to outlast that of the average Zarenyian dalliance. Somewhere on or around the building, a soldier was cranking the handle of a siren for all he was worth.

Grimacing, Cabal clambered painfully back to his feet. 'We must move,' he said. 'We cannot take on the whole Mirkarvian army of occupation. We must focus on our objectives.'

Leonie glanced at the lowering bulk of the *Rubrum Imperatrix* where it hung at anchor. 'Shame they cottoned onto us so quickly. The ramp is way over there, to the rear of the aeroship. That's got to be three hundred yards over broken ground.'

Cabal looked askance at her, specifically at the very professional way she was wielding the rifle. 'You seem very at home with that gun, Miss Barrow.'

She half laughed, half smiled. The smile vanished. She sighted and fired. A shot ricocheted, there was a cry of dismay from the end of the Mall, and the sound of army boots in rapid retreat. Her smile returned. 'After the first time we met, Cabal, my father made sure I knew how to handle myself in a fight. After the second time, I went off and made sure I knew how to handle a pistol. After the third time,

I taught myself how to handle rifles and shotguns. My *curriculum vitæ* makes astonishing reading thanks to your influence.'

'Always glad to be of service.'

Zarenyia suddenly reared up, her abdomen curling beneath her to bring her spinnerets to bear forwards. There was a wet squirting noise that, even in the middle of an armed engagement, managed to sound wholly lascivious. A corporal bringing up some sort of single-shot rocket launcher, a novelty from the Mirkarvian armouries, was hit in the chest by a cable of spider silk as thick as his thumb. He barely had time to register that he was snared before he was jerked from his feet with enough force to cause compaction injuries along the full length of his spine and neck as his body bent backwards under the impetus. The line slacked when he was mid-parabola, and he sailed down towards Zarenyia under the normal forces of gravity and forward velocity until he met her foreleg, crooked sideways, at which moment he was neatly severed atwain.

While the act of bisection itself was neat, however, the immediate aftermath was not. The top half crashed to the floor wetly spilling lungs and stomach contents, but the lower half unloaded a mass of intestines and much blood, which splashed egregiously.

'For heaven's sake, madam!' snapped Cabal. He lifted first one foot then the other from a large and growing pool of gore. 'Less extravagantly, if you please!'

Zarenyia turned to look at him, almost comically saddened. 'I've got man giblets all over my sweater. I'm not sure it will wash out.'

'If we get through this, I shall buy you a whole new wardrobe, but please, will you focus on the task in hand?'

She brightened instantly. 'A whole new wardrobe? Oh, you darling! You heard that, didn't you?' she asked of Miss Smith and Leonie Barrow. They exchanged glances, but said nothing. Zarenyia didn't care; she returned her attention to Cabal. 'I have witnesses!' she said in a righteously warning tone.

'Quite. Ninuka. Reason for us being here. Focus.'

'Yes. Find Ninuka, kill Ninuka, take Holy Grail or whatever this is all about, get new wardrobe. See? I have my priorities all worked out.'

Abruptly, the siren died away. 'Finally,' said Cabal. 'Horst and his constituency have arrived. I was beginning to think it would require an engraved invitation.'

In fairness, the plan had always been a little vague as to what constituted the signal by which Horst was to know when to lead his force of ill-matched vampires into battle. 'You'll know it when you see it' had been Cabal's pragmatic though unhelpful advice. This failed to take into account just how Horst was supposed to see anything when his role was to lead the vampires around to the rear of the armed encampment built within the skeleton of Buckingham Palace, and therefore had no clear line of sight to where his brother and the others were hoping to infiltrate at the front.

He had been considering the wisdom of sending one of his number—which frankly had little experience as vampires and less still as soldiers and could hardly be depended upon once out of his sight—or to go himself and risk his force engaging the enemy out of boredom or, worse still, suddenly realising that their loyalty to the Lord of the Dead lasted exactly as long as he didn't ask them to do anything that might finish with them in dust. The Mirkarvians were, after all, notoriously adept at dealing with vampires, having famously all but exterminated their own population of *nosferatu* for failing to pay its taxes. One of the first acts of the occupation force when faced by the supernatural horrors their leader had cursed the city with was to capture any vampires that tried their luck with Mirkarvian troops, and destroy them in front of the Houses of Parliament, which was a known leech nest right from the beginning.*

The decision was rendered moot by the distant sound, perfectly audible on the still night air even to the dull senses of mortals, never

* And, if one is inclined towards cynicism, long before the Mirkarvian curse was ever visited upon London.

mind those of vampires, of shouts, and then screams, and then shooting. The mournful wail of a siren was simply a confirmation.

'Guns and screaming,' said Horst. 'My brother's definitely in town. Come along, all! England expects, and all that. Tally-ho!'

Feeling more British than he had ever done before in his life—after all, what could be more British than leading a shock force of vampires on a raid into the ruins of Buckingham Palace, short of doing the same but wearing bowler hats?—Horst led the charge.

He needn't have worried about the resolve of his force. They were sadly changed creatures, but not one of them had not examined their own futures and seen nothing but a spiritual death, picking over the bones of a dead country. Perhaps one day they would cease to think as humans, but that time was a long way off, and all had a personal purgatory stretching before them that would finish in an inhuman hell, with no heaven as even a fleeting prospect. They walked, they talked, they fed, and they feared a meaningless death as much as they had ever done, but they all knew that death had already claimed them, and that no amount of walking, talking, and feeding would ameliorate that truth one jot. Varney had told them they were the new lords of London and they would take the place as their fiefdom once the Mirkarvians left as they surely must. It was comforting, but it was a lie, as all knew but for Varney.

Now they had a new leader and he was as they, but he had more life than even the most mortal of mortals should contain. He offered them a vision as grim as it was compelling of likely destruction, but of flickering out in a moment of meaning and not inertia. Everyone dies eventually, even vampires, and while they could remember the families, the friends, the smiles, and the loves that had been taken from them, they would sell this poor counterfeit of life, this undeath, on their terms, and dearly.

It was no platoon of feral creatures that had once been humans that fell upon the Mirkarvian guards patrolling the rear wall of the palace at Grosvenor Place, nor was it a horde of ancient decadents somehow stirred to concerted action. It was a bunch of Britons with fangs and a grievance, and there is no more terrifying sight in creation.

The guards had no chance, and most fell hardly aware of how they were being killed. They were, as was so much of Ninuka's invasion force, conscripts who had few enough chances to even let off a shot in anger, the real veterans being employed in the pacification of the rest of the country. The alarums and excursions at the front of the palace had entirely distracted them, and most weren't even facing the attack on their line when it came. It was over quickly and, though he cavilled at the pragmatic brutality of the order, Horst had told his minions to drain whatever blood they required to be replete. The coming action would require each and every one of them to be at the limits of their capabilities and that meant being fully fed. It was this *al fresco* dinner that resulted in the longueur between the siren sounding and the vampires attacking the palace proper that irked Cabal so.

Once the guards were no longer anything but nourishment, the vampires easily scaled the wall and, pushing themselves to the edge of human perception, moved easily unseen through the gardens. It turned out to be an unnecessary precaution; the gardens were empty of troops, the handful of two-man patrols having abandoned their orders in favour of finding out what all the excitement at the front was. When they saw it was the sort of excitement that involves a body count (including fractions), they found sensible things to do some distance away, where they could take cover, point rifles, and give the impression that they were watching developments in a professional and soldierly manner as opposed to cowering like undertrained conscripts. Perish the very thought.

In any event, the effect was that the vampire horde easily moved to the remains of the palace, infiltrated the ruins, and split into two parties on reaching the barracks. Horst gave brief orders to the section commanded by the City gent, whose name turned out to be Johns; they were to wait within easy sprinting distance of the barracks' rear doors (given that it had until recently been part of a larger building, there was no shortage of rear doors at assorted levels of the half-ruined building, opening out into partial rooms, corridors, and apartments). Meanwhile, Horst and his half of the force would scale the outside of the building to the roof. The silencing of the siren would be the signal for the assaults of the building's interior from above and below to begin.

Buckingham Palace was, by any measure, a building. It wasn't a very pretty one and, indeed, when the Houses of Parliament burnt down in the early part of the nineteenth century, the King offered it to the government as a permanent replacement with unseemly haste. Parliament thanked the King kindly for the offer, but pointed out that it was not suitable for the seating of two large assemblies. They neglected to mention that it also looked like a troll's birthday cake, and that they would personally rather only ever have to go there for garden parties and for picking up the occasional honour. Aesthetically a disaster, the palace sat in the heart of London, fondly regarded by tourists and no one else. The Royal Family always much preferred Windsor or Balmoral to staying at Buckingham Palace, and who can blame them? That the palace had never looked so interesting as it did now, subsequent to an aerial bombardment, says all one really needed to know about the place.

Even the Mirkarvian troops stationed there didn't like it; it was more a collection of rooms cobbled together by an architect sure that what royalty really wanted more than anything was lots of rooms cobbled together. It lacked cohesion and practicality. The troops chafed at the nearness of the former Horse Guard barracks hardly five minutes away, but their grumbling was ignored. The Red Queen wanted to station her flying palace over the ruins of the old, and she wanted her soldiers as close to hand as possible. If that meant soldiers' boots churning up luxurious carpets, and antique furniture being broken up for firewood, so be it. The Red Queen's will was all, and to deny it was to deny life.

The tactical downside of this location compared to a purpose-built barracks was that the soldiers were split into smaller groups rather than the higher concentrations afforded by long barrack rooms. When the NCOs went around to roust the troops at the beginning of the day, it was tiresome but necessary to visit several rooms to bellow loudly at the sleeping men whereas they would have preferred to appear at the end of a single room and practise their generic sexual insults and imaginative threats upon all the men at once. Still, this was the price of keeping Her Majesty happy, and a happy majesty was a majesty not handing out death warrants.

Now, however, the current deployment's shortcomings were to prove fatal. As the man cranking the siren on the roof fell victim to a former washerwoman armed with the strength of ten and needle-sharp fangs, the siren's handle turned unattended, slowing with every revolution as the warning tone grew quieter and lower until it faded into nothing.

Doors were flung open, trapdoors lifted, and the vampires were in. The soldiers within had very little warning and even less chance to defend themselves. Most were unarmed, and an unarmed man against a vampire at the peak of its energies is a poor match indeed. Soldiers fell hardly aware of what had overtaken them, cut down by cabdrivers, shop workers, a terribly conflicted vicar, a renowned West End actor, all working in concert and in awful silence, their progress marked only by the sounds of doors being violently thrown open, and the very occasional cry from those poor souls who saw their fate approaching and knew there was no evading it.

One decided he would not die that way, and threw himself from a window. General Fischer, who happened to be directing his subordinates from the base of the steel ramp that led up to the *Rubrum Imperatrix*'s main aft entry, watched the man fall two storeys to crash to the floor below. Instantly realising that the Mirkarvian ambush had been categorically outflanked, he ordered his men to form a defensive line protecting the ramp and the ship from attackers. But even as he was wondering what could be done to withdraw any surviving soldiers in the routed building, the problem was taken from him. Over the crackle of gunfire he had not heard the humming tones of electrical motors and hydraulic rams. Above his head, he had not seen the silhouettes of gun barrels swing ponderously from their mountings and sponsons. The first he knew of it was when they opened fire.

Explosive shells struck the last surviving wing of Buckingham

Palace in a rapid salvo, the recoil from which made the anchor cables groan with stress as the *Rubrum Imperatrix* shifted under the impulse. A pause of a fraction of a second, and then the walls bulged outwards, inflated by the burst of the shells. Fire roared from windows, bodies vampiric and mortal were thrown out to somersault gracelessly to the hard pavement. The former struggled back to their feet, only to be stitched with raking heavy machine-gun fire from anti-personnel weapon positions studded about the aeroship's underside. Fischer had fought vampires both here and in Mirkarvia, and knew that even that sort of weaponry would only slow a determined specimen. He was therefore astonished to see the vampires bloom in fire, burning briefly but fiercely as a magnesium ribbon burns when held in the Bunsen flame. They screamed as they died, and every vampire hit *did* die.

It was incredible. It was also clearly planned. Furious, Fischer ran up the ramp.

He finally found his queen on the top surface of the aeroship, watching the carnage below with the detachment of an entomologist watching ants fight.

'You knew!' spat Fischer, anger stripping him of diplomacy. 'You knew this would happen!'

'Good evening, General,' said Ninuka without turning. 'You have something to report?'

'If you knew this would happen, why didn't you warn me? Those men . . .' The north end of the palace was in flames. Two more shells struck it in rapid succession and a corner of the wing fell away in a tumble of masonry. Beyond it apartments burnt out of any hope of control. 'Those are Mirkarvians, damn it! Good men! How can you sacrifice—'

'Every time you send your men into battle, you know you will be sacrificing at least some of them.' Ninuka spoke sharply and the general's sense of self-preservation finally caught up with his anger. 'Every man in that building was as good as dead as soon as the vampires entered. This way, their deaths are not in vain.'

'The ammunition our machine guns are using, what is it?'

'Every creature that walks has its weakness, General. I have made it my business to specialise in weakness, to know my enemies at least as well as I know myself. It was an expensive business to find a suitable Achilles heel in vampires, and expensive to manufacture. The levy soldiers could not be equipped with it, but my Imperial Bodyguard has been. I hereby hand their command to you, General. Use them wisely. Hunt the leeches and exterminate every one of them. *Every* one of them, especially a handsome one with a faint Hessian accent and probably a well-tailored suit.'

'You warned me of him once, Your Majesty, but he was not one of the four.'

For the first time, Ninuka's equilibrium seemed shaken. She turned to him as angrily as if he had been unwise enough to personally insult her.

'Impossible! How do you account for that pocket army of leeches otherwise? Of course he's here!'

'With respect, the four that attempted to penetrate the perimeter consisted of a blond man, who does fit the description you gave of one of the likely intruders, but the other three were all women.'

Ninuka looked blank. 'Women?'

'Yes, My Queen. One man and three women pretending to be the two survivors of the *Lammasu* ground support patrol and a pair of prisoners.'

The Red Queen looked off into the fires, an eyebrow cocked in intrigue. 'My, my, Herr Cabal,' she said to no one in particular, 'how your social skills have come on.' She dispelled the reverie with a shake of her head. 'Horst Cabal is behind the attack on the barracks; only he could have led the leeches. He was always fated to become the Lord of the Dead, one way or another.'

Another staccato hammering of automatic fire, another flare. She returned her attention to the battlefield. 'Where are Cabal and these three women throughout all this? I heard shooting.'

'I couldn't see, and the subaltern I sent to find out didn't come back, Your Majesty.'

'You couldn't see.' There was the slightest note of derision. 'All can be seen if you stand in the right place.' She walked towards the aeroship's prow, past the covered shapes of several CI-880 Ghepardo entomopters liberated (or looted, depending on one's perspective) from the Senzan Aeroforce inventory. Fischer glanced at them as he passed by, half longing, half loathing. Mirkarvia's aerial forces had been a joke in the region. ('What is the difference between a spider and the Mirkarvian Aeroforce?' 'People are afraid of spiders.') Air superiority would have been impossible to impose in the wars against Senza and Poloruss. The Red Queen's unconventional forms of warfare had rendered that shortfall moot, and the vastly superior aerofleets of the conquered powers had fallen into Mirkarvian hands.

But, it was all for show. Now Mirkarvia had the weapons that had proved useless to their vanquished enemies, and continued to prove useless in Mirkarvian hands simply because they were often surplus to requirements. Off in battles going on that moment around Britain in such exotic-sounding locales as Uttoxeter, Thetford, and Charnock Richard, such engines of war were being used in earnest. Wherever the Red Queen was, however, they were simply ornaments.

The deck jerking slowly beneath his feet in reaction to another salvo of shells fired into the pathetic remains of Buckingham Palace reminded him that this not entirely true; Her Majesty seemed to have a fondness for aeroships and their effective use. The entomopters may sit unattended and barely used but for occasional reconnaissance flights, but the vessel on which they sat was allowed the privilege of flexing its muscles in anger and of drawing blood. Every station aboard the ship was manned by Queen Ninuka's personally chosen crew and staff. This really was her palace now she had grown bored with the crumbling heap that was Harslaus Castle in Mirkarvia's equally faded capital, Krenz. A very special palace that could go where it was required and, if necessary, level an area the size of a small town once it got there.

Fischer was distracted enough by the entomopters that he allowed Ninuka to get a few yards ahead of him. She therefore reached the rail overlooking the ship's prow first, and so Fischer had the dubious honour of hearing his famously imperturbable queen become perturbed for the second time in five minutes. 'What is *that?*'

He joined her at the rail, and they looked down in mutual incomprehension. A badly formed and rapidly disintegrating cordon line of green soldiers was breaking up under the onslaught of a woman with a rifle, another with a wand of all things, and . . .

'What is *that?*' echoed the general. It was Zarenyia, but they weren't to know that.

'The drained corpses found in the National Gallery.' Surprise was rapidly being replaced by calculation in the queen's mind. 'The webs. It cannot be a coincidence.'

'I shall have the ship's guns redirected upon that . . . thing,' said Fischer, glad of a chance to give orders and feel like a soldier again. He would have pointed out that if the *Rubrum Imperatrix* had been left on its habitual alert levels, lookouts would have spotted the monster immediately after it appeared. As it was, everybody had been ordered by the queen to keep a close eye on the approaches to the ship's aft quarter. He decided that this was neither the time nor the place to criticise Her Majesty, just like every other place and every other time. In the empire of the Red Queen, discretion was a survival trait.

'No!' She was pointing furiously into the middle of the unlikely group of attackers.

A man wearing the uniform of a Mirkarvian commissioned officer but with the air of a civilian was climbing to his feet in the middle of the triangle of forces arranged about him. He took a moment to dust himself down and then—Fischer drew his small binoculars from their case to confirm it—strolled over to an abandoned forearm that lay on the ground not far away. The forearm still wore the lower sleeve of a Mirkarvian uniform, and Fischer judged it as belonging to a major by the rings of rank around the cuff. The hand gripped a service pistol, and before Fischer's astonished gaze, the man placed his foot on the severed forearm and wrestled the pistol free from the dead fingers. Pleased with his prize, the man rejoined the monstrous squad of women and started a conversation with them while placidly plinking 9mm rounds at the unhappy conscripts.

'That is Johannes Cabal!' The queen's teeth were bared. 'On no account is he to be killed or seriously injured, General. Any man who breaks that order will suffer my profound displeasure.' Given the awful fates that had befallen those who merely peeved Queen Orfilia Ninuka, this was not a warning to be lightly ignored.

Very aware that he was likely exposing himself to such displeasure, General Fischer felt compelled to point out the realities of the situation. 'Your Majesty, he is protected by a monstrous spider . . . woman . . . *thing*, a witch, and a woman who seems very comfortable with a rifle. Capturing him may be impossible.' Ninuka turned on him, scenting insubordination. He raised his hands in pacification. 'I speak only of practicalities. The troops we have to hand are green, barely out of training. It would take experienced men to do as you wish, and we have none.'

'None? There must be a few veterans. They cannot all be dispersed around this wretched country.'

'There *were* a few squads I might have trusted to mount a competent attempt to take that man unharmed, but . . .' He nodded aft where the flames of the burning palace rose high into the sky.

Orfilia Ninuka looked at the glowing smoke rising from the unloved palace, and her jaw became set. For a moment Fischer was sure she was going to demand his pistol and, in all likelihood, shoot him dead. It would not have been the first time she had retired troublesome senior officers whom she felt had disappointed her. Instead she smiled. 'Then we shall consider an alternative stratagem. Listen carefully, General.'

Horst did not feel at all lucky to be blown up, yet he was, which only goes to show something or another. The reader is at liberty to draw their own lesson in irony.

Even at his accelerated state wherein hummingbirds seemed slothful and sloths seemed geological, the detonation of an artillery round as it passed through the room into which he was about to enter was still an unavoidable surprise. Admittedly, he saw it as no mortal might with their own eyes—the sudden twitch in the far wall, the ripples travelling across the torn wallpaper, the glow of light around the door frame, then the hot, radiant gas of the explosion ramming in glowing planes under and over the door and even through the keyhole, the shudder in the wood, the eruption as the hinges and lock were torn from the disintegrating frame, the door shivering into smaller and smaller pieces, the floorboards lifting beneath his feet, waves rushing along the carpet as the gas got beneath it, and then the waves turning to smoke and fire as the material flashed—but he stood no chance of escaping it.

The blast picked him up, threw him back down the corridor as easily as if he were a scrap of paper, and then projected him through a window to fall thirty feet. As he lay there, burning, peppered with wooden splinters the least of which was the size of a pencil, and his suit utterly ruined, he did not feel very lucky. Yet he was, for he had been thrown out of the side of the building away from the guns of the *Rubrum Imperatrix* and so did not finish the moment punctured and destroyed by the arcane ammunition devised by the inventive mind of Orfilia Ninuka.

He became aware of somebody appearing over him, and then all became black. He felt some hard textile thrown over him and somehow dredged up the memory of lying on carpet offcuts in a den he had made in the woods near his home when he was perhaps nine or ten years old. Somebody was using a length of salvaged carpet to put out the flames upon him, which was kind of them, whoever they were, and probably not the actions of the enemy. This was reassuring and he allowed himself to relax a little. Presently the carpet was removed, and he found himself looking up into the face of Johns. His morning suit looked the worse for wear, and his top hat had entirely gone.

'Are you all right, my lord?' he was asking anxiously.

'Oh, call me Horst.' He said it vaguely; the blast had taken more from him than he realised. 'What happened?'

'They fired on their own barracks! They must be insane!' Johns looked back at the burning building. 'And they have some kind of special weapon, my Lord Horst. It kills those who are like us. There's only a handful of us left who were lucky enough to be on this side of the building when they opened fire. What shall we do?'

'Lucky?' Horst managed to sit up, but it hurt more than anything had ever hurt him since he had become nocturnal by necessity. He made a mental note to avoid third-degree burns and blast injuries in future.

'Wait here.' Johns vanished into the smoke.

'Righty-ho,' said Horst, and waited there. Presently Johns returned dragging a terribly injured corporal, also a victim of the short-range artillery bombardment.

'There you go, old chap. Tuck in. Got to keep your strength up if we're to confound the Mirkarvians.' He noted Horst's dismay, and added, 'I know, I know. I must admit, I've never really understood how some of our number can be so gleeful about feeding. But needs must and, for what it's worth, he's quite insensible and not long for this world in any case. Poor fella's already lapsed into shock, and I doubt the best doctor in the world could bring him out of it. Go on . . . Horst. There's still work to be done.'

Horst nodded reluctantly, muttered a few words of regret and apology to the comatose man, and fed.

He lifted his head some minutes later feeling physically much better, but mentally much worse. The soldier was quite dead and, even if he was technically one of the enemy, using him as a handy panacea to a vampire's injuries seemed unfeeling at best. But it was done, and there was no point crying over spilt blood.

'I hope the others have made some use of the distraction.' Horst climbed easily to his feet, now as limber as a boy once more. He stepped away from the body, putting it out of sight, and proceeded to attempt to put it out of mind. 'How many of us are left?'

'Including us? Six.' Horst looked at him, dumbfounded. Johns shook his head. 'I don't know if they fired into the barracks simply out of panic and were lucky, or if it was a very deliberate trap. Surely they wouldn't sacrifice their own people like that?'

'They wouldn't. *She* would.' The identification needed no further clarification than that, Ninuka's public relations disasters being common knowledge internationally.

'I'd heard stories of what she did to her own country—'

'All true. She is perfectly capable of any act. Rally the few we have left. We have to make this count before they realise they haven't destroyed all of us.'

Johns nodded, and ran off, dodging through the ruins, seeking cover as he went. He was barely gone a minute before Horst saw him running straight back in as straight a line as he could manage in the terrain. He looked terrified.

'My lord!' Horst couldn't tell if he was calling to him, or sending up a prayer to an uncaring God. 'They're dead! They're all dead! We have to—'

The bullet took him high in the back and went clean through, exiting from the left side of the chest. Horst, who as a vampire had been shot often enough to remove the novelty of it, was momentarily unconcerned; what could a bullet do to such as they? But almost instantly smoke began to issue from the exit wound. Johns looked down at it in uncomprehending horror. Smoke curled from around his collar, and he tore at it as if he believed his clothes were on fire. They were, but only because the body on which they hung was starting to burn. Johns tore away the collar and half his shirt, his waistcoat buttons popping under the frantic violence, and the flesh exposed beneath was already incandescent with escaping energy. Johns started to scream. It lasted barely three seconds before he collapsed in a rain of charcoal and hissing bones.

Eight men appeared seconds later, and they were very different soldiers from the majority of the Mirkarvian forces. They wore steel helmets finished in a matte carmine, and gorget patches in the same shade on the collars of their black uniforms. These were the queen's own Imperial Bodyguard, an elite force used not only as a personal guard but frequently for special operations at the Red Queen's behest. They were well trained, well equipped, and feared by friend and foe alike. There was also the rumour that any new recruit had to endure a ceremony during which the queen took the soldier's soul for safekeeping and to ensure loyalty. Of course, that was just silly hearsay. As if such things were possible.

How stylishly they were apparelled was of secondary interest to Horst at that moment. That they carried ugly, squared-off carbines that could apparently kill vampires with a single shot occupied his thoughts far more acutely. His recent dismay that his feeding upon an, admittedly, already dying man had shortened a life by a few minutes was now replaced by a very pragmatic relief that he had done so; his reserves were full, and that was just as well. By the time the Imperial Bodyguard arrived, there was no hint Horst had ever been there but for a slight breeze in the otherwise still air.

Cabal, Leonie Barrow, Miss Smith, and Zarenyia had sought cover not long after the aeroship lowering nearby laid fire into Buckingham Palace, thereby putting the last vestige of the building out of its misery. It had occurred to Cabal that he had made a mild error in forgetting that the *Rubrum Imperatrix* was positively bristling with guns of assorted kinds and that it might take it upon itself to use them at some point. Thus, he led his party at a sprightly trot to cover by a tumbled wall. It would offer no protection from an artillery shell, it was true, but at least they would be invisible to the gun-aimers.

Cabal peered cautiously around the corner and settled a purposeful eye upon the aeroship's entrance ramp. The top part of it was the vessel's own; a broad deployment point that would touch the earth should the ship set down, or be used for dropping rappelling lines or even at greater height yet, the use of parachutes. These were a new-ish contrivance, and Cabal wondered at the nerve required to bet one's life on a large sheet conducting one from hundreds or thousands of feet in the air down safely to very solid ground. He understood the science of it, but that didn't mean he had to like it.

The lower half of the ramp built to span the gap was a semi-permanent affair of sapper bridge sections raised at an angle, supported by girders, and rooted in concrete. Any sentries that were supposed to have been there had been drawn off by the action or perhaps even taken cover from the effects of the heavy guns over their heads. It seemed to have ceased for the moment at least, and he was relieved to note that every gun barrel was pointing resolutely towards the raging conflagration previously known as Buckingham Palace. He spotted movement at ground level and saw troops leaving the end of the ramp and heading in discreet sections towards the fire. Their professionalism was apparent, and Cabal lapsed into tactical ratiocination.

'Ninuka's sending her bodyguard out.'

The others joined him and watched the figures disappear from view around the sides of the burning building. 'That's a lot of men,' said Leonie. 'She can't have many left aboard.'

Zarenyia regarded the aeroship with disfavour. 'It's going to be full of little corridors, isn't it? Hardly room to swing a baby. I'm not going to have to fold up again, am I?'

'You're assuming that I intend to board.' This was disingenuous; Cabal's distracted air as he weighed up the approach to the ramp made it perfectly clear that this was precisely his intention. 'But, no. I am concerned for Horst and his cadre. We've seen that the Mirkarvians have access to weapons that make short work of vampires. Would you be so kind as to find my brother and any survivors and bring them to the aeroship as quickly as you can, madam? I think they would be both safer and more useful aboard the . . .' He squinted at the vessel's prow. 'The *Rubrum Imperatrix*? Truly? Oh, the utter arrogance of the woman.'

'Yes, that would be entirely alien a concept to you, of course.' Miss Barrow's smirk was distinct, but forgivable. Certainly Cabal had nothing to say to it.

'Give us a leg-up,' said Miss Smith, holding a hand out to Zarenyia. Zarenyia looked at her with astonishment for a brief moment before it was replaced with delight.

'You're coming with me, then, darling?'

'Why not? I sort of enjoyed riding around on you in Hell.' The expression of Leonie Barrow, who was observing this exchange, became one of perturbed puzzlement. 'And this time I'm armed.' She held up her wand, as proud as any child with a wonderful new toy on Christmas morning.

Zarenyia lowered herself and offered a knee, of which she had a surplus. Miss Smith clambered up easily behind Zarenyia's human torso (to distinguish it from the arachnoid thorax upon which she sat) and made herself comfortable, exposing a shameful amount of ankle as her long skirt was pushed up in the process. Ankle all the way up to the mid-thigh to be precise. Stockings exposed to what was surely a scandalised London (zombies and vampires and foreign invaders were bad enough, but just cover yourself up, woman!), she placed a hand on Zarenyia's shoulder and held her wand at the ready in the other. 'I feel like a cowgirl,' she said.

Zarenyia laughed. 'You just *cannot* help feeding me straight lines, can you? I like you, poppet. Shall we go and kill some people now?'

Without waiting for an answer, Zarenyia galloped out of cover.

Cabal watched them vanish in pursuit of the Imperial Bodyguard with naked irritation. 'Wonderful. Now there are only two of us to storm an enemy warship. What could possibly go wrong?'

'I hope that was rhetorical, Cabal, or we're going to be here for quite a while listing things that could possibly go wrong.'

Cabal said nothing, but only checked his pistol. He did it in such an offhanded, inconsequential way, however, that she realised with some surprise that he was procrastinating.

'We are still going to try, though? Zarenyia and Smith can buy us some time, and God knows they'll provide a spectacular diversion, but if we're going to attempt this, we have to do so now.'

Cabal cocked the pistol and checked its safety was on before replying, 'You know me, Miss Barrow. Better than most, I would say. You would not characterise me as given to irrational fancies?'

'Not for a second. If you did have the occasional irrational fancy, you would probably be more likable. What is this about?'

'Well, for one thing, you have a basis for possibly finding me more likable, for I am prey to an irrational fancy.' He looked up at the aeroship hanging impassively before them. 'I have a bad feeling. I cannot characterise it beyond that; believe me, I have tried. I have a sickness of spirit that drains me of any desire to go forwards.'

Leonie Barrow gawped at him. 'Are you saying you're *afraid?*'

He did not deny it, did not quibble with the term. 'I believe so. The Phobic Animus is very much at home in me at the present moment. I fear that my luck is running out. I fear I will not leave that vessel alive. I fear that I shall, at this very late pass, fail finally, totally, irrevocably. I am afraid.'

She went to crouch by the wall by him. 'Well, I suppose that's that, then.' She started thumbing fresh rounds into her rifle's magazine. 'I should have expected it to happen under stress. I *did* expect it to happen under stress. And here we are.'

Cabal looked quizzical. 'You anticipated my failure of nerve?'

'Not exactly. I anticipated the moment when your soul finally settled back into where it's supposed to be, and stopped misfiring every five minutes. You are afraid, Mr Cabal? I am afraid. For all of her hooting and carrying on, I suspect Miss Smith is afraid. We are in danger. Of course we are afraid. Welcome back to the human race, Johannes Cabal. We were beginning to wonder if you'd received your invitation.'

'You are mocking me.'

'I am. But that doesn't mean I'm not telling the truth. Look, just do what you always do—walk in like you own the place, be sardonic, shoot people. It's the only way that we can get out of here and back to the real world. That's the game, Cabal.'

Cabal gave her a hard look, then glanced away while he thought. Leonie, painfully aware that any door of opportunity they had could well slam shut any second, somehow held her silence. Cabal straightened up. 'I shall need another gun.'

'That's my boy.' Leonie clapped him on the shoulder and smiled far too broadly to be ladylike at the vile look he gave her in return. 'Can't go in there with only one gun; there might be *lots* of people to shoot.'

It took an unconscionably long time to run the length of the *Rubrum Imperatrix*. Cabal was aware that much of the subjective time was simply down to how very uncomfortable it is to run beneath a massive flying artefact whose underside is liberally laden with ways of swatting humans into sticky little red puddles. As they ran, he could hardly help but glance up now and then to see if an inquisitive turret had noted them as they scuttled beneath the colossus, and swung its maw to bear upon them. In truth, there were so many turrets bearing machine guns, he could hardly keep an eye on them all, but their run was not interrupted by a rain of lead falling upon them to smash their bones and puncture their internal organs, so he supposed the gunners were still far too interested in the last throes of the burning palace, its walls falling around the inferno, to look straight down.

A long time—subjectively—later, they arrived at the base of the entry ramp. As Leonie took position to scan the approaches, Cabal peered cautiously up the ramp, ducking his head around the edge of a fixing stanchion at the base and back immediately for fear of sharpshooters in the beast's belly. No bullet winged its way at his head. Indeed, he had seen no one. Cautiously he took a longer peek, and confirmed the dispersal area at the ramp's head seemed to be completely abandoned.

'We haven't been spotted on the ground yet, Cabal.' Distantly they heard the sound of Zarenyia whooping happily and the distinctive sound of shattering physics that accompanied the use of Miss Smith's wand. 'But I do not know how long that will last. How many are guarding the ramp?'

'None.'

That gave her pause. 'None? They've left the door to their queen's flying boudoir unguarded? That seems . . .'

'Unlikely.'

'I was going to say "suspicious".'

'Also a good analysis.'

They looked about them, but if there was an ambush in the offing, it was taking its own sweet time in materialising. Leonie made an unhappy face. 'A trap.'

'Certainly, but not here or it would already have been sprung.' He nodded to the ship. 'Our fate awaits us.'

'Still frightened?'

He nodded. 'Terrified.'

'Good. Not just me, then. I don't suppose there's a choice. Off you go. I'll follow you up and cover our back, o Great Leader.'

Breaking cover was hard to do; there wasn't a scrap more to be had on the ramp itself, and they would be exposed to fire for some eighty feet until they were within the shelter of the aeroship's belly, where there was probably an ambush awaiting them. It would not be an enjoyable ascent.

At least the first sixty would be stable upon the ground-mounted ramp. The lowered aeroship ramp married reasonably well with the ground ramp's upper lip, although that they weren't connected by chains despite both lips having holes in them that would have been ideal for the purpose perturbed Cabal. Still, indecision would butter no parsnips, nor aid in likely regicide, so he put a foot on the ramp and began a fast crouched ascent that he hoped might make him less of a target for any passing Mirkarvian. Seeing he was at last committed to the climb, Leonie Barrow let him get ten or so feet ahead in an effort to avoid clumping together and offering an easy mark before starting up herself.

They proceeded with the curious feeling that they were in a play, which—in a manner of speaking—they were. The artificiality of the Five Ways bore upon them as at no other stage of its development, now that they were surely approaching the dénouement. He had already experienced anagnorisis. Presently, there would be a confrontation, a peripeteia, catharsis, and probably some sort of coda. The one thing they could not predict was whether this was an heroic tale, a tragedy, or even a comedy. Perhaps Ninuka would prove vulnerable to a good speech and they could all dance around as the curtain fell. This seemed unlikely. It was a theatre of improvisation that came with a butcher's bill. Well stocked with mechanicals, it also put real lives into jeopardy, or even took them. There seemed little doubt from what they had been able to glean that the core of Ninuka's force had come from the real world along with her. These were real people and they had died real deaths in the pursuance of her grand scheme. Even Miss Smith had been dragged into the trial, and who knew who else that had simply been close enough to the upstage to be perceived. On the plus side, Ratuth Slabuth was as dead as mutton, so the stormy outlook bore at least one silver lining.

No Imperial Bodyguards appeared as Cabal and Leonie ascended, no triumphant cackles to tell them that they had fallen into Ninuka's cunning trap, nyahahaha, etc. They climbed to the accompaniment of the sounds of disagreement as Zarenyia and Miss Smith introduced themselves to the ground troops mopping up the vampires. The disagreements were pithy.

Cabal reached the overlapping lips of the ramps, and hesitated. Strictly speaking, the Rubicon of the venture had been crossed when they first entered the sort-of realities of the Five Ways. There and then, however, the lines of steel across the ramp marked it more physically to his mind. With grand misgivings, he crossed the lines and continued onwards and upwards.

He had barely taken five more paces when a shot rang out from somewhere off to their right. Cabal instinctively dropped flat onto the unforgiving surface, the horizontal tread lines cut into the metal discoloured and marred with ashes and soil trodden in by any number of soldiers' boots tramping back and forth.

'I think there's a marksman at the guard post,' he called back over his shoulder. 'Lay down suppression fire until I reach cover, and I'll do the same for you while you follow.'

He waited, but there was no answer.

He knew what he would see even before he craned his neck to look. Leonie Barrow lay crumpled on the ramp some five feet short of the join in the ramp. She was motionless, her rifle inches from the fingertips of her out flung arm. There was blood on the ramp.

For a moment, he did not only not know what to do, he didn't even know what to think. Theirs was a dangerous undertaking. They had all—with the exception of Miss Smith—volunteered for the task. There had always been the likelihood of injuries and the possibility of death. He had seen enough of it to regard it as just something that happened, thankfully relatively rare but always ultimately unavoidable. He had killed others himself and seen that role as just part of the weave of history.

Yet this seemed wrong. Leonie Barrow could not be dead. She could not. She could not.

The old part of him rankled with disgust at such a romantic view of life. As if anyone was proof to the inevitability of their own mortality. The new part of him, pink as new skin growing from a ruin of burnt flesh, was innocent in its own way, and it did not wish to listen. She could not be dead. She could not be.

It struck him that he had been looking at her body what seemed like a long time, even if it were really only a few seconds. More than long enough for a marksman to chamber a new round. Should he return fire? A pistol against a rifle at range seemed a poor match. Should he try to reach her? The angle of the ramp relative to the guard post gave him a sliver of cover where he lay, but Leonie was close by the ramp's edge. If he went to her, he would be an easy target.

He was debating what to do when there was a dreadful concussion that made the ramp buck beneath him and threatened to fling him from it. He held on for life itself, gripping the deep ridges and wondering what new catastrophe was being visited upon him. He looked to Leonie Barrow to ensure that she had not been thrown off, either, and saw the clouds of concrete dust blowing out from beneath the lower section of the ramp. With a squeal of protesting metal, the lower ramp dropped a few feet and lay off-kilter, the side bearing Leonie's body the higher. Then there was a groaning crash, and the entire ramp fell, and Leonie Barrow fell with it.

He realised the nature of the trap too late to do anything about it. Of course he would be the first up the ramp, eager for confrontation even as it terrified him. One or more marksmen would be assigned to bring the ascent to a halt by firing at the opportune moment once he was past the join between the ramps, but anyone with him was not. Then, to ensure he was isolated, demolition charges set into the lower ramp's base and supports were detonated.

Johannes Cabal, utterly outwitted, alone, and aggrieved, could do nothing as the *Rubrum Imperatrix*'s aft ramp slowly rose up into the vessel's belly on hydraulic rams.

We can forgive Johannes Cabal at that moment. He had rarely felt true despair in his life—it took a very great deal to make him feel even mild despair—and he was host to a mix of emotions whose potency overwhelmed his atrophied sentiments. Given a minute longer he might well have looked around and begun formulating a response, extemporising a plan, and started shooting people, which was often how these things went.

As things were, however, he did not need that minute to reaffirm his self-sufficiency for, to coin a phrase, the cavalry were on the way. An unusual cavalry—consisting of a witch, a vampire, and a devil—but a sort of cavalry all the same.

How Zarenyia and Miss Smith rescued Horst from the murderous intentions of the Imperial Bodyguard is a short tale. The guards were equipped with the curious boxy carbines previously mentioned, odd little weapons chambered to fit odd little bullets comprising a soft lead nose upon a hollow body of an unusual silver alloy that in turn contained a liquid of vile provenance and despicable modes of collection. The troops were told the liquid was holy water, but it was not water, and it was a very long way from holy. The effect of the rounds upon undead flesh (not only that of vampires) was spectacular, as demonstrated by the unwilling Johns.

Horst was keen not to be shot by such a weapon and so had resorted to skulking and hiding while he found a way out of the dense cordon of searchers looking for him and those like him. It was all beginning to look rather hopeless when a witch turned up on a devil's back and proceeded to lay into the searching guards. The bullets would certainly have killed a human should they be struck, but turned out to be singularly useless against Zarenyia's armoured lower body. Thus, she spent a lot of time rearing up to scythe and slice her way through the startled troops, and when she did lower her forebody it was to reveal Miss Smith standing on the thorax, her wand spitting havoc, and wearing an expression that indicated that she was enjoying herself far too much.

The Imperial Bodyguard were well trained by Mirkarvian standards and—if the rumour was true—certainly well motivated to do their best. Training tends to be very specific, however, and somebody had plainly blundered in failing to prepare them for situations in which they would be fighting a small number of very irregular troops, each roughly equivalent to a platoon in the 'making a ruckus' stakes.

While they were trying to think of a sensible way to deal with a witch and a devil, they were not so concentrated upon the vampire problem, which was a shame, as the vampire problem was very concentrated upon them. Horst had not so much enjoyed being the Lord of the Dead as finding himself in the company of people with a similar lifestyle to his, and there was fellowship there. He had even begun to like a few of those he saw as his charges, especially the patrician Johns, who turned out not to be so ghastly when you actually chatted to him. Seeing Johns killed in front of him while—mark it well—he was not running for his unlife but trying to warn Horst had pushed him past a limit. A vampire is a major threat. A vampire with a personal grudge against you is a vast threat. The soldiers of Her Majesty's Imperial Bodyguard turned their collective back upon just such a vast threat, and they paid for that very quickly.

The battle, such as it was, was quite brief and spectacularly brutal. The boxy little carbines were of little use in confined quarters and the soldiers merely ended up shooting several of their own while trying to settle a sight upon the dodging, weaving, blurring in and out of existence Horst as he visited red ruin upon them. Miss Smith dismounted Zarenyia and moved amongst the soldiers, distributing eldritch ends at point-blank range, while Zarenyia took it upon herself to abscond with a few envenomed specimens on which to feed. These she lugged off behind a freestanding wall as a small nod at propriety, or at least, not being shot at while practising succubine rites upon her victims.

There was a sudden hiatus in hostilities caused by a howl of outrage from behind the wall. Zarenyia climbed over the wall's top, legs appearing first as she emerged holding a limp body over her head. She flung it at one of the few vaguely organised clumps of resistance, braining some and scattering the rest.

'They're empties!' she roared in a truly diabolical rage. 'Some little shit has got there first and taken their souls! Of all the bloody-minded, selfish, dog-in-a-manger-ish . . .' And the rest of the imprecation was lost in a new welter of carnage while Zarenyia salved her hurt feelings with multiple murders.

It will be understood that the few lingering vestiges of resistance dried up shortly after this.

After Miss Smith fried the last of the hapless and soulless, the trio made their merry way back to where Cabal and Leonie doubtless waited for them.

'*Mein Gott.*' Horst saw first, and the others looked to him in confusion before they followed his gaze. He saw Leonie lying on the ramp first, saw the blood, saw his brother crouched helplessly just too far away to help. 'No, no, *no!*' The gravel spraying back from his hard acceleration, he sprinted towards the base of the ramp. He had hardly begun to run when the explosion startled him into an untidy halt. The ramp lurched, held, and then collapsed. In agonising slowness, he saw the ramp fall faster than the body of Leonie Barrow, leaving her behind as it fell through dust and concrete fragments. He accelerated again, but he couldn't hope to reach her before she struck the now horizontal ramp. He came to a halt again, albeit a more controlled one this time. His mind burnt through possibilities as he loosened the leash on his vampiric side.

'Miss Smith! Help Leonie if you can! Zarenyia! To me!'

Neither needed a second bidding. Miss Smith drew her skirt up and ran as fast as she could towards the downed ramp. Zarenyia galloped up to Horst and, such was the urgency and the gravity of the situation that she even passed up the golden opportunity to flirt with him over how masterful he was being.

'Oh, the poor poppet,' she said, looking towards the crumpled body in a stolen grey uniform. Then, to Horst, 'What do you want me to do?'

'Johannes is in trouble. I have to get up there and help him.'

She glanced skyward. 'I'm not good in confined spaces, darling—'

'I know. You stay with Smith. I just need you to get me up there before that ramp closes.'

She looked up again, weighed the odds, and nodded firmly. 'Consider it done. Hop aboard, and hang on!'

Miss Smith had almost reached the collapsed ramp when she stumbled. Not badly enough to fall—although she cursed her impractical shoes as she tottered—but enough to spoil the shot that was meant for her and that creased the air just ahead of her where she would otherwise have been. Blessing her impractical shoes under her breath, she wheeled to gauge from where the shot had likely come. The checkpoint on the encampment's perimeter seemed likely, and furtive movement there confirmed it. Miss Smith would love to have visited something especially imaginative on the rifleman who it seemed must have been the one who shot Leonie Barrow, but she didn't have the time. She invoked raw destruction and directed it through her wand. The checkpoint and all its contents, including the marksman, disappeared in a perfunctory but staggeringly powerful explosion that startled birds in Southwark Park into the air over three miles away. Resistance overcome, Miss Smith once more hiked up her skirts and headed for the fallen Miss Barrow.

'Smithie's having fun,' said Zarenyia. Horst said nothing. He was too busy concentrating on not falling off an eight-legged devil dangling upside down while climbing an anchor cable up towards the lowering bulk of the *Rubrum Imperatrix*. It required a lot of concentration. One of the things he found himself concentrating on was how far the cable's hawsehole in the ship's hull was from the steadily closing ramp. Closing far too steadily for comfort. Then the ramp stopped in its tracks. Horst could make out movement close by the pivot and realised that his brother must have jammed the mechanism by some means. It probably would not buy them much time, but perhaps it would be enough.

The best place to cling to an inverted spider-devil, the reader will be illuminated to discover, is under the thorax. Thus, to talk to Zarenyia, he found it necessary to peer past the forward edge of that chitinous surface and up (or down, she being inverted) between her forward legs to look up (or down) at her humanesque upper body. This had another effect.

'I am very sorry,' said Horst, 'but I cannot help but see up your sweater.'

'Don't apologise,' she called back. 'I'm proud of my body. That aside, how can I help you?'

'I was just wondering how we were going to get from the top end of the anchor cable to the ramp.'

'I *was* thinking of walking it, but I'm not so sure now.'

'Too smooth?'

'Oh, please. I can stick to glass if I put my mind to it. No, I was thinking rather more about all these guns and things that are starting to take an interest in us.'

And so they were. Not all, by any means, nor yet even a majority, but enough of the machine-gun turrets were busily buzzing on their bearings to aim at the climbers.

'Oh, this is going to get terribly fraught, isn't it? I doubt the bullets will be much bother for my lower half, but my top bit is all lovely and squishy and not as bulletproof as I might wish at this precise moment. Even if they don't kill me, I don't think I'll be able to hang on.'

'Then wh—'

'Hold on *hard*,' she called, and then, without pausing to check if he was indeed holding on hard (he was; throwing aside manners and embracing her fiercely around the midriff), she threw herself upwards off the cable. For a second time since he'd been blown out of a window of Buckingham Palace, Horst found himself in free fall, and it was only more bearable than the first occasion because, primarily, he wasn't on fire and, secondly, Zarenyia's top bit really was terrifically lovely and squishy.

He was distracted from this by the distinct sensation of his legs being forced apart by Zarenyia's abdomen curling upwards. Then over his head he saw a stream of glistening white fluid shoot past. He hardly needed an accelerated metabolism and associated sensibilities to know what would come next, and hung on for dear unlife.

The stream hit the underside of the aeroship and stuck fast. A small part of a second later, Zarenyia strained under a great impulse as the silken cord drew tight and her shallow downward arc was halted to be replaced with a soaring upwards swing. Horst looked up and saw the narrow aperture of the almost shut ramp section approaching at dizzying speed.

'Now or never, darling! Jump!'

Feeling like an acrobat upon a very eccentric trapeze, Horst waited until the swing was almost over and—at a moment when there was still momentum to be had before the arcing motion came to a halt—he leapt.

Behind him he heard in rapid succession, 'Fly, my beauty! Fly!' then the sound of multiple machine guns opening fire in a panic of inaccuracy, and then, 'Rude!' He had no time to attend to any of that; the edge of the ramp was there just below him, then closer at his level, and then above him and he couldn't see it, only the drop below him. On the far side of the anchorage, he saw one of the *Rubrum Imperatrix*'s anchors disengage, its flukes winding back to unhook from the great iron hoop set into the buckled earth.

He felt his hand catch the very edge of the ramp, but all the speed and strength in the world could not help him against the simple mechanics of leverage and force. He felt his fingers slip and knew it had all been for nothing.

It was a surprise, therefore, a very pleasant surprise when he found himself dangling from the two-handed grip of his brother, heels dug in fiercely against the last lateral gutter of the ramp's surface.

'Pull yourself up quickly!' Cabal grunted. 'I can't hold on . . .'

It took a moment for Horst to find the ramp's lip with his free hand and to expend a few drams of stolen blood to take the weight off his brother. A moment later and they were sprawled together on the safety of the ramp. 'Zarenyia . . .' gasped Horst and rolled over to look down. He needn't have worried; Zarenyia had not lived for such a long time without learning how to frustrate the efforts of those who would do her harm, a very considerable population. She had tucked her forebody up so that it was shielded by the armoured abdomen and thorax. The period of her swing was predictable, but the gunners were not trained in tracking rapidly manoeuvring bodies at close range, few bullets struck home, and those that did whined off the pseudo-chitin of her spiderish body. Then she severed her cable, soared for a brief moment through the air and snagged one of the still attached anchor cables. The aeroship was busily preparing for flight, and cable after cable was being released and drawn aboard, the anchors themselves, flukes flattened, finishing snugly against the aviatory equivalent of a sea vessel's catheads. Indeed, even the cable Zarenyia had settled upon was released a moment after she caught it. She skimmed down it much faster than it could be drawn up, however, and she descended in a shower of sparks stuck between her legs and the steel hawser, screaming, 'Wheeeeee!' all the way down.

'We could all learn a lot from her,' said Horst. 'She has wonderful *joie de vivre*, don't you think?'

'She is far and away the homicidal maniac with whom I most enjoy spending time,' agreed Cabal. 'Now, to action. We have a single goal now: to reach Ninuka. Between us and her are any number of highly motivated gentlemen with guns that can apparently kill vampires. They will undog that door over there sometime in the next minute and endeavour to demonstrate. Do we have a plan?'

'Yes. You go after Ninuka, and I'll deal with the crew.'

Horst said it so firmly that it impressed Cabal, despite which he felt constrained to say, 'Are you sure? You did hear what I said about anti-vampire weaponry?'

'They had surprise on their side last time. This time they don't, it's close-quarter combat, which doesn't favour firearms, and—I have to tell you—I am really angry with them.'

Cabal looked away. 'I couldn't help her. I couldn't even reach her.'

'I know. Just for once, I'm not going to hold you responsible for when things go to hell. This is all Ninuka's doing one way or another. We don't have long, Johannes. I just want to say, in case things go to hell again, I don't blame you for any of this, and I forgive you for everything else. You have always been and always will be my little brother, and I love you. No matter what happens, always remember that.'

Cabal looked at him, vaguely appalled. 'For God's sake . . .'

Horst shrugged. 'Had to be said. They're unlocking the door now; I can hear them trying to be quiet. Good luck, Johannes.'

The Mirkarvian marines opened the door and promptly regretted it. Thanks to the confusion spawned by having a giant spider-lady swinging around under the ship's belly, reports had been fragmentary and inaccurate. The few observers who had noticed Horst had mischaracterised him as a hapless comrade captured by the monster or even that the creature had two forebodies, one male and one female. None had noticed Horst's leap nor his entry into the ship.

The upshot was that the marines entered the ramp's staging area with caution sufficient to deal with one untrained civilian with a handgun. This had all begun swimmingly when they saw him waiting for them on the far side of the chamber, the stolen army tunic thrown aside, and his hands held up in a position of surrender. 'I surrender,' he lied at them.

They moved quickly forwards to cover him, and so did a very poor job of examining the rest of the area, specifically the wall above the door through which they entered. When they were all deployed in an arc, bristling with weapons all bearing on the unthreatening man in the blue-glass sunglasses, the rearmost marines started dropping silently. Five were down before somebody noticed the form of a fellow marine fall in his peripheral vision. He turned his head, and started to shout a warning that was abruptly curtailed by being punched so hard his jaw entirely dislocated.

The marine made a pained sound at this treatment, which attracted the attention of the rest of them, encouraged to do so by Cabal pointing and saying with mountainous disingenuity, 'Oh, what's happened to him? Is he well?'

The sharper marines realised there was a threat behind them and turned their attention in that direction. Even sharper marines might have thought that perhaps there were threats on either side, but none were present.

A pistol going off at close quarters behind them unsettled the marines badly, and by the time they had settled on some form of response, they were largely dead or unconscious. The sole conscious survivor was a corporal who now found himself disarmed and held up against the chamber's forward bulkhead by an angry vampire and a necromancer who was examining one of the discarded carbines of famously boxy design.

'Ninuka,' demanded Horst. 'Where is she?'

When the Brothers Cabal emerged from the staging chamber, Horst was strong with new blood and Johannes was carrying two stolen pistols, a stolen carbine, and stolen ammunition for all of them. He looked back at the pile of dead and unconscious men in the chamber before slamming the door shut and dogging it locked from the outside. He glanced momentarily at the ramp lever on the outside of the doorway, the corresponding one within having been disabled as part of the trap. Horst watched this and read possible intent there.

'Those men are all on the ramp. Pulling that lever would be a cruel thing to do to men who are already having a bad day.'

'I know.' Cabal looked at the lever for a moment more, then shook his head. 'Once I would have done it without hesitation, to cut their numbers, but they're just puppets in all of this. I hold no animus towards them and, let's be honest, their chances of survival are likely thin enough already. Let those of them still alive dream on a little longer.'

Somewhere an alarm began to squall. Cabal smiled sourly. 'In any case, our imposition seems to have been discovered. Attend to the crew, Horst. I shall find Ninuka and bring matters to a conclusion.' He hesitated. 'And Horst . . .'

'Yes?'

'What you said earlier. That thing you said . . .'

'Yes?'

Johannes Cabal smiled. 'You really are a sentimental fool, you know that?'

Horst Cabal smiled. 'I do, and I consider it one of my best character traits.'

'Fare you well, brother.'

'Good fortune, brother.'

And so, like characters in one of the bloodier Grimm's fairy tales, they parted.

Of Horst's progress, little needs to be said. He wandered the corridors until he began to understand how the ship's architecture worked and so began to recognise recurrent features, especially the hatches that led into the ventral gun positions. These he would enter. If he found them unoccupied (as was invariably the state of the larger guns, their work done for the moment), then so much the better. When he found them manned, he subdued the occupants by mesmerism where possible and by force when they proved too unimaginative to take the less painful path. Turrets ornamented by sleeping gunners dreaming of summer days and pretty girls or bedewed with the blood of the recalcitrant were left in his wake. In either case they grew quiet and unresponsive to the increasingly frantic calls for status from the ship's bridge.

Horst had read enough magazines of popular mechanics to know that the practical necessities of an aeroship meant that its vitals were sited on the uppermost decks. This was where one would find the engineering sections that tended to the gyroscopic levitators and the etheric line guides that both harvested energy (probably from a dimension several over from the one he called home, that had more energy than it knew what to do with) and provided forward motion by dragging the ship along the lines of ethereal force that penetrate the world in a complex and unpredictable weave.

Also on the upper decks would be access to the main bridge, at the apex of the surface-ship-like prow, to give a good view of the land beneath. Horst had already discovered the smaller landing bridge in the middle of the lowest deck wherein a pilot would guide the ship in for field landings. It had been empty, but he took a moment to wreck the steering gear so it could not be pressed into service in the emergency the ship would shortly be suffering, if he had anything to do with it.

Occasionally he encountered ship's troops responding to the 'Hostiles Aboard' alert sounding in every corridor. They were noisy, even in the soft-soled deck boots they wore, and he was never surprised by them. Contrariwise, they were always surprised by him. In a single encounter was he wounded, but the bullet barely skimmed his flesh of his left tricep and failed to discharge its fatal contents into his body. That aside, he blurred and dodged, and punched and broke hands and arms in an attempt to disable rather than kill. He left patrol after patrol groaning and weeping in his wake as he made his irresistible way towards the master bridge.

Acting on the information received from the corporal they had interrogated in the staging chamber, Johannes Cabal made straight for the quarters of the Red Queen. His path was relatively short, and he was untroubled by the attentions of the ship's marines. This hardly surprised him; it was necessary for the conclusion of the Five Ways that they meet, for what adventure does not conclude with the protagonist and antagonist face-to-face? Which of them was which was a matter for minds of a more literary bent than his. Every man and woman is the hero of his or her own story, striving for something better. Ninuka's probably lay in the re-creation of the Mirkarvian Empire, an entity seen here in prototype. This was undoubtedly a good thing for Mirkarvians—empires usually are for whosoever gets to put the name of their country before 'Empire' in the title—but unusually awful for everyone else if this was how things were intended to turn out. A vision of men in shiny boots stamping around from the ruins of Albion in the west to humbled Poloruss in the east was deeply unpalatable for all but the Mirkarvians and their queen to strive for. Still, it was always nice to have a hobby.

And for Cabal? He could not even begin to guess how many lives he had caused to be lost or ruined directly or indirectly since he had begun his great project. On the other hand, he had certainly saved the world at least once so, on balance, he was fairly sure that made him the hero. Flawed, certainly, but he seemed to recall that both Ulysses and Jason of ancient legend could be utter arses when the mood took them; he was probably some sort of paragon in comparison.

He discovered Queen Orfilia Ninuka at her desk, waiting patiently for him as was only right. It had all the makings of a set piece; he swept open both of the double doors to her quarters in what he assumed would be the appropriate manner. She was behind the great white-and-gold desk, her back to him in one of the new style of swivel chairs, a sensible choice given the great vista of doom-haunted London spread out below them.

'Ninuka.'

A heartbeat's pause, and the high-backed chair rotated slowly to face him, as perfectly staged as anything upon the West End.* She sat there regarding him with the icy malevolence of a cobra with expensive tastes in couture.

'Cabal.'

There was silence, broken only by the distant sound of the alarm and the universal hum of the levitators thrumming through the hull. The silence drew out, and Cabal began to wonder if he was supposed to have been issued a script, because he was damned if he could think of anything else to do but raise his pistol and kill her. Then she spoke, and he was saved the anticlimax.

'Fate is a curious thing, is it not, Cabal? If we had never crossed paths, my father would still be alive, I would still be happy in my blinkered little world of sensuous excess, and Mirkarvia would still be a rotting backwater where history used to happen. Now look at me. I discovered that the position in society that was my birthright could be used for more than luxury and indulgence; that the social

---

* Which is to say, the real theatre land West End of London as opposed to the Five Ways phantom of it. On that West End, one would find little on the abandoned stages but rats and zombies. Perhaps that's not so different, after all.

skills of gentle persuasion and the powers of subtle coercion I seemed equally born into could be utilised to bring greater prizes than expensive gifts and bedmates.'

'You will recall that those powers failed to work upon me.'

'I do recall, but that was because you are so thumpingly stupid, Cabal. Don't ever try to congratulate yourself on resisting any wiles I may have employed upon you. They only count as wiles if the subject isn't so stunningly dull as to not even notice.'

Cabal's lips thinned; his vanity was a small thing by most standards, but where it stood its ground was on the subject of his intelligence. 'Perhaps—' he began.

'No.' Ninuka raised a hand to stop him. 'If you intend to tell me that perhaps you were playing the innocent the whole time, no. I am very familiar with what 'playing hard to get' looks like, and it was utterly absent in your guileless, clueless face. No. That will not do.'

Cabal considered. 'Are you suggesting that if I had blithely fallen into bed with you on our first meeting, we would not now be flying over a phantasmal representation of the ruins of one of the world's great cities, and many, many of your troops would still be alive?'

She shook her head, then hesitated, her chin tilted up in thought. 'I had not considered matters that way. Perhaps so. Your celibacy may well have consigned thousands to death or the threat of death. Really, Cabal, it's only a dick. Why did you have to be so damned possessive?'

Cabal's mouth opened, closed, opened again. He blinked foolishly, his eyes denoting confusion and discomfort. 'I admit, madam, I was not expecting this interview to unfold in quite such a manner.'

'Nor was I, but I'm glad we've had a chance to clear the air on the matter.' Her hands had been folded in her lap throughout the conversation, but now she extended her right hand towards him, and he saw she held a pistol in it. 'This is my father's pistol. It survived the crash of the *Princess Hortense*. My new friends in the Katamenian banditry recovered it along with his body from the wreck before the Senzans could land rescue parties nearby. The bandits built a funeral pyre for him.' She nodded at the urn in its case, ebony with the

Marechal crest in gold upon it. 'There he is. He goes everywhere with me. I talk to him. Sometimes he even talks back.' She smiled cynically at the expression Cabal was trying unsuccessfully to keep entirely off his face. 'Oh, yes. I'm quite mad. I'm sure of that much. I hold you responsible for that, too.'

She weighed the pistol in her hand, holding it almost casually, but Cabal could see her finger was upon the trigger and that the muzzle never wavered away from him. 'I wonder if this is how this is meant to end, Cabal. Another aeroship, another pistol fight. That seems a little prosaic to me. Banal, even. I was of the impression that the Five Ways might be a little subtler than that.' She raised the pistol, lowered the hammer with her thumb, and tossed the weapon onto the desk. 'If you're going to shoot, Cabal, then shoot. I've seen you kill a woman at point-blank range. I know you can do it.' She spread her arms. 'Murder me, Cabal.'

Cabal levelled his pistol, and centred the barrel upon the plain of her pale forehead.

'That's it,' she whispered, yet still he heard her. 'Shoot me in the brow, just as you did my father. Go on. Fire.' He hesitated. He knew he was entering a trap when he first started up the ship's boarding ramp. Why did he feel that the real trap was only just closing upon him now?

'Shoot. Shoot, you fucking coward.' She said it quietly, without rancour: a benediction rather than a curse.

The steel of the trigger felt warm beneath his finger. He squeezed almost without realising it.

'She's only a simple girl. I think she's telling the truth in most respects,' said Frank Barrow, father of Leonie. Cabal looked at him blankly. He was reasonably sure that Barrow had not been there a moment ago. He wasn't even sure what Barrow was talking about.

'Meaning what?'

'She came to this carnival last night. The very same night she concocts a poison and uses it. I don't think she could have become Lucrezia Borgia at such short notice without professional help.'

Barrow looked meaningfully at Cabal, and Cabal was fairly sure that he was insinuating something. Exactly what he had no idea, so he asked.

'What are you insinuating?'

The sergeant coughed, startling Cabal by the very fact of his presence. There was a British police sergeant and two constables, all uniformed. The damnedest sense of *déjà vu* settled upon him. The sergeant spoke. 'The arcade, sir, if you would. We would like to look at the machines.'

'Very well, but you're wasting your time.' Cabal said it with the greatest confidence, although he was profoundly unsure what the police hoped to find in the arcade. The sense of familiarity troubled him; it was as if a memory was being held from him.

Cabal led the way for the little entourage of three police officers and Barrow to the arcade. He felt in his right-hand jacket pocket for the bunch of keys he knew would be there and unlocked the big, good-quality padlock that sealed the entrance and stepped aside. 'Be my guests.' The party entered and stood in a huddle near the door while Cabal went around and opened the shutters. As each shutter opened, bars of daylight lanced in, but there was something theatrical about the way they illuminated the airborne dust within the arcade. Why was the inside of a travelling carnival's arcade dusty at all?

A travelling carnival. The Cabal Brothers Carnival, less widely known as the Carnival of Discord. This place had occupied a whole year of his life. How could he have forgotten that? Through the unshuttered windows he could see the countryside of Penlow on Thurse, looking surprisingly like artfully painted theatrical flats.

Barrow's eye lit upon the penny tableaux and he went to investigate, followed by the policemen. Cabal leaned against the wall and affected a nonchalance that he did not feel. It was more like hitting his mark. Barrow studied the row, reading the titles as he moved along it. '"The House of Bluebeard," "The Pit and the Pendulum," "The Court of Ivan the Terrible," "The Haunted Bedroom," "Tyburn Tree". Very *Grand Guignol*, Mr. Cabal,' he said disapprovingly.

'It's what people like, Mr. Barrow.'

Barrow had arrived at the end of the row, a machine covered with a tarpaulin and with a sign fixed to it. '"Out of order"? What's wrong with it?'

Cabal had not the first nor foggiest idea. He looked at Barrow and Barrow looked back, tilting his eyebrows interrogatively in a manner not so much inquisitorial as supportive. Cabal glanced around, but there was no worried assistant in the wings clutching a tatty copy of the script, ready to offer a prompt at a beseeching glance. There was just Cabal, Frank Barrow, the sergeant, and two extras dressed as constables. Cabal ventured an *ad-lib*.

'I don't know. Something mechanical. Quite beyond me.'

There seemed to be an almost imperceptible sigh of relief from the others.

'We'd like to have a look at it if we may, sir,' said the sergeant.

'I don't think that would be wise.' He wasn't just saying it, he realised. It really would be unwise to look at the machine. 'You have my word there is no machine like the one that you have described. Isn't that enough?' He said it with too much emphasis. Surely he had been more reserved the last time he had been here?

'We'd like to see for ourselves, sir. The tarpaulin, if you please.'

'I really don't think I ought.'

'That's as may be, sir. But if you'll pardon me . . .' The sergeant quickly undid the tarpaulin and pulled it away.

The penny tableaux machine was stuck in mid-action. In a cunningly wrought representation of a large and luxurious stateroom-cum-office aboard some grandiose aeroship, a blond man wearing blue-glass spectacles was pointing a pistol at a woman. She was young and attractive, though her face was marked with a calm, sardonic distance, and she wore a gorgeous red dress that made her seem very pale. She was sitting behind a massive white-and-gold desk before a great window made of two large sheets of glass. Upon the desk's top lay a military revolver.

From the tip of the man's gun barrel an almost invisible length of wire ran in a straight line to the woman's forehead. Not even a quarter of the way along the wire, a bullet was represented with a small length painted black, followed by an explosion of red and orange, and then the rest of the bullet's track was marked in white. The mechanism was not functioning correctly, however; the 'bullet' kept travelling forwards perhaps an inch only for it to be jerked spastically back with a small metallic *ping* of protest.

The four men watched the bullet fly forwards and twitch back in silence for some seconds. 'What's wrong with it?' demanded Barrow.

Cabal did not know, but he knew it mattered. 'Something mechanical,' he echoed his own words.

'Fix it.'

'Yes, of course.' It mattered more than anything. 'I'll fetch the mechanic.'

'No.' Barrow stepped close to Cabal and glared at him with full loathing. '*You* fix it.'

This seemed unreasonable. 'I don't know how.' Cabal glanced at the cabinet. Carefully but not entirely professionally painted, the title ran across the wooden frame above the glass front; *The Necromancer's Tragedy*. 'I don't know how,' he said, wondering at what tragedy this might be even as he defined it.

'You broke it. You fix it.' Barrow was pale with anger, almost shuddering with it.

'Of course. Of course. Right away.' Cabal fell to his knees on the grimy boards of the arcade floor and took hold of the side of the case. The mechanism cover, a piece of wood two feet by three, didn't seem secured at all, but came away easily when he pulled on it.

A chaos poured out. Blood and wire. Springs and sinews. Bones and cogs. It fell into Cabal's lap, covered it, and yet more came. It was impossible; he gazed at the ruin and could see no way to start a repair, never mind finish it. He looked up at Barrow. 'I don't know how.'

Barrow towered over him, the police officers behind him merging to become a wall of dark blue serge, soaking up the light of an artificial day. 'She's dead because of you. Fix it!'

The red flood was burying him. 'I don't know how.'

'Fix it!' Barrow was shouting at him, spittle raining on the gore and the gears. 'Fix it, damn your eyes, Cabal! Damn you to hell! Fix it!'

The gun kicked in his hand, and he realised he must have shot Lady Ninuka. Odd that there seemed to be an echo to his shot. Except, no; his shot was the echo to another.

Count Marechal was fast, but Cabal was sure.

Somewhere a wire slid forwards a little further, the painted representation of a bullet upon it that much closer to the painted brow of a painted woman in red.

He turned away as Lady Ninuka threw herself wordlessly across her father's body.

He reached down and took Miss Barrow by the upper arm. 'We should leave now,' he said in a terse undertone. There was something wrong, something out of kilter with the situation, but he wasn't sure what. He should get away, and take Leonie Barrow with him. Although, hadn't he been talking with her father a moment before? And wasn't Leonie Barrow . . .

'No! Cabal, we can't. *I* can't.'

She was looking at the surviving passengers: Herr Roborovski pushed back up against a chair, unable to look away from Satunin's body; Miss Ambersleigh, hands to her mouth, trapped in incomprehension; Lady Ninuka, her dark lace cuffs darkened further by blood as she held her father tightly. 'What has happened?' she asked nobody in particular. 'What has happened?'

For his part, Marechal lay with his eyes open and with the calmest expression Cabal had ever seen him wear, his brow now troubled only by a dark hole a mite over 10.35mm wide, the brain behind it forever stilled by the addition of 179 grains of lead. For a moment Cabal thought he saw a length of wire, almost invisible, extending from the wound.

He grimaced at the image, and saw it was just a trick of the light. There was no wire. 'They can look out for themselves. Come on. Every second wasted narrows our chances.'

Miss Barrow was having none of it. She shook off his hand. 'Why did you come back?' she demanded through taut lips.

'It wasn't for you, if that's what you're thinking. Are you coming or not?' They glared at one another.

It was a moment of the purest horror for both of them. Cabal found himself impulsively leaning forwards and, before he was even truly aware that he was moving at all, he kissed her.

'I'm lying,' he said, although he didn't know why. 'I did come back for you.'

She looked at him as if he had just slapped her, eyes wide, mouth open in astonishment. 'What . . . ? What do you . . . ?'

Then she slapped him, hard enough to rock him back on his heels.

'Daddy,' Lady Ninuka said with faint certainty. 'Daddy will make everything right.' Cabal looked at her. He was the only one to look at her. He was the only one that saw. She rocked back and forth, hugging her father, but he was no longer a corpse. Tightly held in her arms was the funerary urn of Count Marechal, ebony with the family crest in gold upon its neck.

The aeroship lurched harshly to one side, almost knocking Cabal from his feet. 'The ship is out of control!' cried Roborovski.

'Oh, my Lord!' Miss Ambersleigh pointed forwards through the broken window of the salon. 'We shall crash!'

Cabal somehow regained his balance, even though the deck was canted over to starboard by some thirty degrees. 'What? No, this isn't what happened.' Yet there it was, clearly visible through the cracked glass, a cliff of exposed rock where the side of a hill had been undermined by a river running by its base.

Travelling at very nearly full speed, the *Princess Hortense* drove headlong into the cliff, crumpled, dropped, and exploded as it crashed heavily to earth.

The fire engulfed Cabal as he was tumbled around the aeroship's salon like a pea in a can. *I truly do not remember dying this way,* he thought as he tumbled, peevishly.

Presently, he stopped tumbling and settled down to death. It was cooler than he had expected, and darker. Also, death smelled slightly musty with a distinct note of burning crab oil.

'Well,' said the voice of the afterlife, 'how'd you like those apples, eh?'

Cabal's eyes opened wide in unpleasant surprise. He was where he had no right, no reason, and no desire to be. He was in the cavern of the Phobic Animus upon the inconstant island of Mormo, a chamber roughly hewn from part of an ancient cave system. Before him was a stone throne, and upon it sat the source of much evil and even more irritation, a thing that sometimes pretended to be a pleasant but dull solicitor called Gardner Bose, Esq., commissioner for oaths, conveyor of houses, destroyer of worlds.

Cabal could do little but stare at it for an incontinently long time. Then he looked at his hands. They were clean, unsullied by gunpowder residue, grime, or burns. He looked back up at Bose.

'Nyarlathotep,' said Cabal, more calmly than he felt. 'You little bastard.'

'Hello, Johannes,' said Bose, otherwise known as Nyarlathotep, otherwise known as the Crawling Chaos, otherwise known as the Stalker Amongst the Stars, otherwise known as the Eater of Grey Lilies, otherwise known by at least 995 other names and appearances, and likely more. 'Learned to pronounce my name correctly, I hear. Good for you!'

'I thought,' said Cabal, crushing down the great and negative emotions he felt at that moment on the basis that it doesn't do to get into a shouting match with an entity that can obliterate one from the very fabric of space-time with a thought, 'I *hoped* you said you were done with me and that we would never meet again.'

'Yes, well'—Bose shrugged—'what can I say? It was hardly my decision. As far as I was concerned, we were done, you and I. But then—who would have thought it?—you go and get yourself involved with the Five Ways. Now, be fair, old man, even I couldn't have known that would happen. I could have asked Yog-Sothoth, but it gets all mystical about telling the future, which is—of course—the *now* as far as it's concerned, and then it won't give you a straight answer, which usually doesn't bother me because, you know, I have quite a subtle mind, and I'm terribly good at the cryptic crossword, but it all gets so very time consuming and, anyway, Yog-Sothoth cheats at cards, too, so I'm not inclined to ask as even I've got my limits, and I think I'm getting a little off the subject. Hello!' Nyarlathotep clasped his hands in front of him and smiled winningly. 'It is *so* nice to see you again.'

'Can *you* give a straight answer to a simple question?'

Bose/Nyarlathotep rocked his/its head from side to side. 'It's happened, now and then. Go on, try me.'

'Is the Trial of the Five Ways your creation?'

'Straight question. Straight answer . . . yes. I devised it a long, long time ago for some pre-human race or another, and just left it running. It simply is the most terrific fun.'

'For you.'

'Obviously.' He laughed. 'You're wondering if the prize is genuine, aren't you? Of course you are, I can see the thoughts swirling around inside your comically tiny ape brain. "Oooh, Nyarlathotep big fibber. Maybe Five Ways big fib, too. Oooh." Well, no. For reasons that must be painfully plain to even the meanest intellect'—here Bose pointed at Cabal with both index fingers and mouthed, *Like yours*—'it makes more sense for the prize to be real. Word of mouth, you see? So important. But, it's a poisoned chalice. Of course it is. Get your dearest wish? No, no, no. It's got "monkey's paw" written all over it.'

'I do not recognise the allusion.'

Bose seemed slightly startled by the admission. 'Really? Perhaps I haven't released it into the world yet. I really must get a diary. In any case, take it from me, it's a stinker. Dearest wishes and utter curses have a lot in common.'

Cabal glared at him; it was the most he dared. 'Nevertheless, I shall have that prize.'

'You see?' Bose clapped his hands in delight. 'I've told you it's heartbreak and damnation, yet still you're going for it. I do love humans. They are *so* stupid. I shall tell you something else, old bean, I'm rooting for you—yes, you!—to win. Ninuka is an open book to me, I've seen thousands like her. She'll use the power to destroy her enemies (which means you, right at the top of her list), bring her daddy back (who will get in the way and mess up her plans because they will both want to be in control), and consolidate her corporeal power (and fail to notice when the rot sets in to whatever governmental structures she sets up and the whole farrago falls down).'

He feigned a yawn. 'Tedious, isn't it? I really could not care less. You . . . I don't know. I think you have a secret project that even I haven't been able to spy. Probably somebody close to you who's dead? Your father, too? Hmmm, no. That isn't it, I think. In any case, secret project aside, you have brought along the most interesting people. Ninuka's original plan was to do it all herself, but she couldn't crack *The One True Account of Presbyter Johannes by His Own Hand*. So she tinkered with it a bit, forged a new copy that removed any of the hints that five was an important number in connection with the rite, laid a simple enchantment of geas, as the Irish say, upon the thing so you would decide you needed four little helpmates along when you attempted it, and then left the book in a place she trusted you to be clever enough to find.' Bose nodded appreciatively. 'I have to say, I quite admire her as humans go. You certainly fell for it.'

'It was hardly an obvious trap.'

'You wouldn't have fallen for an obvious trap. Well, apart from that one that got Miss Barrow killed—'

'Shut up.'

Bose cocked his head and regarded Cabal with a speculative smile. 'Yes. I thought so. You poor chap. Must pain you to lose her. She reminds you so very strongly—'

'Shut *up*!'

Bose leaned back on his throne. 'Perhaps you're right. Perhaps it's time to conclude our business once more. I doubt we shall meet again, but I've been wrong before. To err is human, eh? Good luck, Johannes. I truly hope you win.'

The lights in the crude clay oil lamps and fluttering from the torches grew dim as all the flames in the room slowly died away. In the moment after the room was plunged into total darkness, Cabal thought he saw Bose's eyes glowing in a colour that had no satisfactory name in any human tongue. Then the darkness was absolute.

Cabal waited, but he seemed alone once more. He took a match from the little metal matchbox in his pocket and struck it, but the light seemed hardly to travel at all. He watched in bafflement as the flame shrank quickly, and then he gasped in horror as his strength left him at the same rate. He tried to keep the match burning as long as he might, but it was hopeless. Soon it was gone, and he fell to his knees. He started to fall forwards, but there was something stone or perhaps concrete right before him, and he leaned gratefully against it. Above him, the cave grew brighter, and he looked up, only to see he was no longer in a cave at all, but beneath a starry night.

Ill unto death, he had returned to his strange little isolated house to recuperate, yet could not enter since his front garden was conspiring to kill and eat him. He saw then that his was to be an ignominious death, to slowly shuffle off the mortal coil while propped against the gatepost of his home, mere yards from salvation. It did not surprise him—it is the lot of a necromancer to die, in all likelihood, an ignominious death, and he could only sigh a small sigh of relief that it didn't involve zombies, because that would have been tiresome. So, necromancer that he was, he settled down to rattle out his last breath in as much comfort as he could.

There he expired.

Too late did a potential rescuer arrive, a taciturn figure that stood over the body of Johannes Cabal, and sighed his name with true grief. The figure leaned upon the gatepost in silence for some minutes, then effortlessly lifted Cabal and walked up the garden path with the dead necromancer carelessly slung over one shoulder. At this new presence, the starving unseelie of the garden scattered in fear, because that which is supernatural and nasty knows supernatural and nastier when it sees it.

The front door was a hefty artefact of English oak and triple locked with a London bar device to resist kicking and battering attacks. The figure, a man, kicked it clean out of its frame without even troubling to put down the body, and entered. He stood for some seconds upon the black-and-white chessboard tiling of the hallway, taking in the ambience of the house. It was not the curious glance of an intruder he turned upon the mundane details of the visible house, but the slow, absorbing regard of nostalgia and memory; this had once been his home. Then, with the resolve of one on familiar ground, he made his way through the hall to the kitchen at the rear of the house, and thence down to the cellar.

Here he placed Cabal's corpse carefully upon the workbench in the corner and went to the far wall where, after a little searching around the nitrous stonework, he found and released a hidden catch. An apparently effortless shove swung a heavy secret door open, revealing a hidden laboratory larger than the mundane cellar that concealed it. The man pushed the operating table that dominated the centre of the room to one side and briefly examined the floor beneath it before finding a recessed ring in the centre of a large slab of stone flooring. He glanced up at the lifting gear suspended from the ceiling usually employed to lift the slab, but decided against it. Instead, he hooked a couple of fingers through the ring and, taking a moment to get good purchase on the floor, heaved with quite literally superhuman strength. The slab lifted sideways with a splintering grating of the edge of the slab snapping off shards as it became a pivot against the surrounding floor. It ruined it as a place of concealment, but that was all right; it would never be used again. The man allowed the slab to fall past the tipping point and it crashed to the floor, but did not break further. He noted in passing that only the top surface of the slab was made of the same stone as the rest of the floor, while the underside was pumice, presumably to reduce its weight. Perhaps so, but lifting it by brute strength had still been a prodigious feat.

Beneath the slab lay the glass coffin. The man stood silently looking at the woman within for several minutes. He had known her in life, and it was horrible and wonderful to see her again. Horrible that here she was, preserved like an exhibit in a museum of natural history, yet wonderful that the preservation was so perfect that she looked like she might open her eyes any moment, and it would be a moment of joyous surprise, not of horror. But that would never happen. Not now.

The glass coffin was sealed carefully all around its upper edges to safeguard the preservative qualities of the strange colourless yet glistening liquid in which she lay suspended. To break the seal was to immediately restart the process of decay that had been halted all those years before. The man did so without further hesitation, tearing away the waxen substance that was not wax around the coffin lid and then levering it up just as he had done with the stone slab concealing it. Unlike the slab, the lid broke when he let it topple, into three large pieces. The man did not care. He was far past caring about such trivia now.

He went back out into the cellar and returned a moment later with Cabal's body, which he laid alongside the open coffin on the fragments of glass. He stood back to look at the scene. It wasn't enough. He knelt by Cabal and gently slid his legs off the glass into the liquid, and then his midriff. The upper body followed naturally in, and the man gently moved Cabal alongside the woman. There wasn't enough room for both bodies to face upwards, but they finished floating face-to-face, and that was good. The man stood and looked at them. They would never be reunited in life; reuniting them in death was the best that he could do. He said their names. He said goodbye.

From the cellar shelves, the man fetched down a storm lantern, its reservoir kept filled and its wick trimmed in case the house's electrical generator should fail. The man took it and the box of vesta matches lying by it upstairs. It didn't take long to scatter most of the lamp's contents around the front room of the house. With no further lingering, he walked out of the house, lit the lamp, and flung it through the front window. For some seconds he wondered if the throw had extinguished the light, but no, there, a flickering illumination appeared, making the bookshelves glow. A curl of smoke, a sudden crescendo of light as the oil caught fire. The left-hand curtain started to flutter as the heat in the room began to draw air through the broken window. The man had made a point of leaving the doors open; the fire would spread easily. A suitable funeral pyre for Johannes Cabal.

The man turned and walked away, and a ghost watched him.

'No,' said Cabal. He raised his aim, a wire snapped, and all outcomes were reshuffled.

Lady Ninuka stared at him as if just realising she had no idea what he truly was. She lowered her arms. 'Why?'

'Because I may be your enemy, but you are not mine. You may be my nemesis, but I am not yours. I grow tired of these games, Orfilia Ninuka; yours and everybody else's. I am just a scientist, and I am conducting an experiment.'

He turned to face the urn containing the ashes of Count Marechal. Ninuka realised what he intended a second before he did it; she cried out, jumped to her feet, and reached for her own gun. It was all too late. Cabal fired once. The shot was deliberately placed off centre and the urn was untouched by the passage of the bullet. The glass shattered, leaving the urn still firmly affixed to its shelf by the locking collar around its base.

'Ah, ah,' warned Cabal, swinging his aim to Ninuka as he walked to the urn. She froze, her hand over her pistol. 'Good. I am tired of killing, but not so much that I will not kill to preserve my own life.'

'Save me, Orfilia!' implored the urn in the voice of Count Marechal. 'Cabal means to steal me!'

Cabal raised his eyebrows. 'Your Majesty, amongst all your other myriad talents, do you happen to include ventriloquism?' She did not answer, but her face told him all he needed to know. 'I thought it unlikely. And, yes, to clear away any uncertainty on your part, I did hear that urn speak to you. This is unusual behaviour for urns, you may be sure, and bears investigation. Step back from your desk, please. I would hate to have to shoot you before this business is concluded.'

Ninuka stepped away from the desk and watched him stonily, her arms crossed. Satisfied, he released the locking device from the urn's base and took it down from its place. He regarded it thoughtfully. 'You realise how unlikely it is that your father's body was recoverable from the wreck of the *Princess Hortense?* I watched it burn. I cannot know for sure, but I think somebody has been playing a game with you for a long time now. Don't let that upset you; I have been a pawn in it, too. I hope this is the end of it.'

Resting the urn on an occasional table by the wall, he removed the urn's lid and looked inside. A brief smile passed over his face, equal in parts sardonic, relieved, and sad. He reached in and extracted a small crystal phial filled with a dram of colourless liquid, its cap sealed with white wax. He replaced it and tilted the urn to show the inside to Ninuka. Within there were no ashes, and never had been. Instead there was a bed of black velvet into which was embroidered a golden pentagram. At each vertex was a small padded well into which a phial lay embedded.

'The Five Ways,' said Ninuka. There was a longing in her eyes, a hollowness in her tone.

'I am told that they are cursed articles of the "Be careful what you wish for" variety, but the entity that told me is not always reliable. We shall see. And by "we", I do not include you. You have lost.' He extracted his cigarillo case from his pocket, opened it on the table, and stowed the five phials there, using the cigarillos as bumpers to keep them safe. As he closed the case and returned it to his pocket, he said, 'The trial is at an end, I think. I advise you to return to the mundane world with alacrity, along with whatever remains of your force. This world will soon collapse like a house of cards.'

As he retreated towards the door, she walked slowly to the table, took up the urn, and examined it. 'I don't think so. You're right, Cabal. The game is over, and I do not care to be drawn into another.' She dropped the urn carelessly. 'I am retiring from the field the only way I know how.'

Cabal was at the door. 'That is your prerogative.' He knew there was no point in asking her to consider the lives of her men. She hadn't considered them when she had dragged them as auxiliaries into the Five Ways; why would they trouble her now?

Just before he left, she said, 'You say you don't hate me.'

'I do not, Your Majesty. I dislike you as a damnable nuisance, but hate is a strong emotion, and I have little time for such. No, I do not hate you.'

She crossed her arms. 'I'm sure I shall manage to stir such an emotion even in your frozen sarcophagus of a heart, Cabal. I shan't say farewell. I hope that you encounter all kinds of misfortune.'

Cabal decided he had wasted enough time upon her, and left without another word.

Ninuka looked at the dropped urn, turned her heel upon it, and walked to her desk. She took up the revolver and looked at the crest of the House of Ninuka in Marechal upon the white grip. As slowly as an image developing upon a photographic plate in the chemical bath, a smile formed upon her mouth.

'I *know* you will encounter all kinds of misfortune, Cabal,' she murmured. 'I *know* that you shall hate me.'

The bridge door of the *Rubrum Imperatrix* was flung open, and the officers swung around in astonishment to see the door's guard slide at great speed across the floor to finish with a solid hit upon the binnacle, making both his skull and the brass casing ring.

Horst Cabal entered, smiled, and waved. 'Hello, everyone! Here's the thing: in all the rush to get airborne and everything, my brother and I have been separated from our friends who are still at what's left of Buckingham Palace. I don't really fancy walking, so I was wondering if you'd be kind enough to turn the bus around and go back?' He shrugged apologetically. 'I should point out that, although I phrased that as a request, it's more in the way of an order, really.'

The captain stepped forwards, a hatchet-faced man with a goatee sharp enough to stab a badger. 'My authority comes from Her Imperial Majesty, Queen Orfilia Ninuka, and I obey her orders and those of my lawful superiors only, sir!'

Horst nodded. 'I can understand that, but one of your vermin shot a friend of mine, and I'm just about out of sympathy. So, I'll use whatever particles of it I still have to reiterate. Turn this ship around, or I will kill every single one of you Mirkarvian bastards one after another until somebody realises that perhaps turning around is actually a terrific idea. I am going to start with you, Captain, because your goatee offends me.'

'You would not.' The captain said it defiantly, but stepped back all the same.

'I would, you know. In case you haven't been keeping up with current affairs aboard your ship, you'll find none of your gun positions respond. I've left the engineering section alone, because they seem rather important to keeping us in the air. More important than you by a long chalk.'

'Impossible,' said the captain. Then to his first officer, 'Get on the telephone; check the gun positions.' He turned his attention back to Horst. 'You're lying, of course. It would require a full boarding party to achieve what you claim. No single man could manage it.'

'Ah, well, in that case, I think I've spotted the flaw in your thinking.' He bared his teeth and allowed his fangs to extend.

The captain paled. Unaware, the first officer called over from command station, 'None of the guns are responding, sir! I can't get any reply from the security details, either.' He belatedly realised his captain was staring fixatedly at the interloper, looked himself, and then swore.

'Turn the ship around,' said the captain. 'Return to our last anchorage.'

'Captain . . .'

'Do as I say!'

'There we go,' said Horst, clapping his hands once and smiling winningly, like somebody who has just reconciled a silly dispute over a neighbour's property line. 'Now I don't have to break anyone's neck. I don't enjoy it, you wouldn't have enjoyed it . . . Now everyone's happy, yes?'

'Happy' was overstating matters, but nevertheless, orders were given, and the vast edifice of the *Rubrum Imperatrix* turned to the starboard until its heading was steadily back towards the exciting redevelopment opportunity formerly known as Buckingham Palace.

The sound of movement behind him made Horst spin, only to find Johannes Cabal coming towards him along the corridor in a dogtrot. 'Hail and well met, brother!' said Horst.

'We're done here,' said Cabal. 'We need to leave as quickly as possible.'

'All in hand. I've prevailed upon the captain to take us back. We're making best speed now. Quick enough for you?'

Cabal entered the bridge to stand by his brother. He looked out through the great panes in the flying bridge cockpit, and did not like what he saw.

'Not nearly quickly enough.'

The navigator cried out, 'Captain!' He rose from his position and pointed towards the horizon.

The bridge crew and the Cabals saw a darkness there, a great black smudge that seemed to be growing. 'What is that? A storm cloud? I've never seen the like.'

'No storm cloud, Captain,' said Cabal. 'Look at the city beneath it.'

As the blackness expanded, the buildings of London seemed to fall into pieces at the edge of the void. The blackness deconstructed them, the rear of the buildings being stripped down to girders and floorboards while the face remained intact, the component parts falling away to be lost in an infinite distance. Soon enough, the wave stripped away the rest of the building and even the very earth on which it stood. Sewers, gas lines, and water lines were exposed beneath the disintegrating pavements and roads before they, too, tumbled into oblivion.

'This world of shadows was never intended as anything more than a temporary stage for us to play our roles,' said Cabal.

Horst eyed the billowing void with growing concern. 'It isn't half shifting. Johannes, I don't think we can outrun—'

'Not in a bloated flying fortress like this, no. Happily, there is an alternative. Come with me. Smartly now!'

This new disaster had handily focussed the attention of the bridge officers forwards, so none noticed their erstwhile hijackers leave the bridge, find an access stairwell, and quickly climb the narrow spiral stairs to the uppermost part of the ship.

'If you're expecting me to sprout bat wings and fly us to safety, I've told you before—I can't do that. I wish I could, but y'know, even vampires only get to be just so wonderful.'

'Hardly,' said Cabal. He had reached the top of the staircase inside what appeared to be a large letter box. He opened the hatch and climbed out. Horst followed to find his brother already going along the row of parked entomopters. '*I* shall be the one flying us to safety. Let me see, interceptor . . . interceptor . . . ah! A reconnaissance variant with two seats. More comfortable than having to strap you to a weapons wing.' He detached the covers and flung them aside. 'I'm fairly sure I can remember how to fly one of these things. Much like a bicycle. Probably. Are you coming, Horst?' He nodded at the nothingness that was devouring London. It was barely half a mile to the aft of the running ship and steadily catching them. 'I'd advise against dawdling.'

The entomopter was fuelled and ready for a rapid scramble alert. As Horst strapped himself into the forward seat of the tandem cockpit, Cabal cast his eyes over the controls. Its systems were noticeably more advanced than the basic Symphony trainer that was his only flying experience to date, but he was sure he would pick up the niceties of its handling soon enough. Given that the alternative consisted of being dismantled by an oncoming cloud of nothing, he appreciated that he had better. The lack of a cartridge ignition system baffled him for a moment, and there was an agonising thirty seconds of him searching through the unfamiliar panels while Horst said, 'Johannes . . .' repeatedly every few moments, each rendition slightly higher than the last, but then he found an ignition chamber system, took a few seconds to work out how to use it ('Johannes . . .' 'Johannes!' 'JOHANNES!'), charged, pressurised, and fired it.

It worked first time.

'Well, that was easy enough,' he commented as the entomopter lifted and sped forwards, even as the aft rudders of the *Rubrum Imperatrix* were devoured by the blackness.

Throttle opened as far as he dared with a cold engine and with the airspeed indicator rising satisfactorily, Cabal risked a glance back through the aerocraft's high-visibility bubble canopy. His last sight of the great aeroship was of the prow windows directly below the bridge. There, standing in the angle of the glass, he saw Orfilia Ninuka, resplendent in red, her arms crossed, and unafraid. Momentarily, Cabal wished that there could have been some other resolution. Momentarily, he thought she was magnificent. Then he turned away.

Zarenyia and Miss Smith had retired to the relative safety of a gun position on the former perimeter line for the *Rubrum Imperatrix*'s anchorage, now rendered a perimeter line for a lot of smashed and burning buildings since that vessel's precipitate departure. Zarenyia had been forced to readopt a trimmer body so that the sandbag walls were actually high enough to shield her, and Miss Smith—who had belatedly discovered that throwing around vast magical energies was severely taxing upon the constitution—had discovered the joys of support weapons while she recovered her strength. The heavy machine gun she was currently manning was tremendously noisy, but also good fun, not least because of the not entirely kind commentary that Zarenyia—who was keeping the gun's ammunition belt feeding smoothly into the breech—kept up about the hapless Mirkarvian soldiers who we trying to assault their position.* It was all high jinks of a homicidal sort, and it helped distract them from the body under a blanket behind them.

They were further distracted by the approaching distinctive engine tone of an aviation engine overlaid by the vicious buzzsaw-like hum of entomopter wings. Miss Smith was just hauling over a light machine gun to provide anti-aerocraft fire when Zarenyia cried, 'It's the boys! They're alive and not dead! Isn't that nice?'

Miss Smith returned to the first gun. 'It would be nicer if they

* 'Run for it, darling! Run for cover! You can make it! Not far now! Fleet of foot, and strong of . . . Oh, bad luck. Still you made it further than your friend. Oh, there's another! Run for it, darling!' And so on.

could drop some bombs or something on this lot.' She sighted down the barrel, then lifted her head in bemusement. 'Oh, that flying machine has scared all the soldiers off. Look, they'll all running away. Feels wrong to shoot them in the back.' She shot one just to check. 'Yes, I didn't enjoy that at all.'

'Darling.' Something in Zarenyia's tone made Miss Smith look over. Zarenyia was facing the direction where the stolen entomopter was setting down, but that wasn't where her gaze led. The sky was vanishing. The city was vanishing. Belatedly, Miss Smith realised that the Mirkarvians weren't running from her at all.

The Cabal brothers climbed from the entomopter and ran towards them, Horst leaping the sandbags and Cabal rolling over them in his haste to join the women. He almost fell on the covered body. He stepped back, startled, and demanded, 'Is this Miss Barrow?'

'I'm sorry, Cabal.' Miss Smith abandoned the gun and went to him. 'There was nothing we could do. She was already gone when we reached her. I'm sorry.'

Cabal looked at her with genuine perplexity. 'Why are you sorry? You didn't shoot her, I trust?'

'Of course not. But I know what she meant to you.'

Cabal shook his head irritably as if dissuading a determined fly. 'What she means to me? She's a colleague. A reliable ally.' He started checking his pockets for no discernible reason.

Miss Smith glanced at Horst, who shrugged, and Zarenyia, who pulled a face and offered, 'Are all humans so bloody abstruse?'

Cabal produced a cigarette case or similar. Miss Smith held out a hand. 'If you're going to spend the last few minutes before the world ends puffing on a gasper, I want one, too.'

But instead of a cigarillo, Cabal removed a tiny crystal phial, sealed with white wax. He snapped the case shut, dropped it back into his pocket, and whipped away the blanket. Feigning ignorance of the ragged bullet wound in her side or its larger exit wound, ignoring the great deal of blood she must have lost as she haemorrhaged to death with no one to save her, he lifted her head, opened the sealed cap of the phial with his thumb, and poured the contents into her open mouth.

'What is that?' asked Miss Smith, fascinated.

'A miracle. I hope.' Cabal regarded Leonie Barrow's face closely, but there was no flicker of muscle action, no change in the dull, corpse pallor. 'Come on,' he whispered. 'Come along, Miss Barrow. I went to a great deal of trouble to get this. Kindly oblige me by not being dead any more. Come on . . .' He slapped the corpse across the face. 'Come on!'

'Johannes!' Horst snapped. 'What do you—'

Cabal's hand was already back ready for another blow when the body's hand reached up and grabbed his wrist. Leonie Barrow's eyes flew open. 'If you slap me again, Cabal, I will break your bloody nose.'

'Well,' said Zarenyia, 'there's something you don't see every day. Or, indeed, at all.'

Leonie was glaring at Cabal, sparing some ire for all these people gathered around her. 'I was just knocked out. I was climbing up the ramp and I slipped, that's all. I am perfectly well, thank you. Never felt better.'

'Actually,' said Miss Smith in the confidential tone of a friend who is going to broach the subject of an unexpected personal hygiene problem, 'no. You were stone dead.'

Leonie looked at her sharply. 'I was not.'

'Take it from a professional, Leonie—yes, you were.'

Leonie Barrow's anger fell away. She glanced at Cabal. 'Was I?'

'Yes,' he said simply. 'You were shot and bled to death.'

'I thought . . . I thought you couldn't resurrect the dead perfectly, Cabal. I thought . . .' Her eyes widened. 'Oh, God. I'm not a zombie, am I?'

'If you are, you're chattier and more introspective than any I've met before.' Seeing her expression, Cabal added, 'No. I am confident that you are completely restored to us. Ladies, Horst, we have won. The prize of the Five Ways is ours. Your share, Miss Barrow, is why you are no longer dead.'

'Johannes.' Horst pointed to the darkness. It was no longer a linear wave, but seemed to have broken around the area at the end of the Mall, sweeping around as a wave does upon a rock. The horizon turned dark all about them. 'I don't wish to spoil the party, but what are we going to do about the imminent end of the world?'

'Nothing. It is not necessary; when this reality fails, we shall be spat out into our own. We are the victors here. To destroy us now would spoil our benefactor's joke.'

'Benefactor?'

'You truly don't want to know. In any event, we are safe'—he turned to Miss Smith—'but for you.'

Her face grew taut. 'What do you mean, Cabal?'

'You were never intended to be part of the trial. You were dragged along as scenery. There are no guarantees for you. You don't even have a body to return to. If this world ends and you cannot reach the Dreamlands—and I shall be frank, I see no mechanism by which you might—you will be destroyed in the dissolution.'

Miss Smith sat heavily by the sandbag wall and slumped back against it. Her eyes flickered about distractedly as she sought solutions and failed. 'It hardly seems fair to die twice when it wasn't my fault either time.' She looked at Cabal. 'Well, fuck.'

Cabal crouched before her, opened his cigarillo case and produced another phial. 'Orfilia Ninuka shall not be needing hers. I cannot be sure it will help you, but given the alternative . . .'

Miss Smith leaned forwards and snatched it from his hand with a speed and precision that would have made vipers applaud, if only they had hands and a sense of graciousness. She tore off the stopper and swallowed the contents in a second. Only after she had ingested the fluid did she find pause to look abashed. 'I'm fed up of dying,' she said.

'Well, I hope it goes well by you, Miss Smith. If it . . .' Cabal frowned. 'Madam, you are becoming less substantial.'

'What?' She held up her hand to study it. There was indeed something of the translucent about it. 'Is this right? Is this supposed to happen? Am I dissolving or becoming invisible? Invisibility will not help me right this moment, Cabal! Not with that coming!' She waved a decreasingly apparent finger at the oncoming void. As she spoke, despite her excitement raising her voice, there was an ineffable yet definite sense that it was simultaneously draining away, as if she was being upset at a distance.

'I cannot say,' admitted Cabal. 'Every phial may have a different effect, depending on the recipient. Oh, Miss Smith!'

But there was nobody to talk to. In mid-harangue at an implacably bloody-minded destiny that seemed set on dissolving her by one means or another, her voice dwindled to nothing, and her presence with it. Her clothes collapsed by the sandbag wall and the empty phial clattered to the ground.

'Did . . . she just die? Again?' asked Horst.

'No.' Cabal was certain. 'I strongly doubt she did. But bear in mind that she was never truly with us, but merely a dreamer's body gathered from the Dreamlands. And these'—he prodded the very solid seeming dress—'are Dreamland clothes, yet they remained here. I think Miss Smith may well have returned to the corporeal world. Whole and well, I hope.'

'And naked!' said Zarenyia cheerfully.

'All the best people are resurrected from certain doom naked,' said Horst, also cheerfully. 'Well, I was, and that turned out all right.'

A sudden sense of *presence* at his elbow made him look down. At his right elbow stood the ghost of a frightened little girl.

'Oh, Minty . . .' In all the excitement, he had quite forgotten about her, and the inattention stung him with guilt.

'Wha's 'appening?' she said. 'Where's London goin'?' Her eyes were wide, her speech hurried and panicked.

Horst knelt to look her in the eye. How could he tell her that she was nothing more than a shadow of a shadow, a facsimile of a phantom, a stage prop in a murderous theatre?

'We've undone what happened here,' he told her. 'The Red Queen is dead. It will be as if none of this ever happened.'

She blinked at him. 'Will I be alive again?'

Horst nodded. He could see that motes of pale light were starting to stream away from her towards the darkness as London died.

'But . . . bein' alive 'urt,' she said. 'Bein' like this'—she held up her hands—'nothin' 'urts. Nothin'.'

The motes had become a stream. She was diminishing, emptying away before his eyes. Miss Smith's vanishing had been a far less cruel thing than this.

'Minty, I've been alive, and I've been dead. Being alive is better, believe me. When you return to life, you won't remember any of this, but perhaps you'll remember this much. To have a good life. It's brief. It's often troublesome, but it's a great deal better than the alternative. We're all a long time in the grave, we poor creatures. Make what you can of those years when the spark is in you.'

She turned then, and saw her essence being drawn away. She looked back at him. 'Take me wiv you, Horst! *Please!*'

And she was gone.

The void was almost upon them. 'Here,' said Cabal with urgency. 'It would be as well if you all had your share of the prize when the void reaches us.' He quickly handed a phial to Zarenyia and one to Horst. Horst took it from him silently, still looking into the darkness where a small light faded.

Cabal returned the case containing the last to his pocket. 'You are already your own proof, Miss Barrow.'

'Should we hold hands or something?' she asked, the gun redoubt rapidly becoming the only point of reality left in an infinity of nothing.

'Oh, let's!' Zarenyia grasped Leonie's hand and Cabal's. 'Everyone hold hands! We can sing a song!'

'I'd rather we didn't . . .'

'*Ging gang goolie goolie goolie goolie watcha . . .*'

At which moment, the last world of the Trial of the Five Ways was snuffed out, and that was probably just as well.

THE FALL OF THE HOUSE OF CABAL

Vlatez and Muk had enjoyed their camping holiday. Of course, as Katamenian bandits they had lived the larger part of their adult lives bivouacking in forest clearings or in handy caves. Relatively few of their nights were spent under the rooves of houses and these they regarded as novelties, sure enough, but never likely to catch on. Thus, as previously noted, any camping vacation was in the manner of a busman's holiday for them, but at least it had been conducted in a country not their own, or just over the borders of a neighbouring state.

They had been given a good sum of money, return tickets to England, and very explicit instructions. For a period that might be as short as a few days or as lengthy as a couple of months they were to monitor any activity around the house of Johannes Cabal and to keep a watch on the railway station that served the village an hour's walk away. In case of certain situations arising, they were instructed to do this, that, or the other. In the meantime, they were given basic rules of conduct and strongly worded warnings as to what would surely result if they failed in even the smallest aspects. Given that the orders had been personally given by Her Majesty herself, and the superstitious—and sensible—awe in which her Katamenian mercenaries held her, there was never any question that Vlatez and Muk would do their very, very best. Their honour demanded it, and their senses of self-preservation were very much in favour, too.

Their cover was simply that they had always wanted to visit the English countryside and that they were happy to simply wander the byways, admiring the flora and fauna. They were to remain at least reasonably sober at all times, they were to indulge in no criminal activities no matter how many soft targets crossed their paths, they were to maintain friendly contact with the locals as and when it was unavoidable, but should otherwise shun any company but their own.

Thus, once or twice a week, one of the bandits would wander into the village in the ludicrous 'rambling' outfits that had been pressed upon them after a brief read of some old magazines and a battered Boy Scout's manual, and there they would purchase rations. The locals became familiar with the sight of either the cadaverous Muk or the apelike Vlatez appearing in the grocers dressed in baggy brown shorts or green corduroy trousers, short-sleeved shirt or tank top, and a broad-brimmed canvas hat, and buying assorted staple food items in broken English, occasionally pausing to smile brightly and comment on the weather.

The villagers rapidly came to the conclusion that the visitors could only possibly be interested in the only unusual thing to be found in the area: Johannes Cabal. Given the heavy-handed attempts at portraying themselves as nothing more than innocent hikers, they were presumably up to something clandestine and almost certainly injurious to Cabal and his interests. This was fine with the villagers; anything awful that befell him was something wonderful by their lights, he having failed to ingratiate himself with the locals. This is an understatement; on more than one occasion the locals had tried to get rid of him themselves, but failed for a variety of reasons, often by being talked down from the peak of righteous fury by the words of the local policeman, Sergeant Parkin.

Parkin, it should be pointed out, did his duty in this way for dual reasons: it was his job to keep the peace, and lynch mobs were distinctly not peaceful; and he was very happy to have his salary bolstered by regular bribes from Cabal precisely so he never forgot that duty.

Parkin was not only sharper than the Katamenians believed, but even than the locals knew. He had understood that the 'hikers' were a threat to Cabal the moment he clapped eyes upon them, and set about identifying them. The men were cagey about saying from exactly where in Eastern Europe they hailed, but Parkin noted both men possessed unusual tattoos of the sort associated with prison yards and memorised one in particular that both men bore. It was an ugly thing, and badly done, but the design was distinct: a skull, its crown removed, sitting in a campfire. Either the campfire was very small, or the skull very large, for the flames barely licked up past the level of the upper teeth. Propped in the skull's open brainpan could be seen the handle of a spoon or a ladle. It seemed an impractical way to serve broth, but Parkin guessed it referred to some local legend or popular tale.

Whatever its provenance, it was distinctive. Parkin took down his copy of *The Big Police Book of Criminal Organisations Around the World* and spent a hair-raising morning examining the indicia of sundry gangs, mobs, and syndicates of many lands. Working his way through those of Eastern Europe in particular, he finally located a drawing very similar to the tattoos he had seen both foreigners sporting on their forearms.

EUROPE: EASTERN: KATAMENIA: KATAMENIAN BANDITS

'Oh, dear,' said Sergeant Parkin. He made himself a fresh cup of tea and settled down to examine the text. During the reading, he had cause to say, 'Oh, dear' several times more; bandits as an occupational grouping tend away from the wholesome, but the Katamenian variety seemed to go out of their way to dabble in the ghastly.

Presently, when he had finished reading, Parkin closed the book.

He took a long draught of hot tea and blew a sigh of steamy breath through his walrus moustache. 'Sorry, Cabal, old son,' he said to the empty room. 'You're on your own this time.'

It was in an early morning in the fifth week of their vigil that Muk was to be seen speeding away from the railway station upon a bicycle (the bicycle was hired as per their instructions, despite them so very much wanting to steal one instead). A study in angles, Muk arrived in an area from which they had previously been kept by their orders: the environs of Cabal's house itself. Casting the bicycle aside, he waved like a human semaphore up at the hill that faced the house. He remembered the hour, drew a pistol from his pack, and fired it skywards, then took a red flare, ignited the fuse against the striker cap, and capered excitedly around. Some five minutes and another couple of skyward shots later, he was rewarded by the sight of Vlatez making his way at a steady jog through the gloom towards him.

The burly man arrived with a question on his lips, but it died when he saw Muk's grim expression. Still, he had to be sure.

'The queen . . . she has not arrived?'

Muk shook his head. Through their long surveillance, it had primarily been the thought of pleasing Her Majesty that had kept them keen. The conditions for ending their mission had been threefold and explicit. If nobody comes to the house in the space of three months, they were to return to Mirkarvia by the next available packet. If Queen Ninuka or one of her recognised senior ministers or advisors arrived, they were to be conducted to Cabal's house with all possible speed, for the necromancer was dead or captured, and his house and its contents were declared bounty to the new Mirkarvian Empire. If, however, Cabal or one of his colleagues were seen to return . . .

They both knew this boded poorly for their beloved monarch, whom they loved more than life. With a dark hatred growing in their hearts for the probable assassin of Queen Orfilia Ninuka, they opened their packs and removed the pieces of equipment they had hoped never to need.

* * *

It was a tired necromancer and his subdued vampire brother who left the milk train at the station and, finding no cart to be hired, nor even any bicycles to be had, they settled down to walk the few miles to the house. 'He was luckier than us,' said Horst, nodding at the angular man in ill-chosen shorts haring off down the road on a bicycle. He looked to the sky and checked his watch against the station clock. 'Oh, well. Should be back with a few minutes to spare before dawn, in any case.'

Cabal and Madam Zarenyia had popped back into existence in Abyssinia, Horst and Miss Barrow in Constantinople. As previously arranged by Cabal in a tortuous but ultimately sensible plan of meeting places and *poste restante* addresses, they rendezvoused in Venice. The plan was for them to travel on together back to England, but Leonie Barrow had said she needed a holiday to recuperate from the adventure in general and being dead in particular, so she would remain on the Continent for a few weeks more. Zarenyia had said that sounded delightful and, as she herself was probably *diaboli non grata* in Hell for the next few millennia, she would be honoured if Miss Barrow would allow her to be her travelling companion and bodyguard. 'We can broaden one another's minds, darling. You can teach me to be a little bit good . . . and I can teach you to be a little bit wicked.' Madame Zarenyia said this, and smiled lazily. After securing Zarenyia's oath not to kill people willy-nilly, extracted with a great deal of dibbing, the Cabal brothers waved goodbye from the Orient Express to the ladies on the platform as the train pulled away safely after dusk with a coffin stowed in the baggage car.

Thus, they found themselves back in England, walking home. They walked largely in silence (Horst being in an uncharacteristic melancholy mood), but for Cabal once saying apropos of nothing that he hoped the dose of the prize that had gone to Miss Smith had done her good.

'What do you call "good"?' asked Horst.

'Returned her to life, of course. A life worth living, that is. Her last fragments of physical existence in this world are bobbing around in formaldehyde in my laboratory. If that's what her spirit has been forced into, I would not regard that as "good", for example.'

'You've got bits of Miss Smith in bottles?'

Cabal nodded. 'It was a courtesy of sorts. I don't expect you to understand.'

Horst didn't, and so that line of conversation dried up.

They were within a mile of the house, although it was hidden from view by the curve of the small valley in which it resided. Horst paused. 'Something is wrong,' he said with a certain gravity that impressed his brother.

'Wrong? How so?' He peered off into the darkness. The day was coming, and the ridges of the hills were rimed with pre-dawn light. The birds were stirring in the trees, and there was dew upon the grass. It seemed commonplace enough, but Cabal felt his hackles rise.

Horst closed his eyes and stood with his head cocked as if listening. Then he drew in a deep breath through his nose.

'Smoke. I smell smoke.' His eyes opened wide and he stared at Cabal with horror. 'Fire.'

'Run! Run!' Cabal had no time for niceties. 'I will catch up. Run, for heaven's sake!'

Horst burnt a lot of his blood reserves to go as fast as he possibly could, and that was very quickly indeed. He tore through the intervening mile in a time more easily measured in seconds and parts of seconds than minutes, and turned the edge of the hill upon whose lower slopes Johannes Cabal had somehow shifted the house some years before. It was alight, the window of the sitting room on the ground floor and that of Johannes's bedroom on the first both shattered, smoke and flames showing through the frames.

He ran to the house, noting an abandoned bicycle lying by the path through the valley some twenty yards from the wall. Instantly put in mind of the figure cycling away from them with such urgency at the station, he started to get a vague understanding of what might be afoot.

He hurdled the front wall into the house's small rose garden and found the little folk of the garden engaged in a cleanup job. Assorted body parts were being dragged under the rosebushes. Horst noted a rapidly vanishing leg, extant only from the knee down, wore a bicycle clip. 'What happened here?'

'Is not our fault,' chorused the tiny, cute, ineffably dangerous denizens of the garden. 'They weren't postmen. Johannes only said not to eat the postmen! We have been good!'

'I said'—Horst allowed his own ineffable dangerousness to wash into his voice—'what happened here?'

Taking the hint, the garden folk said, 'They climbed over the wall! They had metal rocks and threw them. *Poom!* The metal rocks went *poom*! And things went on *fire*! We said, "Hey, you! Stop throwing around metal rocks that go *poom*!" And they went, "Whaaaaaat?" And then we ate them because they weren't postmen. That is what happened here.'

Johannes Cabal arrived, panting heavily and his jacket discarded somewhere on the way. 'What,' he wheezed out, 'has happened here?'

Horst reached down and lifted up the leg despite the squeaks of protest from the garden fey and tapped the bicycle clip significantly.

Cabal glanced at the fire and grimaced with open anger. 'Ninuka! *Such* a poor loser.' Now he weighed up the fire more carefully and how good its grip on the fabric of the building might be.

'The house is doomed,' he said almost immediately. 'But we can still save much. Avoid opening doors when you can, keep the rooms short of oxygen.' He nodded at the house. 'The sitting room and my room will be lost first. Mine contains little of import, but from the front you must get all the books from the second and third shelves, and save the three boxes on the deep shelf by the fireplace.'

'Really? You want me to save your head collection?'

'My reasons are sound, hardly sentimental. Meanwhile, I shall fetch Dennis and Denzil. They may for once turn out to be useful.'

'Johannes, wait!' Horst pointed at the eastern sky. 'The sun's almost up. I can't help you. I have to find cover.'

Cabal did not hesitate. 'Drink your phial. It will make you human again, I think.'

Horst shook his head. 'You think. And what about Alisha Bartos? No, the phial is for her. I failed her, I will save her.'

'Miss Bartos shall have mine. You take yours now. Consider it the fulfilment of the promise I made when I first released you from the Druin crypt. You deserve life, Horst. A real life.'

Horst gawped at him. 'Yours? But . . . what about—'

'If we don't act now, all is lost. You say you failed her. No, she understood the danger and risked it, anyway. But you, I failed you at that crypt. You had no idea into what peril I was taking us. This time, when I say, 'Trust me,' I mean it with every thread of my being. Use your phial. Time is against us.'

Without waiting for a reply, Cabal ran down the side of the house to the shed where he kept sundry tools, a quantity of firewood and coal, and two blissfully happy zombies called Dennis and Denzil, who found *post-mortem* existence very much to their liking.

Horst reached into his waistcoat pocket and fished out the small crystal phial. He regarded it with unreadable expression for a moment, his awareness of the imminent sun rounding the earth to blast him to ashes growing by every tick of his pocket watch. Then in precipitate action, he tore away the stopper and threw the contents into his mouth.

He had long since forgotten what it had felt like to become contaminated by the taint of vampirism, or so he told himself. It was not true; he had felt the corruption flood every cell, felt his humanity come under a spiritual assault unlike anything he could ever have imagined, felt his very body change as it prepared him for an existence that made him both the most alpha of predators, and the most wretched of parasites. He had felt all these things, and then he had spent the subsequent years of imprisonment assiduously wiping every conscious memory of it away. All he had was that he was Horst Cabal, who was so very human, and people liked him. This was the stanchion to which he clung while the world turned upside down, and it had worked. When he finally emerged, he was not the thing of whispered horror he might have been. He was still Horst Cabal—good old Horst—and if it was only an act, it was good enough to fool even him.

That pretence was stripped away now, as the shadow was lifted from him, the corruption burning from his cells, and as it did so, he plaintively realised that, to an extent, he had enjoyed being a vampire. The strength, the blurring into motion so rapid as to be almost invisible, the mesmerism, the psychical invisibility, it had all been useful one time or another and, he had to confess, often a great deal of fun. He would miss all of that. Now he would just be himself again, he would age, and he would die. That was fine, he supposed, but he would really miss being something extraordinary.

He was shocked by how much he had become habilitated to the taint, however; his mortality returned to him like a golden flood of true, actual life. It was ecstasy without a hint of the accursedness that had troubled his feeding as a vampire. He fell to his knees and shuddered under the impact of life.

Cabal returned a minute later with Dennis and Denzil pottering along good-naturedly hideous and dead in his wake, each clutching a bucket. 'Go to the stream, fill your bucket, bring it back, throw it'—Cabal realised he was just setting them up for Saturday morning matinee antics unless he was painfully specific in his orders—'throw the *water* from the bucket onto the fire, and then return to the stream to do the whole thing again. Keep doing it until I tell you differently. Go on! Off you go!' He watched the wretchedly preserved pair totter off in the direction of the stream. 'And don't fall in!' he shouted after them, more in hope than expectation.

Glancing at the state of the house—the fire had become noticeably more entrenched even in the minute or so he was away—Cabal helped his brother back to his feet. 'Well?' He looked to the east. The sun was almost cresting the hills. There would just be time to get Horst to the shed and away from the sun's rays if the contents of the phial proved to have failed. 'Did it work?'

His brother looked at him. Cabal realised something he never had until that moment; just how much of the colour had left Horst since his unfortunate change in lifestyle. When he had first seen him as a vampire, Horst had been trapped underground for over eight years, and Cabal had unconsciously rationalised his changed complexion as something akin to prison pallor. Then he had grown used to it, not least because the practicalities of vampiric life meant that he had only seen him by artificial light, by candle or fire, and occasionally by the light of the moon subsequently.

Now there was colour in his face, pinkness in his cheeks, and the gleam of his eye was less unnatural, less feral and feverish.

'I think it did, Johannes.' Horst said it slowly, as if waking from a dream. 'I think it worked. I feel different.'

'Human?'

Horst shrugged. 'I don't know. My memory's not that good.'

The acid test was upon them a moment later. The sun finally spilled its light over the horizon and bathed the pair of them in its brilliance. Cabal squinted against it and regretted having dumped his jacket in the run to the house; it might have done to shield Horst and give him an extra few seconds if necessary. But Horst was standing there, looking at his hands in the full onslaught of the new day and, wonderfully, there was no smoke leaking from them. He turned to face the sun, and the only shield he needed was his hand to his brow.

'*Mein Gott*,' said Cabal. 'It worked, Horst. It actually worked!'

Horst turned back to him, looking perplexed. 'There is one thing, though.'

'Which is?'

Horst opened his mouth to show his teeth. Nothing seemed unusual. Then, presumably as the result of a small act of effort on Horst's part, his fangs extended. 'Wha's all this abou', eh?' he asked, as of one having a conversation with the dentist.

Cabal looked at him, little short of aghast. He looked at the sun, which was definitely up, definitely real, and definitely sprinkling its purifying rays all over his brother. He looked again at Horst, who was definitely alive, definitely befanged, and definitely not bursting into flames. It was a conundrum.

'Horst,' he said, theorising frantically yet failing to settle on any specific conclusion, 'I'm not entirely sure, but I think we may have inadvertently disturbed the natural order of things.'

Horst closed his mouth and made a sour face. 'What? *Again?*'

'In any event, we have no time to discuss your newest and most baffling change in taxonomy. The house is afire and'—they watched as Dennis, soaked to the skin, padded past, threw a half-filled bucket of water into the flames, stood admiring his work for a few seconds, turned, and padded happily back off to the stream—'and I have no great hopes of bringing it under control. Come on!'

And so saying, he ran to the front door, tested the handle to see if it was hot, and entered, Horst close on his heels.

They cleared the burning sitting room first. Horst gathered up armfuls of the indicated books and journals while Cabal stood on a chair to recover the three head-sized wooden boxes from the deep shelf by the fireplace.

The work progressed quickly, punctuated by the occasional sprinkle of water as Dennis or Denzil flung the remaining contents of their buckets through the smashed window. Cabal also noticed, but did not comment upon, just how many books Horst could carry at a time, ferry them out, and return for more, all without even breaking a sweat. The prize of the Five Ways truly was staggeringly powerful. Returning Leonie Barrow to life exactly as she had been before she was shot had demonstrated its extraordinary capabilities, but if Horst truly had been turned into a creature with the advantages of a vampire but with all the marked disadvantages removed, that was perhaps an even greater miracle. Had such a creature ever existed before?

The upper stories of the house were in the greatest danger, so they headed upstairs for their next job. Cabal had next to nothing he couldn't live without in his room or anywhere on the first floor, and he was in and out the former to grab his backup travelling bag, a hidden bag of cash garnered from the year of the Carnival of Discord's operations (he had a feeling he would be needing a lot of money in the near future), and—somewhat to Horst's surprise and pleasure—a framed picture of their mother and father. That was it for the first floor.

The topmost floor consisted of Cabal's main attic laboratory. Here Cabal flung a shelf full of notebooks and journals into an old Gladstone bag, and then moved along the shelves rapidly and without vacillation choosing those things that would be very hard to replace. These were dropped on top of the notebooks, those things that he did not require being left to burn.

There was one point where he paused before a row of jars half filled with a clear liquid, almost colourless but for a hint of yellow. That he stood staring at them for more than a few seconds was enough to draw Horst's attention, busily loading a tea chest with pieces of equipment his brother had asked him to save.

'What's in those jars? Something important?'

'It's what's *not* in those jars that astonishes me, and gives me hope.'

'Hope?'

Cabal turned his head, and Horst saw he was smiling slightly. 'Miss Smith.'

Horst looked to the jars as understanding dawned. 'Ohhh . . . Well, fingers crossed for a happy outcome there.'

'Indeed so.' Cabal returned to selecting those things to be saved with a new vigour. 'Indeed so.'

The attic laboratory scoured of all that was useful required three journeys. Cabal was sweating and dishevelled at the end of it, but Horst was still disgracefully unruffled. Cabal began entertaining thoughts that the phial had magically imbued his brother with the power to be more irritatingly perfect than even he had previously believed possible. On the last sortie, the stairwell had been difficult to negotiate, both in terms of the smoke noticeably thickening since the last one, and the choking effects it had as it gathered at the head of the well. Cabal glanced up at the skylight that illuminated the stairwell; as and when the fire broke it, then it would become beyond any hope of control. Between the broken windows and an open window at the top of the house, a convection flow would surely develop, feeding the flames with fresh oxygen and turning the building into an impromptu furnace.

'We don't have long left,' he told Horst as they put down the last load of salvage from the attic by the garden gate.

'Put out the fire! Burney fire! Ouchey fire!' chanted the garden folk as Denzil and Dennis ambled past, bearing buckets. They lined up in front of the sitting room window and attempted to fling water through the broken glass. Denzil underdid his swing of the bucket, and watered the base of the wall. Dennis overdid his, and ended his swing with the bucket on his head. Denzil regarded him for a moment, put down his own bucket, and tried to dry Dennis off with his hands, a hopeless venture given both of them had already fallen in the stream a half dozen times each. Finding his fingers wet, Denzil tried flicking water droplets from them at the fire.

The Cabals watched them, paragons of firefighting. Johannes Cabal shook his head. 'There's no point in trying to sort them out. It would take hours. The fire will spread very soon and threaten the fabric of the house. The cellar; nothing is more vital now.'

Cabal wetted his handkerchief on a passing zombie and tied it over his nose and mouth. Horst demurred to do the same; he apparently felt few ill effects from the heat and smoke. Then they entered the house in which they had grown up together for the last time.

They made their way with the surety of long familiarity through the smoke in the hallway, across the black-and-white tiles of the corridor, across the parquet from the base of the stairwell, and so to the kitchen. There Cabal opened the door to the cellar and flicked the light switch. Electric lights glowed slowly into life, draining the last few minutes from the emergency storage batteries even as the automatic generator was coaxed into life by the demand for power. By the time they were halfway down the stairs, the generator had coughed a few times and was now chugging along quite contentedly. The light strengthened, and they looked around the first cellar, neatly arrayed with shelved assorted household oddments, storage boxes, fuel cans, and boxes of tinned food. They ignored them all, but for a large barrel. Here, they hesitated.

'It's bigger than I remember,' said Horst.

'We got it down here easily enough. We just reverse the process. You are more than strong enough to—'

'I *was* strong enough. That was before I swallowed the contents of the phial.'

Cabal stared at him. 'But . . . you still have your fangs. You've been carrying around great piles of books and equipment without obvious effort. I thought—'

'No. I've changed. *Something's* changed. I can feel it. I'm not as strong as I was.' He looked around, found a large sack of potatoes, gripped it by the neck with one hand, and hefted it up.

Cabal pointed. 'That is no small feat.'

'Any decent circus strongman could do this.' Horst gasped with exertion. 'This would have been nothing to me an hour ago. Now I'm really labouring to manage it.' He dropped the sack. 'I'm not even half as strong as I was. That barrel, plus all the liquid in it, plus poor Alisha, how much is that going to weigh? I can't do it, Johannes.' He nodded towards where the hidden laboratory lay behind its secret door, his evident despair deepening. 'And this thing is a feather's weight compared to the glass coffin.' He looked helplessly at his brother. 'What are we going to do?'

He may not have been possessed of fangs and fashion sense, but Johannes Cabal was not without notable qualities, too. One of them was that he was rarely caught at a loss for more than a moment, no matter how dreadful the situation, no matter what the possible repercussions. In the house of his mind, the servants of his personality had permanent standing instructions that, not only was Herr Cabal never at home to Mr Panic, but that Mr Panic should be afforded a good larruping and sent away with a flea in his ear.

Thus, with no more time to think than was necessary for him to look away, sniff, and nod, a scheme was hatched and committed to wholeheartedly.

Cabal went to an old workbench in the corner, sorted through a small crate sitting on the corner of the bench's top, and returned with a short crowbar of the sort known as a jemmy. He handed it to Horst. 'You can do this more quickly than I. Open the barrel.'

'We're doing this now?'

'We have little choice.' Above them, something thudded heavily to the floor, making them both glance up. They looked at one another, their thoughts the same. Cabal nodded at the barrel. 'Quickly, please.'

Horst required no further assurance. He drove the bar's beak into the edge of the lid and levered violently. Perhaps too violently; the topmost hoop strained against the forced stave and threatened to snap. Horst paused, but Cabal said, 'Break it,' so he did. Without requiring direction, he shifted his attention to the band around the barrel's equator. This refused to break, but the stave Horst was levering against moved in, and a curious fluid escaped, colourless and transparent, but seemingly flecked with tiny motes of light, pouring to the floor. Cabal joined in then, taking up a lump hammer from the workbench and smiting the neighbouring staves until they, too, loosened.

The liquid was escaping rapidly now, and the pressure against the inside of the barrel was diminishing. Horst loosened more staves from where the hoop had dug into them and was finally able to get a good grip on it and pull it up and off the barrel altogether. Without the metal band to hold them in place, the staves required little persuasion to disengage from the barrel's bottom and fall outwards like the petals of a wooden flower. The brothers leapt back, but were still soaked from the thighs downwards. In the centre of the flower lay the naked corpse of Alisha Bartos, former Prussian spy, former agent of the Dee Society, and victim of a *döppelganger* ambush.

'I'm glad at least one of us has a jacket,' said Cabal, kneeling by her in the pool of thaumaturgical liquid. 'She's going to get very cold otherwise.'

'Johannes, what about . . . ?' Horst nodded at the secret laboratory.

'Berenice will be safe. I constructed her resting place with a mind to possible disasters, especially fire. The ceiling is heavily reinforced, as is the cover of her tomb, and I diverted a brook to run through around the walls of the glass coffin to keep it cool. She will be safe. She has to be safe.'

'But all this was *for* Berenice, really! I mean, wasn't it? If you use that phial on Alisha—'

'Zarenyia may still have her prize,' said Cabal. 'There were five ways. If she no longer has her phial, then I shall find a sixth somewhere, somehow. Now hush. Necromancer at work.'

He took his cigarillo case from his trouser pocket and opened it. Snuggled safely between a pair of the black cigarillos was his share of the prize. He extracted it, lifted the corpse to a sitting position by him, and leaned back her head so the dead mouth flopped open.

'Oh, gods.' Horst turned away. 'I can't look at her like that.'

'My brother the squeamish vampire,' said Cabal in an undertone. He flicked off the phial's lid and, with no ceremony whatsoever, dashed the contents into the cold, lifeless mouth and throat.

They waited expectantly. After a few moments, Cabal rolled back one of the corpse's eyelids for something to do in what was becoming a fraught silence. The exposed eye bore the unpromising blue-white glaze of the very dead.

'Any signs of life?'

Cabal shook his head. 'I admit, I'm very disappointed. Miss Barrow regained life with great promptitude. Perhaps being within the weave of the Five Ways was part of that effectiveness, or perhaps the length of time *post-mortem* may—'

He was interrupted by Fräulein Bartos's eyelid snapping shut as she reared up in his arms and vomited a spectacular quantity of clearish fluid speckled with silvery glowing motes. 'That was a third possibility I was considering,' he told Horst.

Horst was crouching by her in a second. 'Alisha! Are you all right? Can you speak?'

'What . . . ?' She stared wildly at them. 'What happened?' She looked around. 'Where are we? The monsters—'

'The monsters are dead. You're safe.'

'A very relative statement, given the state of the house,' muttered Cabal.

'Safe? They speared me, Horst! Straight through me, here!' She looked down to indicate a place over her heart, and paused.

'Why am I naked? And wet?'

'That,' said Horst cautiously, 'is a long story.'

'And we do not currently have the leisure to explain it to you,' added Cabal. 'Here's a jacket. You're welcome. May we cut along now?'

'Wait, wait.' She looked narrowly at Cabal. 'This is your doing, somehow. You've done something.'

Cabal sighed. 'We are in a burning building. May we cut along now?'

She looked around her again. 'What?'

'You've been . . . ill, Alisha. A . . . coma! Yes, you were in a coma, we've been looking after you, you're all better now, and the house is on fire. We really had better go.'

'A coma?'

Cabal sighed. 'My brother's new euphemism for "dead". But he's right about you being all better and the house being on fire. May we cut along, now, before we're all dead? Please? Yes? Splendid.'

Alisha Bartos's legs were weak under her, but Horst was more than delighted to carry her out, at first in an heroic cradle lift and then, after he managed to crack her head on a support beam, in a less heroic but far more practical fireman's carry, and crabbing his way up the stairs.

Behind him, Johannes Cabal hesitated and looked across to the unassuming section of wall that hid the entrance to the second laboratory. 'It's a setback,' he whispered to the dead, 'but it was the right thing to do. You would never have forgiven me if I'd let Fräulein Bartos boil in her barrel. So close. I will never give up.'

He followed Horst out of the cellar.

The hallway was impassable to mere mortals, so they went the back way and out into the small garden and paved yard there, and thence down the side passage to the front of the building. There they found Dennis and Denzil still engaged in throwing pitiful amounts of water through the broken window, despite Denzil himself being on fire. It was only a small patch of his ancient and horribly stained Casey Jones hat, but it promised to spread over him as surely as the fire was claiming the house, so Cabal told them to desist from fighting the fire and confine themselves to trying to put out Denzil's hat. This proved challenging until Dennis hit upon the happy strategy of using soil rather than water, the former being more immediately to hand. Denzil sat and patiently waited while Dennis threw handfuls of soil and clods of earth in the general direction of his head. Remarkably, the fire was doused by a lucky hit quite early on, but by then Denzil had forgotten why it was necessary to have soil thrown at him, and Dennis had forgotten why he was throwing soil at his colleague, but as both remembered it pertained to something important, they continued to do so with stolidity and perseverance.

As Dennis slowly but surely proceeded to bury Denzil (hardly prematurely), Johannes and Horst Cabal stood and watched their home burn down, while Alisha Bartos sat naked but for a gentleman's jacket and still with no clear understanding of how she came to be there.

'Wait,' she said. 'Horst, the sun's up. Why are you . . . not—'

'Bursting into flames? Ah, well, now, that's quite the story.' He tried to look wise and failed. Alisha looked to Cabal for elucidation.

'My brother has experienced a transfiguration akin to your own, Fräulein, but whereas yours has brought you cleanly and perfectly back to full life and health, even your injuries healed in their entirety, it has done something rather different to him.'

Horst nodded. 'Transfiguration,' he said to Alisha. He still didn't look wise.

'I will need to conduct a few experiments upon him,' continued Cabal, causing Horst to give him a hard look, 'but my belief is that his mental state affected what happened to him. I do not believe he entirely wished to give up the perks of being a vampire. Would that be true, Horst?'

Horst looked shamefaced. 'It's not *all* bad,' he admitted. 'Actually, most of it's pretty good. It's just the daylight thing and all the business with the blood makes it a bit off-putting.'

'So, the effects were moderated in him. Instead of becoming merely human like you or I, he has become something that has aspects of what the Albanians call a *dhampir,* which is to say, a vampire without all the usual problems.' He looked at Horst, who was smiling brightly at this diagnosis, dispassionately. 'The *dhampir* are also associated with unbridled sexual habits, so that will suit Horst very nicely.'

Horst's smile vanished. 'Don't listen to him,' he told Alisha.

She hugged the jacket more closely around herself. 'Nobody's told me why I'm naked yet.'

The brothers had returned their attention to the burning house. 'Oh, because I took your clothes off,' said Cabal with regrettable offhandedness.

'*Why?*'

'Because they would have contaminated the preservative fluid.'

'Don't worry,' said Horst. 'My brother's seen lots of naked women.' They watched the fire a little longer. 'Admittedly, mainly dead naked women, but still . . .'

'Whereas my brother has seen plenty of living naked women, usually while naked himself.'

'Don't listen to him.'

'Lacrosse team.'

'*Johannes.*'

The remainder of the day was absorbed in storing the books and paraphernalia away in the woodshed and warning Dennis and the recently disinterred Denzil not to touch anything. As to the matter of putting a roof over their own heads, Cabal had applied a little thought to the matter, and led Horst—carrying Alisha Bartos to protect her feet from sharp stones and her legs from brambles more than anything—up the hillside overlooking the house. There they found the well-established encampment of Vlatez and Muk, recently re-provisioned and with a store of freshly washed clothing, a Katamenian bandit regarding cleanliness as being next to beastliness. Vlatez was about the same height as Alisha, and so she appropriated his garments.

Cabal and Horst decided to sleep under the sky, the weather being clement enough, leaving the two-man pup tent to Fräulein Bartos, at least for the time being. The daylight was beginning to fade as Cabal busied himself making a meal of bacon and eggs, washed down with tea. Alisha, recovering slowly from her recent resurrection, commented that she was surprised that he could cook so assuredly, to which Cabal replied that making three plates of bacon and eggs was hardly testing, and that, in any case, cookery and chemistry are very much the same thing.

Three plates of food were required because, to his amazement and pleasure, Horst found himself salivating as his brother made the food, requested a morsel, ate it, and ate some more. 'This is wonderful!' he said, laying into his fourth rasher. 'I'm not dependent on blood any more.'

'You may still be,' warned Cabal, 'simply in smaller amounts. I suspect that it is necessary for your more superhuman feats. That said, it makes your life a great deal more practicable.'

After they had eaten, Alisha Bartos began to fade with fatigue, and Horst suggested that she had endured quite a day, all things said, and that she should get some rest. They would make plans for how to reinsert her into her old life with minimal fuss, even if it meant concocting some story about only being in a coma and having been abducted by the notorious Johannes Cabal for nefarious, nebulous reasons. He was, after all, a necromancer of some little infamy.

When she was abed and asleep, Johannes Cabal and his brother, Horst, settled on the hillside and admired the view, marred though it was by a house in the latter stages of burning down. The bandits had chosen an excellent lookout point that gave them a perfect view of the House of Cabal without being too obvious themselves.

Cabal had avoided looking at the house more than necessary, but Horst saw he did so now in the manner of a man grasping a nettle.

For all his words of assurance, Cabal could not be entirely sure that his precautions would prove sufficient, and that the hidden laboratory's ceiling or door might not be breached by the fire or collapsing masonry. But, there was nothing to be done now. Not until the fire burnt down and the ruin cooled.

'Awful to see the old house go like that,' said Horst. 'I have so many happy memories of the place. I'm surprised nobody from the village has come out to see what's going on; the smoke must be visible for miles.'

'They are fractious creatures, the villagers, and Sergeant Parkin is probably keeping them from investigating until he has had a chance himself. We shall see him on the morrow, I have no doubt. Without his intervention, there would be a party down there even as we speak. Yokels roasting potatoes in the ashes of the necromancer's house.' He nodded in the direction of the village. 'The tavern will be doing very good business this evening. They think they have something to celebrate.'

'And do they? What will you do now, Johannes?'

His brother was silent for a long moment. Horst looked across and thought he saw a tear at the corner of his eye, but that might just as easily have been an effect of the light of the low sun. That was how he decided to interpret it, at any rate.

Johannes Cabal took a long breath, exhaled, then said, 'I shall rebuild. The same site, I think—I like it—but something perhaps a little larger this time.'

'That will take time and money, won't it?'

'Less than one might suppose. I shall use the same methods to construct a new house as I used to bring the old one to that place. The employees work remarkably quickly and do not require payment.' He took out his cigarillo case, offered one to Horst—who demurred—selected one himself, and lit it up. He smoked in silence for a while. 'Not in money, anyway.'

Treading carefully, Horst said, 'What . . . just playing devil's advocate here, brother, but what if the cellar—'

'Then it is all moot.' Cabal said it with finality.

Horst didn't know how to reply to that. So much depended upon what they would find in the morning, but fretting would not bring the hour a whit closer. Yet for all his apparent phlegmaticalness, Horst could see every passing second until that moment of discovery dripped upon his brother like acid.

A crow settled upon a nearby tree. 'Kronk!' it said in an over-familiar tone. Both of the brothers ignored it.

They sat in silence as the house burnt dully, the sun kissed the horizon, and Cabal lit another cigarillo.

'And you, Horst,' he said suddenly, startling his brother. 'What are your thoughts?'

Horst grimaced a little, home to a disagreeable consideration. 'I wonder how awful a life must be for death to be more enjoyable.'

Cabal glanced across at him. 'You speak of the ghost girl.'

Horst nodded. 'Do you think Minty really exists, or was she just something fabricated by the Five Ways?'

'It seems likely everything we saw in that London was a reflection of the real world, such as it is. Even Lord Varney, should you wish to reacquaint yourself.'

Horst's grimace returned. 'In his case, I'd rather not. She was so bright, though. Could we do something to help her?'

Cabal blew smoke out of his nostrils. 'A well-dressed man wandering the stews of East London enquiring after a young girl. I am sure that your intentions couldn't possibly be misconstrued.'

'There has to be *something* we can do. I know this world's Minty has no idea what the ghost version of herself did in the false London, but I still feel we owe something to her. She deserves a better life. Can we do that?'

'Let us rebuild the house first; building materials will still have to be bought, even if the labour is cheap. Then I shall examine my . . . *our* finances, and see what we can do for her. You're right; there is a debt there, and I dislike feeling indebted.' He blew a smoke ring, which travelled a full yard before an errant breeze tore it to wisps. Cabal watched it disappear with equanimity. 'Any other thoughts?'

Horst considered the glowing eastern horizon before them. He leaned back upon the hillside, his hand behind his head. It looked altogether too louche a posture for Cabal, who remained sitting upright upon the grass.

'I was thinking how beautiful the sunset is, and how nice it is not to burst into flames while watching it.'

Cabal considered this, and assented with a thoughtful nod. He turned his face also to the setting sun, and his pale skin glowed in its light.

'You were ever the poet, Horst,' said Johannes Cabal.

AFTERWORD

And there you have it.

ACKNOWLEDGEMENTS

I acknowledge nothing but the burnished shine of my own golden genius.*

* Contributory to that golden shine, I am apparently morally obliged to mention my editors, Peter Joseph with the dauntless assistance of Melanie Fried, and copy editors, Chris and Sara Ensey with ScriptAcuity Studio, for said burnishing; my agents, Melissa Chinchillo of Fletcher & Co. in the United States and Sam Copeland of Rogers, Coleridge, and White in the UK, for their roles in the nefarious conspiracy to put my work into the hands of people to whom it may do great moral harm (one hopes); and the artists Michael J. Windsor and Linda "Snugbat" Smith for making the finished product rather prettier than it might otherwise have appeared. I would also like to thank Gareth L. Powell for the literary equivalent of grasping my lapels and bellowing, 'Pull yourself together!' in my face during a crisis of confidence. I needed that.

I would also like to thank you, reader. It's been a long haul to reach this point, and your enthusiasm is noted and appreciated. Unless, of course, you're reading a pirated copy, in which case may you die alone in misery and poverty, and the little children dance upon your grave in the potter's field.

Printed in the USA
CPSIA information can be obtained
at www.ICGtesting.com
LVHW090523100624
782803LV00005B/217